Thomas is an Australian engineer, writer, and reader with too many books on the shelf waiting to be read and too many ideas scribbled illegibly in notebooks waiting to be written. When he's not staying up too late (sometimes writing, more often procrastinating) he can be found eating vegemite toast, watching old sci-fi shows, or getting far too invested in the footy (that's Australian rules football for the internationals).

Thomas lives in Melbourne with his partner and their dog. He writes (almost) every day flitting between crowd sourced flash fiction experiments, science fiction short stories, strange, unsellable novellas, thriller-leaning novels and the occasional unfinished, untitled fantasy epic. Most of which can be found on his website: thomasklee.com

Project Gateway is his debut novel.

Kickstarter Supporters

The wonderful people listed on these pages are my very first supporters: friends, family, colleagues, and even a few generous strangers who were willing to chip in a few dollars to support an unknown, first-time author. This book wouldn't have made it out into the big wide world without them.

So, my thanks to you all.

———— ● ————

Jade C Wildy
Luke Eric Applebee
Ben D-W
Henry Neilsen
André Furstenrecht
Thomas Greeley
Kara Tan Bhala
David Grubb
Prasoon Premachandran
Toby Roberts
Leanne Drzewucki
Carmel Corrigan
Lendyn Philip
Nandita Fernandes
Tegan
John and Pam Garrity
Grace Moloney
Christena Maurer
Joel Beeson
Richard
Hannah Ervin
Alexander Legaree
Dominic Fabri
David Lukas
Sam Dowle
Nerida

Patrick Hay
Luke Weavell
Michael Slee
Therese Slee
Allyson Woodford
Ryan
Clayton
Paul S.
Margaret E Heaphy
Alisha Ashley
Kelsie Clarke and Nicholas Werrett
Milfred G.
Uncle Les
Matthew
Tony
Lex
John Coates
Zack Fissel
Julie Hamilton
Megan Sutcliffe
Christy S.
Breona
Dan Balkwill
Chris McKitterick
Mary Wilson
Chris Bristow
Peter Bell
Bert
Starlit Swan
Anonymous
Heather Lampshire
Val Mooney
Robin Johnson
Manny Lykourinos
Divyarani Mruthyunjaya
Alison Biram
Adam Boratyn

PROJECT GATEWAY

Thomas K Slee

REFRACTION PUBLISHING

For Caitlin, who liked my hustle.

1

—·—

BRITA'S PHONE BUZZED IN the pocket of her blazer. Again. She ignored it. Again.

Whoever it was would just have to wait.

She rocked back in her chair and kept both her gaze and her breathing steady. Across her desk, silhouetted against the bright London skyline, Richard Solomon thumbed his way through the contract.

He was tall, lean, sun hardened, and well dressed, like a cowboy plucked from the prairies his forebears had called home. As if he hadn't concreted them over and built a gleaming tech campus in their place. As if he was still the world's favourite tech billionaire, still the hero for the digital age, and not the head of an ailing, monopolistic platform squeezing every last dollar it could from its dominance.

On another day, Solomon's insistence on leaving his entourage at the door to her office, on negotiating one on one, might have flattered her. She had a reputation of her own; they both knew it. Today, though, Brita's nerves and the studiously disinterested eyes of her executive team, who hovered on the far side of her office window, kept her focused. She kept count of the pages, knew just which clause had triggered a twitch in his brow and which warranty had made him lay a finger between pages twenty-five and twenty-six, the pages he'd flicked back to once he'd reached the end.

"Hmm." He purred like a well-oiled engine as he pulled a fountain pen from his pocket and circled the offending clause in green ink. *Of course Richard Solomon writes in green ink.* He slipped the contract back onto the edge of her desk, the clean white paper stark against the void-dark glass.

"Strike that, and you've got yerself a deal."

He eyed her with an impenetrable calm, and Brita did her best to match it. She didn't flinch, didn't smile, didn't even hint at looking down.

"No."

She didn't need to look. She knew the sticking point. It was plastered across every piece of stationery on her desk, every meeting room in the building, every

1

engineer's polo, and every email signature. Etched into the casing of her phone, two million more across Britain, another twenty across Europe. Hell, she could even see it reflected from atop her building in the freshly polished windows directly across the Wharf.

Five letters, burnished copper against navy: *Stora*.

Her phone buzzed again, incessant. She whipped it from her pocket and silenced it, face down, against the glass.

Stora.

A nonsense word, chosen by her father one night in his shed. A name he had turned into a brand, built up until it was worth a hundred billion dollars. A legacy he'd then trashed. That she'd resurrected. Stora had dominated her entire life.

Well, not anymore.

"No?" Those wiry salt-and-pepper eyebrows lifted in surprise.

"No."

Solomon leaned forward, his fingers steepled beneath his chin. "That name carries somethin' special. A reputation."

Brita shook her head, a sad smile on her lips. "It used to."

"It will again." Solomon stared at her as if he were making a solemn vow.

"No. It won't."

"How much is it really worth to you, buryin' that name?"

"Twelve point nine billion pounds," Brita said without a moment's hesitation. "Do you want our hardware or not?"

Brita knew that he did. Solomon was a software billionaire, his empire built on his users' data. Hardware didn't matter: he was everywhere, scraping, listening, selling ads. Then AI arrived, and suddenly hardware mattered again. Everywhere he looked, his competitors controlled the gates: computing belonged to Microsoft, smartphones to Apple and Android, the cloud to Amazon. OpenAI was gaining, and NVIDIA had already left him in the dust.

Solomon didn't just want her hardware. Her patents, her engineers. He needed them.

"Haw," Solomon chuckled. "Yes, I surely do." He relaxed his hands. In a different world she could see him resting against a fence post, chewing on a hay stalk and contemplating the horizon.

Brita pushed the contract back towards him.

"Then it sounds like we have a deal."

"Yes, Ms. Gundersson. Ah think we do."

The tension she'd been holding at bay rose up and threatened to boil over as she watched him flick to the final page, slide the lid from his pen, and sign his name. Heat prickled behind her eyes, and a surge of unexpected emotion welled up within her.

Finally, after all these years, after so many setbacks and broken relationships. It was over. She could move on.

Solomon passed her the contract, and there was a flurry of movement from out in the foyer. Garfield, her CFO, had broken through the ranks of functionaries and was headed for the door, his phone pressed to his ear. Mariska, her GM of Investor Relations, was hot on his tail.

Brita cleared the phlegm that suddenly clogged her throat and tried to focus on the contract. Whatever Garfield wanted could wait. Solomon's signature sprawled in vibrant green against the sharp black text, and beside it was a blank space just waiting for her own.

She plucked a pen from the holder on her desk, and her hand hovered over the page, Solomon's words ringing in her ears: *How much is it worth to you, buryin' that name?* She sucked in a deep breath, pen trembling in her hand. *More than you know, Richard. More than you know.*

"Brita." Her office door hissed across the carpet, and a blinding flash of reflected sunlight crossed her vision. Garfield Overton's red-flushed neck bulged over the collar of a too-tight shirt. He held his phone, another Stora of course, tight against his chest.

"I said no interr—"

"It's your father."

Brita's stomach, which had been coiling itself tighter and tighter with every passing second, collapsed through the floor. Behind Garfield, Mariska scowled. He had wedged the door with his well-heeled bulk, and she was blocked off, unable to intervene.

"Problem?" Solomon asked.

"No. Not at all," Brita said, as if she believed it, but inside she was spiralling. Her father? They hadn't spoken in years, not since...and he was calling now? Right now? She flipped her phone over, knowing exactly what she would find. Seven missed calls. Hugo Gundersson. That man had impossible timing.

"Garfield, hang up on him."

"He says—"

"I don't care what he says. Mas, get him out of here. Now is not the time." Brita waved her past away, as if that was where it would stay. Her mouth was dry. She poured all her attention onto the contract and tried to regain control of her hands, her lungs, her beating heart.

"Sounds like he doesn't want you to consign his legacy to history," Solomon drawled, and it was that, more than anything, that drew her back from the brink.

"He lost that right eleven years ago." Brita snapped, fixing Solomon with a murderous glare. Stora was hers. Hers to save and hers to let go.

She snatched the pen up from where she'd dropped it, but the door was still ajar. Mariska's manicured fingers tugged at Garfield's jacket, but he refused to move.

"You're still here."

"I'm sorry, Brita, but a promise is a promise." Garfield's chin trembled as he spoke, still clutching the phone tight to his chest. "He knew you wouldn't answer, so he came to me."

Her pen hovered agonisingly close to the paper, but something, some base instinct, stayed her hand. Even now, after all he'd put her through.

"We have a deal, Ms Gundersson." Solomon shifted in his seat and eyed her with growing ill ease. She knew he could sense a deal slipping away. "And ah have an awful long memory."

Brita stared at Solomon. Sitting at her desk, in her office, and he dared...She turned back to the man standing at her door. "What is it, Garfield? What does he want?"

Her CFO swallowed. Beneath the ruddy cheeks he was starting to turn green.

"He only wanted you to know one thing: Gateway. He says it's working."

2

JORGE STOOD IN THE wings of the studio, just beyond the reach of the lights. Roger, his producer, buzzed in his ear, rattling off talking points. "Make sure you get an answer on what exactly broke the deal. And don't forget to grill her on her relationship with her father..." Jorge let it all flow over him, the crazy hubbub of writers and technicians, cameras and microphones. He clutched his dog-eared notes tight in his fist. This was his chance. A real interview. A real story.

The notes, the talking points: yes, they were important. He'd been out of the game for a long time, but not so long as to have forgotten the fundamentals. He still knew that the most important thing was to watch, to listen, to not miss a thing.

Brita sat at the opposite end of the oversize desk, her hands clasped in her lap. Her eyes were closed as Suzie fussed over her foundation, Andy teased at her hair, Hal picked flecks of dust from her dark navy jacket, and May adjusted her mike. Four people, so close she would be able to feel their cloying breath on her skin, and she let them roll around her and right on by, like they were water and she was a stone. The so-called stars he interviewed these days revelled in this sort of treatment, and the power brokers, policy makers, and tycoons he'd stared down in his youth had hated it. He had used that fact to his advantage more than once in the old days.

But that tactic would not work today, it seemed. Not on Brita Gundersson. She had sat opposite that thug Richard Solomon. Looked him in the eye and told him no. Not today. Jorge shivered and slapped his notes against the palm of his hand. He couldn't tell if his nerves were fuelled by adrenaline or jealousy. *If I could have seen Solomon's face at that moment...*

The enemy of my enemy is my friend.

This was going to be fun.

He stepped out, and the heat of the studio lights rippled down his back. Usually the spotlight made him woozy, reminding him of the quiet back rooms and surreptitious phone calls he'd been forced to leave behind, but today he was hungry. The glare brought everything into focus. Today, this set was his domain.

"Are you listening?" his producer squawked in his earpiece. *"I want fireworks, Jorge! Make it happen!"*

"Quiet, Roger." He waved a dismissal to the control booth, way back in the shadows. "I've got it from here."

"You begged for this. Don't fuck it up," Frank Darabont, the usual host of the *Darabont Report*, snarled.

Oh, I won't, Jorge thought, turning on his million-pound grin, letting it flow right up to his eyebrows. *As long as you let me do my fucking job.*

He glanced over at the clock. One minute. Time to introduce himself. He stepped up onto the stage. Flimsy panels, painted black, creaked beneath his feet. Brita was a picture of calm amidst a sea of chaos. If she was troubled by having just reneged on the promised sale of her company, against the wishes of her board and her major shareholders, and by being forty-five seconds from having to defend that backflip on live television, she didn't show it.

"All right, Suzie, May, you can let her be." The Perspex table creaked as he leaned against it. "She looks great."

Brita blinked, squinted up at him against the lights. With a final flurry of brush and comb, they were alone. Well, as alone as interviewer and interviewee can be with three HD cameras pointed at their faces.

He held out his hand, and she took it. "A pleasure."

"We'll see about that." Brita smirked. She had a firm grip. He held her hand for a beat longer than was normal, wondering if he might detect something, but no. There was not even a hint of nerves.

"I was surprised you accepted my invitation."

"If it was up to me..." She peered into the darkness beyond the stage, to where her entourage waited nervously, her lips pursed. "You have my head of Investor Relations to thank for that."

"So it has nothing to do with you, very publicly, making an enemy of Richard Solomon? Nothing to do with our sordid history?"

He watched her carefully for any reaction and could only chuckle at her exaggerated sigh, at the exasperated eye roll she sent his way. *This is not about you,* she was telling him. He held up his hands in apology.

"In that case, I owe your head of Investor Relations a beer."

"She drinks champagne. But let's wait until after this is over to see if she deserves it."

He laughed, but still, in the back of his mind, he wondered what she knew of his past. About his own run-in with Solomon, all those years ago.

"Big shoes for you to fill tonight. Finance isn't your usual beat, at least not anymore. Was Frank busy?" Brita did not chuckle, did not smile. Her gaze was backed by a steel he'd not faced in a long time. Butterflies tumbled in his stomach. Why, suddenly, did he feel as if he wasn't ready?

Internally, he admonished himself. *I've been wasting away here, playing games with celebrities for too long.* This was exactly what he needed. A story he could sink his teeth into, loosen those long-dormant investigative muscles.

Externally, he exuded Spanish charm. He smiled, winked, stood, held a finger to his earpiece. "Even fossils deserve a night off, every now and then. I hope you'll enjoy the change of pace."

"*You keep that up, Jorge*—" Frank blustered in his earpiece, but Jorge ignored him.

"You reading us okay, Roger?"

"*Loud and clear, killer.*"

Jorge cringed, put them out of his mind. "Excellent. Ten seconds, Ms Gundersson. Good luck." He took his seat and aligned his papers. "You're going to need it."

He could feel her eyes on him as he ran through his vocal warm-ups. He tried to imagine her looking down on him, the little TV presenter playing at hard-hitting journalism, lining up his gotcha questions, trying to trick her into an unfortunate sound bite.

"Five seconds." A producer, in his earpiece.

But it wasn't Brita looking down on him. It was Roger. Frank. The faceless producers and senior editors. Thinking he would let them down. That he was past it. A hack.

"Three."

But he still had it. He knew he had it.

"Two."

He would prove it.

"One."

The studio was silent.

He snapped his eyes open, smiled directly at the red flashing light, and their doubts, his past, all of it was gone. Music blared, cameras swung and zoomed. There was nothing but the bright white lights, and he was in charge. Not the producers, not the editors, not his guest. It was just him, his questions, and his wits.

"Good evening, London, and welcome to this special edition of the *Darabont Report*. I'm Jorge Elorza." On the teleprompter, his script scrolled smoothly by. He didn't need it. "Tonight, I'm here with Brita Gundersson, CEO of Stora Telecom and daughter of Hugo Gundersson, the company's famous and reclusive founder. Brita, welcome."

"It's a pleasure to be here, Jorge, thank you for having me." She smiled, it seemed to him, through gritted teeth. Her lips had pinched just a little at that jab about her father. Good.

"Let's get into it, shall we?" He glanced down at his notes and skipped his first question. He'd get back to that once he had her off balance. "It's been a whirlwind twenty-four hours."

"Yes, Jorge, it has. And I'd like to—"

"I'm sure you would." *Not so fast,* Jorge thought. *We'll get to your talking points when I'm ready. Not before.* "But first, I think we need to set the scene a little for our viewers. Stora is not the household name it once was."

"If that's how you've been told to play it, Jorge..." Brita's hands twitched as if she wanted to cross her arms, but decades of media training had kicked in at the last second.

"No games, here, Ms Gundersson, just questions." He flashed an impish grin at the camera, playing to his audience, the butterflies churning like a hurricane in his gut. "Now, if we were to cast our minds back to the nineties, we'd find Stora was the dominant mobile phone manufacturer in the world. Everyone, and I mean everyone, had a Stora mobile phone. Mine even survived the Balkan War. Fast-forward fifteen years, though, to when you ousted your father, and Stora was still a respectable third place behind Apple and Nokia, with a young Samsung snapping at your heels. Tell me, where does Stora sit now?"

Brita blinked. Once, then twice. "Actually, I'm glad you've asked this. It's better to make sure everyone knows the facts before we get to the gossip." He held her gaze, and he was almost certain that she meant it. "Based on Q3 sales data, Stora is seventeenth, between Motorola and HTC. Up from nineteenth the last year."

"That's quite a decline."

"From ten years ago? Yes, it is." The admission slid out as if she'd practised it a thousand times. She ignored the cameras, focusing solely on him. "But over the last three years—"

"Sales data can be misleading, can't it, Ms Gundersson. Both Motorola and HTC are valued at around fifty billion pounds, more than four times Stora's market capitalisation."

"If you're saying we're undervalued by the market, then I'd agr—"

Jorge cut her off, dropping the informal, conversational tone. "Why did you back out of the Solomon deal?"

Brita sat motionless for a moment. Not because she was stunned, but because she was calm. Because she wouldn't be rushed. "How about we take this one question at a time?"

"All right, let me rephrase. Given you're now an industry also-ran, why turn down an offer most analysts agree was too good to refuse?"

"We're not an also-ran, Jorge." Brita's eyes sparked. "And your analysts are wrong."

"Are they, Brita? You've overseen an 87% decline in sales during your tenure—"

"If you want to ignore the consistent year-on-year growth over the past three years, and the significant changes to our platform that have underpinned that growth, that's fine by me. The market has, as have your precious analysts. And, in my opinion, so did Richard Solomon."

"So you're saying the Solomon deal was unfair?"

"Richard Solomon was chasing a bargain. He's a savvy investor, always looking for value. I took his offer as proof that we're competitive again—"

"A savvy investor? You're making Richard Solomon out like he's Warren Buffet or Charlie Monger, someone who's carefully crafted an empire over decades through smart acquisitions, when the last few years have revealed him to be a ruthless monopolist, using his market dominance to squash competition and buy innovation." Jorge scoffed. There was so much more he wished he could say. "Are you claiming that Solomon saw you as competition?"

"Are you quite finished?" Brita asked, eyebrows raised, and waited for him to concede that he was. "Thank you. And no. I don't think Richard looked at Stora and trembled in his cowboy boots."

"So he wanted you for something you had and he didn't?"

"I can only assume so."

"Come on, Brita." He rapped his pen against the table. "Don't play coy. You know exactly why Solomon wanted Stora."

"No, but it seems you do. Why don't you enlighten us?"

"All right." Jorge smiled, though this time it didn't quite reach his eyes. She'd backed him into a corner. He'd let her. There was only one thing to do. "I'll bite. Richard Solomon is a data billionaire in a world that's beginning to realise that maybe it shouldn't be giving away its data for free. He owns an app, where his competitors own platforms. More than that, they all have hardware to fall back on. All of them except him, and not for lack of trying either. So Richard Solomon does what he always does. He tries to buy what he can't create himself."

You're getting nowhere, Roger growled in his ear. *Solomon's not here, she is! You need to change tack.* He gritted his teeth, Roger's patronising tone grating all the more because he was 100 percent right.

Brita chuckled politely. "That's quite the story, and I'm sure it will play well in the tabloids. All I can tell you is that Richard's offer was outside confirmation of something that my team and I already knew. That we deserved to be taken seriously again." For the first time in the entire interview, she leaned forward, facing directly into the camera. "That Stora is back."

Jorge let her answer hang in the air. *You want me to change tack, Roger? How's this for a change of tack?* "So Stora is back, you think? Is that's why your father convinced you to scrap the deal? To preserve the family legacy?"

Brita blanched, and Roger's aggressive exclamations buzzed in his ear. *That's more fucking like it, Jorge old boy! She doesn't like that one bit. Keep at her!*

"Well, Ms Gundersson?"

"I haven't spoken with my father in over a decade." She fidgeted with her hands, smoothing her skirt, crossing her legs, but she maintained eye contact the whole way through. "What I will say, however, is that after careful consideration with my team, we decided that Mr Solomon offered short-term value to our shareholders only. And unlike some of our competitors, we're in this for the long h—"

"A decision made with your father's full support, of course."

Brita pursed her lips. "I guess I shouldn't be surprised. Everyone always wants to talk about my father, his achievements, his legacy, when the reality is that Stora only exists today because my father is no longer in charge. Without a decade's worth of incredibly hard work from every one of my employees, both Stora and Hugo Gundersson would be footnotes in the history books."

"A lovely sentiment." Jorge grinned, Brita's firm, measured responses only whetting his appetite. God, he had missed this. He clicked his pen and circled the word *estranged* on his note sheet, giving her a moment to stew. "But you didn't answer the question. Did your father support the Solomon deal?"

"I've seen the same quotes in the paper that you have, Jorge. Why don't you tell me?"

"I—"

"No, don't answer that." Brita shifted in her seat, and Jorge waited, allowing her irritation to manifest. "My father's thoughts on this are irrelevant. Stora has been my company for a decade, and I rejected the deal. Not my father, not the board. Me. And I will wear the brunt of that decision, whether time proves it to be right or wrong."

He let her anger roll over him, and, despite the baying in his ear from the control booth, he allowed her a moment to compose herself. If he was being honest, he'd gotten himself all worked up over Solomon, and he needed the moment too. Besides, there had been something in the way she'd jutted her jaw in defiance in that last statement. Something beneath the surface she wanted to crow about, and in this moment of calm, he could smell it. Time to let it simmer.

"All right, let's set your father to one side. Why are you so confident that the analysts are wrong? What do you know that the analysts don't?"

"What do I know?" Brita smirked, leaning back and crossing her legs. He could tell she knew this was just a temporary stay. "I know my people, I make a point of it. And I know tech buyouts, better than most, from the inside. I know what would have happened to my employees once Stora was absorbed into the Solomon corporate behemoth. They would have been stripped of their assets, their IP, given a pat on the back, and shipped off to the scrapyard. I couldn't put them through that."

She almost spat Solomon's name, as if it were something slimy, and Jorge could not help but smile. She knew. *She sensed it, just as I had.* "You make it sound personal."

"How can it not be? Stora and I practically grew up together. I've known many of my employees since I was a young girl. I have no hesitation in doing the right thing by them, even if it costs us money in the short term."

"Of course, but, uhh..." Jorge had to glance back down at his notes to remind himself that he was pushing Brita on her company, not looking for yet another angle on Solomon's. "But should it be so personal? Can you honestly say you're thinking in the best interests of the business, and of the shareholders?"

"I don't subscribe to the theory that one needs to be ruthless to be a good leader." She raised her eyebrows suggestively, as if referring back to her previous comments about Solomon. Had she seen something beneath his mask? Had he let something slip?

"Sometimes tough decisions need to be made to save the company, and as you've so tactfully touched on tonight, I've had to make my fair share." She paused a beat, taking a breath, and he realised that no, he was safe. "I've proven I will do what's best for Stora, regardless of my personal feelings. More than most CEOs have had to prove, wouldn't you say?"

She stared pointedly his way, and he nodded with a wry grin. Just for a moment, he caught a glimpse of what it must have cost her to swing Stora's board against her own father, to run him out of the company he'd built from the ground up. There was no denying that Brita had her shareholders' interest at heart, back then at least. The question now: Was that still the case? He held her gaze for just a moment longer, as she relaxed back into her chair once more.

"But all that's beside the point. Solomon's offer was decent, but not outstanding. Stora is in good financial shape. Again, not outstanding, but stable and most importantly improving, with highly promising developments already in the pipeline. Accepting a buyout, from Solomon, at Solomon's asking price, would have been about short-term shareholder profit at the expense of the business, our employees, and our customers. And that's not the way I operate."

"And it's admirable. Really." Jorge extended his hand in an almost conciliatory gesture, the silver pen between his fingers sparkling under the studio lights. "And I imagine your actions during and since your installation as CEO earned you significant credit with your shareholders. What do they think of your most recent change of heart?"

"Calling my decision a change of heart isn't quite fair, Jorge. I've said before, and I'll reiterate right now: I'm open to receiving a fair offer for Stora, as any CEO worth their salt should be. But in the end, Solomon's offer didn't stack up, and that's that."

"And the shareholders?" Jorge prodded. She was developing a habit of not quite answering his questions.

"Look, many were disappointed, I'll grant you, but they've been on the journey with us for a long time; they're not about to jump ship now. And remember who the largest shareholder is." Brita gave a self-deprecating grin. "I forwent more than anybody else to reject Solomon's deal. Well, except for Britannia Bank, but I'm sure they'll manage in the short term." Brita's eyes burned from across the plastic desk. "In the long term, I promise Stora will repay the faith."

He could sense her starting to relax again, but there was something else, something she wasn't saying that underwrote her confidence. Jorge had seen that same subtle smugness a half dozen times before, in politicians who thought their connections, their money, their position, made them safe. It always unravelled before the end. He pushed on.

"How long term? Are you expecting a turnaround in the near future?"

"I am."

There it was again. A little smile, saying, *You don't know what I know.*

"How soon? Let's put it on the record."

Brita paused. The wheels were turning, her inner fire pushing against the game plan that had surely been laid out for her by that executive hovering in the wings. *Hit these five points, play a straight bat to everything else, don't mention your father, and get the hell out.* Totally unambitious. She shifted her weight forward, and her words from before rang clear as a bell in his ears. *This is my company, not my father's, not the board's. Mine.* He found himself holding his breath. The game plan was going out the window.

"All right. You want a number and a date? Here it is: within five years, Stora will be back on top. Samsung and Apple had better watch out."

He thought he heard a squeak from that executive behind the sound stage, and he knew he heard one from Roger, wheezing ecstatically into his earpiece. It was all too much, and Brita sat back with a self-satisfied grin as his jaw flapped aimlessly.

"Say something, you Catalonian nitwit!"

Roger's scream jerked him back to reality. He fumbled with his papers, cleared his throat. "Ah...well. Fighting words from our guest Brita Gundersson, Stora CEO. We'll be back to discover whether there is any substance to them, right after these messages from our sponsors." He held his smile for a full second, letting it drop only once Roger signalled the all-clear with a mouthful of expletives.

"You don't think I can back it up?" Brita demanded, once she was certain they'd gone to commercial.

"Well, shots fired. I hope Solomon, Tim Cook, and Lee Jae-yong are watching from their penthouses." Jorge flicked off his earpiece and sighed with relief. "You've surprised my producer, that's for sure." A staccato burst of footsteps from behind made Brita turn around. "And some of your own, I see."

An entirely silent exchange occurred between Brita and one of her fiercely glaring hangers-on, who had stormed right up to the edge of the sound stage. Subtle movements—a nod, a raised eyebrow—and Brita had talked her down without saying a word.

"Dissension in the ranks?" Jorge asked, as innocent as he could manage.

"I think Mariska would prefer I say nothing at all."

"That was Mariska? The lady I owe for this interview?"

"The very same." Brita smiled, a hint of pride in her eyes. A protégé, perhaps? "It's nothing I've not said publicly before, but still. She worries."

"She shouldn't have booked an interview with me if she was worried. And I doubt you've threatened to topple both Apple and Samsung in five years before. You want to throw Google in there while you're at it? Amazon too?" As he spoke, Jorge began jotting down rough calculations. Despite the earpiece dangling by his collar, he could still make out Roger's exasperated shouts: *"Current market share data! Growth rates! Where will the revenue come from?"*

"Hah, I know my limits."

He looked up at that. He had the numbers right in front of him, and he wondered if she really did.

"Pity. Well, get ready. The party's just getting started." Jorge glanced up as a producer frantically signalled the five-second warning, and the studio once again fell silent. Behind Brita's shoulder, at the edge of the sound stage, Mariska hovered, her arms tightly crossed. He wondered if she would be more effective standing behind him, where her boss could see the deadly warning in her eyes.

Jorge held Brita's gaze for the full five seconds, flicking the earpiece back up just in time. As the count switched from verbal to disappearing fingers, he let what he thought of as his languid Mediterranean charm fade away. By the time he'd released her and turned back to the camera, Brita was no longer smiling. Perhaps she'd realised that the Jorge Elorza that had been nominated for a Pulitzer from the Yugoslavian front lines all those years ago was still alive, still kicking. He tapped his pen on the table, switching his smile back on for the camera.

"Welcome back. This is a special edition of the *Darabont Report*, and I'm Jorge Elorza, sparring with Stora CEO Brita Gundersson. Now, Brita, before the break you made a bold prediction. Would you mind repeating it for the viewers?"

Jorge beamed at her, eager for her to bluster, backtrack, anything he could latch on to. She did nothing of the sort.

"I don't think it was bold at all, Jorge. I said that within five years we'll have retaken our position as the world's first-choice mobile communications technology, unseating both Apple and Samsung, and I stand by it." She clasped her hands together, pressing her thumbs tightly to stop them from shaking. "Stora is not the kind of company that gets bought out by the first bloated corporate behemoth to come knocking when the market gets tough, no matter their 'credentials.' We stand up for ourselves, our values, and we fight back."

"I bet your PR team had fun coming up with that one." Jorge chuckled, flashing a wink at Mariska and the camera. "But we'll come back to exactly how you plan to grow Stora from its current 0.8% market share to the thirty plus percent you'll need to overtake Apple or Samsung in a moment, but first I want to touch on what you just said: 'retake our place.' It wasn't that long ago that Stora was the company with the thirty percent market share. More, in fact. Can you distil, for our viewers, exactly how you lost your dominance?"

Across the desk, Brita's shoulders relaxed, and in his ear, Roger squawked, lambasting him for going soft. *Does the man have no patience?* No, Jorge realised, of course he didn't. He was a TV news producer, stuck in a downward spiral of sound bites, gotcha questions, and clickbait headlines. He tuned Roger's accusations out and let Brita ease into her boilerplate answer.

"The first wobble was the release of the iPhone. It was a game changer, one we really weren't prepared for. The second was the financial crisis, which followed shortly after. It was a case of horrendous timing for us—we were debt heavy, and demand fell off a cliff. Suddenly we couldn't pay our bills. Like many businesses at the time, there were real worries about whether we'd make it. It took eighteen months of tireless work and significant sacrifice to right the ship.

"Those eighteen months cost us dearly. Sadly we lost a quarter of our workforce, but we survived. However, by the time we'd regained our footing, it had been thirty months since Apple had changed the game, and we had no viable, competitive product to match it. We'd been outstripped, and it took us another eight years and a number of false starts to reverse that trend."

"So it was a case of unexpected hardware innovation and poor timing that kick-started Stora's ten-year decline?"

"In a nutshell, yes."

"And what was it that arrested that decline in the end?" *Can you see where I'm going yet, Roger?* Jorge thought, smiling at his slightly bemused guest. *Can you, Ms Gundersson?* She knew he was lobbing softballs, and he could see in the slight furrow of her brow that she was wondering why.

"The turning point was abandoning our proprietary operating system and combining our hardware with Android software. It turns out we'd missed two boats. The hardware leap was one we could handle in house; however, the network effects of the Apple and Google platforms we just weren't equipped to navigate on our own."

"I see." Jorge made a show of marking off two of the questions on his list, questions from a script long abandoned. What he wanted was a moment of silence while he laid his trap.

"So now Stora is hitched to the Android bandwagon, just one of dozens of manufacturers both old and new. Your younger competitors are fighting for market share with innovative design, while you're trading on past glories and better-than-average hardware. And all that seems to have done is help you reclaim a percentage point here, another point there. Is that fair, would you say?"

"That's one very negative way to characterise the efforts of my people to return Stora to both profitability and growth over the last couple of years."

"Okay"—Jorge raised his palms in muted apology, as if he hadn't meant every word—"but you'll admit it's not the kind of strategy that will deliver you the one hundred and ten, one hundred and twenty percent year-on-year sales growth that you'll need to catch Apple and Samsung over the next five years?"

"Yes, I'll concede that, Jorge."

"So what am I missing? What will be the game changer? What will be Stora's iPhone?"

Brita smiled, the kind of confident, knowing smile of a person with a secret. And not the dark kind of secret that his politicians and kleptocrats had harboured, their grubby fingers and their grubbier pies. The good kind, the kind that the holder was desperate to let you in on: the promotion, the long-hoped-for pregnancy.

The breakthrough.

Jorge clenched his fist tight about his pen. *I knew it.* Now to tease it out of her.

"That's exactly it, Jorge—there hasn't been a major disruption in this industry since 2007. That's more than a decade of incremental change." The smile that had slipped through her defences was gone, and Brita had rolled into her keynote-speaker mode. "Sure, phones now have curved bevels, more megapixels, fun colours, but it's still the same damn phone we've all been churning out since 2010.

"We've all been working on our own 'game-changers'—you've seen the foldable screens, metaverses, chatbots—the latest in a long line of gimmicks. That's not what we're about. No, we're targeting something more, something actually life-changing here. Nothing less will do."

"Targeting? Or building?" Jorge asked. Roger had, at long last, fallen silent.

"I'd prefer to keep that card close to my chest, Jorge."

"But you do have cards to play?"

"Of course."

"Come on, Brita. You don't think your shareholders deserve a hint of what you have planned?"

"Our shareholders trust me, and I will repay that trust by playing my hand when the moment is right. And not a moment before."

Jorge changed angles. "Do you have prototypes?"

Brita flicked at a strand of hair that had fallen from behind her ear, pulling it back with a slender hand. For a hint of a moment, the smile was back. "No comment."

But you want to, don't you. I know you do. I can see it. You're ready to burst.

Jorge knew where the pressure was building, and just where to prod.

"I'll take that as a no."

"You can take that however you like, Jorge. It doesn't change the facts."

"Facts." Jorge couldn't stop his eyebrows from arching. He licked his lips. "Now there's an interesting phrase. The only facts that have been put on the table thus far this evening are that Solomon made you a multi-billion-dollar offer for Stora, and you turned him down. Everything you've said since then..."

"I stand by every single word, Jorge."

"Of course you do. And your sincerity makes such outlandish deflection that much more believable. But I won't fall for it, Brita. And neither, I daresay, will your shareholders."

"Jorge." Brita's fists clenched beneath the cover of the Perspex desk, where he could see them and the camera could not. Her gaze and her voice were steady, but the set of her jaw left no uncertainty as to what she was feeling. "I've actually enjoyed this interview. You've pulled no punches. But I draw the line at baseless accusations of dishonesty."

Jorge's heart pounded. He was on the edge of the seat now, notes, teleprompter, cameras, and producers entirely forgotten, the opening Brita had just handed him hanging there, waiting to be exploited.

"How about we put this to the viewers?" Jorge pointed his pen directly at her. "Think about Fred and Frances, sitting at home on the couch. Which seems more likely to them? A dinosaur like Stora climbing off the canvas to deliver knock-out blows to both Apple and Samsung? Or an embattled CEO bluffing in the face of waning interest and circling creditors, turning down a helping hand out of pride?" Jorge held up his hand as she opened her mouth to speak. "Ms Gundersson, Stora hasn't made a significant technological breakthrough since the early nineties. The nineties! That's almost thirty years ago!" He paused for dramatic effect and watched as her cheeks reddened, even beneath the heavy makeup. "But that doesn't mean you haven't talked about these radical changes. Your father certainly did, he couldn't help it! You ousted him after he spent years spruiking his mysterious projects, with nothing to show for it but billions of wasted dollars and declining sales. Or did you think we'd have forgotten? That we wouldn't wonder what's changed between then and now?

"But then it's obvious, isn't it? You said it yourself. You grew up with Stora. You're too close. The world has moved on, and you've lost, but you can't tell the stalwarts of the past that their time has come. It's not 'the way you operate.'

"Let's be honest, just for a second. If you had a game changer in your back pocket, you would have used it already, and Solomon wouldn't have let you walk away from negotiations as easily as he has. Why haggle for the eighteenth-largest mobile phone manufacturer when he could just buy the nineteenth or the twentieth? It's time to play your cards, Brita. No more holding out. Tell me I'm wrong. Or are you really just your father's daughter?"

The normally quiet studio was deathly silent. Roger, camera operators, technicians, even Frank bloody Darabont must have been holding their breath. Jorge waited, and Brita crouched, her feet planted, her whole body tensed. She stared at him, but she wasn't looking. Wasn't seeing. The muscles in her jaw twitched, and Jorge knew he'd gone too far. Pushed too hard. Roger squealed with delight in his ear. Exactly the kind of fireworks he'd been looking for: flashy but empty. Brita would never talk now.

He'd blown it.

There was only one thing to do, and he felt sick to his stomach. He shook his head in exaggerated disappointment and leaned into the stereotype of the gutter TV journalist, proud of his empty kill.

"So, Ms Gundersson, finally faced with a question that doesn't have a rehearsed answer, we get nothing. I hope you'll give better answers to your shareholders in private than you've provided for our viewers tonight."

This final insult was like a spark to a gas cloud. In an instant she was on her feet, her fists pressed into the desktop. She loomed over him, her hair hanging loose about her face, obscuring her fury from the cameras, so that only he could see.

"I am directly responsible for over seventeen thousand employees. Seventeen thousand people, just like your Freddy and Frances. Do you get that? I will not divulge confidential, business-critical information simply because you ask me to. I will not!" Spittle formed at the corner of her mouth, and she ripped the mike and battery pack from behind her back. "I've read up on you too, you know, and despite your past history with Richard Solomon, I thought you were better than cheap gotcha journalism and might actually leave the spurious attacks on both my integrity and the capability of my employees to the tabloids."

She dumped the microphone on the desk, and the crackle through his earpiece made him wince.

"I hope this sham rates highly for you, Jorge, I really do. It certainly hasn't done anything to rehabilitate your reputation as a journalist." The cameras followed her as she stormed from the set.

For a moment, Jorge could only watch as Brita stormed past a shell-shocked Mariska, dragging a swarm of panicked assistants in her wake. He blinked once, then twice, before years of habit drew him back to the camera.

"Well, folks, it looks like that's our interview for this evening. Brita Gundersson, CEO of Stora. Sticking to her guns, quite admirably, if I may say so. I'll be watching this story as it evolves, with interest."

He held the camera for two more beats, an excruciating smile on his face, until the studio broke into an absolute buzz of activity. Roger exploded from the wings to slap him on the back, but Jorge couldn't focus. All he could see was Brita's little smile as she avoided his questions. A smile that all her bluster and false bravado could do nothing to dispel. What was she hiding? What did she know that he didn't? That Solomon didn't?

There was something there. A story.

He could feel it.

3

BRITA STOOD ON A bustling Whitechapel street-corner and pressed the buzzer next to a nondescript grey door. She thanked her lucky stars that the crowd of young workers rushing past was totally oblivious to who she was, to the fact that she'd just imploded on live television. Jorge's final accusation was still pounding in her ears: *Are you just your father's daughter?*

She'd ordered her entourage away the moment she'd left the sound stage. Even Mariska had been too shocked to argue. *Let them figure it out for once!* She'd stalked past her car and her driver, hopped into a cab, and let it whisk her away. Then she'd sent one message, just one, and set her phone to silent. Now it dangled by her side, the endless stream of notifications flashing uselessly into the night.

Despite the burning in her gut, she knew it was only temporary. The Solomon deal, the pressure from the board, the shareholders, that fucking reporter. He'd seen right through her, and still it didn't matter. She shook her head, unable to quite believe that despite the turmoil, despite the PR nightmare she'd just unleashed for no good reason, it didn't matter. None of it mattered. Gateway was working. She'd seen it. Held it in her hand.

Understood what it meant.

She toyed with the back of her phone as she waited, tracing each letter of the Stora logo with a fingernail, and let her imagination wander, let the interview fall from her mind. Thinking about Gateway was so much more fun—

"Brita!"

Anita burst through the door, engulfed her in a glamorous cyclone, and tugged her inside. For a half second, all eyes on the street were drawn towards them, and then the door slammed shut. Brita was safe inside Anita's house.

"Sorry. This is such late notice—"

"Sorry? What for?" Anita ushered her down the familiar hallway and out into the spacious, impeccably appointed, and rarely-used kitchen. "Do you want wine or whisky?"

19

"What makes you think I need a drink?" Brita said, plopping down onto a barstool. Anita turned, one hand on her hip, the other holding a bottle of Bordeaux. Despite everything, the look of absolute incredulity that bloomed onto her face drew a laugh. "Fine. Whisky."

"I thought so." Two tumblers, two fingers. Brita knocked it back without even blinking and held Anita's priceless antique crystal out for a second round. This one she sipped, savouring the burn.

"How much did you see?"

"Enough to know you went on live TV looking like this." Anita waved a vague hand and tutted, eyeing Brita's tailored and tastefully plain suit with comic disgust. "No wonder it all went to hell."

"Yes I did, and yes it did. But you know exactly why I have to wear these things, so don't go all heiress on me. We're here to drown my sorrows, not talk about them. I did quite enough reliving on my cab ride here." Brita took another sip and let the whisky absorb her anger. Anita didn't deserve it, and she didn't need it.

"Listen, what he said..."

"It doesn't matter," Brita said, a little too fast, as Jorge's sneering face fought its way back to the surface: *Are you just your father's daughter?*

"We're not our fathers, Brita." Anita took her hand. Held it. "You've got this, no matter what that punk reporter says."

Anita smiled, a knowing little smile. She knew what it was like to be the daughter of a famous father, the heir to a business empire, successor to a pioneer of British innovation. For Anita it was aircraft; for Brita, telecommunications. Both industries 'vital to the national interest.' For Anita, though, the transition had been different. Not easier, but... her father had passed away, and she'd inherited. Stepped up, taken over. Seamless.

Until two days ago, if Brita was feeling particularly honest with herself, she'd been a little jealous. She'd even thought, in private, guilty moments, about how much neater it all could have been, if he'd just... Even now, her cheeks burned with shame.

"It was him, you know." Brita knocked back her drink, and raised her glass for another.

"Who?" Anita raised her eyebrows.

"Dad. He convinced me to back out."

"I thought it must have been." Anita nodded, the bottle of Gordon & MacPhail dangling from her hand.

"He called. While—wait, you did?"

"You were so set on selling, on being rid of it all." Anita shrugged. "What else could it have been?"

"I was about to sign the contract." Brita mimed her pen, millimetres from the countertop. Then she barked a bitter laugh and looked away.

"What did he say?"

Gateway. It's working. The knowledge of what those words meant to the world burned within her, desperate to escape. She couldn't let it out. Not to Anita, not to anyone. No matter how much she wanted to.

"No? You can't even tell me?" Brita pursed her lips, and Anita whistled. "But you can let slip that you're gunning for Apple and Samsung, both at the same time? He must have made one hell of a sales pitch."

"Jesus. I really said that, didn't I." Brita looked down into her tumbler, swirled the whisky, and watched the long, thin legs clinging to the crystal before draining away.

"Yeah, you really did. I can just imagine Mariska's face, too."

Anita contorted her very British lips into a surprisingly accurate impression of Mas's surly Hungarian scowl, and Brita noticed for the first time what she was wearing. She was all glitter and sparkle: a halter neck gown, heels, half made up but with perfectly styled hair. Her skin shimmered in the kitchen lights.

"What are you all dressed up for?"

"Just for you." Anita watched her carefully for a moment, as if she was deciding whether to let her change the subject. Then, decision made, her face broke into a rakish smile. "But no, I'm meant to be at a fundraiser, for red squirrels if you can believe it. Dame bloody Westover…"

And Anita was off, regaling Brita with the latest high-society gossip. It washed over her: friends, acquaintances, and even the odd rival, from school and from college. Who was getting into bed with whom, for both business and pleasure. As far as Anita knew, what Brita needed right now was a moment. A moment to exhale, to relax, to laugh, and Anita delivered, as only Anita could.

A third whisky followed the second and, bit by bit, Brita found herself unwinding. At first it was a giggle and a snicker, then a crackle, then an "Oh my God, no way, do you remember when…" By the time her fourth tumbler was poured, Brita was rolling too, swapping story for story. And even though Brita's stories were all old, from far too long ago, it didn't matter. Not for now. She hadn't known how much she needed this.

Anita got a call; Brita made a jibe, wondering out loud whether the squirrels were missing her as she turned to take it. In the silence, Brita absent-mindedly flipped her phone back over, having completely forgotten what was hiding underneath. One hundred and thirty-seven missed calls: from Mariska, from Garfield, from Lloyd, her banker, a dozen numbers she didn't recognise, and a dozen more she didn't want to. Concern. Bewilderment. Frustration. It all came roaring back, and then:

A message from her father. Ghostly green, glowing in the warm light of Anita's kitchen.

Dad

Let them scoff.

They won't survive what's coming.

She stared at the message, blood pumping in her ears. She glanced up at Anita, staring out into her private courtyard, and watched her gesticulate into the phone as if the voice on the other end could see. Something about delays to an aircraft order. With a sudden, stabbing insight, Brita realised just who her father was referring to when he said they wouldn't survive what was coming. Brita clutched her phone so hard that it hurt. This was already messy, and it was only going to get worse.

Ding-dong.

"Anita—"

Din-din-din-din-ding-dong.

"I...I'll go get it." Brita stood, a steadying hand on the table. The doorbell continued its incessant dinging, whoever was pressing it having no intention of letting it rest. She took a deep breath, the smooth steel of the dead bolt cool in her fingers. She twisted it, and it made a satisfying clunk.

"Brita! What the fuck is going on?"

Brita jumped, having to fight every instinct not to slam the door back in Mariska's face. The Hungarian curl her protege had fought so hard to eradicate from her vowels was back with a vengeance. They always slipped back in when she was angry.

"You can't just run off like that! They're all in a panic!"

"Mas, listen—How did you find me?"

Mariska rolled her eyes and held up her phone to show a photo of a pair of whisky tumblers, empty, with lipstick on the rim. Taken by Anita, in her kitchen, and posted less than half an hour ago. Brita groaned.

"So?"

"Look, I know you're frustrated—"

"Frustrated?" Mariska's heavy eyebrows shot right up to her hairline. Her lips pulled back, baring her teeth. "Yesterday, I was frustrated. Thirteen billion for our shareholders, thirteen million for me, my new—" She stopped herself midsentence and took a sharp, agitated breath. "All of it gone because your dad calls for the first time in forever. Sure, that's frustrating, but Stora is your company, not mine. But now? What kind of bullshit was that? On live TV? You couldn't have made my next fortnight harder if you'd been bloody trying! Give me one good reason why I shouldn't quit right fucking now!"

"Listen, come inside." Brita pulled her into the hallway and was unable to stop herself from grinning as she closed the door, cutting the bustle of the street to nothing. "And, if you want just one reason, your stock options will never be worth less than they are right now."

Mariska threw her hands up in the air. "You think this is funny? Maybe this is a game for you, a few million here, twelve billion there. Not everyone was born with your silver spoon."

Brita fought her smile down, grabbed Mariska's hands, and drew them together. "I'm sorry, you're right. You're one hundred percent right. I know how hard you worked to bring that deal to fruition, and I can imagine what it looks like, my going off half-cocked tonight."

"Emotional, Brita. That's how it looked. Like it had all gotten the better of you." Mariska's features softened. "You and I both know that's the last thing a woman in your position can afford."

"I know."

"So what's going on? What on earth did your prick of a father say?"

"Yes, Brita." Anita swanned down the corridor. Brita and Mariska had hardly made it beyond the coatrack. "What did your prick of a father say?"

Brita smiled. "Anita, look who decided to drop by."

"Stop dodging the question." Anita jabbed her in the ribs.

"Whatever it is, it's commercial in confidence." Mariska pouted. Anita just rolled her eyes.

"Mas is right, I'm afraid."

"You're lucky I'm not a shareholder." There was mischief in Anita's grin, but also genuine curiosity. Brita couldn't bear to look at her.

"After this evening's performance, you're lucky you're not." Mariska said. In the awkward silence, she nodded towards the exit and placed a not-so-subtle hand on Brita's back. "Come on. I have a cab waiting."

"Whisking her off to limit the damage?" Anita smirked.

"Something like that." Mariska opened the door, and the cool night air puckered Brita's skin. Before Mas could tug her through, Brita pulled her old friend into a hug. "Thanks for having me. I really needed that."

"Anytime."

"Send my regards to Dame Westover and her grey squirrels."

"Red squirrels, darling. The grey ones do *not* need our help." Anita grinned as she waved goodbye.

Mariska led her between nighttime revellers, relaxing only once they reached the silence of the empty cab. Mariska looked as tired as Brita felt.

"You still haven't answered my question." Mariska leaned her head back against the padded leather and closed her eyes. Brita had a feeling she knew there would be no satisfactory answer. How could there be?

"No, I haven't." The driver asked where they were headed, and before Mariska could answer, she gave him her father's address. "But not because I don't have one. You just need to see it for yourself."

4

What a trainwreck.

Mariska hunkered down into the back seat of the cab, her arms tightly crossed, her gaze resolutely focused on the city whizzing by. Brita was smiling. Just sitting there, grinning like an idiot, after everything that had happened. She just couldn't face it.

Why? Why did I think Jorge and O2TV would be a good fit? Because he was a hack. A hack that still carried a semblance of respectability from the nineties, who would make it look like Brita was facing the tough questions, without presenting any real risk. As long as Brita played ball.

Mariska scowled as they crossed the Thames, the bright copper Stora logo like a mocking beacon in the rearview mirror. A live TV interview was such a stupid risk. Why would Brita play it safe? She never had before. Because the board and the shareholders were pissed? Jorge was right, she was too much like her bloody father. Two hours Mariska had wasted talking blindsided executives down from the ledge, somehow plugging the leaks, calming the banks, staving off the collapse. For now at least. She'd even hunted her boss down, dragged her away from that toff Anita Kingston, and for what? To have her intelligence insulted? To get nothing but cryptic answers and knowing smiles?

Fuck that.

She glared at the back of the cab driver's head. She wanted to tell him to stop, right here, and let her the fuck out, but she knew she couldn't. Buried within the folds of her coat, she balled her hands into shaking fists. Why couldn't she just be angry? Why did she have to be so goddamn curious as well? That phone call, those three words: *Gateway. It's working.*

What did it all mean?

The cab turned off Lambeth Bridge and rumbled over cobblestones. Whatever it was, it had gotten under Brita's skin so deeply that she'd torn up a deal she'd been desperate for and melted down on live TV. And now she was smiling. It was unbearable.

The cab jagged down a narrow side road, and Mariska's breath caught. She slumped back into her seat, unable to tear her eyes from a very familiar terraced house. White sandstone, black iron fencing, black door. Was Brita being intentionally cruel? She risked a quick glance across at her boss and realised that no, of course not. Hugo lived in Knightsbridge; that was all. She tried not to pine as the softly lamplit stair faded into the night.

Dammit, Brita, that house was perfect. Papa would have hated every bourgeois inch of it.

"Trust me, Mas. In an hour, that little apartment you're pining over will look like a hovel."

Compared to where you grew up, everything looks like a hovel! Mariska wanted to scream it into Brita's face, but she bit her tongue. Bottled it up and swallowed it down. Yelling wouldn't bring the Solomon deal back from the dead. And it wouldn't satisfy her curiosity.

There will be other deals. Other houses. Other bosses.

Burning bridges was a desperate tactic, and she wasn't desperate. Not yet, anyway.

— • —

The cab pulled up to the curb, and reluctantly, Mariska swung the door open and stepped out onto the tree-lined street. The paving, the stonework, the ironwork, all of it was old. Old money. So ancient you could smell it. Next to Hugo's towering residence, her little terrace seemed positively tacky. Brita strode up the steps, and Mariska fully expected the front door to swing open and a silent butler to usher them inside.

But that's not what happened.

Brita tried the handle, rapped the knocker hard three times, then three times again. She pulled out her phone.

"You don't have a key?" Mariska asked, hugging herself tight against the falling chill. Now that she was out of the cab and loitering in the street, "antique" and "historic" were becoming "musty" and "damp" and "chilly."

"Hah, very funny." Brita tossed her answer out there as if this was totally normal and pressed her phone to her ear, glancing up at the black window on the second floor.

"Yes. We're out the front." An exasperated sigh. "Mariska. Yes, I told you about her. Yes—No—Just look out the window!" There was not even a hint of movement. "Fine, don't look. Just come down and let us in. Christ." Brita muttered, only after she'd violently disconnected the call.

Mariska tried to remember the last time she'd seen Hugo Gundersson, not as he was on the promotional photos and corporate histories, but live. In the flesh. Or even on TV.

She couldn't. Every image she dredged up was of Hugo the founder, tall, full head of white hair and carefully groomed beard. Barrel chested. Vital. There must have been footage from after, the way the paparazzi hunted down any scandal in this bloody country, but it had been expunged from the corporate records. She had only ever seen him smiling.

She took in Brita, bathed in the dappled light of a streetlamp half-hidden behind a drooping oak tree. She'd tucked her phone away, and now her shoulders were tense. Her cocky smile was gone, and Mariska felt a pang of sympathy. This must be, what, the third time Brita and her father had spoken in over a decade? The second? She exhaled softly and clenched her teeth. At least he was still around to cause stress. Mariska didn't even have that.

The lock clicked once, then twice, and the door opened onto a dark hallway. Mariska squinted, but she could make out nothing beyond the doorframe. Brita stepped through it and disappeared, only for her face to reappear a moment later.

"Are you coming or not?"

"I'm coming, I'm coming." Mariska nodded and jogged up the stairs, pushing aside the sudden nerves that had taken control of the back of her neck, and the feeling that once she crossed the threshold, there would be no turning back.

⸺ ⁕ ⸺

Mariska blinked, her eyes failing to adjust to the dingy interior. There was no butler dressed in black with polished leather shoes. The hall smelled of musty papers and dust. Hugo apparently didn't even have a cleaner. Someone brushed past her and pushed the door closed, the lock ramming home with a heavy clunk.

Then there was silence.

"I don't like this." The voice was as dry and dusty as the hallway, and despite the years and the damage, there was no mistaking the clipped Swedish cadence. Hugo Gundersson. He sounded old.

"Then you shouldn't have opened the door." Brita sounded impatient.

"I don't trust her."

"You've never met her."

"It's too early—"

"No, Dad. Just no. You're the one who called me. There's no going back. This is happening." The double click of heels on timber broke through the muffled silence, and light flared from a cobwebbed chandelier. Brita stood by the stairs, a bright and vibrant figure amongst stacks of grey paper and sheet-covered furniture. "So let's get on with it."

"You're not in charge of this," Hugo growled from behind Mariska's ear. "Gateway is mine."

"If the Gateway was yours, you wouldn't have had to beg me not to sell." Brita jabbed her finger at her own chest, her cheeks flushing with anger. "After everything you've done, after everything this has cost. You owe me."

"I owe you?" Hugo blanched, knocking into Mariska as he pushed past her. She caught only a glimpse of his features, but it was enough. The hearty, charming man from the photos on the office walls was gone. His hair was ragged, his beard patchy, his cheeks sunken, those broad shoulders hunched beneath a knitted sweater, marked with stains and far, far too big. If she hadn't been in his house, hadn't heard Brita call him Dad, she wouldn't have recognised him. He'd spent the last decade wasting away, until all that remained was resentment. She could see it twisting and coiling beneath his every movement.

He stood in front of his daughter, stood over her, and Mariska waited. What was he going to say? What was he going to do? He raised his hand, and Brita did not move. Didn't even look at it. She met his glare, but not with anger. Her face softened. She almost looked sad.

"No matter how much you want it to, Gateway won't bring back anything that we've lost." She reached out and took his hand in hers, curled her manicured nails around his grimy fingers. "The best we can do is make something new."

Reluctantly, Hugo nodded.

"And if we're going to do that, it can't be just us. We're going to need help. Okay?" Her boss didn't wait for an answer. "Good."

Brita nodded up the stairs and placed an encouraging hand on her father's back. It was only when she turned to give her an apologetic look that Mariska realised she'd been staring, jaw hanging open, and dropped her gaze to the floor.

"I'm sorry you had to see that."

"No, that's, umm..." Mariska looked back up, not sure what she was going to see, but Brita's eyes were clear, her features open. Almost excited. *And I thought my relationship with my parents was strained.* The thought flashed into being before she could stop it, and it caused a tightness behind her eyes. She was no one to judge.

"Come on, Dad's workshop is just up here. What he's about to show you will be worth it."

*What he's about to show me...*Mariska grabbed the handrail. "Gateway?"

Brita nodded, her eyes sparkling.

"What is it?"

"You'll see soon enough."

"Ugh," Mariska muttered, glaring partial daggers at her boss's back as she followed her up the stairs. *When had Brita become so smug?* Her thoughts oscillated between the things she'd very much like to do to Brita's neck, and an increasingly mad spiral of imaginings about the nature of this mysterious "Gateway." Is this what it had been like, sitting in the audience awaiting the launch of the iPhone? Steve Jobs standing there in his obnoxious black turtleneck, grinning because he knew things the rest of the room did not?

"Oh, wow."

Mariska stopped, stuck on the final step. She could only stare.

The entire second floor of the terrace had been gutted. Plumbing and wiring hung exposed from the ceiling, and the gaps in the plaster ran like jagged scars where the walls had been ripped out, leaving the beams exposed, the floor above supported only by crude props. There was no furniture, or no furniture that you would expect in an eighteenth-century terrace. This was no longer a drawing room or a dining room. This was a lab.

A stainless steel bench ran along three of the walls, the fourth painted a sterile, almost liquid white and covered in scrawled equations and diagrams. The room's centre was filled with rack upon rack of equipment. Arcane machines humming quietly in their corners. Wires, circuit boards, boxes with knobs, boxes with lights. It was chaos, and yet it was also ordered. Everything that needed to be stored or categorised had been, and everything else had been left to rot. It reminded her of a past life, of old and new fighting for supremacy and her parents caught in the middle—

"Here, hold this."

Hugo shoved a heavy block into her hand. The back was rough, a cobbled-together mishmash of industrial plastic and copper wiring. And yet the underside was so smooth against her palm. She flipped it and blinked. It was a phone. A Stora phone, a Komtil model, maybe six years old. The hardened glass screen was smudged with grease, and it had what looked like a massive auxiliary battery pack jerry-rigged to the back.

"And do what? What is this?" Mariska asked, but Hugo had already retreated to the other side of the room and collapsed into a well-worn swivel chair.

"That's Project Gateway."

"Project Gateway?" She glanced pleadingly at Brita, but her boss simply shrugged, maintaining that infuriating, inscrutable smile.

Project Gateway. She flipped the phone again, inspecting the battery bank. Whatever it was, surely this couldn't be the reason for the death of the Solomon deal, and for that outburst with the Spanish reporter. It looked like something out of a horror movie.

The phone's rear panel had been discarded completely, and the screen's usual smooth bevels had been covered over by a battered copper rim. The power and volume buttons, the charge port and the phone jack, they were all inaccessible, and dotted around the back were a dozen soldered connections to wires that snaked out from beneath the pack. Two cable ties, ratcheted tight across the screen, held it all together. Just.

It vibrated in her hand, the original casing buzzing against the new copper rim. The screen flickered to life, showing an incoming call from an unknown number.

"Go on, answer it," Brita urged.

Mariska snuck a glance over at Hugo. He had a similar-looking contraption clutched in his lap, but he was watching her. Intently. Something very strange was going on here. Very strange indeed. Her finger hesitated over the pulsing green circle, the roof of her mouth suddenly parched. She swallowed, gulped in a lungful of air.

"What are you waiting for?" Hugo demanded, at once eager and resentful.

Mariska didn't have a good answer. And yet... He leered at her from across the cold, empty room, as if daring her to back out, to leave him and his daughter in peace. *Fat chance of that, old man.* She closed her eyes and swiped.

The phone pulsed one more time and then lay dormant in her hand. If anything, she could have sworn there was a faint rush of air. She opened her eyes, and the muted grey graphics had been replaced by a crystal-crisp image of the underside of Hugo's beard.

"That's..." She lifted the handset closer, studied the individual hairs, in particular a small section with hard twisted ends, where a soldering iron had clearly gotten too close. She could almost smell his musk. *Christ, it's as if he's sitting in my lap.*

"That's a remarkable picture." Hugo shifted his grip, and the image shifted with it, absolutely flawless. "And not a hint of digital compression. What is it? A new screen prototype? A new network chip of some kind?"

"Ha, not quite." Brita smiled. "Show her, Dad."

"You might want to sit her down first."

Brita shared a secret grin with her father as she brushed a stack of textbooks from a lonely folding chair and fetched it over, which only made Mariska study the image all the more carefully. Hugo's flat instruction had rasped from the phone so cleanly that she almost didn't care that he'd spoken of her as if she were a child. She rotated the contraption to one side, wondering if there were larger speakers embedded within the battery bank, but she could see nothing, and she allowed Brita to guide her down onto the edge of the seat.

The chair creaked and groaned beneath her, but she barely noticed. She'd turned the phone back over and now studied the edges of the screen, or rather, the lack of edges. The close-up of Hugo's face bypassed the bevel completely, and there wasn't even a hint of the recessed home button and print scanner at the bottom, or the front-facing camera and notification LEDs at the top. The image covered the entire surface bounded by the copper rim, impeded only by the two cable ties stretched taut across it.

"I think she's ready."

Ready for what? Mariska wondered, as Hugo raised his phone from his lap so that it showed the entirety of his face. Every line, every crease, every bloodshot vessel in the whites of his eyes. She leaned forward, as if the phone had its own gravity. Hugo lifted his free hand, one finger pointed as if to tap a notification, and then it kept coming.

And coming.

Coming through.

Mariska froze, unable to reconcile what her senses were telling her with the reality she knew. *That can't be real. Can't possibly be real.* She shook her head, mouth open, with nothing coming in or going out. Somewhere in the background she registered her boss's glee, Hugo's smug pride, but her mind rejected it. All of it.

The phone slipped from her grip, and as it tumbled in slow motion, the evidence of her eyes became irrefutable. Protruding from the phone's screen, no, from where the phone's screen should have been, was Hugo's hand. One sun-spotted finger extended, three more curled into his palm. Soiled fingernails, coarse white hairs. His bony wrist. The faded wool of his sleeve. The whole damn thing.

Coming through the screen of the phone, arcing slowly towards the floor.

His falling fingers, five yards distant from their owner's arm, brushed her leg, grasping desperately. There was a yell. Then two. His hand reared, spasmed, snapped back, like a deep sea eel retreating into its cave. She looked up to see Hugo wrenching his hand from out of his phone as if it had been down the sink and the garburator had whirred to life.

And then the phone she had dropped hit the floor. Blinding white sparks flared outwards, accompanied by an electronic shriek.

And then silence.

At her feet, the phone was just a phone again. No impossibilities. Just a blank screen, with smoke curling from the ugly contraption strapped to its back. But she had seen what it had been before, and her world was not the same.

5

—·—

"Dad!" Brita rushed across the cavernous workshop, a great knot coiling inside her chest. "Are you all right?"

He held his trembling hand before him as if it were a ghost, his chest heaving, the blood almost completely drained from his face. The Gateway phone was still clutched tight in his other hand, his grip like iron, his knuckles white.

She stopped two steps short of him. Despite everything, she was still unable to bring herself any closer. She slumped against the workbench, the sudden, unexpected flood and then release of emotion leaving her weak. There was no blood; all fingers were accounted for. His breathing steadied as he curled his hand into a fist.

"Dad?"

Very carefully, he set the Gateway-enabled handset on his bench, before stalking by without acknowledging her at all.

"What in God's name did you do that for?" Hugo roared, all of the fear that had taken him now hardening into malice, directed at the distraught, uncomprehending Mariska. Brita shoved her way past her father and put her body between them.

"Stop!"

"I could have—"

"She didn't know that! How could she?" Brita relaxed her hands, which had somehow found their way to being pressed against his chest. "You're lucky I didn't drop it when you did the same thing to me."

He softened, just a little, his gaze sliding from Mariska down to the still-smoking handset lying on the floor. "Well. You're Gundersson stock. We're made of stronger stuff."

Brita knelt down. The Gateway unit was warm to the touch, but not burning hot. She hefted it, placing a hand on her friend's knee. She passed her father the broken handset, and his brow furrowed as he slid a battered pair of spectacles from his pocket and inspected it, tutting all the while.

"I'm sorry, Mas, that was a cruel thing to do. Two days ago, he did the same thing to me, and I reacted just about the same as you have tonight. I saw how much perverse pleasure he took in my reaction, and I guess I wanted to be the one on the other side."

Beneath her makeup, Mariska was as pale as Brita's father had been. She breathed out slowly, her lips still shaking. "Brita, what on God's green earth was that?" A touch of colour returned to her cheeks. "And don't just say 'Project Gateway' and expect me to cop it. No more glib bullshit. Okay?"

"Okay, Mas. I'm sorry. What you just saw—"

"Jesus!" Hugo wailed from over at his workbench.

"Dad, will you just give me a minute?"

"She's busted three of the connections between the containment fie—no! Four! Jesus Christ!"

"Are they hard to fix?"

"No—"

"Then stop whining, and start working." Brita snorted loudly, expelling her frustration, visualising it floating away on her breath. *Spare me.* She ignored his protests and turned her attention back to Mariska. "Right, where were we."

"You were explaining whatever the fuck I just saw." Mariska bent forward, elbows on knees. "Because it looked like a goddamn magic trick."

Brita smiled. In fact, she beamed. How could she not? It was exactly like a magic trick, except it wasn't a trick at all. "You saw exactly what you thought you saw. My dad called you from across the room, and you answered. The moment you did, a connection was made between those two phones, what Dad calls a Gateway. It's as if..." She paused, her words failing her. She called out to her father. "How did you explain it?"

"The Gateway connection folds space, like two faces of the same sheet of paper." Hugo remained buried in his work, the soldering iron tracing delicate repairs. "So at the same time, the phone screens were both six yards apart, and flat against one another. Back to back."

"How?" Mariska's eyes were wide open, but there was a tension there, behind the wonder. As if she didn't quite want to believe.

"The how isn't important. That's Dad's domain. What matters is that it's real. That was Dad's hand coming through the screen. And it doesn't have to be a hand. It could be anything. Food delivery. A package. A scent, an experience. Oil. Light. Heat. Anything. With the touch of a button."

Mariska shook her head. "No. I don't believe it."

"If you hadn't dropped it, you wouldn't have to believe it. You could have tried it for yourself."

Brita rolled her eyes and had half turned to scold her father, but Mariska beat her to it.

"Would you give it a rest, Mr Gundersson? What did you think would happen?"

"Give it a rest? Give it a rest!" Her father spun, brandishing his soldering iron like a weapon. "Don't you get it? Gateway is my life. My *life*! Ever since—"

"And for the last twelve months the Solomon deal was my life, but that doesn't seem to matter to either of you," Mariska spat, bitterness and fatigue and shock twisting her words into nasty shapes.

"But you see why I had to kill it now." Brita said gently.

"No. No, I bloody don't." The chair scraped back violently as Mariska got to her feet. "And I don't care to find out. Usually I'd say it was a pleasure, Mr Gundersson, but under the circumstances I'm sure you'll understand if I just see myself out."

A hot, futile anxiety coiled up Brita's neck as she watched her investment chief pull out her phone and stalk towards the stairs. She knew what she'd seen; she just didn't want to accept it. And Brita got it: she'd felt the same way. Worse even. To be so close to getting out, and then to hear her father's voice for the first time in a decade. To see his face. Gloating, like he'd proven himself right after all these years. She'd wanted to break his smug fucking nose. But she hadn't. She'd come around. There was just no denying the Gateway's potential.

But would Mas be able to do the same? Everything that had happened these last few days, the deal, the interview, the aftermath. They were all out of Mas's hands, actions that Brita had taken. Mas only dealt with the fallout. To her, right now, Gateway was just one more shitfight. One more crazy thing she couldn't control. Walking away was something she could. Even if it would be the biggest mistake of her life.

"I thought you said she was smart, Brita."

Mariska's stride faltered, just for a moment, and the knot in Brita's stomach squeezed that little bit tighter. *Will you just shut it, Dad. Just this once.* She held her breath. She could see from the effort Mas was putting into every step that she was right on the edge. "She is smart. It's just—"

"Well, she certainly isn't acting like it."

With her hand on the banister, Mariska stopped dead. The knot that had been building and building in Brita's stomach fell through the floor.

"You know what's smart, Hugo? Extracting myself from whatever the fuck is going on between you two. Your petty bullshit has already blown up a thirteen billion dollar deal. Why on earth would I want to hang around to watch the rest of this fucking trainwreck?"

"Mas, whatever's between my father and I—" Brita began, but her father cut her off.

"Don't bother, Brita. If she can't see the bigger picture, then we don't need her."

"Bigger picture? What bigger picture!" Mas was beside herself, her eyes wide, but, Brita noted, she had stepped back into the room. "All I see here is the latest cycle of a fucking family squabble, over a bastardised conjuring trick held together with cable ties. Your 'Gateway' is nothing. It's a mirage."

"A mirage?" her father exploded, snatching the handset he'd been working on up from the bench. "Where did you find this fucking imbecile—"

"Dad, you're not helping."

"No, Brita. I'm out." Mariska waved her hand. Her father's insults had been the final straw. "Good luck with...all of this."

"Mas—"

"Let her go." Her father placed a heavy hand on her shoulder. It was the first time he had initiated contact in over a decade. "We can do this on our own. You and me, that's all we need."

Tears pricked at the corners of Brita's eyes. How she wished that were true. But there were so many roadblocks. Funding, regulation, competitors, the government. God, if anyone caught wind of this, even a whiff, before they were ready. Sharks like Solomon were already circling, and what had she done? Issued a challenge to their biggest competitors on national TV! What had she been thinking?

"No, Dad. We can't. It's not the sixties anymore. We need help." She turned back to the stairs, but Mariska was gone, her heeled footsteps echoing down the hall.

"You really trust her?"

Brita looked up at her father. He looked tired. Like he no longer wanted to fight. "I do."

"All right then." He swiped at his handset, dialled a number, and handed it over. "Tell her that."

The phone vibrated softly, once, twice, three times. Mariska's footsteps fell silent. Brita listened for the telltale clack of the bolt on her father's front door sliding open. It didn't come. Instead, the Gateway hummed, and the phone screen shimmered and vanished. What she held in her hand was a portal into her father's dusty hallway, the must intermingling with the subtle scent of Mariska's perfume. The only light was what flowed through the Gateway, a diffuse rectangle illuminating her protege's squinting, exasperated face.

"What."

"Gateway is real, Mas. It exists. You can see that, I know you can. And not just see it. You can smell it. Feel it." Brita paused, hoping Mariska would say something, make some concession, but she simply stood there with her hands on her hips, her jaw set. "But you're right, too. It might be real, but it is definitely not ready. To make Gateway a *reality*, for Stora, we need your help. I need your help."

Mas stayed silent for a long time. Brita bit the inside of her lip, counted her heartbeats, and studied Mariska for any sign of a tell. Her dark hazel eyes gave nothing away, until they softened, just slightly.

"I want that apartment."

Brita's cheeks flushed with relief. "It's yours."

Mariska nodded, and then she was gone. Brita pressed the button on the side of the battery pack. The Gateway collapsed with a small pop, but the smell of the hallway lingered, and Mariska's approaching footsteps echoed up the stairs.

6

HUGO SHUFFLED BACK OVER to his workbench and allowed himself to fall down into his chair. This evening was veering off course. *And how had you imagined it going, hmm? Did you think your daughter would just accept you seamlessly back into her life, back into the company? Let you run things again? With one phone call? One dazzling invention?*

He watched her, leaning up against one of the scaffold supports that held up the roof, her head tilted to one side. The dormant Gateway dangled from her hand. *She looks almost as tired as I feel.*

The echo of sharp heels on oak changed timbre from a muffled clack to a deeper thump. His daughter's assistant, whatever her name was, had just reached the bottom of the stairs. Maz? Mas? Something like that. He smiled to himself. She certainly had guts, calling Brita, her boss, out on her bullshit. Maybe working with her wouldn't be so bad after all.

"What apartment is she talking about?" he asked.

"Hmmm? Oh, a little place she had her eye on. Across from St John's Garden. She was going to buy it, once the Solomon deal went through." Brita twisted around, waggling the handset in his direction. "Why do you have a Gateway set up in the hallway."

Hugo shot a guilty glance at the silver filing cabinet against the wall, inside which he kept his old hunting rifle. He swallowed. "Just in case."

Mas topped the stairs and stopped, her hand resting on the banister. As if she still wasn't convinced, and might turn around and leave at any time. "Did you get it working again?"

Hugo swivelled on his chair back to his workbench. The repairs looked ugly, lumpy globs of solder holding strips of copper together, discoloured from the heat. But the whole thing looked ugly. He nodded to her. It would work.

"Let me see." She strode across to the workbench, taking the Gateway handset out of Brita's hands as she passed. Without quite knowing why, Hugo found himself backing out of her way.

She set them up side by side, and with a quick double tap on the repaired Gateway handset's screen, she initiated a call. The vibration rattled through the steel of the workbench, sending loose screws dancing across its surface. Then, with that characteristic shimmer, that soft, unobtrusive puff of air, the Gateway connection sprang into being.

I'll never tire of seeing that, Hugo thought. He'd been chasing the Gateway for longer than he could remember. Narrowing his focus so that only the research mattered. Nothing else. And now it was real. Proof that he was right.

He took in his workshop with new eyes. Brita, standing a pace or two back with her arms crossed, curious at what Mas was attempting, and surrounded by this cavernous space. A space that he had gutted, and filled with every tool and contraption that money could buy. A space that had once held her bedroom. The window that he'd blacked out had been in her library, and her nursery before that. She'd had a cushioned bench beneath it and had read all day there, overlooking the trees in the back garden.

He glanced at his daughter. She caught his look, and she smiled at him, the movement creating wrinkles in the corners of her eyes that travelled all the way back to her temple. How long had they been there? And when had she started wearing so much makeup? He took her in as she was now, rather than as the daughter he had known, and realised that she'd begun to grow old. Like him. That's not how it had been, back before—

Hugo coughed, forcing a shiver down his spine. Following that line of thinking would only dredge bad memories, and worse, up from the depths. He turned his attention back to Mariska, the two handsets, and the open Gateway, both portals showing him two aspects of his tattered, crumbling ceiling.

Mas scooped up a handful of screws and held them above the right-hand Gateway, and through it he saw a second version of that hand from below. She opened her fingers and the screws tumbled down, and through, and then shot right back up into the air. They sparkled in the harsh fluorescent light.

"Wow." He crouched down, ignoring his protesting knees, until his eyes were level with the open Gateways. Four stainless screws climbed to the top of their apex and paused, as if to take in the view, before gravity dragged them back down, only for the Gateway to intervene. Instead of landing on his benchtop, they fell through the open portal and, for them, gravity flipped. They jumped half a foot sideways and went from falling to climbing again, only for gravity to reassert itself, forcing them into a never-ending loop. It was mesmerising.

The screws fell, jumped, then rose once more, but this time Mariska was waiting, and she snatched them right out of the air. Whatever anger, frustration, and defensiveness there had been were now totally forgotten.

"All right, Hugo, you've got me. Walking away would have been the dumbest thing I ever did. But"—she jabbed a manicured finger at his daughter—"nowhere near as dumb as what you actually fucking did tonight. Why? Why would you ever let slip that something like this was coming?"

"I..." Brita stammered, a red flush rising in her cheeks. She glanced at him, nervous.

Let slip? Hugo chest tightened, and his eyes flicked involuntarily to the Gateway, to *his* Gateway, and then the blacked-out window and the world outside that wanted to take it away from him. To the rifle he stored in the closet. He turned back to his daughter, and an accusation croaked from his mouth. "What did you do."

Brita was pleading with Mariska. He could see it in her eyes.

"Brita. What did you *do*?"

"He doesn't know?"

"Dad? You sent me a message. I thought you knew."

Brita's eyes bulged, and Hugo felt like his were about to explode. "Know what! What don't I know?"

Mariska smiled. A wicked, malicious little smile. "Your daughter was on TV tonight."

"Dad, I was defending the decision to kill the Solomon deal, and I..."

"And you what? What, Brita?" An uneasy energy drove his feet. He was pacing. He didn't know what to do with his hands.

"She threw down the challenge to Apple and Samsung, Hugo. Said Stora would blow them out of the water within five years. You should have seen her. She sounded like a fucking loony toon..."

Hugo was no longer listening. He could barely even see straight. They were going to come for the Gateway. He knew they would, he fucking knew it! They were going to come, and they were going to take it away, and all that work, all that effort, the sweat, the blood, the sacrifice, the *years*. All of it would be for...for...

The room was spinning, and he was floating, sliding sideways—

—■·■—

Hugo blinked. Brita's face filled his vision. His daughter. Why had he called her? She'd stolen his company. Taken away the only thing that had really mattered to him. That made *him* matter at all.

Her mouth was moving. What was she saying?

"Dad?" A glass of water appeared at his lips. He gulped at it. When had he last drunk water? Or eaten? "Dad, what was that? Are you all right?"

"All right! All right?" He shook his head, the words not coming. He clutched the glass in both hands to stop them from shaking.

She looked down on him with pity, like he was an old man. They both did. It was happening again. He'd opened the door for her, let her back into his life. She was barely through, and already she was up to her old tricks. Planting seeds. But he knew her game. Gateway was his, and unlike Stora, it would remain his. *I should never have opened that door.* He'd slammed it shut for a damn good reason.

"I didn't say a word about the Gateway. Not one." She crouched down, so that she looked up at him. Like she had when she was a kid. She reached out for his hands, but he pulled them away. "I'm sorry. Mas is one hundred percent right. It was stupid. I went off script because I was mad, excited, and so, so sick of being told I don't know what I'm doing. I made myself look desperate, like I was clutching at straws. I—"

"She sounded like you, Hugo." Where his daughter's expression seemed designed to placate and reassure him, Mariska's glare was hard. Uncompromising. "Like the Hugo Gundersson that almost ran Stora into the ground."

"That's not fair."

"It is fair. Jorge was spot on. He read you like a book, and it was a lucky thing, Brita. For once all this family bullshit worked in our favour." Mariska waved a hand in their general direction. "No one fucking believed you."

"Hah!" The barking laugh burst out. Hugo couldn't stop it. He looked from Brita to Mariska and back again, his daughter suddenly on the defensive. Pulled down a peg or two.

"Don't think you're getting away scot-free, old man. Three hours ago what your daughter said was absolute nonsense, but now that I've seen this"—Mariska pointed to the still active Gateways, humming quietly on the workbench—"She was on the money. Apple and Samsung won't know what hit them. If we do this right."

Old man? Hugo scowled. He was just starting to like her, too. "We'll do this right, don't you worry."

"Worrying is my job, Hugo, and you worry me."

"Mas—"

"You both worry me. You've not spoken to one another for what, twelve years? Let me ask you a question—whose fault is that?"

Hugo stared at his daughter, and she stared back at him. He crossed his arms. He knew who's fucking fault it was, and it wasn't his. He'd been the one to break the silence after all. He'd called her.

"Mas, now is not the time."

"No, Brita, you're right. Of course. Much better to let this fester away for later, when there's actual capital on the line, decisions that have been made, and contracts to be fulfilled."

"Mariska, look. I get that—"

"Why did you hire me?" Mas cut his daughter off, and Hugo noticed the colour rising in her cheeks. She was getting flustered. He fought to keep a smile from appearing on his lips.

"That's not the point—"

"Why did you hire me?"

Brita sighed. "Because you can read people."

"Because I can read rich white men, like him." Mas jabbed a finger directly at him. Hugo shifted in his seat. "And because I can read rich white men like him, I know that the two of you need to have a conversation, right now." Mariska turned and grabbed another chair. She dragged it across, metal legs scraping across the bare floorboards, and plonked it in front of him.

"I know what I want. Money, lots of it. And the power that lots of money will give me." She stepped back, leaned against the workbench, and crossed her legs. "What do the two of you want?"

Hugo shifted his weight back in his chair and set the empty glass on the ground. Meanwhile, his daughter stood, slowly, her hand on the back of the chair Mariska had dragged over. She couldn't quite meet his gaze.

"Don't look at me." Mariska laughed. It wasn't a pleasant sound. "Talk to each other. Figure it out." Then she turned around, fished a screw from her pocket, and set it looping through the Gateways again. *As if she's forgotten we're here at all.*

Hugo turned his attention to his daughter. If someone was going to take the lead, it should be him. It had always been him. Her body faced him, knees together, hands resting on her thighs, but her head was turned towards her subordinate. *The way her hair gets caught behind her ears…* Hugo blinked. *Lord, she looks like her mother.*

And then she turned, and the memory was gone. She was his daughter again, with the set jaw and defensive gaze of the woman that had ousted him from the company he had built from nothing.

This had been a long time coming. Too long.

"I like her." Hugo said, making himself relax and nodding Mariska's way. "Even though she called me an old man."

Brita almost smiled. "You are an old man."

"I know. But she didn't need to remind me."

The smiles lingered, then faltered. Words and sentences chased one another around, but Hugo couldn't seem to grasp them. Twelve years of burying himself in the Gateway so he didn't have to think about what she'd done to him, and about what he'd done to himself, were coming home to roost. He looked down at his hands, nicked and calloused from decades of work, nails stained with grease. Hands that had created something amazing.

Hands that didn't want to let go. That had never wanted to let go.

"I—"

"Dad—"

They both spoke, but stopped. Both laughed, nervously, and waved the other on. Then he looked her in the eye, and saw something there he recognised, deeply: regret. He sat back and let his daughter speak.

"Dad, I'm sorry for what I...for cutting you out. For going behind your back. It...it wasn't easy."

"I didn't make it easy." *And nor should I have!*

"No. You didn't." She looked at him, looked away. "But I shouldn't have let that...Look. Just because it's been broken a long time doesn't mean it can't be repaired. I want to make us whole. You and me whole. Stora whole. That's what I want."

"You were going to throw it away. Without even talking to me, you were going to sell it to some Yank."

"I was. I really was. And I was happy about it. Ecstatic. I figured...I'd done all I could. I'd fixed what you'd broken. It was time to make something of my own. Then..." She smiled, sweetly, with a twinkle in her eye. "I got your phone call. I'm so glad I did."

Hugo tried to discern what was going on behind the mask, behind the bitten lip and the remnants of the TV studio makeup. Was she calculating her every word? How much of this was real? Could he trust her? The rising heat in his chest told him he wanted to, so much more than he realised. The tightness in his gut fought against it, begging him not to. Not again. Not ever.

Then why did I make the call? Why did I pick up the phone and dial the number?

"You know, when I got them working, I didn't even hesitate. I didn't even think about it. Calling you was the first thing I did."

"Why?"

Because the original sketches and diagrams, the foundational research, is all still in Stora's archives, that's why. Because I'm still listed as an honorary director, so Stora owns it all. You own it all. Because you would have sold it, ripped it all out of my hands again, for a handful of silver. Not ever knowing what you'd done. I couldn't have that.

Hugo fought to keep his hands open, his shoulders relaxed. His smile pleasant. Understanding. "I called you because, after all these years, I'd had enough of the silence. I—"

"Bullshit!"

Hugo jumped. Mariska was perched against the workbench, elbows down, back arched, legs crossed. Behind her, a continuous arc of screws, capacitors and twists of wire looped gracefully from portal to portal. Which she ignored, instead watching him with a cynical smile.

"Complete and utter bullshit. The second you thought Brita had let slip about Gateway, you almost had a fucking stroke!"

"I didn't!"

"Dad, you absolutely did." His daughter laid a hand on his knee. He could feel the pity leaching into him, and he wanted nothing more than to kick it away. "The only reason you didn't hit the floor is because we caught you."

"Brita..."

"Hugo, tell her what Gateway really means to you. Or I walk."

Hugo's gaze flicked between the two women. His daughter, anxiously waiting, and Mariska, domineering, commanding the room. Mariska, this woman he'd never met, but who seemed to know him better than his own daughter.

Or, a malicious little snake whispered, *does Brita see through me too? Is she playing me? Are they both playing me? Testing me, probing my weaknesses, so they can figure out when and where to strike?*

"Dad?" Brita looked concerned. For him, or that he might be past it? Too old, too broken? That she might have to cut him out all over again, for the sake of the company?

"All right, fine. Fine. You want the truth? This is it." *Part of it, anyway.* "I called because I hate what you did to me. What I forced you to do to me, and what Stora became as a result. I spent twelve years locked away, working, because I wanted to show you, and show the world, that I'm not dead. Not past it. Not yet."

For a moment, neither of them reacted. Not Mariska, not Brita. Hugo held his daughter's gaze, not daring to look Mariska's way, lest he see that she saw through him. That she knew he'd left out the most important part. That the Gateway was his chance to take back what was his. Once and for all.

"Dad. We'll bring Stora back. Better than it ever was. I promise." The intensity, the need in her eyes made Hugo shift uncomfortably in his seat. He had to force himself to hold her gaze, to not succumb to doubt.

"Good." Mariska clapped, snapping him back to the room. To the task at hand. He breathed a sigh of relief. "Now that that's out of the way, I have one question."

She carefully lifted one of the Gateways off the bench, keeping it level, making sure the odds and ends continued to loop from one handset to the other, until she held it in front of her. One by one, each object fell, disappearing down the Gateway, before they reappeared, hovering over her shoulder as gravity yet again halted their ascent, before dragging them back down, back into the never-ending loop.

"Just one?" Brita quipped.

Mariska grinned, and Hugo could almost see the pound signs rolling behind her eyes.

"Can you make them bigger?"

7

"BIGGER?" BRITA RAISED AN eyebrow at her friend. "You already need two hands to carry one. Surely they need to be smaller?"

But Mariska wasn't looking at her. She was looking at her father. Waiting for his response as he eyed her with...with what? Brita knew that look, that combination of curiosity and challenge. It set her pulse racing. She'd grown up with that look beaming down on her over breakfast, over homework and assignments, over home projects. And then later, much later, she'd come to recognise it in herself. But then it had disappeared, and it wasn't until now, seeing it again in her father's haggard eyes, that she understood how much she'd missed it.

Finally, her father spoke. "How much bigger?"

"Wide enough for a chef to pass a plate of steaming hot goulash with dumplings from his kitchen in Budapest, straight to my dining room? For a forklift to pick up a pallet of shoes from India, a pallet of oranges from California, then a pallet of microchips from Taiwan? For a brand-new Porsche, rolling off the production line in Stuttgart and right into your garage?"

Her father nodded as Mariska spoke, and his gaze lost focus as the technical problems began to take over. "Yes...yes. There's no reason the size of the Gateway opening has to be tied to the size of a phone screen, none at all. There would be implications for power draw, but the plate is definitely doable. And the others—"

"They're the obvious next steps." Mariska set the Gateway back down on the workbench, far less carefully this time, and the cascade of screws and transistors collapsed, scattering themselves across the floor. "If we don't take them, someone else will."

"Someone else?" Brita blurted. The idea of competition shocked her, though it shouldn't have. *I've been too wrapped up in the idea to even think about the implications.* She glanced at her father. *We both have.* Mariska was the perfect person to snap them back to the real world.

"The Gateway is mine. There is no one else."

"For now. But the moment we launch…"

Brita glanced worriedly at her father. The mere mention of her slip-up on Jorge's show had sent him into a tailspin just half an hour before. But not now, it seemed. Even beneath his ragged beard she could see his jaw was set.

"Our launch will blow everyone else away." He was so confident.

"Dad, Apple may have done that to us with the iPhone—"

"Not just us."

"But not everyone. Samsung reacted, fast and hard. Took advantage of the turmoil, and others followed. First mover's advantage is shorter than ever these days."

"For a new phone maybe, but not for the Gateway! Did you hear what she said? This isn't a new type of screen or a better camera. This is the combustion engine! The silicon chip!"

"And who invented the combustion engine, Dad?" Brita pushed herself to her feet, leaving the squeaking folding chair behind. "It wasn't Toyota, or Volkswagen. Did Maersk invent the shipping container? No. Did Google invent internet search? Did Richard Solomon invent social media? Things have changed. The moment we launch, a million engineers from California and Shenzhen to Delhi and Taipei and Amsterdam will be ripping the Gateway apart to figure out how it works. Figuring out how to do it better and cheaper."

"We'll patent it!"

"You're patent won't mean jack shit in China, Hugo, and you know it." Mariska's voice was stern. "We have one chance to do this, and do this right."

"What would you know about doing it right!" Brita's father shot to his feet, sending his swivel chair crashing into a filing cabinet across the room. "You've only known it existed for an hour! I've lived and breathed this for a decade!"

"I know that if we're going to turn Stora into the biggest company the world has ever fucking seen, we're going to need more, and we need to hit the world with it all at once. A whole suite of solutions, consumer, business, logistics, military. Solve everyone's problems, right out of the gate. Don't give the competition a chance to swing before we take them out."

Brita squeezed her eyes shut as Anita's rakish grin rose up, unbidden, her familiar face just one example of the many industries a fully realised Gateway would crush.

"That will take years." He father's voice broke through, and she forced her eyes back open, her guilt back down out of sight. He stood rigid in the middle of the room, panting, his sweater askew. They locked eyes, and Brita saw the implication hiding behind the words. *Years I may not have.*

"Yes. And it will turn billions into trillions." Mariska crossed her arms, as if she were determined to combat Hugo's increasing agitation with a relaxed contempt. "Trillions, Hugo."

Her father straightened his back and smoothed down his sweater. Brita took the opportunity to break the cycle, just a little. "Dad, this is your project. What are your next steps?"

"Well." He cast around for something to hold in his hands, settling on a battery pack from a nearby shelf. "I wanted to improve the power packs. It's damn clunky at the moment. And"—he sighed—"Mariska is right. I need to separate the Gateway from the phone as a platform. To allow for growth."

"Great. I'll get you all the help you need."

Her father stuck his hands in his pockets. "I don't need any help."

Mariska rolled her eyes so severely that it was almost audible. "Hugo, do you want to do this or not?"

"Of course—"

"Then take the fucking help. You called us, remember?"

"I called her, not you," her father said, in a tone that made it clear he regretted doing even that.

"Dad, every scientist or engineer on the planet will want in on this project at the ground floor."

"I don't doubt it."

"Then what's the problem?"

"Three people in the world know about this. Three people! And even then, it almost gets blabbed on national TV." Her father slapped the battery pack he'd been waving about into the palm of his hand. "Every person you bring in increases the risk that the secret gets out."

"We can't do this on our own!" Brita turned to Mariska in exasperation.

"No," Mariska began slowly, "but perhaps a slow, careful start is not the worst idea. Going straight from your taunts at the competition to poaching their best engineers would be something of a red flag."

She felt the bright warmth rising into her cheeks once more. *Goddamn it.* They were both right. "Fine. At least this gives us a chance to do some planning in the meantime."

"Planning? What sort of planning," Hugo asked, warily.

"You know exactly the sort of planning." She counted off her fingers. "What this might turn into. Who to bring in and when. How to make it. How to market it. How to pay for it all."

"Pay for it all?"

"Yes, Dad, pay for it all." Brita snapped. He couldn't possibly be this naive. "Nothing in this business comes for free, or have you forgotten that after all these years?"

"You're not going to take this to the banks!"

"I don't know, Dad, but probably—"

"No, no way. I'm not giving over control of Gateway to anyone from fucking Lombard Street. I'll sell this place, sell everything before I give up control."

Mariska cut in. "Hugo, that won't be enough."

"I'm a fucking billionaire! How is that not enough?"

"Because we need more than just prototypes, you senile old man! You know! I know you know!"

Brita was taken aback at the force of Mariska's outburst.

"You know this has to stay secret until no one can ignore it, because you know what will happen if the Saudis find out that suddenly you don't need a car to get to work, or the beach, or fucking anywhere. If the airlines and hotels and shipping lines find out that overnight, their business model is defunct. If the cartels find out that there is a new way to get drugs across the border undetected. If the CIA catches wind. MI5. The Chinese. The Russians. ISIS. Christ, the QAnon freaks. If anyone hears a whisper before we're ready to launch, then at best, the Gateway is gone. Out of our hands.

"At worst..." Mariska let the implication hang there for a long, long moment. Letting the reality sink in. "And even then, at launch, we need to be ready to fucking go. We cannot risk being another Theranos, making promises we can't deliver. If we're going to survive the first week while our rivals and our governments try to shut us down, we need to be able to *ship product, immediately, to anyone that wants it.* We need to be fucking ubiquitous. Straight away. Selling this"—she waved her hand at the shabby plastering, at the gutted ceiling and the scuffed floorboards—"won't nearly be enough."

Brita stared at her head of Investor Relations, her mouth ajar. She was right; of course she was right. Every inkling she'd thought she'd had about how big the Gateway might be was vastly, impossibly wrong. If her father could make the Gateway large enough, not only would they not need cars—they wouldn't need roads. Everything would change.

Everything.

People would lose money. Governments would lose control.

They wouldn't let the Gateway be owned by some billionaire halfway across the world.

How could she prove to the world she could be trusted?

"Brita, don't you even think it." Her father's demand, more of a hiss than a sentence, snapped her back to the cold and quiet of the makeshift workshop. The battery pack he'd been holding was on the floor, and he was stalking towards her, finger pointed straight at her throat.

"I'm not thinking anything!"

"Yes you are, I know you. I know you, because I raised you. I know you're smart, and determined, and more than anything, I know you're a coward. That's why you wanted to sell, because you're scared you aren't up to the job, and now your little friend has outlined the risks, you're scared of the Gateway too!"

"A coward! Was I a coward when I stood up to you and your lackeys, your fucking yes men, and saved Stora from your mismanagement? Was I?"

Her father growled, towering over her, and for a terrible moment she thought he would strike. But instead swerved past her, intent on his workbench.

"Dad—"

"Hugo, calm down! Please!"

"Calm down? Calm down?" He glared at Mariska, and she ducked out of his way. He killed the still-open Gateway connection and gathered the two handsets up in his arms. "I should never have made that call. Should never have let you back through that fucking door."

Brita hovered on the edge of the precipice. He was spiralling, and she'd only made it worse. He'd obsessed over the Gateway for too long, spent years in the details, so many that he'd lost sight of the bigger picture. So much so that now he refused to see it. She had to snap him out of it. She had to act. She pushed the air from her lungs in one short, sharp burst, and stepped over the edge.

"Dad! Look at me!" She forced her way between him and the cabinet as he fumbled for his keys. She grabbed his head with both hands and forced him to look. "Look at me. Just breathe. We're not trying to take the Gateway away from you. Not trying to bury it. But in the wrong hands, Gateway could be dangerous. We have a responsibility to do this clean, to do this right."

His cheeks were slick with sweat, his eyes narrow and suspicious, and he pulled away from her. He rammed the keys into the cabinet door and stashed the Gateway units into a safe tucked neatly inside and bolted to the floor.

Brita stepped back and felt Mariska at her side. Had she noticed the rifle in the cabinet corner too? What had she gotten them into? And would she be able to get her father out of it?

Her father slammed the safe, and then the cabinet shut, and shrugged on his coat.

"Gateway is mine. If either of you dare go behind my back..." Her father pointed a crooked finger at her from the top of the stairs and curled it into a fist. "I'm going for a walk. Don't be here when I get back."

8

THE FAINT BLUE OF his screen was the only source of light in Jorge's apartment. It was dominated by an empty page, the blinking cursor an insult, confirmation that he had nothing to say. He picked at his takeaway vindaloo, only for his fork to emerge totally empty. He'd finished it hours ago.

"Maldita sea!"

He tossed it aside, the plastic fork clattering across the linoleum floor, and clicked away from the unfinished, unstarted piece. He blamed the empty page, but it was Brita's knowing smile that he couldn't forget. Roger and the other producers, of course, had focused on her dramatic exit. On the salacious comparisons to her father and his ignominious "retirement" from Stora at her hand. But that wasn't the real story. That was just fluff. The kind of brain-rotting gossip that rated, that he was forced to waste his time on. That distracted from the truth...

I'd prefer to keep that card close to my chest, Jorge.

That was the story, right there. He'd known it straight away. And what did he have on it? Nothing. *Nada.* And no ideas on where to get more.

Well. No *good* ideas.

Unbidden, his hand moved his mouse over to his oldest obsession, a compulsion from which he'd managed to abstain for almost a month. But, he told himself, it wasn't unhealthy to go back. Not this time. It was research.

He balanced back in his chair, his bare feet up on the desk, and his wireless mouse couched in the softness of his stomach. He clicked on the news alert he'd had set up for longer than he could remember, and a month of headlines filled his screen:

Solomon's Omni Misses Revenue Target for Third Straight Quarter

Solomon's Wisdom: Can the Tech Mogul Turn Green into Gold?

Campfire, Omni's Response to ChatGPT, Fizzles Out

Solomon's Judgement: Congress Threatens Omni with Record Fine

The puns weren't even original. He opened a couple of the articles, skimmed them, but there was little of interest. The past couple of years had seen the first chinks in Solomon's armour exposed, and still these supposedly critical articles amounted to little more than puff pieces. Not a single journalist willing to pry, to expose the murkiness beneath the corporate sheen.

Not that this surprised him. Jorge knew what happened to those who dared, all too well.

He scrolled to the bottom, to the most recent headlines:

Stora Stalls Solomon

Solomon's Stora Play Squashed

More fluff, rehashing the same three statements from Stora, from Brita's media team, and from Solomon himself. The same three statements he'd read a dozen times in preparation for the interview. Absolutely nothing of substance. He swapped to the flight scanner, which confirmed that Solomon had already jetted back to the States. *Hopefully with his tail between his legs.*

He kicked away from his desk, sending an empty bottle rattling away into the corner. His dress coat, the one he wore in the studio with makeup stains on the collar, had ended up on the ground beside his beautifully polished shoes. He needed space to think. He slipped into a well-worn pair of boots as he hunted for his favourite jacket, and then he was out the door, into the late-night London air with his camera slung over his shoulder.

Jorge's apartment exited onto an alley, right in the heart of the city. It was on the dividing line between the affluence of Kensington and the highly charged centres of government and finance. As far as places go, it was one of the nicer parts of town, but that's not why he chose to live here. There were far cheaper, far less stuffy neighbourhoods, but this was a place where he could keep his ears to the ground. On nights like this, when the story wouldn't come, he holstered his fingers and let his feet, his eyes, and his ears take control.

On nights like this he could imagine he was still the man he used to be. The uncompromising, unflinching newshound on the prowl.

He turned south. You never knew who or what you'd run into in these dark hours. These Englishmen just didn't seem to be able to handle a late night, not like the politicians, cops, and businessmen back home in Madrid. Everything he saw on his midnight excursions he noted down and filed away. And once every now and again, he'd stumble onto something real.

His feet took him down towards the river, and his thoughts wandered backwards, to similar walks when he wore the same boots, same jeans, same jacket. Carrying the same camera.

He'd just ghosted out of a hotel bar, a dreary function in downtown Brussels, where not even the free booze could keep him interested. Computer scientists, a notoriously egotistical bunch. He'd had high hopes, but all they'd talked about was algorithms, processors, and server farms. Just confirmation that science wasn't really his beat. Back then he'd wanted scandals, corruption, the tensions and power struggles that bubbled away beneath the calm surface of the European Union. He wandered aimlessly down the back streets, behind the hotels and bars. They were always more interesting. He saw a pair of familiar faces. Dangerous men arguing. They jagged his intoxicated attention. One was Stanley Adams, Richard Solomon's skeletal chief of staff. The other face he knew but just couldn't place. He'd groped for his camera, but by the time he was ready, the mysterious stranger was turning away. So he'd filed the chance encounter away, thinking he'd taken photos of an empty doorway...

A beggar lurched from behind a dumpster, interrupting his reverie. Jorge skipped around the poor fellow with his hands in his pockets. He ignored a slurred plea for a bob or three, and emerged out onto the main drag, the Thames glittering under the midnight city lights.

His route took him, via the back streets of course, through the grounds of a well-lit but empty parliament house and across Westminster bridge. He passed bars with revellers spilling onto the streets, house music pumping. Beautiful people stumbling, dancing, singing—making the most of the late-night stars. He soaked in the atmosphere, watching and reminiscing, but eventually moved on. Not much of interest ever happened out in the open.

Back in his hotel room he'd started on the minibar (back when his publisher had gladly covered his expenses) and was absently flicking through his photos. A blurred mess of overfilled bins; a grimy doorway marred by the flare of a fluorescent alley light; the back of Stanley's head, and...He zoomed in. A man with severe, Slavic features—gunmetal grey hair, pockmarked skin, and hard eyes—was just barely visible, illuminated in the shadow by the glow of his cigarette.

It took him three days to attach a name to that face: Volodymyr Uvorvykishki, and it would take months of digging to uncover why Solomon's fixer had been meeting with the Donetskaya Bratva's money man. That one of the most ruthless crime syndicates in the world was a major investor in Solomon's Omni, and had been from the very beginning.

Solomon scowled as he rounded a corner and stumbled into the smug gaze of a three-metre-tall Frank Darabont, his fatuous colleague having apparently taken up residence on the walls of Waterloo station. *If I hadn't caught Volodymyr in that photo, I might never have met you, Frank. Half my fucking luck.*

Jorge shrugged his coat tighter over his shoulders and ducked down a side alley, out of Frank's sight. Light spilled from a weary café, and he dodged it instinctively. In fact he was almost past it when a glimmer of recognition stirred.

Was that...?

His step faltered, just slightly, but he forced himself to carry on, taking a long, slow loop of the block. His mind raced, and as he approached the window once more, he found himself biting the inside of his cheek.

He walked past Darabont's poster as if he hadn't a care in the world, his head buried in his phone, sparing only the briefest glance for the café's interior, its bored-looking waiter, and the only two customers. He didn't react, didn't panic. It was as if he'd seen nothing at all.

He made his way to a bench on the opposite side of the lane, his back to the light, and pulled out a battered paperback, opening it somewhere in the middle. Over the top of his book he had a perfect view through the grimy café windows, the soft lighting spilling out onto the dark street, and the lonely occupants within, uncomfortable at a rickety table. Of the two men, he could see the face of only one, and it was one he knew all too well.

His skin seemed a little greyer, and what remained of his hair was the same length as the stubble on his chin, but Stanley Adams's eyes had lost none of their intensity.

What was Solomon's chief of staff, his fixer, his bagman, doing in a central London café in the middle of the night? With his thin fingers coiled beneath his chin, an untouched coffee at his elbow, and an unknown guest at his table? While his boss was on the other side of the Atlantic?

He checked left and right before lifting the camera to his lap. After adjusting the lens, he snapped a series of quick photos. Whoever this guest was, he was clearly agitated. He gesticulated animatedly, Stanley's coffee rattling in its saucer. Stanley interjected with a quiet word only once, and was otherwise unmoved. Jorge searched for a mirror, a reflective surface, so he could get a good look at this mystery man's face, but there was nothing.

From the deep wrinkles in the back of his neck, the gnarled fingers showing the first hints of arthritis, Jorge knew that Stanley's accomplice was old. In his seventies at least. He wore a threadbare knitted sweater with what looked like a hole burned into the right-hand side. Bedraggled white hair and a heavy grey beard. Honestly, this man wasn't so dissimilar from the vagrant that had surprised him from behind the dumpster.

Jorge pulled a crinkled notepad out, jotting down the address, the café's name, the time, and the protagonists: Stanley Adams and his mystery guest. He tried not to think about the aftermath of his last late-night encounter with Stanley Adams, and settled into his jacket. He set the tools of his trade away, out of site, and reopened his novel. Judging by the length of the guest's monologue, it looked like being a long wait.

Jorge would have made it through at least three chapters by the time Stanley stood to leave, if he'd actually been reading. He checked again to make sure he was alone and slid the camera up to his lap. He snapped away as Stanley dropped a five-pound note on the table. Just before he left, he shook hands with his mysterious companion. Jorge blinked. That didn't look like the handshake of two men leaving on good terms.

He let go of his camera and hid it behind his novel. Stanley hurried past without a glance. Jorge decided against following him. If he could find out who he was meeting, he might be able to find out why. Besides, Stanley would be based out of Solomon's permanent suite at the Savoy Hotel. He already had access to the CCTV that covered the lobby. He could check up on Stan anytime he liked.

Decision made, he packed up his things while keeping one eye on his mark. Those thin shoulders hunched as he lingered over his coffee. If he was going to follow this character, sitting on this bench reading a book was a bad way to start. He sidled away from the café, up a slight hill, on a hunch. He set himself up against a dark lamppost, where he could watch over the café entrance. He pulled his phone out, lamented for the hundredth time giving up smoking, and waited.

The mystery man exited five minutes later, fully illuminated by the light from the café door. Jorge almost dropped his phone from shock. He knew who that was. He'd spent the best part of his morning studying him. Or, at least, studying him as he'd been twelve years ago.

Hugo Gundersson had gotten old.

More to the point, Hugo Gundersson hadn't been spotted in public since the day Brita had ousted him as CEO. What where the odds he'd turn up tonight? The same night his daughter had broadcast to the world that she had a secret? A secret so valuable that she'd made an enemy of one of the world's most powerful men in order to keep it? Hugo glared out into the empty street.

He'd just met with Solomon's most trusted confidant.

Even that glorified mouthpiece Darabont would have realised this wasn't a coincidence.

Hugo glanced back at the café, as if he couldn't quite believe what had just happened. He lived in Knightsbridge, Jorge knew, in a mansion just across from Hyde Park. He'd turn to his left and head downhill towards the river, back towards the city, towards Lambeth Bridge. Jorge would let him go, wait until he reached the end of the street to push off his lamppost, and settle in for a long walk, about half a block behind.

Hugo turned right. Straight towards him.

Jorge stiffened and wedged his camera tight behind his elbow. He felt the over-bright glow of his phone illuminating his face from below, the looming presence of Frank Darabont hovering behind. There was no hiding from it. Hugo was ten paces away. He flicked away from his e-reader and opened Omni in the hope that the light from the app's forest green logo would disguise his face.

"Spare a fag, guv?" Jorge asked, slipping into the most clichéd cockney accent he could manage. Hugo turned up his nose in disgust and bustled past without a second look. *Spare a fag? Jesus.* Jorge shook his head with a wry smile. Where had that come from?

Hugo crossed the front entrance of the station and turned off Waterloo Road as soon as he was beyond it. Jorge trailed along behind, catching sight of Hugo hurrying down the station's cab road. He dawdled past the turn-off and took the next right at a jog. There was only one way the old man could go, and if he hurried, Jorge could head him off.

Dashing through the cool night air with Frank's cardboard cutout disappearing into the distance and a mark in his sights, something shifted. He wasn't Jorge Elorza, entertainment reporter for the UK's fifth-largest news network. With his camera in one hand, the wind rushing through his hair, he was back in Kosovo. Capturing a truth that people like Hugo, like Solomon didn't want the world to see.

He slowed back down to a walk as he approached the entrance to Lambeth tube station, his chest heaving. Okay, so London wasn't Kosovo, and he was no longer in his twenties. And sure, Hugo was no Milosevic. But it sure as shit beat interviewing yet another generic popstar about their upcoming album/tour/who cared what—*Ah, there he is!* A block and a half down the road. He pretended to study a menu stuck inside a café window and watched him stride confidently between black cabs and electric scooters as if they owed him obedience.

Jorge lingered, expecting Hugo to reach the footpath and come towards him....*Shit!* As soon as he'd reached the other side of the road, he was gone, off down another alley. Where was he going? Jorge squeezed past a trio of stumbling lads, wincing at their enthusiastic but off-key rendition of "Blue Is the Colour," and settled into a run.

His footsteps echoed off the walls of the mostly empty streets, only to be overwhelmed by the clatter of a train racing away from Waterloo station. By the time it had passed the long laneway that Hugo had entered, that ran under the tracks and towards the St Thomas's Hospital, it was empty.

"Fuck."

He'd lost sight of Hugo for no more than five seconds. How far could he have gone? Hands on hips, Jorge stood at the laneway entrance and quickly scanned the nearby buildings: another café, a pair of apartments, a bicycle shop, and—

Jorge ducked behind a teetering stack of pellets. Hugo was just across the courtyard at...he poked his head around the corner. A self-storage facility? He crouched down, caught his breath, and watched. Hugo slipped a key into a roller door and lifted it halfway, revealing an empty darkness beyond. This time he looked left, looked right, before ducking under it with a grunt. As the roller door crashed back down, an internal light blared, just in time for Jorge to see Hugo's feet turn and stalk down a sterile corridor.

Now that there was no risk of being spotted, Jorge pulled himself upright. Why had the old man come here? What was he hiding in there? The choice of café for his clandestine meeting couldn't have been a coincidence. And if Hugo had chosen the café so he could come here after, then the odds were he'd come to work, not a quick pick-up or drop-off.

A short jog, no more than two minutes, confirmed that the self-storage warehouse had only one entrance, and one exit. There hadn't been a train, nor had there been another telltale crash of the roller door slamming shut. He crossed back over to the Waterloo station side of the street, found himself a window seat at the Walrus Bar, and ordered himself an overpriced Shiraz.

He set his camera on the windowsill, sipped his drink, and winced. How long the bottle had been open and sitting underneath the counter he didn't want to know. But no matter. Hugo Gundersson was across the road. What the old man was doing in there was a mystery, but he'd find out.

First the daughter, now the father. Keeping secrets, playing dangerous games with dangerous people. He rubbed his hands together and settled down to wait.

9

"How long?" Mas asked.

"Fifteen minutes."

Brita slipped her phone back into her pocket and crossed her arms. Her driver was way across town. *That's what I get for slipping the net, I suppose.* She scanned her father's workshop, scattered with tools and experiments, blueprints and resentment. It was hard to imagine this had been her bedroom, once. She shivered, and wondered if there was any way of recapturing what had been lost. Thrown away.

Mas's eyes were still on the cabinet where her father had stashed his Gateway handsets. Those devices, and her father's absence, were a malign, suffocating presence in the cavernous room. She needed to get out of here; they both did. So they could think.

"Come on," Brita said, making for the stairs. She felt the need to make a decisive act, something to change the mood. "I'll make you a cup of tea while we wait."

"Tea?" Mas raised a sardonic eyebrow.

"Good point. Dad always kept a little something lying around."

Moving up one level was like rolling back through time. The hallway, the dining room, the kitchen—it was as if they'd been preserved in a layer of dust. She made a beeline for an oak-panelled cabinet, nestled in the kitchen corner, and tried to ignore the memories niggling away in the back of her mind.

"Found anything?"

"Right where he left them!" Brita called back, crystal tumblers clinking as she extracted an antique decanter. She pulled the stopper, allowing the delicate aroma to waft gently upwards. Scotch, single malt. That would do nicely.

"Christ, you'd think he'd be able to afford a cleaner."

"As if my father would trust a cleaner." Brita sloshed two fingers of amber liquid into a pair of tumblers and set the decanter down in the middle of the kitchen table. A small puff of dust curled into the still air. Mas stood in the kitchen doorway with a crinkle in her nose.

Brita held out a tumbler. "To trillions."

Mas grinned, and the ring of crystal on crystal filled the air. "To trillions."

The scotch rolled down her throat, still smooth as silk after who knew how long forgotten in that cabinet, spreading its warmth down into her core. Brita closed her eyes as it worked its magic, sapping away the stress of an insane forty-eight hours.

"So what do you think he meant?" Mas asked, leaning gingerly against the least-dusty part of the kitchen bench, in front of the microwave.

"By what?"

"You know, 'If either of you go behind my back...'" Mas hunched her shoulders, made her voice gruff, like his.

"Knowing him, he's probably got some sort of in-built kill switch."

"Kill switch?"

"Something in the trusted hardware layer that only he knows about." Brita shrugged. "That he can trigger when he feels threatened, turn all his prototypes into bricks."

"He'd do that?" Mas asked, eyebrow raised.

"Oh yeah. One hundred percent."

"Do you think he'd really do it?"

Brita shook her head. "He can't afford to."

"And tonight's performance?"

"He couldn't delegate at the best of times. And he's an old man now..." Brita glanced down at the table where she and her father had sat and planned out her career. *Go and learn. Run a team, run a company. Then, when you're ready...*She took another sip, let the soft burn wash the memory away. It all felt so long ago. "He's been on his own for a long time. He just needs time to adjust."

"How much time?"

"Probably more than we can afford." Brita sniffed. The sheer scale of the Gateway project was numbing. Every time she tried to wrap her head around it, it shifted and changed, unveiled another complexity, grew another layer of pitfalls and traps. There was so much to do.

She cupped her tumbler in both hands and looked across the table at Mas, staring down into her own drink, lost in her own thoughts. Brita couldn't imagine a better person to have by her side through all this.

"You'll have to touch base with the shareholders tomorrow."

Mas glanced up, her eyes rolling back as if she dreaded the prospect. "My phone hasn't stopped buzzing all night. I should be talking to them right now."

"How do you think they'd feel about us keeping a hold of our dividends this year?"

"Even less favourably than you ruining their payday, and then throwing a tantrum on national TV." Mas smiled into her drink. "Why?"

"Every other pound is allocated or already committed." She'd told Jorge that Stora was now a tight ship. No loose spending. Which meant nothing to spare for a rainy day. Or an opportunity. "If we hold the half-year disbursement, it would at least give Gateway some seed capital. Tide us over."

"And signal to the world that Stora is broke? That we should have jumped at the Solomon deal when we had the chance? Garfield is already gunning for your job. He'll gladly twist the arms of a few shareholders if he smells an opportunity."

"If we doubled down on the breakthrough narrative..."

"And give your father an aneurysm?" Mas drained her glass and slammed it on the crowded bench. "Hugo would jump across to Garfield's side in a heartbeat if you did that. And I wouldn't blame him. This needs to be kept as small as fucking possible right now, until we know what we're doing."

Brita looked away and gulped the remainder of her suddenly bitter scotch. It burned, but not enough to displace the knowledge that Mas was right. Garfield was a thorn she could do without, especially with a sensitive group of shareholders just waiting for an excuse.

"Give them a cuddle then. We'll have to find another way."

Her phone buzzed against her chest, and as she checked the notification, she set her glass on the table next to the decanter. Where her dad would see.

"Car's here. You ready?"

Mas nodded and slid her tumbler onto the table to make a pair, before following Brita down the stairs. The house was dark, but the stairs still creaked in all the same places. It was so strange being back here. Like nothing had changed in a decade.

Then, in the darkness, she spied the outline of a Gateway handset mounted to the wall. Surveilling the front door. Guarding it against unwanted attention. This house was no longer her home. It was her father's fortress.

She opened the door, ushered Mas out onto the street, and found herself hesitating with the door halfway open, halfway closed. Would her father ever let her back in? Everything had changed, and with the Gateway it would keep changing. She exhaled, let the door close with a soft click, and slid into the low warmth of her sleek black Mercedes.

There would be no putting the genie back into the bottle. There never was, no matter how much she might want to.

"Where to, Ms Gundersson?" Henry, her driver, asked. He'd been with Stora since her father's days.

"Mas's place first, then home, thanks, Henry."

Mas sat opposite her, facing away from the car's direction of motion. She flashed a brief smile of thanks, then buried her head into her phone. They both had hundreds of emails, messages, and calls to deal with, but Brita decided hers could wait. Instead she watched as London slid by the window, the bright signs of the UK's and Europe's corporate giants shining like beacons in the clear night sky. Virgin, Barclays, BP, Britannia Bank. From down on the ground, they were bright enough to blot out the stars.

"I'll talk to the banks. Tomorrow." If they could secure a series of small loans, enough to get them started, it would at least buy them time. Time to come up with a plan.

Mas raised an eyebrow. "Even after your dad's meltdown? Do you think that's wise?"

"I'll just have to share the alternatives with him, like you said before." She chuckled to herself, imagining the exact shade of beetroot he would turn at *that* suggestion.

"Actually, I did have another idea."

"Oh?" Brita eyed the back of Henry's head. He'd been with them so long, but even still. She held her fist to her chest, and Mas nodded. "Do tell."

"Well, if we're to become a threat to certain parties..." Mas let the implication hang there. The auto manufacturers, the hoteliers, the shipping magnates, the oil barons. Anita. "Perhaps we could take advantage of this. Charge a premium for advanced warning of what's coming. Form a strategic partnership, an opportunity to reshuffle portfolios in preparation for what's coming—"

"No." Brita cut her off, her throat tightening at just the suggestion. What Mas was suggesting... wars had been fought over less. "No, I don't think so. Widening the tent to give our competitors room to move is not the right play."

"Don't think of them as competitors. We would be the combustion engine to their horse. The steel to their bronze. Think of them as...compelled investors. If we pick the right kind, they could even make Gateway better."

"Investors? In Stora?" Brita asked, wide eyed. Mas nodded. "With whose shares? Mine or my father's?"

Mas shrugged. "We can sort out the details later—"

"Giving up even 2% could cost me control of Stora altogether," Brita shot back, memories of board challenges crashing in. Her and her backers on one side of the table, her father and his on the other. "That's not a 'detail.'"

"Fine, point taken. But we should talk about it. Once your father's cooled down at least."

"You want to give him another stroke? No, he'll try to kick you out all over again."

"I don't know..."

Brita shook her head. "Well, I do. This is a bad idea, Mas. Gateway is too important, too volatile, to use this way." As a weapon. As a threat. As a vehicle for her father to inflict his vengeance on the world. "We need to do this clean. Aboveboard."

Mas pursed her lips but stayed silent. In the muted darkness of the Mercedes, her face underlit only by the blue glow of her phone, her expression was impossible to read. But still, Mas radiated with a sudden tension. This wasn't over.

Henry swooped down narrow, deserted lanes, and Mas typed out response after mollifying response. Brita's phone buzzed each time her subordinate hit send, but she didn't look. There was no point. Not tonight. The shareholders could wait until tomorrow. In a year or two's time, when the Gateway launched, they would be glad she spent the night thinking instead of pretending to be at their beck and call. In fact, they probably wouldn't even remember it.

The Mercedes slowed to a halt, and Mas stepped out with a terse farewell. They would speak tomorrow. Have this fight again in the cold light of day, she was sure. But for now Brita just wanted to be home, in her shower, to wash all of the day's stresses away with steaming hot water. To climb into an empty bed and forget about shareholders and prices, reporters and headlines. About her father, and how lonely he had seemed. How bitter she'd made him.

10

"STORA IS NOT THE kind of company that gets bought out by the first bloated corporate behemoth to come knocking when the market gets tough, no matter their 'credentials.' We stand up for ourselves, our values—"

"Pause," Solomon said, turning his back on Brita's gigantic, overly earnest face, the video window hanging suspended in the air above a high-fidelity re-creation of his family ranch. It was dusk, the sun half hidden behind wisps of cloud. Cicadas hummed in the distance.

"—and we fight back."

"I bet your PR team—"

"Pause, ah said!"

"—had fun coming up with—"

"Pause video, goddammit!" Solomon barked, closing his hand into a fist, and finally the video stopped with Jorge's face frozen in the middle of one of his smug, holier-than-thou grins. "Jesus Christ. Open command logs." He glanced around wearily, found only open plains, and sighed. "Ah said 'open command—' thank you."

A second window belatedly popped into existence, and Solomon, swiping down with one finger, scrolled down through the input logs. Then, finding nothing, he swiped the window away. *That hand signal works, at least.* Why it took multiple attempts to get the Omniverse controller to recognise his voice commands, though, remained a mystery.

He strolled over to a gnarled fence post, a ranchworld interpretation of the balustrade on his office balcony. With each footstep, the atmospheric algorithms output a crunch of dry grass. A jarring contrast with the smooth tiling in his real-world office, which was actually beneath his feet. He leaned on the fence post / balustrade, tried to ignore the buzz of anxiety as reality clashed with what was being projected into his eyes and his ears, and gazed at the supersized journalist floating before him.

"Fast-forward video, three minutes."

The sun sank below the horizon, and still images of Brita, then Jorge, jumped back and forth, shining a ghostly light across the plains. The video returned to stillness with Brita sitting on the edge of her seat, hands before her as she spoke. He tried to reconcile the enthusiasm on display here with the Brita he'd sat across the desk from, practically begging him to wipe her company from history.

"Play video." Nothing. *For fuck's sake.* Solomon had to stop himself from rolling his eyes. Who knew how the Omniverse headset's sensors would react to *that.* "Play video. Play—"

"*—on our own 'game-changers'—you've seen the foldable screens, metaverses, chat-bots—the latest in a long line of gimmicks. That's not what we're about. No, we're targeting something more, something actually life-changing here. Nothing less will do.*"

"*Targeting? Or building?*" Jorge was just as engrossed as Brita, probing away, trying to pry something loose, and Solomon couldn't help but smile. Having a reporter of Jorge's quality wasting away in infotainment. Such a shame.

"*I'd prefer to keep that card close to my chest, Jorge.*"

"*But you do have cards to play?*"

"*Of course.*"

"Pause video," Solomon whispered, and for once the Omniverse listened. Play-back stopped, and Brita's smile filled the darkening sky. A smile that said *Yes, Jorge, I've got pocket aces, and everyone else at the table is bluffing.* "Open Stora Negotia-tions—March 17, 2024."

A black rectangle sprang into existence, little more than a play button and a progress bar. He stabbed at it with one hand. And again. "Jesus, play recordin', you stupid fuckin'—"

"*—like he doesn't want you to consign his legacy to history.*" The recording was fuzzy, partially muffled by his jacket pocket. Even after decades spent in the public eye, Solomon couldn't acclimatise to the dissonance between his voice as he heard it and as it actually sounded to the rest of the world.

"*He lost that right eleven years ago,*" Brita snapped, irritated at the interruption. Not the reaction of a CEO with pocket aces. "*You're still here.*"

"*I'm sorry, Brita, but a promise is a promise.*" Brita's snivelling little CFO. He would have been one of the first out the door had that deal been signed, and he knew it. "*He knew you wouldn't answer, so he came to me.*"

"*We have a deal, Ms Gundersson. And ah have an awful long memory.*"

And Solomon was back there, eyes on Brita's pen as it hovered above the dotted line, the patents, the technicians, the know-how he needed to get the Omniverse fucking working just a signature away. And then the pen lifting. The moment gone.

"*What is it, Garfield? What does he want?*"

"He only wanted you to know one thing: Gateway. He says it's working."

Solomon swiped the recording away, leaving only the cicadas in the distance and the memory of Brita's knowing smile. Gateway, Brita's pocket aces. That one word from her father had taken her from desperation to outright arrogance. But what was it?

"Excuse me, Mr Solomon?" Alex, his assistant, coughed behind him. He turned his back on Brita to find Alex's avatar standing about five yards behind him, his feet hovering six inches above the grass and his glassy eyes staring a foot to the right of where they should be.

"What is it?"

"I've got Senator Guerrero on the line. Would you like me to direct the call in here?"

"In here?" Solomon winced. "God no. Get him hooked up on a regular video call, and get the logs of this session over to Martinez over in R&D. Voice command is still touchy, and hand signals are even worse. And we have to do somethin' about the haptic feedback. It's all over the place."

"Of course, sir."

Alex turned to go, and Solomon reached up for his headset, ready to pull it from his head. "One more thing. Get me everything we have on Hugo Gundersson, and an update on Brita since the deal fell over."

Alex's avatar pursed his lips. "The full package, sir?"

Solomon nodded. "By the time ahm done with the senator."

"Yes sir."

Solomon closed his eyes and pulled. When he opened them again, the ranch had disappeared and he was back in his office, all smooth slate and polished glass. Beyond the horizon, the sun still bled light into the darkening sky, and the cicadas were still audible in the distance, but the wide-open plains were long gone, buried beneath design hubs and laboratories, Astroturf and server farms.

He tossed the headset to one side and ran a hand across his scalp, feeling for the dimples left by the straps and annoyed with himself for caring. Guerrero had come to him, not the other way around. He hit the blinking light on his dial pad and broke into his most charming smile.

"Senator, to what do ah owe the pleasure?"

"Richard, the pleasure is all mine." Senator Guerrero, one of the last surviving southern Democrats, was in his sixties and had a full head of unrealistically black hair and shockingly white teeth. "I was sorry to hear about the Stora deal falling through."

"Yeah, well, there just ain't no accounting for that British temperament, is there." Solomon leaned back, smiling beatifically. "And it sounds like ah might be in need of some of that dough, what with your little brothers down in Congress. Ah hear they're talkin' billions."

"I wouldn't worry about that—"

"No, ah don't suppose you would. Ah, on the other hand, might start wonderin' why my good friend wasn't able to prevent, or even warn me about, such an unpleasant surprise."

"We're friends because I help you avoid actual surprises." Guerrero clucked his tongue, as if he was dressing down with a junior staffer. "This is nothing more than opportunistic posturing. Representative Jackson is just chasing headlines, as per usual."

And a not-so-subtle challenge to you, mister head of the judiciary committee. You and your friendship with people like me, Solomon thought. *Representative Jackson wants yer senate seat.* "You don't need to spout yer talkin' points to me, Senator. Save it for the press gallery. Why'd you actually call?"

Guerrero shifted in his seat, his fingers unconsciously tugging at his collar. An actual surprise then.

"The DOJ is pulling together an antitrust case against Omni."

"Aw hell, is that all?" Solomon emitted a performative guffaw, designed to hide the sudden tightness in his throat. Guerrero was right—this was exactly why Solomon had insisted they become friends. To one side, his personal mobile phone rattled against his polished mahogany desktop. He silenced it without checking who it was. "They've been threatening me with an antitrust suit for the last two administrations. Ah've bought 'em off before, Ah'll just do it again."

"A briefing paper came across my desk this afternoon, laying out the candidates for special counsel." Guerrero swallowed. "Heavy hitters, Richard. One solar farm isn—"

"So ah'll give 'em ten. Batteries, pumped hydro, whatever the president's little green heart desires."

"Richard, I don't think your little greenwashing projects are going to cut it this time."

"Well, in that case, Senator, ah'd be glad to hear yer suggestions." Solomon's phone buzzed again, and this time he flipped it over. Stan. For him to have called again after being dismissed the first time, it must be important. "Listen, my sincere apologies, but somethin's just come up. I'll have Alex send you the full package on our favourite headline chaser right away. Wouldn't want him cramping your style in November." Guerrero started talking, but Solomon had already moved on. The senator would send him the names on the DOJ's list, and the gears of obstruction would begin rolling. "I'll be in touch."

With a touch of a finger he terminated the call. "You catch all that, Alex?"

"Yes sir." Alex's voice sounded tinny through the intercom, but was that any worse than his avatar levitating like a wall-eyed idiot? Just thinking about the Omniverse made him grind his teeth.

"Good. See to it, and screen my calls. London's callin', and ah don't want to be disturbed."

"Yes sir."

Solomon cut off the intercom, picked up his phone, and headed for the balcony. The sun was fully set now, but the bright streetlamps extended daytime long into the night on the Omni business campus. He dialled Stan's number.

"Ah just blew off Guerrero. This'd better be important."

"I just met with Hugo Gundersson."

Stan's voice was as thin as cigarette paper, but his words hit as if they were made with iron. It took Solomon a moment to drag his eyebrows back down to their normal resting place. "Did you now? And how, pray tell, did you wrangle that?"

"He called me. Agitated. Wants to meet, so I say sure. Name the place and I'll be there. Gives me the address of some shitty little café off Southbank and half an hour later there he is, looking like he's just gone ten rounds with a grizzly."

A grizzly, or his own daughter. Solomon knew which he'd prefer. "Out of the blue, just like that, huh?"

"Just like that."

Solomon waited, frowning, but Stan didn't continue. It wasn't like him to bury the lede. "What did the old man want?"

Stan sighed.

"Hey, you called me. Is this important or not?"

"All right, but I'm just warning you. This smells messy. Like a family shitfight."

Solomon held his tongue and considered himself warned.

"He wants his company back. Wants your help to oust his daughter and reinstate him as CEO."

"Well, yer not wrong. That fuckin' reeks." *And it adds another data point to the Gateway conundrum. Who holds the cards here? Clearly Hugo, if he thinks he can just get her out of the way.* "Why me? Why not the other shareholders?"

"He gave me a spiel about how he sees you as a fellow innovator, someone who understands the value of inspired leadership. You know, the usual bullshit to cover the real reason."

"That he thinks ah hold a grudge. That because his daughter shafted us both, we're natural allies."

"That would be my guess."

Solomon dropped the phone to his chest for a moment. Stan was right—this was family bullshit, through and through. But it was also an opportunity. Two days ago,

Stora had been little more than a source of patents and engineers. A resource to be mined and abandoned. But now? This Gateway, whatever it was, had him intrigued despite himself.

Brita Gundersson was a lot of things, but she wasn't the kind of leader to buy into the hype. She'd never let marketing drive the technology in the way her competitors had. A weakness even Apple had fallen prey to of late. Solomon glanced back at the Omniverse headset discarded beside his desk. Scowling, he shoved it out of sight.

Under her watch, Stora had always focused on core functionality. Their new flagship was brilliant, but fucking boring. Which made her arrogance, and her subsequent meltdown, on Jorge's show all the more intriguing.

"Did he mention Gateway?"

"No. And I didn't push. I didn't want to scare him off."

"Good. That's good." Solomon tapped the stone balcony with the tip of a pointed shoe. "Did he give any indication of havin' a plan?"

"Honestly, more than anything, he seemed to want someone to rant to." Stan paused, and Solomon stood up a little straighter. "By about ten minutes in, I got the impression that he realised he shouldn't have called me. That sitting down with me was a mistake."

"Good instincts." Solomon chuckled.

"A little late, though."

"Yeah, well. Perhaps it runs in family." Two blunders, from two members of the same family. From two holders of the same secret, all in the space of six hours. "So he didn't give anythin' away?"

"No, I wouldn't go quite that far." He could almost hear the skeletal grin spreading across Stan's lips. "He did mention something about their bank's holdings being gettable, which would open up some options."

"Yes. Yes it would." Solomon turned his back on the Omni campus and the activity bubbling along below. His mind was racing. "Did he say when he needed to hear back?"

"No. All I promised was that I'd pass his request up the chain."

"Good, that's good." Solomon fell silent for a moment, thinking. Stan knew well enough not to interrupt, but that didn't stop a ping from erupting from his laptop. He rapped his phone against the handrail and turned back inside. "Yer instincts are right as usual, Stan. There's nothin' to be gained from engagin' in this. Not formally, anyway."

"How long should I wait before letting him know?"

"No later than tomorrow afternoon."

"Consider it done." He heard Stan stand up in the background and knew he was already moving on to the next item on his agenda. "I've sent you the recording, and if you want to keep tabs on this, I'd suggest ordering the full package on Hugo…"

"Already done." Back at his desk, Solomon clicked into the waiting file. Brita's update was comprehensive. Location data, search history, proximity data—practically everything she'd done online for the last week captured in a database. And Hugo's…Hugo's was empty. "Actually, you might want to give our Slavic friend a call. Hugo is goin' to need some attention of the analogue variety."

11

—·—

"Name?"

"Jorge. Jorge Elorza." He flashed the desk sergeant his best television smile, hoping it might dispel the ramshackle image he knew he was presenting. "Can you please let Detective Inspector Turnbull know I have some information for him."

"Is he expecting you?"

"I doubt it. But I know he loves surprises."

The desk sergeant snorted, the burst of air rustling the greying whiskers of his moustache as he hooked his phone between his ear and his shoulder. "A Mr Elorza, sir. Says he has some information for you." A pause, his beady eyes judging, from the mess of Jorge's unwashed hair down to his tattered runners. "No sir, not as far as I could throw him, sir."

He set the phone back down. "Have a seat, Mr Elorza. DI Turnbull will be down shortly."

"Many thanks."

Jorge sat in the far corner, where he could watch the comings and goings through the front offices of the City of London Police department. Uniformed officers, plain-clothed detectives, and civilians, on both sides of the law, all intermingled. It was a strange place, a melting pot, filled with hushed conversations and nervous glances. He settled down to watch, and rehearsed his pitch one more time.

"Jorge!" DI Turnbull burst out into the open and let go of his swipe card, which raced back to his hip via his retractable lanyard. He propped the door open with one foot and waved Jorge over. "Quick, come on through."

He stood, suddenly conscious of his wrinkled shirt and unkempt hair in the face of DI Turnbull's starched collar, tie, and impeccably parted hair. The detective studied him with a quiet intensity.

"Thanks for seeing me at such short notice."

"With the quality of your info, I'm happy to make the time." The door hissed shut behind them as Turnbull hurried through the busy corridors. He glanced back, a grin on his face. "The hair and makeup team over at O2 must be fucking wizards."

"You should see Darabont before they've waved their magic wands."

"Hah, I'll bet."

Turnbull led him around a corner and through an open-plan office, one wall stacked to the ceiling with filing boxes. In front of it, DCI Marlowe, Turnbull's boss, was directing a gaggle of bright-looking young investigators through pile after agonising pile of documents. Before Turnbull could hurry him out of sight, Jorge spotted at least six documents bearing the official watermark of Brittania Bank. He filed the titbit away for who knew when, and allowed himself a smile. There was no turning off the journalistic instincts. Even for a dinosaur like him.

"Looks like Marlowe's got you working on something big, Harvey," Jorge said as DC Turnbull ushered him into his office.

"I can neither confirm nor deny, Jorge." Turnbull rolled his eyes. "If she finds out I even let you, a verified hack, walk through that room, she'll have my balls, which means I'll be forced to have yours in retaliation." Turnbull held his tie in place with one hand as he relaxed into his chair, his grin belying the seriousness of his words. "Now, what have you got for me?"

Jorge cleared his throat. "A proposition."

"A proposition? I thought you had information?"

"I will have information, but I need your help."

"This had better not be about—"

"It's not." He hesitated, unsure how much to reveal. "It's about Brita Gundersson and Stora."

"Ahh." Turnbull laced his fingers together across the tail of his tie. "I did catch a minute or two of your interview. Thought you were a mite unfair, if I'm honest, though I imagine your bosses were very pleased."

Jorge rolled his eyes. Roger had been so excited he'd needed a moment all to himself. "Harvey…"

"No, no, I get it. We've all got to earn a crust somehow, don't we. And holding the rich and powerful to account is a step in the right direction, compared to what you've been stooping to lately."

"Not by choice."

"No, but that particular cloud had quite the silver lining. For me anyway, Jorge. Those investigative instincts needed an outlet, and so here we are. What have you got in mind?"

"At the moment? A glint in the eye, a coincidence, and a totally unsubstantiated hunch."

Turnbull frowned. This was not the way these meetings usually went. "What do you need?"

"CCTV footage." Jorge pulled his notepad from his pocket. "Unit CC4983A, between six p.m. last night and six a.m. this morning."

The detective glanced across at his computer. Jorge knew that the footage he needed was only a few keystrokes away. "That's all?"

"That depends on what the footage throws up."

Turnbull wiped his hand across his brow.

"Come on, Harvey, have I ever steered you wrong?"

"Not me, though your old editors over at the *Times* might beg to differ."

"I wasn't wrong about that. If I'd written that story now—"

"Yeah, yeah, Solomon's no angel. I was only teasing." His hand dropped to his keyboard, hovering over the keys. "What are you expecting to see?"

"Hugo Gundersson's front door. I want to know if he had any visitors last night."

"After your interview."

Jorge nodded. "After my interview."

"And if he did? What then?"

"That depends on who shows up." Jorge considered leaving it at that, but Turnbull's fingers had begun to retract from the keyboard. There was no point holding cards for the next round. This was the game, right here. "All right, all right. You want to know what I'm thinking, that's fair. There's something fishy going on with Stora and the last-minute decision to balk at the Omni buyout. I think Hugo has something to do with it, and I think something Brita said last night got a little too close to the truth."

Turnbull nodded. "So that's the hunch and the look in the eye. What was the coincidence?"

"That's why I like you, Detective Turnbull. You actually listen to what I say." Jorge pursed his lips and looked at his watch, trying not to let his frustration, or his enjoyment, show. "Let's just say that I know where Hugo was about nine hours ago, and it wasn't at his house in Knightsbridge."

"All right. All right." Turnbull's fingers flew across the keys, and with a flourish, he lifted his hand to the edge of his monitor. Jorge licked his lips as he waited for the detective to spin the monitor around, but instead he received Turnbull's most serious look, with both barrels. "I'm giving you this on faith, Jorge. Because even though you're a sleazy bastard, you're a good reporter, and you care about justice as much as the scoop. But before I let you in, I need to reiterate that this is a two-way street. If you uncover evidence of criminal wrongdoing, it comes to me before it goes on the air, and I can kill the story if I think it might blow our chances of a conviction down the track. Is that clear?"

"As crystal, Detective." Jorge nodded. They both knew how this worked. He leaned forward, and Turnbull, finally, swung the monitor around.

The footage was grainy, the branches of a gently waving oak tree obscuring the top third of the screen. However, the glossy black panels of Hugo's front door were immediately recognisable to Jorge. He'd been there only hours before, hoping for and eventually finding a CCTV camera: CC4983A. In the bottom corner of the screen, ugly white digits declared the date and time: 18:01 08/19/2024.

"Perfect." A black cab rolled silently by. "Can you speed it up?"

"Sixteen times?"

"Can you go thirty-two?"

"You got somewhere to be?" Turnbull asked.

Jorge shrugged without looking up. He had a production meeting in a little over an hour, but he could be late to that. He often was. "I just don't want to take up any more of your time than I need to."

"Why thank you, Jorge. Your kind consideration is duly noted."

The graceful sweep of the tree's branches, caught in the autumn breeze, became staccato jumps across the camera's field of view. They were lucky Hugo's street was quiet, the exclusive domain of the ultra-rich. Who, it seemed, often weren't home. It made the black cab's appearance and disappearance, its screen time lasting no more than a second at thirty-two times speed, stand out like a calm moment in the heart of a storm.

"There! Go back." Two ghosts had appeared at Hugo's door. By the time Turnbull had slowed the footage down, the door was closed and the street was empty. The timestamp flashed 20:06. Then, slowly, the black door opened, and two figures reversed out onto the street. "Who have we here?"

"Looks to me like the highly anticipated Brita Gundersson." Turnbull grinned. "Who's her friend?"

Jorge squinted and leaned closer, reaching out to tap Turnbull's space bar as the second figure's gaze swept about across the empty street. A flash of recognition. "That's Brita's head of Investor Relations. Mariska Farkas. She spent the entire interview fuming in the wings. I'm amazed she didn't rush the stage and pull her boss off the air herself."

"And that's what you wanted to see?"

"It's a start." Jorge dragged the keyboard across the desk, ignoring Turnbull's disapproving huff. He started the footage rolling once more and watched the two women slip back inside. The corridor was dark, and then it disappeared behind an implacable black door. He set playback at sixteen times speed, and was unable to keep the smile off his face.

"What are you thinking?" Turnbull asked.

"If Brita brought Farkas, then whatever is going on inside is a business meeting. Odd timing, given she knifed the old man over a decade ago, wouldn't you say?"

Turnbull merely grunted and checked his watch. The late-summer light finally faded and the street fell into a darkness, illuminated only by the soft light above Hugo's front door. 21:00 passed, then 22:00, then 23:00.

"What else are you looking for? Haven't you got—"

"Not quite." Jorge slapped the space bar, and the image froze with Hugo Gundersson stalking off-screen, halfway through wrenching an overcoat about his shoulders. The same overcoat that had been draped over the back of his chair at the café. *So Hugo left first.* "He doesn't look like a happy camper, does he?"

"Three hours, and the old man suddenly storms out at eleven p.m.?" Turnbull raised his eyebrows.

"I've got you intrigued now, don't I?"

"You've always had a nose for this sort of thing. I'll give you that."

Jorge set the footage rolling again, dropping it to eight times speed. He'd barely finished noting the times of entry and exit down when a sleek black Merc rolled up, and both women slipped out the door. He paused, inspected the faces, but they were hidden in shadow. Inscrutable. He noted down the time and the vehicle registration.

"So that's it then. You've got everything you need?" Turnbull asked, reaching for the keyboard.

"Just humour me, a couple more minutes. I just want to make sure Hugo makes it home safely." Jorge pulled the keyboard just a mite farther out of reach, eyes on the screen. 00:00.

01:00.

02:00.

"Jorge…" Turnbull began, but the words had barely left his mouth when another black cab flashed onto the screen, disgorging another figure and leaving her sitting on Hugo's doorstep. Jorge slowed it to normal speed and met Turnbull's suddenly riveted gaze.

Mariska Farkas had come back.

They watched in silence as she waited: 02:15, 02:30. Clearly she was waiting for Hugo. But why? And behind her boss's back? Jorge's mind raced. Whatever was going on, he had to get to the bottom of it. He had to. And then, she stood. Jorge dropped the footage back to normal speed.

Then he hit pause, mouth open in disbelief.

The door had opened, and there was Hugo. Inside the house.

"Did you…?" Jorge asked, eyebrows raised.

"No. Rewind it a bit, maybe we missed it."

They rewound, right back to eleven p.m., Hugo shrugging into his jacket once more and pounding the pavement. Nothing. They played it forward again, slower this time. Brita and Mariska leaving. Mariska returning. But no Hugo. Not until he appeared inside the front door.

"There must be an alternative entrance, a house that size." Turnbull rubbed his eyes with his fingers.

"Yeah, surely…" Jorge nodded and hit play, whilst privately scrutinising his timeline from last night. He'd been certain that Hugo had been locked away inside that storage facility until at least 4:00 a.m.; he had the lack of sleep to prove it. But clearly not.

He returned his attention to the video feed, to Hugo and Mariska. The old man was shocked, his pose defensive. Mariska spoke with her hands raised, as if to placate him. And then, Hugo cocked his head. Was that a smile? His stance softened, and he invited her back inside. Jorge hit pause, the image frozen on Hugo's bearded face disappearing into the shadow of his hallway. He let out a long, slow breath.

"More than you bargained for?"

"You could say that." What in God's name was going on?

"Well, you can label me intrigued." Turnbull extracted the keyboard from Jorge's grip and swivelled his screen back to its normal orientation. "I'm glad I could help."

Jorge blinked, and then grinned, slapping his notebook against his palm. Whatever it was, it was certainly better than sitting through another production meeting with Frank and Roger.

"Harvey, you didn't just help. You're a star. An absolute star. However, I do have one more *tiny* favour to ask."

12

—·—

BRITA SCANNED A DRAFT press release, her red pen culling and tweaking, while Anna prepared coffees for Sunil and Luan, Mas's protégés. They were waiting for her to finish. The sun was barely above the horizon, shards of light glinting off the neighbouring skyscrapers. It had taken all her willpower to choose her water bottle over a second coffee. But, as her father had always said, back when they'd actually worked together: if you can't be well rested, be hydrated. So she took a long pull of the crisp, chilled water, savouring the shiver as it trickled down her throat.

"Ah, Mariska. Perfect timing." Her office door swung open and Brita passed over the amended press release. "Here, tell me what you think of this."

Mas took the paper with one eyebrow raised. She was, as usual, perfectly put together: painfully high heels, deceptively simple makeup, not a hair out of place. There was no way of knowing that she'd had barely four hours sleep.

She appraised the memo without sitting. "The gang's all here."

"After last night's excitement, we needed an early start."

Anna had met Brita in the car park, ready with a summary of everything she'd missed since the interview last night. She'd been halfway through digesting it when the lift doors opened on the top floor to reveal Sunil and Luan, draft press release at the ready.

"Hmmm." Mas held out a hand, and the younger of the two, Sunil, passed her a pen. She made a couple of additional comments and then dumped both the draft and the pen back to Sunil. "Get that typed up. It's pretty close."

Brita watched Sunil scurry out the door, the more experienced Luan smoothing his jacket and bowing slightly before following his colleague out of her office.

"How'd you sleep?" Brita asked.

"Sleep? What's that?" It had the structure of a joke, but Mas wasn't laughing. She sank down into the chair opposite. "Overton rang me on my way in. He's on the warpath."

"Good. Bring it on."

"You've seen the pre-trade movements?"

"I have." Brita glanced Anna's way. She'd provided a comprehensive overview of the expected impacts of last night's excesses on Stora's share price. "I'm ready."

"If he's called me, he's called everyone." Mas pulled her phone out and raised it to her ear. "He's coming for you. For us." She shot back to her feet, a strained smile replacing the look of dour warning. "Hello? Lloyd! Glad you called, how are you? Yes, yes—mmm..."

Mas stepped away, towards the window and the orange-tinted views down across Canary Wharf. Brita took another slug of water and heard the elevator's soft ping. She had a feeling she knew who would be coming around the corner. She stood and slipped back behind her desk. She needed to present as both calm and in control. This was her desk, her office, her company.

Sunlight flashed across the room as the door was flung open, leaving a momentary bright spot in her vision. By the time it had cleared, Garfield Overton was bearing down on her.

"I don't know who you think you are, but if you think you can go on live TV, pull that shit, and then not answer any of my calls—"

Brita ignored his bluster. Instead she held up a finger and clacked away at her keyboard with one hand, as if she were writing an email.

"Brita—"

She hit send with finality and closed the lid. Only then did she look up. "Garfield. Nice of you to join us. Have a seat, Mas will be with us shortly." She glanced over at her assistant, giving her a wan smile. "Anna, would you mind?"

"What in God's name are you playing at?" His cheeks, his nose, even his neck, spilling over the lip of his too-tight collar, were bright red.

"Garfield, will you take please take a seat?"

"I demand answers—"

"Sit down, and you will get them! I will not be dictated to in my own office."

Garfield's mouth flapped like a fish on the hook, but he finally caught sight of Mas over by the window, watching him bluster with a dispassionate ire, and thought better of continuing with his spectacle. He pressed his lips together, his hands into his lap, and sat sharply, looking as if he'd swallowed a lemon.

"Thank you. Now, about last night. I am sorry about that. A few of the things I said may have been a tad premature..."

"Premature!" Garfield scoffed, his eyes turning to the ceiling as if in prayer. "Premature? I'm sorry, Brita, but 'we'll topple both Samsung and Apple within five years'? You sounded, frankly, out of your depth."

Less than five years, Garfield, Brita thought. *And you'll be watching and weeping from the sidelines.* "Like I said, it wasn't ideal, but let's not overstate it."

"The pre-trade data is forecasting a 13% fall. Thirteen!"

"It's an overreaction."

"That may well be true, but our shareholders don't care! They just don't. They care about one thing, and that's the little green arrow, pointing up. And what are they seeing instead? Negative 13%, the ticker tape bleeding red. They want answers, Brita. Answers I can't give them." He balled his fists in a pitiful display of manufactured exasperation. He thought he was playing this like a pro. "If you don't kowtow, I'd not be surprised if they wanted heads. Maybe even yours."

"Kowtow, Garfield? This isn't the eighties anymore. The shareholders don't run the company; I do. And although I regret going a little too early with last night's comments, I stand by them. One hundred percent."

"But the numbers—they just don't—" Garfield stammered. Then he stopped, snapping his mouth shut and springing to his feet. "No. No, I'm not engaging. You've run this company like it's your own personal fiefdom for far too long. You're living in the same fantasyland that swallowed your father. This ends now."

Brita stood too. He was flustered, backing towards the door but not quite committed to walking out on her for the final time. As he'd been speaking, his agitation had given her an idea. The investors wanted to run. What if she let them?

"Remind me. What are our sales forecasts for the next quarter? And for next year?"

"You know that as well as I do, Brita. Strong." He glanced briefly over at Mariska, still whispering in the corner.

"And how has last night's storm in a teacup affected those numbers? No, don't answer. I'll tell you." She followed him around from behind her desk. "Not one bit, Garfield. Not one. Nor will it affect our embedded cost reductions. Nor the increases in production efficiency we've seen in the last six months. The uptick in brand awareness, in customer satisfaction. The share price is one thing. Stora's actual value is another. At the moment, they are only tangentially linked."

"I know, Brita." He looked desperate. "But the shareholders are panicked."

"Then let them panic." She sat on the edge of her desk and crossed her arms. This was her hammer blow, and, if she played it right, it might just solve two problems with one strike. "I'll be more than happy to buy them out at such a steep discount."

"But...ah. Oh." Overton paused, his brow furrowed, the fingers of his right hand counting off as he ran the calculations in his head. He slid across to the couch, gently lowered himself down, and crossed his legs. "That's actually an interesting thought. We'd have to be quick, though. I expect the extremes of this drop will be temporary. Maybe a week. And we're capital constrained, as you know..." Brita let him mumble along, figuring it out for herself. She watched his eyes, waiting for the moment they popped open, for his jowled chin to wobble its way into a grin. "But if we could secure a series of medium-sized loans..."

"Great thinking, Garfield. How about seven loans, separate banks? Fifty million pounds each? No, let's make it one hundred million." She stood abruptly, clapping her hands in excitement.

"Really? I..."

"Excellent. Give me your shortlist by lunchtime, and I'll start making calls." Brita helped him up and ushered him gently towards the door, where Sunil and Luan were waiting patiently, their reworked press release ready to be approved. "I'll leave it in your capable hands."

"Nicely done," Mas whispered as she slipped past, following her flustered CFO out the door. "I'll drop by after my ten o'clock. I have some ideas." Heels clacking on the polished concrete floor, she intercepted her eager subordinates. She stalked towards the lift, pen already scratching further revisions, leaving Brita in silence.

She smoothed non-existent wrinkles from her blazer and patted at imaginary stray hairs as she strolled back to her chair. The sun now hung well above the tops of the tallest skyscrapers, and already she'd had two wins. Only one thing left to resolve. One big thing, anyway. She sank down into her chair, pulled out her phone, and called her dad.

Brrrp brrrp. Brrrp brrrp. Brrrp brrr—

"Hi." Her father's voice was rough.

"Morning, Dad. I didn't wake you, did I?"

"No, of course not." A stifled yawn. She obviously had. "I suppose you've hardly slept, putting out fires?"

"It's been a productive morning. Listen." She bit her lip, an uncomfortable wave of nausea rolling up her throat. "I wanted to apologise for last night, again. Gateway is yours, and you came to me. I'm sorry if I got carried away."

"Thanks. I uh, I appreciate that."

A silence hung between them, as Brita waited. *Is there anything you wanted to say in return, Dad? Anything?* The silence stretched.

"I've, um. Look, I had a good think on my walk last night. I think bringing that Mariska on board is going to work out, but that's all for now. We should move slowly. Carefully."

"Good, Dad. I'm glad you like her. She's the right kind of person for this kind of project. Big picture."

"And aggressive. I like that." A pause. "She's got guts."

A little too aggressive, sometimes, Brita thought, remembering Mas's final suggestion of the night, in the back of her car.

"Listen, I think I've come up with a solution to our funding problem. To begin with, anyway."

"Oh?"

"I've convinced Garfield to start scoping out some minor debt raising, with an eye to complete a series of buybacks."

"Oh." She heard a paper rustling in the background. "Ah. That's clever. He'll never get them in time to make the most of the fall. It won't even last two days."

"I know. So sad. What will we spend that money on?"

"Hah! Very nice." A slurp of something, and a chink of metal against china. Coffee? Or maybe it was whisky, and that had been ice against crystal. It was impossible to tell. "I've had a few ideas myself, so I better go, but thanks for letting me know."

"No worries, Dad. Anything you can share?"

"Not right now." Another silence, stretching, stretching, just like the last. For a moment, Brita thought he'd hung up. But then: "I'm glad I made the call, Brita. I'll be seeing you."

Brita set her phone down on the desk, very gently, and savoured another long pull of chilled water as a hot tear prickled at the corner of her eye.

13

THE ENTRANCE TO THE Savoy Hotel swarmed with paparazzi. Jorge groaned. He'd dreamed of one day standing on these steps, leading the press pack, hounding a certain Texan billionaire as his carefully constructed facade crumbled to dust. But Solomon wasn't even in town.

A rabid photographer elbowed him in the ribs, imagining he'd seen a glimpse of the man they were all here to see. Jesus, if it was this bad out here, it would be even worse inside. Officially sanctioned photographers and anointed "journalists," queuing up for their ten minutes locked in a soulless little room with a mass-produced "star" to help spruik his latest movie.

And today, he was one of the anointed. Roger had even expected to be thanked for bestowing upon Jorge such an opportunity. A privilege. *After that interview, hombre, you've earned it.*

Fucking prick.

Externally, the Gundersson interview had been a raging success, but internally, it had done little but remind Jorge who he'd used to be. And to make matters worse, Turnbull had turned up very little, and both Hugo and Solomon had gone to ground. He was fresh out of leads. The media cycle had moved on. Stora's share price had even begun a half-hearted recovery.

So this was his lot. He closed his eyes, sucked in a deep breath, and held it, as if instead of a luxury hotel, he was about to enter a cesspit.

"Hey, Jorge!" A hand slapped him on the back, belonging to an Old Etonian face, but with distinctly American teeth. "Great interview last week."

"Gracias." Jorge raised his eyebrows with faint recognition and gave off a wan smile. He knew this idiot "worked" for *Glamour*, or *Vogue* maybe. He was always at these fucking things, but what was his name? Gilbert? Albert?

"Didn't realise big business was your go, but you really gave her a deserved what-for." Gilbert/Albert gave him an encouraging punch in the arm. "Still, must be a relief to get back to the home turf."

"Yes, quite." Jorge's brows lifted once more, in apology this time, and he excused himself. He'd barely started, and already he wasn't sure how much of this he could take.

He checked his watch: 9:40. Christ, the press junket had been rolling for two hours already, and his slot was in fifteen minute's time. A harried PR assistant arrowed in towards him, armed with a clipboard and mirror-black heels. If movie stars weren't so universally vapid, he'd have almost felt sorry for them.

"Elorza? O2 News?" She yanked his press pass out of his hand and spoke without even looking up. "The next in queue is late, so I'm shifting you up. We'll squeeze you in before we break for morning tea. You're on in...three minutes."

"Three minutes? I'd be happy to wait until morning tea," Jorge offered, but to empty air. She was already gone, off hassling some poor photographer who had strayed over an imaginary line.

Ugh. Before morning tea was the worst possible slot. Fresh off a half dozen reporters asking the same half dozen questions, with another seven or eight hours to come, his interviewee would no doubt be in the foulest of moods. He checked his notes. Hank something. Robard? Yep, Robard. Starring in yet another movie with a number at the end.

Fantastic.

"Two minutes." The PR assistant was back, tugging him towards an ostentatiously guarded door. "Remember, make sure you discuss the release date, Hank's new co-star, and the kiss we've all been waiting for. We need all three, and we'll be checking the footage before we release it to your masthead."

"Well, that's very kind," Jorge muttered, but she was gone again, leaving him alone with a musclebound security guard. He folded his arms and offered the guard a nod, receiving nothing in return. From across the room, Gilbert/Albert gave him an enthusiastic thumbs-up.

Jorge could only glower at the absurdity of it all.

His phone buzzed. Buzzed again. Turnbull. About fucking time.

"Jorge—"

"Where have you been, man? I feel like a jilted lover, pining and waiting."

"That's, erm, an evocative image." Footsteps in the background, echoing in a corridor. Turnbull was on the move. "Busy week."

He sounds flustered, Jorge thought, *like something big is about to unfold. I wonder...* "Finally making your move on Britannia then?"

"How did you—"

Jorge grinned. He could imagine Turnbull's red cheeks flushing even redder.

"It doesn't matter. I got your report this morning. Everywhere Ms Gundersson's driver has taken her over the last seven days. Ordinarily I would have waited until tomorrow, given how busy I am, but it would appear our investigations have become intertwined."

"Intertwined?" The hairs on the back of Jorge's neck prickled with tension. Britannia Bank was the third-largest Stora shareholder, after Brita and her father. And if the City of London Police had BB in their sights, well. Jorge gave the impassive security guard a look of mock intrigue. This could be interesting. "Don't keep me on tenterhooks, Harvey. Spill."

"One minute!" the PR demon squawked.

"It seems your pal Brita has been hitting up just about every banker in town. Private meetings."

"Just about every banker? But not..."

"No." Turnbull paused. "Well, not yet."

So Brita was looking to fund something. A something that triggered the collapse of the Solomon deal. A something that would, if Brita's PR was to be believed, bring Apple and Samsung to their knees. A something she didn't want a major shareholder to get a whiff of.

"There's a but, isn't there, Harvey. I can hear it in your voice. What's going on—"

If Turnbull answered, Jorge didn't hear him over the PR assistant and her weaponised clipboard. The very secure door was opened, and the guard simultaneously extracted a very pretty and very flustered TV reporter from Hank Robard's clutches, and shoved Jorge into them.

"In you go, Mr Elorza," the PR assistant chirped. "Ten minutes, and remember! Release date, co-star, kiss!"

The door slammed shut.

"Hi—"

Jorge held an impatient finger up, right in Hank Robard's face. "Harvey, you still there? What did you mean, 'not yet'?"

"Sorry, buddy, gotta go. Just make sure it's me that's front and centre on the news tonight, all right? I'm counting on you."

"Excuse me—"

"Harvey?" Jorge pressed his phone hard against one ear, plugged the other, and completely ignored Hank Robard. "Harvey! Dammit!"

The line was dead.

Jorge tapped the phone furiously against his chin. What did he know? Turnbull was going after Britannia Bank, and somehow Brita had gotten herself entangled in the investigation. Was it just their shares in Stora linking them, or something more?

"Hey!" Hank's beefy hand landed on his shoulder and wrenched him around. The actor towered over him, impossibly handsome with his blue eyes and perfectly coiffed hair. A barely contained anger twisted his features. "You'd better start show-ing a little respect—"

"Oh, go away," Jorge snapped, shrugging Hank's hand off. "Can't you see I'm working?"

"Go away! Go away? Not even Quentin gets to talk to me like that..."

Jorge drowned out Hank's affected Tennessee drawl, his mind racing. It had to be more than just the shares, it had to be, otherwise Turnbull wouldn't have been surprised when he got Jorge's report on Brita's movements. And then suddenly his investigation into Britannia Bank and Brita's movements had come together. There was only one thing it could be. He swiped at his phone, desperately trying to dredge up Roger's number.

"Hey!" Robard made another grab at his jacket, but Jorge dodged out of reach. "I don't know who you think you are—"

"I don't think about *you* at all." Jorge glared, for just long enough to know that the insult had hit home, and then he pressed the phone back to his ear. "Roger. Listen—"

"Hey, *hombre*! How's that Yankee hunk Robard? His PR bitch isn't giving you too hard a time, I hope—"

"Fuck Hank. I've got something bigger."

"Bigger than Hank Robard and *Starkiller 6*? I'd like to see that—"

"Hey, fuck you too, buddy! I've had enough of this." Behind him, Hank ripped the door open and bellowed for the PR assistant.

"Wait, *hombre*, tell me you're not calling me mid-interview?"

"Roger, forget Hank. You need to get a news crew out to the Britannia Bank head-quarters. Now—huunghh!" The security guard's hands slid beneath his armpits and lifted him bodily into the air, but Jorge didn't let that stop him. "Something is about to go down, Roger, I'm telling you. City of London Police are up their eyeballs in this."

"Jorge, if you've put a fucking *toe* out of line with Hank Robard, I swear—"

"Swear all you like, Roger. Just, no. You know what? Forget it." Jorge hung up before Roger could get another word in. The entire press gallery, little sheep with their passes, their notebooks, and their complimentary snacks halfway to their mouths, stared as he was carried through the throng. Jorge, though, barely noticed. All he could think of was Roger. Christ, he was shortsighted. Wouldn't know a story if it bit him in the arse.

Jorge motioned to the marble floor, just on the other side of the press junket's velvet cordon. "Here will be fine."

The security guard plonked him down.

Behind him, Hank Robard had been physically restrained, the veins and sinews on his neck pulsing as he screamed profanities across the lobby while his horrified

PR team looked on. Gilbert/Albert was filming it all on his phone, grinning as if this was the best day of his life.

"Your pass." The security guard held out his hand, and Jorge realised he was trying not to smile.

"Oh, yes. Of course." Jorge handed it over, winked, and brushed himself down.

Then, he turned towards the taxi rink and allowed himself a little smile at the chaos he'd created. This was what Roger wanted, wasn't it? Fireworks? There was no doubt Hank's continuing tantrum would make the six o'clock bulletin. There wasn't a PR manager in the world who could prevent it from leaking. It just wouldn't be on O2 News.

But honestly, who cared?

He raised his hand for a cab as he flicked through his contacts, found the name he was after, and hit dial. "Gabrielle? Jorge Elorza. You still at the *Broadsheet*? Fantastic. Get a camera crew out to Britannia Towers. Yes, right now. Yep. Yep—Gabrielle? I promise this is legit. Yes. I'll meet you there."

14

"Brita, my dear. What a pleasure." Lloyd Hargreaves greeted her with an overly familiar handshake, and ushered her forwards with a hand at the small of her back. Even through her jacket, Brita could feel the heat from his chubby fingers. "It's been too long."

Despite Britannia being Stora's banker, and Lloyd Britannia's CEO since her father had been in charge, Brita had never actually visited Lloyd in his office at the top of Britannia Towers. They'd always met in conference rooms, board rooms, publicity events, and soirees. However, in light of the sensitivity of her proposal, she had invited herself up to his private office. Already she was regretting it.

Stepping into Lloyd's office, encompassing almost the entirety of the Britannia Towers top floor, was like stepping back in time. More than the oak panelling that had replaced the brushed steel and polished glass of the rest of the building, more than the lush carpet, or the fireplace that *surely* wasn't to code, was the smell. Leather-bound books, a fastidiously oiled desk. Stuffy. Closeted.

Exclusive.

Lloyd Hargreaves could not have designed himself a more fitting edifice.

"It's quite something, isn't it," Lloyd said, beaming at the shocked expression she'd let slip past her defences. He traced a loving finger along the corner of a heavy mahogany desk. "It's all real, you know. This desk belonged to Hubert Asquith. Came straight from Number 10."

"Really? *Hubert's* very own desk?" Brita urged her features back into order, despite the sheer improbability of Lloyd's statement. "Very impressive. And he brought it straight here?"

"Yes, well. Via Sotheby's, of course," Lloyd conceded, sinking into his leather seat without skipping a beat. He indicated the matching chair opposite him. "Please."

"Thank you, Lloyd." The leather felt just as old as she'd expected. Well worn, and well cared for. "Were these Asquith's as well?"

"The chairs? Heavens, no." Lloyd chuckled, in that affable way only those born into society knew how, with a rakish twinkle in his eye. "No, no. Chamberlain's, actually."

"Ah," Brita said. *Of course they are.*

She sat and tried to ignore just how comfortable the chair was. The uncluttered expanse of the desk was so vast that she felt compelled to lean forwards, while he rocked back wearing a very familiar self-satisfied grin. That smile, and everything that sat behind it, snapped her back to the task at hand.

Every one of the half dozen other CEOs she'd met across the past week had worn the same smile as they welcomed her into their lairs. And each office had been, in a slightly different but unnervingly similar way, a symbol. A desperate attempt to cling to a world and a hierarchy fast slipping into history.

A hierarchy in which she didn't belong.

Well. That was never going to change. But the world was. She was going to change it.

"So, Miss Gundersson. What brings—"

"One hundred million pounds," Brita interrupted, her hands folded across her lap.

"One hundred million pounds?" Lloyd blanched. Just gently, but enough. He shifted in Neville Chamberlain's seat. "That's a lot of money."

"Not really." Brita shrugged.

"Well, might I ask what for?"

"No."

Lloyd's intercom, a modern comms setup disguised as an antique, buzzed. He waved it away.

"No? Not even a hint?"

Brita shook her head. It buzzed again, and he silenced it with affable irritation.

"I must say, this is highly irregular. When I worked with your father..."

"My father is out of the picture, Lloyd. And totally irrelevant." The fire cracked behind her, sending a bright flare across her opponent's cheeks. "This is not a business matter. Not Stora, anyway."

"So, personal then?"

She kept her features neutral, and he sat up a little straighter. Intrigued, she could tell, despite himself. "Well, as you know, we're not in the business of making personal loans of that magnitude for just anyone, and without the backing of Stora's credit rating..." He waved his hands, and his eyes narrowed. "Unless there is a *new* opportunity in the works?"

Brita sighed. Seven times she'd had this same meeting, and seven times it had followed almost an identical script. Feigned shock, a superficial pretence at due diligence, before the greed took over. The realisation that this might be just the first of many. It was depressingly easy.

"Perhaps, Lloyd. There's a lot of water yet to flow under the bridge."

"Of course, of course." He tapped his nose, an entirely ridiculous gesture. "Say no more. Now let's talk collateral—"

The door creaked open, letting in a harsh fluorescent light that turned the antique furniture ostentatious and gaudy. Brita held a hand up to the glare as Lloyd blustered.

"Mae, I thought I told you no interruptions—"

A woman stepped into the doorway. She was no more than a silhouette.

"Lloyd Hargreaves?"

"Mae, what is—"

"Lloyd Hargreaves, my name is Detective Chief Inspector Marlowe, with the City of London Police. I'm sure you know what that means." The woman thrust out a hand. "I have a warrant to search the premises."

"A what?"

"A warrant, sir."

Brita stared, frozen. DCI Marlowe stalked towards her in slow motion, the warrant held before her like a shield. How? How did she know? Had one of the other bankers turned her in? Had Mariska? Her father? No, not her father. He was even more paranoid than she was.

DCI Marlowe approached Lloyd's desk.

Accusations, explanations, excuses formed and jockeyed for position in her mind. It wasn't like the Gateway was illegal. They had no right! And anyway, she didn't even have a Gateway on her! She forced herself to breathe, but...but that wouldn't matter. Not if they knew. If the secret was out...

Her hands cramped, her nails digging into leather, and the pain shocked her back to her senses, to the weight of the UK government bearing down, to the end of the Gateway before it had even begun.

"—pen those filing cabinets for me, Mr Hargreaves."

Hargreaves? Brita blinked, the detective's words finally breaking through the blood pounding in her ears. DCI Marlowe and her colleagues didn't even seem to know she was in the room. They were arrayed around Lloyd, who had launched himself from his seat and extended himself to his full height. All five feet, seven inches of it. He somehow managed to both glare down at Marlowe despite being a good four inches shorter, and totally ignore the warrant she held in front of his face.

"I'll do no such thing."

Marlowe shook her head, dark-brown hair wound into the tightest of buns. She folded the warrant and slipped it into Lloyd's front pocket.

"I'm afraid you will, sir."

They're here for him! For Britannia Bank!

"My lawyer—"

They aren't here for me!

"He's right here, sir."

"He—"

"Over here, sir." Brita peered over Marlowe's shoulder, towards a downtrodden shill in a Saville Row suit. He was shaking his head. "It's all aboveboard."

Lloyd could only stand there red faced, trying and failing not to look at the hand-carved filing cabinets arrayed behind him. Particularly the third one, from the left.

"But, Winston—"

"Best you keep quiet, sir, and let DCI Marlowe do her job."

Lloyd sagged back into his chair and stared ruefully at DCI Marlowe. Just, Brita imagined, as Chamberlain had done when his resignation had become inevitable. What exactly did Lloyd have to hide? Surely no more and no different than the other bankers lined up along Canary Wharf. Suspect clients, no doubt, with suspect deposits and suspect loans, granted with scant oversight and—

Suspect loans. Just like mine.

Brita watched as the constabulary wheeled trolleys into Lloyd's office, loaded with empty boxes. Boxes that would soon be filled, with papers, with hard drives. And if there were constables up here, then there would be police cars down there. Flashing lights, blue and white tape. And that meant cameras. Reporters. Scandal—

"Ma'am." DCI Marlowe was crouched before her, looking up at her. Kindly. "Ma'am? Do you work here ma'am?"

"What?" Brita just couldn't focus. Whatever happened here would affect the others. Britannia would drag everyone down with them. Share prices would plummet. Compliance officers would get cold feet. "No." Brita shook her head, more at her own troubles than at anything DCI Marlowe might have said. "No, I'm, uh. I'm a client."

"Right you are, ma'am. I'll just get one of my constables to get your contact details, in case we need to follow up with anything, and then you can be on your way."

Someone helped Brita to her feet. She didn't know who; it could have been anyone. She gave her name, her phone number. In return they gave her a slip, and she was ushered out the door. There were more navy blue uniforms, more trolleys, more boxes in the process of being filled. She wasn't sure what she expected, a mad scramble to get documents to the shredders perhaps, but not this: forlorn staffers watching on as the evidence of their hard work, their steadfastness, or maybe their wrongdoing was carted away.

She rode the lift down with a chipper detective. He gave her a wink. "Sorry you had to get all caught up in this, Miss Gundersson. Bad timing is all."

She offered a wan smile and tried not to look at her reflection in the polished mirrors. The detective had his hands thrust triumphantly in his trouser pockets, thumbs resting on his belt. He looked like a man who was in the midst of delivering a long-planned project. One that was going very, very well.

"Oh, and don't let that Jorge get you down. He's a bit of an attack dog, I know, but he's a good egg."

"I…" She eyed the screen. Still twenty floors to go. Why did Lloyd's ego demand he have his office at the top of the wharf's tallest building. She didn't quite know what to say. "Thank you?"

The lift slowed to a stop; the doors chimed, then opened. Not a moment too soon.

"And keep an eye on that father of yours."

The detective's words stopped her in her tracks, and she was buffeted by a brace of constables, hurrying past her, so they might reach the upper floors and the evidence therein.

"I'm sorry, do I know you?"

"Not at all, ma'am." He put his hand on her back and directed her towards the door. "This way."

"Then why should I…" Brita started, but then she caught sight of the scene beyond the lobby windows, and her words drained away. The plaza, where the ice rink was during winter, was cordoned off. Constables guarded the entrances and exits, keeping worried employees in and holding overeager passers-by at bay. The detective ferried her through the revolving door and stopped at the top of the stairs.

All she wanted to do was scuttle down the steps, but the detective held her there for what seemed like an age. There was just one camera crew, the lenses of their cameras trained inevitably right towards them. She did her best let her hair, the wind, the glare of the sun obscure her face. But if there was one crew, though, there would soon be more. It was time to leave.

"Just down there, ma'am." A troop of constables carrying heavy equipment marched up the steps, and the detective pointed over their shoulders, down towards the far corner. Right in front of the camera crew. "Show that slip to young Templeton down there. He'll look after you."

He patted her on the shoulder and melded into the crowd of police officers busily combing through the records of her largest shareholder. For a moment, she was totally alone.

She didn't look back. Halfway down the steps she already had her phone pressed to her ear. "Henry, where are you?"

"I'm barricaded in the carpark, ma'am. The police are here, and—"

"I'm sorry, ma'am, you'll have to stay inside until the collections teams have completed their sweep." The constable she'd been pointed towards, Templeton, couldn't have been a day over twenty. His shoes were so new they still shone. He held the straps of his police vest, as if it didn't yet feel normal.

"I don't work here," Brita said, watching over the constable's shoulder as another camera crew careened around the corner. She hung up the phone. If her driver couldn't get to her...

"Be that as it may, ma'am—"

"I can't stay here. I have this." She shoved the slip that she'd been given upstairs into the boy's hand and lifted the police tape.

He grabbed her arm. "Ma'am, you can't just—"

"It's all right, Officer. You can let her go. That's it." The officer's grip loosened, but Brita's heart sank at the very Spanish inflection on the word *you*. She knew that voice. "You saw DI Turnbull directing her down here, didn't you? Read the slip, there's a good lad."

"Oh! Oh, my apologies, ma'am." He lifted the police tape, allowing her to duck underneath. "Hope we haven't put too much of a dent in your day..."

Brita let herself be dragged away, out of the reach of the City of London Police and the shadow of Britannia Towers. Into a quieter part of the plaza, where her rescuer could speak to her in private.

"Now, Miss Gundersson," Jorge asked, once he had sat them both down. "Just how have you gotten yourself tangled up in yet another scandal?"

15
— . —

MARISKA STOOD BEFORE HUGO'S workbench, and for once it was covered not with tools, fasteners, and electronic components but with photographs. Specifically headshots, stapled to their accompanying bios, which detailed how rich each head was, and, crucially, just how those billions had been earned. Seventeen in total, fifteen men and three women. Mariska held another eleven over the bin.

"So we're agreed. This is our target group."

"Yes. I think so." Hugo stood with his hand buried in his beard, intent on the photos. "There's got to be five mugs in this lot that will go for it."

Mas dropped her stack of rejects into the bin with a satisfying thunk. "But we don't want mugs, Hugo. We want people with vision, who can see the big picture. And the writing scrawled across it in dripping red paint...hold on."

Her phone buzzed in her pocket, the staccato rhythm she had set especially for her boss. Christ. What timing.

"Brita." She raised her eyebrows at Hugo and held a finger to her lips. "What do you need?"

"We've got a problem."

"Oh?" Mas meandered towards the far window, until she was well out of earshot.

"Have you seen the news?"

"News? No. I've been deep in a strategy session," Mas fibbed, quickly flicked the phone to speaker, and scrolled through her feed. "Jesus."

"Exactly." Brita's tinny voice barked out of the phone's speakers, echoing off emptiness in the corners of Hugo's workshop.

"And the photos..." Mariska could hardly believe her eyes. Police tape cordoning off the entrance to Britannia Tower, vans loaded with box after box of evidence. All that was missing was that twerp Hargreaves being frogmarched out in handcuffs. Then her well-honed corporate instincts kicked in, and she flicked across to the market. "FTSE is down sixteen points already, Christ." She glanced at her wrist. Not even 1:00 p.m. She let the ticker scroll through. Britannia down thirty-one. RBS, DB, Barclays, Lloyds all in the red, and sinking. "When did this happen?"

"Uhh, just before lunchtime. Eleven, eleven thirty?" Brita sounded flustered. With good reason, she supposed. "Does it matter?"

"No. I guess not." Mariska rolled the price chart back, pinpointing the beginning of the crash. 11: 49 a.m. The fuzz had kept a tight lid on this one.

She perched herself against one of Hugo's overstuffed equipment racks, unlocked one of his blacked-out windows, and swung it open. The hinges screeched in protest, revealing a sad rear courtyard. Dead flowers and long grass, overrun with weeds. Brita had had eight banks lined up for £100 million each, one of which was Britannia. So seven banks, now. She checked the banking index and sucked a breath in through her teeth. Sixteen points in just over an hour, with more to come. Surely, if that continued, seven would become zero. Surely.

"Any idea what Hargreaves was up to?"

"Lloyd? No." Mariska heard Brita shake her head, her hair rustling over the phone microphone. "Whatever it was, though, he won't have been on his own. The others will be getting nervous."

Mariska smiled. So Brita was already thinking it too. She glanced back at Hugo, bent over his workbench, poring over the headshots. Ready to swoop in and save the day. *But I can't push too hard. Not yet.* Brita would have to come around on her own.

"How nervous? You don't think—" Mariska was interrupted by a screaming car horn, and a foul-mouthed cockney tirade. "Wait, where are you?"

"Taxi." *A taxi? What happened to Henry?* "And I don't have to think. I just got a call from Andrew over at RBS. They're out."

"Already?"

"They would have known this was coming. Or at least suspected."

There was something in Brita's voice. A hesitancy. Was it...resignation?

For a moment, Mas heard only the muted sound of London traffic, as transmitted by Brita's phone. It was strangely comforting compared to the cold silence of Hugo's workshop. An empty belly of a once-grand old house, long fallen into neglect. That night, when Brita had first brought her here, this house and Hugo seemed to match one another, but now...

When Brita finally spoke, Mariska realised she wasn't even listening. "Hmmm? What did you say?"

"I said I was there. In Lloyd's office, when they came."

"Jesus." Mariska held the phone to her chest, just for a second. On the one hand, she'd never heard her boss sound so small. On the other...She clenched her fist tight and bumped it against the peeling window frame. This couldn't have turned out any better. "Did anyone see you?"

Another pause. "Jorge. He was the first reporter on the scene."

"You didn't talk to him." Mariska worried that Brita would hear the smile in her voice.

"Of course I spoke to him. He had a camera crew! If I'd tried to cover my face, or run..."

"It would have looked like you were involved." Mariska nodded. It was good thinking. "What did you say?"

"That I was meeting with Lloyd to discuss financial arrangements for an upcoming project, that it was startling to witness a police raid, in the flesh. That Britannia has been a long-term, valued business partner. That the City of London Police were both courteous and thorough, and gave no indication to me as to what they were looking for, or what they alleged Britannia may have been involved in, and that beyond that, it was not for me to comment on what is clearly an ongoing investigation. What else could I say?"

"Good. That's good. Solid." Mariska rolled her eyes. Not a single thing for Jorge to latch on to. Why couldn't she have stuck to the script with Jorge the first time? "But, it's let the cat out of the bag, hasn't it. The other banks will know that your approaches weren't...exclusive."

"Mariska...I thought the police were there for me."

"For you? Why?"

"Come on, Mas. Use your imagination," Brita snapped.

Thinking about it just a little, it was obvious. How would she have felt if the last in a series of clandestine meetings, designed to winkle hundreds of millions of pounds out of greedy bankers' hands, in service of a project that would give any police force, any *government*, nightmares, was interrupted by a posse of detectives waving warrants?

I would have been sweating bullets.

"Right. We're in the deep end, aren't we," Mariska said, the reality of the games they were playing beginning to sink in.

"Yes, we are. And we're bleeding."

"Bleeding? Sure, Britannia is a loss, but seven hundred million pounds is more than enough to get started..."

"Six hundred million. I just lost RBS too, remember."

"Still..." Mariska allowed the doubt to linger in her voice. Maybe they could stretch six hundred million just long enough until the banks recovered...She checked the stock tickers again, knowing Brita would be doing exactly the same; watching the banking sector shrink before their eyes. It couldn't have been worse timing. For Brita, anyway.

The tenor of the call's background noise changed: fuller, messier, interrupted by soft, rapid tapping. Brita had pulled the phone away from her ear and begun typing. Mariska pressed the phone into her ear, straining her hearing. She could have sworn, beneath it all, she'd heard Brita curse under her breath.

"Anything else I should know, boss?"

"Umm...Christ." Mariska waited for a flurry of furious typing to pass. "Look. Mas. I know what you're thinking. Just—fuck. I've got to go. Come see me as soon as you can."

The line was dead. Who had Brita been emailing? Another of the banks pulling out? Or maybe Garfield, trying to figure out if this crisis could be used as leverage? Mariska smiled at her reflection in the black window, and at the empty courtyard beyond. Whatever it was, Brita's funding plan was dead. It was only a matter of time.

"I need you to close that." Mariska jumped. Hugo had appeared right beside her.

"What?"

"The window. Close it." Hugo stared. "Oh, get out of the way."

He pushed past her, stuck his head out into the courtyard, then slammed the window shut and rammed the catch home. The brief intrusion of sunlight into the harsh fluorescence of the workshop had been snuffed out, and Hugo seemed to visibly relax.

"What was all that about?" he asked.

"The phone call?" Mariska decided not to comment on the window, and the obvious paranoia. "Oh, nothing major. Just a banking crisis."

"Another one? Who?" Hugo brushed his hands against his slacks and turned back to his workbench and his rickety old chair.

"Britannia."

"Lloyd?" he ventured, and Mariska nodded. "Well, I'd be lying if I said I was surprised. His father was a crook, and that apple is still clinging to the tree. Brita panicking?"

"Not yet. But she's worried." Mariska grinned, and Hugo returned it. He knew what this all meant. "Made any progress?"

"I think so." Hugo tapped his thigh with a closed fist and turned back to the headshots. He'd split them into six even stacks. "I realised there's no point having more than one rep from the same industry. The whole point is to tempt these schlubs with the opportunity to get an edge on their rivals. Can't do that if they're all in the same room." He shook his head and laid a finger on the first pile. "What we need is a spread. Hotels. Shipping. Automotive. Airlines. Tech. Oil..." He paused on the headshot of a Saudi princeling, before sliding that stack into the bin. "On second thoughts, let's leave oil out for now. Bringing them into the tent could be dangerous."

Mariska nodded. Hard to disagree there. She traced an eye over the remaining photos. "So these five, they're your favourites?"

"You could say that." Hugo gave a mischievous little chuckle. "Not that Brita is going to like it."

"I'm not sure I like it either." She reached out and pressed her finger down on photo number five. Richard Solomon. "I'd prefer some infrastructure exposure over letting him back into the tent. I mean, the internet will still exist, but roads? If anything, we'll be ripping them up."

"Exactly. Demolition and rehabilitation takes just as much effort and manpower as construction. More, even." Hugo jumped in, the argument rolling off his tongue a little too easily, as if it had been pre-prepared. "But Solomon? Every reason he wanted Stora before is just magnified by Gateway. He's a big data guy on the wane, outpointed by his competition. He needs another angle, and he knows it. He's perfect."

"But why Omni? Why not Apple, or Samsung? Someone we'll actually hurt?"

"What, and give them a head start on replicating us? The whole point of this strategy is to get the jump on our competition. That's why Solomon is perfect. He'd already proven he can't build hardware to save himself."

"But he can buy it. He's a takeover guy, Hugo. That's what he is. This is too big a risk." Mariska bent down, fished the stack of infrastructure billionaire photos out of the bin and slapped them down on top of Solomon's. "We need people who aren't like us, who don't play in our swimming pool. Solomon's too close."

"But—" Hugo protested, but Mariska was having none of it.

"But what? Are you going to storm off every time you don't get your way? Try it, see how far that gets you. If you think I'm doing this to protect your daughter, or screw you over, you're dead wrong. I'm here to make bank. I'm all in. And so's Brita—she just hasn't realised it yet. And we can't afford little ego plays that might put her off." Mariska waved a dismissive hand at Solomon's photo and stared Hugo down. "I plan on using every advantage we have. Do you?"

Hugo stammered, looking like he'd been caught out in something. Mariska rolled her eyes. She didn't have time for these games.

"Look, I need to head back to the office." She snatched her coat and handbag from a folding chair. "There will be more fallout from this Britannia fiasco than just your daughter's little financing scheme, which means I'll have actual work to do."

"Actual work? I've been—"

"Yes, Hugo. Actual work. At Stora, my employer. We can't have people getting suspicious." Mariska tossed the comment over her shoulder as she marched towards the stairs. "Forget Solomon, and forget Brita. You keep working on your upgrades."

She flashed him one of her charming smiles, the kind that never quite made it up to her eyes. "This has to work, Hugo. No second chances."

16

— · —

"Anna!" Brita was giving orders the moment the elevator doors opened. "I need you to find Garfield and have him meet me in my office—"

"—Yes, Brita, but—"

"—and track down Janet, from Regulatory and Oversight." She caught her reflection in the opaque glass windows of her office and paused, just long enough to pat down the worst of her stray hairs. "And maybe Sylvia too—"

"—Of course, but Brita...wait, Sylvia C or Sylvia M?"

"What? Sylvia M." Brita opened the door to her office. "And clear my schedule for the rest of the afternoon—"

"Ms Gundersson. Finally." Garfield sat in her chair, his feet up on her desk. "Been out on a nice walk? Getting some fresh air?"

Just breathe, Brita. Just breathe. Don't rise to the bait. She nodded to Anna, acknowledging her assistant's mouthed apology, and relaxed her fingers. The door handle slid from her grip and swung closed behind her. *At least the windows are already blanked,* Brita thought. *Small mercies.*

"Garfield." *You smug bastard.* The primal, vindictive part of her wanted to tear strips from him, right then and there, even though that was exactly what he wanted. Besides. She had a better idea. "I'm glad you're here. What's our exposure?"

"Our... our exposure?" Garfield's smile faltered.

"Yes. That is why you're here, isn't it?" Brita sidled up to the chair opposite her own. The chair Solomon had been sitting in when she'd given him the bad news.

"Uh, yes. Yes, course." Garfield swallowed, smoothed down his tie. Brita sat.

"Excellent. I'm all ears." She leaned back. She wanted to watch him sweat.

"Well. Right. Well. As Britannia is our largest shareholder—"

"Equal second largest. With my father."

"—outside of your good self, of course." Garfield used her interruption as an excuse to push himself to his feet and totter out from behind her desk. He was such an oddly shaped man. At times like these, she marvelled that he managed to stay upright. "And they're the issuer of note for over seventy percent of our debt—"

"Do you think I don't know this already?" Brita snapped, watching to see if he flinched. "What I expect from you is analysis. Of Britannia. What have the police got on them? How close are they to the edge? And if they fall, who picks up their assets? Their liabilities?"

"Well, yes, but I..." Garfield stuttered, then visibly pulled himself together, grabbing the edges of his lapels with his manicured little hands. His head wobbled slightly from side to side as he lobbed his next sentence across the room. "I'm surprised Lloyd didn't tell you himself."

"Oh, get out of here, Garfield. My meeting with Lloyd wasn't a secret. I gave an interview when I left the building, for Christ's sake. Next time you decide to use a banking crisis to play games, at least pretend to have come prepared..."

"It was secret from me!"

"Oh, and I wonder why I would do that. Ah, Janet. Silvia." Brita swivelled with a tense smile at the sound of the office door clicking open. "Perfect timing. Garfield needs some help hashing out the implications of the kerfuffle over at Britannia. See what you can pull together. I want a briefing by...three o'clock."

She arched her eyebrows, and Garfield scowled. That should keep him busy for half an hour at least. She waited until the door was closed again before rising to her feet and collapsing down into *her* chair. Behind *her* desk. She tried to ignore the uncomfortable warmth in the leather that Garfield had left behind.

She pressed her fingertips to her temples and allowed the chair to list lazily to her left. What an awful, awful day. She hadn't even looked at what Lloyd's arrest had done to the share price. She'd seen what it had done to the FTSE, and that was enough.

Out the window, the major players and their polished edifices reached up into the low, overcast sky. Britannia and RBS, they were already out. Barclays, Deutsche, Santander, Rabo. Which would be the next domino to fall?

She replayed the whole sordid thing in her mind. Lloyd preening, and then the ashen horror that had descended as DCI Marlowe marched into the room. No, not quite then. A little later. When his lawyer told him to shut up and do as he was told. That was the moment. The moment Lloyd had realised he was in trouble, and Brita had realised she was not.

"But that's not true, is it?" she muttered. This entire project was trouble. Fantastic, world changing, revolutionary. In a market that strove for a consistency of profit that only monopolies could provide, that sought to quash competition (whatever the Solomons of the world might spout publicly about moving fast and breaking things). Stability was good for business. Innovation, other people's innovation, had a nasty habit of ripping your profit margin right out from under your feet.

That's what Gateway would do. If she could get it ready. Get it out there. Without someone like Jorge asking too many questions and sniffing out the truth, or one of the many, many people they'd need to bring into the fold to make this thing work letting slip the wrong thing to the wrong person at the wrong time, bringing the wrath of the government down on their heads. If she could just do that...

"But it feels a long way away right now." Brita sighed.

"What does?"

Brita jumped in her chair but had the presence of mind to refuse to turn around. Mariska.

"How long have you been here?" Brita asked.

"Not long. Though I did see Garfield skulking away, looking like he'd been bitten."

Brita smiled. "Good." She checked her watch. "He should be back in about fifteen minutes. What have you got?"

"How are we tracking on the, ahh..." Mas perched herself lightly on the edge of the desk and folded her arms. Her head cocked towards the horizon, the prominent logos and the barely contained panic that was surely engulfing the executive suites just below them.

"Lord, I haven't even checked." Brita whipped her phone out from her pocket and groaned at the never-ending list of notifications. Hundreds of emails. Dozens of messages and at least as many missed calls, including two from Oscar, over at Barclays, and another from Clinton at Rabo. She killed the screen, and slipped it back into her pocket.

"Not good?" Mas asked.

Goddamn it, Lloyd. Brita shook her head and stared out the window. She didn't care so much that Britannia had been caught doing...whatever it was they'd been doing; laundering money, probably. That's what Jorge had been pushing her to say, anyway. No, Lloyd was getting what he'd deserved.

*But I tried to get Gateway started without sullying our hands, when I easily could have...*She glanced across at Mariska, her arms crossed, deep in thought and staring at her feet. *But I didn't. I did the right thing, and look where that's got me.*

"Shit."

"Look, Brita," Mas began, unusually tentative. Brita knew in her gut what was coming. "I know you wanted to do this clean..."

Brita wondered if Lloyd was still in his office, watching on as DCI Marlowe scoured his files with a magnifying glass and a fine-toothed comb. Was he fretting? Scheming with his lawyer to find an underling he could toss under the bus? Or was he staring out his window too, wondering where it had all gone wrong? Perhaps they'd they already hauled him away for questioning. Escorted him out through the executive carpark in an unmarked van, so as to avoid the media scrum waiting outside.

I really don't want that to be me. But...

Brita made up her mind.

"I did, but it didn't work." She turned to face her protégé, to look her in the eye as they crossed the line. Together. "I want you to promise me one thing. No oilmen."

"But..." Mas scrunched up her nose in confusion, and then a tiny smile tugged at the corners of her lips. "You don't want to tangle with OPEC."

"And no oligarchs. They're too used to working outside the law. Or CCP shills. We'd basically be letting the Chinese government in the front door. We want outsiders."

"Right. Good call. Anything else you want to...?"

"And no Anita. I don't want her caught up in this."

Mariska raised an eyebrow, as if wanting to object, but she cut her off.

"Look, this is your plan. I trust you to handle it. Just tell me when it's ready." Brita glanced at her watch and spun back to face her laptop, and her emails, needing to put the unsavoury business out of her mind. "Garfield will be back any minute. You want to stay?"

"While watching that oaf try to weasel his way out of another cock-up is always fun, we're already behind the eight ball. I'd better get started." Mas pushed herself to her feet and made her way towards the door. "I'll leave you to it."

"Good luck," Brita said as the door hissed closed, unsure whether she meant it. There were so many things that could go wrong, and only one way they could go right.

17

"I DON'T THINK ABOUT you at all?" Roger bellowed, spittle clinging to his bottom lip for dear life. "I don't think about you *at all*? I can't…Why in God's name would you say such a thing? To Hank *fucking* Robard?"

"Honestly? I don't understand why you care." Jorge shrugged, and all the riggers, technicians, and cameramen stared. Usually, Roger contained his tantrums behind closed doors. "I offered you exclusive footage of the Britannia raid over an hour before anyo—"

"Britannia? *Britannia?* Who gives a *fuck* about Britannia! It's just one story! About a bank, for fuck's sake!" Roger pounded the table, narrowly missing some poor woman's lunch tray. Even still, her fork jumped from her plate and clattered to the ground. "Hank Robard keeps the goddamn lights on around here."

"Is that so?" Jorge rolled his eyes. "Well, I can't say I'm surprised. You've never been able to see past the end of your fucking moustache."

"I, what—"

"Who has the two highest-rating stories this year, I wonder? About a boring fucking phone manufacturer and a *bank*, no less?" Jorge leapt to his feet, sending his flimsy chair flying backwards. "You're always glaring over at ITV and Sky News, agonising over the ratings, coveting their 'reputation,' and yet there I was, offering you the chance to actually rise to their level, and what do you do? You panic, because I had to ignore some overinflated, self-important 'actor' to get it for you."

"Oh fuck you, you pretentious twat!"

"Fuck me? Fuck *me*?" Jorge was beginning to enjoy himself, and he couldn't keep the indignant smile from his lips. People had begun to cluster around the dining room door. *I hope that facile idiot Darabont is getting a good view.*

"Yes, fuck you!" Roger rolled his eyes up at the ceiling and flopped his hands at his wrists, his face twisted into a nasty snarl. His curled his voice too, with a mocking Catalonian lisp. "Look at me, everyone! I'm Jorge! I think I'm better than you because I was nominated for a Pulitzer in the fucking nineties!"

"Yeah I was. And yeah, I do," Jorge snapped. "And I'm right."

"Yeah. Maybe you are. But you know what else you are? You're the man who's cost us millions in sponsorships. Millions!"

"I'm sorry, what?"

The kitchen was silent.

"You heard me. Robard isn't just a star. He's the head of the actors guild. Your spiteful little stunt has cost us dozens of interviews. No movie his production company touches will come near us. No star his agent represents will answer our calls. Because of you, *hombre*."

Jorge stepped back from the table. For the first time since Roger had barged into the kitchen, a hot anger rose to the back of his throat. *Hombre.* He could feel the eyes of the room all over him. A dozen, a hundred small voices murmuring, wondering just how much of it was bluster, and how much of it might be true. What that might mean for their jobs. Their livelihoods.

"I truly hope that is so, Roger." Jorge spoke quietly, evenly, so that his colleagues had to lean forward in their chairs to hear what he had to say. "It might force you to act like a real news organisation for once, and maybe not waste these people's talents on such frivolous, mind-numbing wank."

Squaring his shoulders and shooting his cuffs, Jorge smirked. That was it. That was the line. He'd stuck it to the man and showed the rank and file he was on their side. But there was no chorus of support. No rousing cry of solidarity. He glanced around, his confidence wavering. Not even a murmur.

"I think you'd better leave." The colour in Roger's cheeks receded, and Jorge faltered. "Right now."

"You can't—"

"No, Jorge, you're done." Roger didn't blink. "You'll never work at this station again."

— · —

The instant Jorge was through his front door, he kicked off his pretentious Italian leather shoes and dumped his overpriced jacket on the floor. He felt as if he was shedding a polished but shallow costume, one that he'd worn long past its welcome.

Good fucking riddance.

He wiped the foundation from his brow and pulled on a well-worn pair of jeans. Walking home had been a good idea, even if it had started out as a furious march. It had given him time to think. This was exactly what he needed.

He was on a hot streak. Two high-profile stories in the space of a week, and an oh-so-tantalising lead. Brita Gundersson and Stora. They deserved his full focus. Roger could take his Hollywood-pandering bullshit and shove it up Frank Darabont's arse.

He flipped open his laptop and, with a wry smile, logged onto an encrypted server. The link was a gift from Harvey, a little thank-you for Jorge's undivided attention at the Britannia raid. A little blue bar crept across the screen, and he was in.

There were four cameras, showing live feeds: the main entrance to Stora HQ on Canary Wharf; Hugo's front door in Knightsbridge; a long shot down Chesterfield Hill in Mayfair, with the main entrance to Brita's apartments firmly in the centre; and a grainy image of a grey roller door. Hugo's storage locker just behind Waterloo station. And then there was the tracker.

A live text file that updated every time Brita's driver passed a camera, anywhere in London.

Jorge shook his head. The police really had too much power here. He hunkered down into his chair and lifted his camera out of his bag. Whenever Brita or Hugo made their move, he would be ready.

— • —

Jorge stared at his empty wall, and at the grainy cameras transmitting nothing but empty streets and the tedium of corporate foot traffic, entering and exiting a building. Gabrielle was on the line, congratulating him enthusiastically, while he nodded along, not really listening. He both yearned for and dreaded the end of the call and everything he knew would follow.

"All right, fantastic. That's great. Yep. Yep." Jorge nodded, his forced enthusiasm like little razors, slicing at his pride. "Thank you for the opportunity. I'll see you Monday, bright and early."

He tossed his phone away in disgust, and it landed in a haphazard pile of Styrofoam containers. Vindaloos. Chips and gravy. Stodgy pasta. Kebabs. Three weeks, sitting on his arse. Watching, with nothing to show for it but page after page of useless notes and a bank account dangerously low on funds.

Jorge tossed his head back, hands in his hair, and stared at the ceiling. He had been so goddamn sure.

The fruitless CCTV feeds mocked him from the corner of the room, but he couldn't bring himself to turn them off. Not just yet. A trickle of workers filtered in and out of the revolving door at the top of the stairs to Stora HQ as he sank to his knees, black bin liner in hand, and began clearing three weeks of mess one container at a time.

He'd stopped trying to catalogue the Stora employees over a fortnight ago; there were just too many. If anyone had come to visit Brita at her office, he'd missed them. And no one had visited her at home. No one of note, at any rate. She had a weekly stream of gardeners, cleaners, food delivery, but the only activity on that secluded Mayfair lane had been that same black car, picking her up in the morning and dropping her off at night.

Jorge's fingers landed on something soft. He shifted his weight to the balls of his feet and pulled a soiled jacket from the remaining containers. A white streak of...yoghurt, maybe, stretched from the lapel down to the left pocket. Shit. He'd have to get that dry-cleaned before Monday.

He tossed the jacket over the back of his chair, the sleeve draping over the lens of his dormant camera. Christ, what a waste of time this had been. Four long, cold nights he'd spent camped down the end of Hugo's street after an alert that Brita's car had dropped her off. What had he been hoping? To catch them in the act on his doorstep?

And in the act of what? He tied the bin liner off, tossed it into the corner, and grabbed another. What had he been hoping for? A new conspirator, maybe. Or a hint at what had driven Hugo to meet with Stanley, and Brita to eight banks in four days. *And what do I have instead?* A memory card full of useless photos and the controller to a drone he would never get back. That was all. Brita and Mariska darting from the front door to her waiting car. A dark blur that he knew was Hugo, hovering in the shadows, visible only for the second required to let his guests out before he slammed the door shut again. Close-ups of blacked-out windows, front and back. Even the internal fucking courtyard. He had half an hour of footage after his drone had gotten tangled in a snaking vine. A teetering video of a sliver of light behind a black window as the vine swayed in the breeze.

Fucking useless. Hugo had never even returned to the storage unit. *Or maybe he had,* Jorge thought. *I never did figure out how he managed to get past me that first night.*

He blinked and realised that at some point he'd sat down on the back of the couch and started watching again, the clutter not even half cleared. He shook his head and turned away.

I should turn it all off. Forget about it.

His new job at the *Broadsheet* deserved his focus. The Britannia scandal had staying power. Turnbull's raid had triggered leaks. Gigabytes of data. Spreadsheets, emails, memos, the works, with hundreds of tantalising connections between dirty money and important people. It was a real story, unlike his wild goose chase with Stora. A real scandal. Something tangible he could sink his teeth into. And his impulsive call to Gabrielle that morning had given him an in.

So he tidied, cleaned, washed. Gathered all the clothes that needed dry-cleaning, organised years of haphazard notes. He even showered, for the first time in a week.

A smelly man wrapped in a trench coat and huddled on a street corner was easily ignored. But he didn't need that any longer. God, it felt so good to be clean. He wrapped the towel around his waist and ran his fingers across his three weeks' worth of stubble. It was almost a beard. He smiled to himself. The Jorge in the mirror smiled back. He kind of liked it. And not just because Roger would never have let him grow such a thing.

He didn't want to lose it just yet.

He closed the drawer containing his razor, the shaving cream, sauntered back out into the living room feeling like a new man—

His towel, unsupported, fell to the floor.

There was a truck parked outside Brita's apartment. A catering truck, and it was Mariska, not Brita, holding the door open as the caterers carried their supplies inside. When had all this happened? He leaned in closer, trying to make out the name on the truck, but it was too side-on, too blurry. He shifted the camera from his chair and sat.

And watched.

Brita's car pulled up to her father's apartment, and for the first time since that first night, the first time in three weeks, Hugo left his house. He had two duffel bags, one held over each shoulder. He got into the car, and it drove away.

The tracker pinged with each new entry as Brita's car passed Knightsbridge station, Hyde Park Corner, Park Lane, Curzon Street...And then it appeared at the end of Brita's street. Mariska met him at the curb and accepted a duffel bag, and then the car and Hugo sped off. Back the way he came, and then beyond. Brompton Road. The A4. The M4.

Heathrow.

Jorge checked his wrist, but there was no watch. He was still naked, covered in goose bumps. This was it. Finally, after weeks of waiting, something was happening! The tracker pinged. It had left Heathrow, and presumably Hugo too. Whatever was going on, whatever they'd been planning, it was happening at Brita's. Tonight.

That Hugo wouldn't be there seemed strange, but his absence, and the bag he had handed to Mariska just before he was whisked away: it just added another intriguing twist to the mystery.

He checked his phone. One p.m. If the caterers were only arriving now, then the guests, whoever they might be, would be coming tonight. He had plenty of time. He put his phone on charge. Checked his camera battery, his memory card, and shrugged into a comfortable pair of jeans and his only stain free sweater.

He sat back at his desk, unable to wipe the grin from his face. He'd showered too early, but that didn't matter. His jacket had absorbed the odour of the street.

Coupled with the beard, the overlong, uncombed hair...Brita's guests would walk right past him.

And he would be watching.

18

—·—

BRITA SAT AT HER dusty, underutilised vanity, her hands shaking as she applied her eyeliner. She usually paid someone to do this, when she bothered with it at all. But not tonight. It had taken a full week just to convince her father that caterers were necessary for a dinner party, and that she couldn't just cook everything herself.

"There." She angled her face to the right, then the left, studying the roughly symmetrical black lines that she'd flicked up from the corners of her eyelids. "Not too bad."

Her notes rustled in her lap as she crossed her legs and opened her mascara. Eyes wide, staring at the ceiling, she started again on her pitch. "Thank you all for coming. I know the intimacy of this evening has got you all intrigued, and I can't tell you how much I've enjoyed watching you wonder and speculate throughout dinner...ugh."

Her phone buzzed, rattling against a bottle of foundation. She pulled the black wand gently away from her eyelashes so she could safely glance down. A message from her father blinked up at her.

Dad

All set, ready for testing

About time. She turned her eyes back up to the ceiling and returned to her whispered preparations "...how much I've enjoyed watching you speculate and wonder over dinner: Why are you here? Well, wonder no longer. It's time I introduced you to Project Gateway."

She blinked once, twice, and checked herself in the mirror one last time. A quick run-through with a brush to tidy up her forever-escaping loose ends, and everything was set. She was as ready as she was going to get.

She ran through her checklist: intro, security, demonstration, allow time for awe, for the inevitable questions, then it was time for business.

They had the perfect guest list: logistics and microchips, hotels and defence, automotive and manufacturing, construction and infrastructure. More importantly, her guests were not like Lloyd Hargreaves, clinging to a golden past that could only be seen through the rearview mirror. Sandeep Pridha, Ming-Xia Peng, Phil Greenberg, and Sato-san had already guided their businesses through torrid technological and geopolitical transitions. They would see Gateway and know exactly what it meant.

She breathed out through her nose, a wave of anxiety rising from deep within. Her father and Mariska had done a superb job setting everything up. It was a good plan. The best they could hope for, under the circumstances. *Then why do I feel like I'm about to be sick?* Gateway was the star, but she had to be the saleswoman. She had to make sure they were ready to be blown away. She set her jaw, straightened her back, looked herself in the eye.

I have done harder things than I plan to do tonight. Much, much harder. Her reflection blurred, and instead of forty-seven-year-old Brita sitting across from her, it was her father, betrayal etched deep in every wrinkle. But then his face changed, shifted, grew older, less bitter. *Because Gateway is an opportunity. A game-changer. It brought us back together. It is not the end of things, but the beginning of something new.*

And then she was back, her memory of that horrid day just a memory, and her nerves had fallen away. From downstairs, she heard a celebratory whoop. She set her notes aside and slipped her phone into the pocket she'd had fitted in her gown especially for this evening.

"Mas?" She strode out into the corridor that led from her bedroom suite, down winding stairs to the dining room, which a moment ago had been full of voices but was now silent. She rounded the corner to find Mas alone, draped in a stunning gold gown that seemed to defy gravity and glaring triumphantly at an empty doorway. There was an unusual whiff of spice and dry sand. "Mas? What's going on?"

"It worked, Brita. It fucking worked." She snatched her water bottle from the beautifully decorated dining table: minimalist place settings of earth and clay and copper, a stark contrast against a carved and fluted water feature centrepiece that seemed to float atop a rippling mirror. Mas sucked down the last of her water and crushed the bottle in her fist. Emphatically. "They don't stand a fucking chance."

— • —

Jorge thanked his lucky stars it was a clear afternoon, and that he'd caught onto whatever was going on down the far end of Chesterfield Hill early enough to snare an outside table. He rested an overstuffed backpack on an adjacent chair, spread out his ostentatiously large tourist map, weighted the far corners down with a pint and his trusty camera, and warded off the odd friendly local with a "Lo siento, no hablo ingles" and a smile.

A wild flurry of activity had brought him here: silent curses at the meandering politeness of the midafternoon tube traveller and a frenzied march through the Mayfair backstreets with his eyes glued to his phone, fast-forwarding through the missed minutes of security footage in which the catering truck and who knew what else had disappeared.

But that had been it. Just a pair of cooks—Chinese, judging by the blurred characters scrawled across the side of their van—hauling the last boxes of food out the rear door and down the steps that led to Brita's submerged entrance, a minute after he'd hopped on the train, and a lone hand reappearing to drive the van away.

A second pint followed the first, but the afternoon dragged and the last mouthful went flat in the sinking sunlight. *It's okay*, Jorge told himself. *I expected this.* This wasn't like the other four nights wasted shivering outside Hugo's house, alone but for a homeless man who seemed to shuffle an endless loop around Knightsbridge. The caterers. Mariska's shimmering gown. Hugo's mysterious handover only to disappear to the airport.

Something was happening. He had to remain patient. And vigilant.

Despite all this, the fruitless weeks spent watching and the thousands of useless photos weighed heavily on his mind.

To keep his doubts at bay, Jorge watched the passersby, profiling each one with no more information than the way they walked and the clothes on their back. Two women with fistfuls of designer bags, who must have taken a wrong turn and wound up in Mayfair's less-glamorous backstreets. An oddly familiar, harried-looking technician, air-conditioning by the look of the red-and-blue swirling logo on his navy shirt, shuffling away from him down the footpath, straight past Brita's house. A man on his phone, snapping curt replies to whoever was on the other end. People who looked like they had places to go. Places to be.

The shadow cast by his pint glass grew until it reached all the way across his tourist map, and the streets changed. Men and women in wool suits and understated blouses emerged as if from nowhere and streamed past him, office bags slung over their shoulders. Not a single one of them made eye contact or chatted with the person next to them. They all looked down at the pavement and made a beeline for the tube station, and for the first time in a long time, Jorge felt a twinge of homesickness.

This kind of exaggerated, solitary focus would never happen in Madrid. Of course, everyone would still be at work at this time, but in an hour or two, when the workday was done, colleagues would make their leisurely way to a late-night dinner, laughing all the way. Even in the Balkans, in the middle of a war that split cities along ethnic lines and tore communities apart, never to be rebuilt, he realised he'd never been so lonely as he was in London.

He reached for his ale. It seemed the only reasonable response to such a thought; then he grimaced as the last bitter dregs hit the back of his throat. The streetlights flickered and sprang to life, and a black Mercedes crawled down Chesterfield Hill. He set his empty glass back down in disgust.

Maybe it was time for a change. What had he achieved in London, really? He hadn't rehabilitated his reputation, that was for damn sure, and this new gig Gabrielle had landed him wouldn't help, no matter how positively his friend had spun it. *Just think of it, Jorge! Gigabytes of data. Terabytes!* she'd said. Financial records, emails, memos, and spreadsheets, all of it leaked in the aftermath of the Britannia Bank collapse. *And there's gold buried in there somewhere, I'm telling you. Maybe even a nugget or two about your old friend, hmmm?*

Perhaps, Jorge had thought. And he'd thought back to Brita's robotic, straight-down-the-line answers to his probing outside of Britannia's headquarters. *Perhaps there would be nuggets about his new friend, too.* And that had been enough to get him to say yes, even though he knew Gabrielle's bosses didn't want him, Jorge Elorza; they just needed a body, and he was cheaper and more accurate than an algorithm. For now at least.

Jorge gazed absentmindedly as an elegantly dressed Asian woman with slick black hair and bright-red lips stepped from the black Merc, adjusting the shoulder straps of her glistening white jumpsuit before closing the door and nodding to the driver. Korean? Or Chinese maybe? She looked familiar too—

Jorge lurched for his camera when he realised that she was already on her way down to Brita's front door. *Christ!* He fired off a dozen quick shots without even picking it up, just hoping that the setup he'd done hours ago was still okay, and then she was gone.

"Goddamn it, Jorge, get out of your own head," he muttered, flicking through the photos one by one. Damn. What a waste of an afternoon. Not a single usable shot, just blurry shadows of that white silk against whitewashed sandstone.

But he'd known that face. And not just in an "I've seen that lady somewhere before" kind of way. It was an important face, a face he *should* know. A face that expected to be known. A face that didn't just randomly show up at private dinner parties in Mayfair without a bloody good reason.

So what is that reason, then? Jorge wondered. He signalled the barman for another pint and settled his camera back down, rechecked the focus and adjusted the exposure to account for the low light.

With beer in hand, he brought up a *Forbes* list of Asia's wealthiest and most powerful. He scrolled, sipped, and stopped. That was the face, every arched eyebrow and intelligent smile. Ming-Xia Peng, scion of Malaysian Hotel magnate Sumayr Peng, who'd rescued her father's squandered billions, then leveraged them into becoming

Southeast Asia's largest defence contractor. *Is that the reason, Ming-Xia? Is this all in your honour? Or are there other billionaires, too? Who else has Brita ensnared in her web?*

—·—

"It's sort of quaint that we're serving our own drinks tonight, don't you think?" Ming-Xia Peng quipped through a strained smile as she poured herself a generous martini, one that she'd mixed herself. Clad in a stark white, tailored silk jumpsuit, she mixed her drink with an olive she'd plucked from a small silver bowl behind the bar. Brita could only agree. Being forced to mix Sandeep, then Sato, and then herself a drink had given her nervous hands something to do, helped break the ice. An added bonus to the real reason: keeping the number of people in this room to an absolute minimum.

"Cheers," Brita said, crystal ringing high and clear as their glasses touched. Ming-Xia knew this as well as she did, of course, and was letting her know that she knew. Brita drained her glass, then slammed it down on the counter a little too hard. God, she hated this game of double-speak.

"I heard you've had to drag your father out of retirement." Ming-Xia sipped at her martini, giving herself a little nod of approval, then scanned the other three faces in the room. "Will he be joining us tonight?"

"Unfortunately, no." Brita resisted the urge to bristle at the phrase *had to*. She should be more concerned that Ming-Xia had heard her father was involved at all. "He was called away at the last minute."

"A shame. My first-ever phone was a Stora. Father was an early adopter." A strained smile. "Pity. I would have liked to meet him."

"Do you still have it? Original Stora models are rather rare these days."

"What? Oh no, I wouldn't have thought so..." Ming-Xia was not really listening. She was eyeing the other guests, lips pursed with a questioning air, and Brita followed her eyes around the room. Mariska had been bailed up by the other two guests: Sandeep Pridha and Sato Katsubashi. Mas was listening politely as Sato excitedly expounded on something only an automotive billionaire could care about, nodding and interjecting with the odd question. Sandeep wasn't listening at all. From the direction of his gaze it was clear that, so far, Mariska's outfit was far more to his liking than Japanese manufacturing philosophies.

Brita fingered her necklace self-consciously and glanced longingly at the bar. No, one drink was enough for now. Another would just dull her senses and loosen her tongue. That, she didn't need.

She wished that her father could be here, right now, instead of halfway across the world. *God, when was the last time I wished that?* She took a glass of water and drained it in three gulps. Five billionaires (well, four, plus Mas) in one room, with one more to come. She could feel the tension, each of them watching the others, sizing one another up. Just having her father here would have made it that little bit calmer. Evened the odds. Levelled the playing field.

"If you're father's not coming, who's late?"

"I wouldn't want to spoil the surprise," Brita said, with a knowing smile. "But don't worry, I'm sure he'll be along soon."

"Just one more?" Ming-Xia eyed the table, and Brita followed her gaze. "Not two?"

"Hmm?" Brita rolled her wrist to check the time, even though she wasn't wearing a watch, and deep down a knot that had been simmering just below the surface grumbled to life. Ming-Xia raised an impeccably plucked eyebrow at the dining table's bubbling centrepiece. The burnished gold cutlery. The ochre dining plates.

All seven of them. Not six. Seven.

"I, uhh..." Her eyes snapped across to Mariska, still caught up in whatever innovation Sato was pitching, a wry, knowing smile hiding beneath her tactfully engaged exterior, and the knot reared to life. She glared at her protégé, only to receive a confident wink back. *Mariska, what have you done?*

"Brita?"

She forced a smile to her lips, and, with far more confidence than she felt, turned Mariska's wink back on her guest. "Ming-Xia. That would be telling."

"Ah, well." Ming-Xia took another delicate sip. "Then your assistant in the gold dress wasn't lying when she said this promised to be a night of surprises."

For you and me both, Brita thought. To Ming-Xia, though, she said, "I wouldn't call Mas my assistant within earshot if I were you." Even though, right now, Brita would rather have liked it if she had.

"No?" Ming-Xia waved a manicured hand in vague apology. "Even so, there's some serious money in this room, Brita. And more to come, I would wager. She really is the odd one out."

Hmm, Brita thought. *That was unusually blunt. For Ming-Xia, anyway.* Typically the Malaysian heiress was far more circumspect. They'd met on a few occasions, benefits and gala dinners mostly, and her initial impression had been of a shrewd businesswoman, well practised in the machinations of high society. Not one to reveal her cards needlessly. The air of secrecy must have had her on edge. Strangely, that made Brita feel a tiny bit better.

But not so much better that she didn't jump when the doorbell rang, its chimes resonating across the high ceilings of her dining hall. Her heart pounding, Brita made an uncertain start for the door only for Mariska to wave her away.

"No, no, Brita. You stay right there." She bobbed demurely for Sandeep and then Sato. "If you'll excuse me, gentlemen."

The four of them drifted together as Mariska disappeared around the corner, her pointed heels echoing down the hall. Brita held her breath and counted the footsteps, listening out for the clunk of the dead bolt drawing back and the soft hum of the outside world as the door swung open to reveal...who? Phil Greenberg, building the world's roads and bridges? Or someone else? Mariska's surprise interloper? If her guests speculated, she didn't hear them.

Mariska's laughter pierced the mottled silence, and the door clicked closed. Was she delighted? Surprised? Whatever it was, she didn't normally laugh like that. Brita strained her ears to catch a word, even a grunt, but all she heard was two sets of footsteps: Mariska's sharp heels, and a flat clack matching her step for step. Not heels, but not dress shoes either. The whisky, the only thing in her stomach, threatened to climb right back up her throat as the footsteps approached the corner, and only ancient instinct and a deeply ingrained sense of manners drove her to step forwards in greeting.

And yet even that wasn't enough to ensure the greeting she'd been preparing made its way past her stunned smile as Richard Solomon strode around the corner, with a studiously unflustered-looking Mariska trailing along behind.

Brita stared.

"Miss Gundersson. Mah sincere apologies for mah tardiness. Ah can't tell you how pleased ah was to receive your invitation." Solomon grinned his Cheshire grin, an almost perfect picture of southern charm from the closely cropped bristles of grey hair on his head to the snakeskin boots on his feet. "If only you'd seen fit to deliver it yourself, it would have been all the sweeter. Though, ah must admit, Miss Farkas makes a mighty pleasant substitute."

He bowed, outwardly gracious, though each successive word that had left his lips pushed Brita a little closer to the edge. Then he glanced past her, and he fairly beamed. "And Ms Peng, Mr Pridha, Sato-san! Ah wasn't sure what ah was walkin' into tonight, but already, mah expectations have been well and truly exceeded. Has our gracious host hinted yet at just why we're here?"

"Not a word," Ming-Xia said. "She won't even let slip who our fifth and final accomplice might be."

"Is that so?" He stepped forward and extended his hand to the other guests in turn. "Well, ah can't say ah'm surprised. Ah've sat across the negotiating table from

Miss Gundersson, and, well. Let's just say ah wouldn't want to be playin' poker against her heads up."

"Richard, if I'm hard to read, then you're worse than a doctor's handwriting," Brita said, forcing herself to relax. He was right. She might hate it, but she could play the game as well as anyone in this room. Better than anyone in this room. *And*, she told herself, *none of you know it, but I have the joker secreted in my pocket.* She met his gaze and saw not the unexpected interloper, the unplanned-for wrinkle, but the big tech blowhard who'd tried to buy her out and failed. "You're a bourbon man, isn't that right?"

"That's right."

"Neat, on the rocks, or with a twist?" Brita asked, signalling to Mariska to join her at the bar.

"So it really is just us tonight? How intriguing." Solomon smiled. "Ah'll take it neat, please and thank you."

And with that, Solomon melded into the conversation with the other three billionaires, while Brita retreated behind the bar, dragging Mariska in her wake. She grabbed the bourbon, wrenched the cork from its neck, ready to crush the stopper to nothing in her fist. Then she froze, her hands caught in the twin trap of an anger that needed to be expressed and a need to keep that anger hidden from her guests. Her soon-to-be investors. She had no room for error.

Mariska plucked two tumblers from the cupboard and slid them across the bench. "Breathe, Brita," she whispered. "Just breathe. This doesn't change the plan."

"Oh, is that right?" The bottle rattled against the tumbler, and bourbon sloshed onto the counter, but at least she was moving. "Was keeping me in the dark part of the plan, too?"

Mariska took the overfilled tumbler from her grip and swiped a sliver of lemon rind around the rim. "Solomon was your father's idea."

"My father's!" Brita's knuckles were white around the neck of the bottle. Of course it was. Jesus Christ, anyone would think he wanted her to fail.

"Careful," Mas cautioned. "Sandeep is watching. Give me that glass." Mariska took the second, empty tumbler and dropped a square of ice into it, making a show of mixing up a bourbon cocktail for herself. She smiled sweetly and laughed, as if Brita had just told her a joke. "I told him not to, that it would be too big a risk, but he must have..." Mariska trailed off, as if trying to imagine how and when Hugo could have slipped this one by her. "Anyway, he might not be perfect, but he's still a good fit."

"A good fit? Bullshit," Brita snapped back, matching sickly sweet smile for sickly sweet smile as she took the half-made cocktail, poured herself two fingers, and raised it to her lips. "He shouldn't be within a thousand miles of this room. Gateway will hurt his competition, make him richer. The second he hears about it, he'll unbalance everything."

Mariska pursed her lips, eyeing her lost drink. "You're thinking of the image Solomon projects, not the reality. Omni's profit base is shrinking. Just because Gateway won't directly hurt him doesn't mean—" Mas stopped, and her demeanour changed abruptly. "Ms Peng! What can I get you?"

"An escape from the you-know-what measuring going on over by the window, for starters." She cast a scathing eye back at Solomon and Sandeep facing off, like two exquisitely tailored bulls locking horns. "Poor Sato. He's just not in our league."

"Perhaps not, but which of that trio would you prefer to work with?" Brita asked.

Mariska glanced across at her, and she nodded. Without another word, her infuriating protégé whisked Solomon's bourbon away and glided across the dining room to intervene. The effect of her dimpled Magyar smile and her bare shoulders above her shimmering gold gown were instantaneous. She slipped between them, handing Solomon his drink, and allowed Sato to slide quietly away.

"So that's why we're here? To work together?" Ming-Xia asked with a self-satisfied smile. Brita hid her annoyance with the rim of her glass.

"Later, maybe," Brita conceded. Not that it was really a concession. She'd never have been able to gather such an exclusive crowd otherwise. "For now, though, we're here to enjoy a drink, a meal from my favourite chef, what I'm hoping will be like-minded company, and a private place to talk."

Brita glanced back at the hallway, knowing that there was one more guest still to come and hoping that she still knew who it was.

"Well, I suppose I can handle that." Ming-Xia finished the last drops of her martini and sauntered behind the bar as Sato made his final approach. "As long as I don't have to sauté my own prawns. Sato-san. What can I get you?"

"Do you have sake?" Sato asked, his eyes darting from Ming-Xia to Brita and back again, his *v*'s sounding much more like *b*'s.

"Of course," Brita said, pointing Ming-Xia towards a bottle she'd procured just for tonight. "What kind of host would I be if I didn't?"

"Ah." Sato gave a sharp little bow, his hands pressed together and his eyes sparkling. She could feel Ming-Xia grinning by her side. "My favourite. How did you know?"

"We did our homework," Brita said as Ming-Xia undid the stopper and poured a couple of fingers into a ceramic pot.

"Oh? What did you learn about me?" Ming-Xia asked as she handed Sato his drink and started gathering the ingredients for another martini. "Apart from my favourite brand of vermouth?"

"That we have more in common than I thought, actually. Infamous fathers who, ah..." Brita trailed off, unsure quite how to say then next part.

"Had good ideas, once upon a time, but were unable to let them go?" Ming-Xia suggested.

"Yes. Something like that." Brita passed her the olives and the toothpicks. "It's a bit of a theme, really. Your father was hotels, right? Mine was phones. Pridha Sr was ships and Katsubashi-san was cars."

Sato nodded. "And now we are all trying new things. Richard-san is the odd man out."

"Oh!" Ming-Xia exclaimed, her wide smile disappearing behind her glass. "I think I've just figured out why we're here!" She placed an excited hand on Brita's wrist, her eyes sparkling. "We're going to find out just what you have up your sleeve to take down Apple."

Brita, her stomach coiling in knots, was saved from having to do more than laugh and deflect Ming-Xia's jibe by her chef, Cho Shi Wang, emerging from the kitchen, balancing a tray of delectable morsels for the guests. The focus of the room shifted, and she sighed with relief. Rich or poor, CEOs or schoolkids, it didn't really matter. Everyone's eyes lit up at the sight of a roaming platter of finger food. Cho Shi stopped by Solomon's party first. By the time he reached the bar, most of his bounty was gone.

"Cho Shi, I'm pleased to introduce Mrs Ming-Xia Peng and Mr Sato Katsubashi."

Cho Shi placed the tray on the counter and gave a tight bow.

"Mrs Peng, of Kuala Lumpur?"

"The same."

"Ah"—Cho Shi beamed—"I believe I have once cooked for a relative of yours, a Mr Sumayr Peng, many years ago."

Ming-Xia's smile froze, her eyes widening slightly with a not-quite-so-pleasant surprise. "My father."

"Ahh. Then it is my honour to prepare a meal for a second generation of your distinguished family."

Brita's chest tightened in sympathy. They both knew how difficult it was to take on the family legacy, and she took the opportunity to jump in and change the subject. "What have you planned for us tonight, Cho Shi?"

The little chef's chest puffed out at the chance to discuss his food. "Quite a sumptuous feast, if I do say so myself." He nodded towards the depleted tray. "We start with a marinated beef cheek on betel leaf, followed by steamed prawn dumplings. I also have a Szechuan twist on an old Japanese staple—agedashi tofu for our vegetarian guest." He eyed Sandeep briefly.

"And for the seated meal, I have slow-roast duck, an oak-fired rainbow trout accompanied by a rice broth—an old family recipe, and sides of seasonal vegetables, presented three ways." He winked. "I don't want to spoil the surprise."

"Delightful, I look forward to it." Ming-Xia was gracious, but coolly formal in her dismissal. Cho Shi again offered a succinct bow and hurried back through the kitchen door.

A tension hung in the air, something causing her to withdraw. Sato must have noticed it too, and the silence lingered. Ming-Xia held her empty glass at her lips, and instead of drinking she clenched and unclenched her jaw. Her gaze was lost in the distance. The same distance as Sato's, perhaps? And then Brita knew what they must be thinking. The pressure that came from growing up the only child of a successful family, the heir to a legacy. The self-doubt, the constant straining to prove your worth—to your family and to yourself. And yet those on the outside seemed to think it came so easily.

"Can I get you another drink?" She rested a hand lightly on Ming-Xia's forearm, a small symbol of solidarity. "You look like you need it."

The gesture pulled Ming-Xia from wherever her mind had dragged her. "Please." She looked as if she were about to say more, but held herself back.

Brita added a double serving of sloe gin—a soft pink variety from Western Australia, going by the label—to the cocktail shaker, and followed it with a classic vermouth, slowly stirring the cocktail with a few blocks of ice. She turned to Sato to see whether he also wanted another, but he'd slipped away, phone in hand, the bright screen lighting his face blue from below.

Ming-Xia held out her glass, and Brita poured.

"I don't know what you've collected us all here for, Brita—but you've got me intrigued. And that's half the battle these days." She raised her glass. "Cheers."

Brita offered nothing more, returning the salutation only with a knowing smile. Her tumbler was almost empty, her second for the young evening. Already at her limit. The next one needed to be water, if she was to make it through the twists and turns to come—

There was a soft click, and for a moment the murmur of the world outside filtered down the corridor. Phil Greenberg, the final guest, must have arrived. Five of the six heads swivelled, and Mas, the only one not looking, caught Brita's eye. She was biting her lip, and Brita's breath caught in her throat. Was it Greenberg? Would he even be the last if it was?

The door thudded shut, and a vibrant, effervescent pair of heels danced down the hall. Brita squeezed the tumbler so tight she was amazed it didn't shatter in her grip.

She would recognise those footsteps anywhere.

"Woah, what a welcoming party!" The tall, slender form of Anita Kingston burst into the room. "Brita, darling, so good to see you!" She stalked a path straight across the floorboards, arms outstretched. Brita wrenched her jaw from the floor, forcing her lips into a smile, one that she knew wouldn't reach her eyes. Her mind whirred as she stepped out to greet her old friend.

"Hi," she stuttered, her mouth dry, useless. Anita, as usual, was a whirlwind. A luxurious fur coat hung off one shoulder, handbag dangling loosely before being ditched unceremoniously at the corner of the bar. The other guests had drawn together, conversations abandoned. Anita swooped in, kissing both cheeks before pulling her into a fierce hug, makeup be damned. It was all Brita could do to not blurt out the only thought on her mind: Why are you here? Instead she managed, "I'm glad you could make it."

It was certainly not what she felt.

Anita pulled back, giving her an appraising look. "If only Mas had given me more notice." She shrugged. "I moved a few things around. Love the dress, by the way. Great colour." Then she glanced around, taking in the other guests for the first time, now collected in a loose arc with their backs to the window that overlooked the internal courtyard garden.

Unexpectedly, Anita flushed pink. If Brita had but one word to describe her friend, it would be *brash*. Embarrassment was an unusual accessory for her.

"Hi everyone, I'm Anita," she offered, with a small, awkward curtsy. "Mas, Sandeep, Ming-Xia—good to see you again. And...Richard Solomon?" She raised a conspiratorial eyebrow Brita's way. "We've not met; however, I know you by reputation."

"That goes both ways, Ms Kingston," Solomon said, tipping his hat without a hint of a smile.

"Well, isn't that lovely," Anita said, her smile faltering only slightly as she came to Sato.

"Sato Katsubashi, Ms Kingston," he muttered from the bottom of a deep bow.

She reached across, clasping his hand in both of hers. "Ah, of course! Dooitashimasute! Brita, you'll have to seat me next to Sato-san. I have so many questions!"

"I'm sure Mas will be able to sort something out. She's in charge of seating arrangements," Brita said, a hint of a snarl in her voice, glaring at Mariska across the table.

"Grand. Absolutely grand. Now—Brita, is your glass empty? Tsk, tsk, we can't have that." Anita swivelled and tossed a mischievous grin at the watching crowd. "If you'll forgive me, our illustrious host owes me a drink. I'll be sure to continue our acquaintance once that particular debt has been serviced."

Brita found herself leaning against the bar for support, her heart pounding. Her empty tumbler rattled as she set it on the stained cedar bar top, unable to keep her hands from shaking. She tried to focus on selecting a good whisky, taking deep breaths to calm herself, but she could barely even see the labels.

Mas, what the hell have you done?

Anita reached past and selected a Scottish single malt, heavy on the peat, and pressed it into her hands. "Don't forget to swirl the bitters before you add the scotch."

And with a snort, Brita was back. "Like I don't know how to make an old-fashioned." *Maybe having Anita here won't be so bad after all.*

A counterweight.

A murmur of conversation filled the room, the other guests having re-formed their previous small clusters. Anita was watching her closely. She tilted her head to one side, shrugging slightly, as if to imply...

"Do you want to make it?" Brita snapped, frustration bubbling to the surface.

"Sorry." Anita reached over the bar and squeezed her hand. "I'm sorry. Did Mas not tell you she'd invited me at the last minute?"

Brita sighed, hating that it had been so obvious. "Not really, no." She returned the squeeze, before swirling the tumbler to coat the inner surface with the raw sugar and bitter slurry.

"No, I'm sorry. Tonight is a big night for us, and you're a little unexpected. It threw me off kilter a little." She dropped a large ice cube and followed it with a generous splash of the scotch. A twist of orange peel, balanced on the lip of the glass, and she was done. She drew a terrible energy from the biting, peat-ash aroma before passing it over. *Forgive me.*

Anita inhaled the heady bouquet before sipping gently. "I should never have doubted you."

Brita pressed her toes into the bottom of the bar and pushed down the guilt. There would be time for that later.

"I don't know what you've got planned here, but you've certainly got me wondering. It's not like you to get rattled by a little thing like an unexpected guest."

Brita regarded her friend briefly, examining her profile. Simple pearl earrings clasped to her lobes, partially hidden under a wave of chestnut hair, and familiar fine lines creeping from the outside corner of her eyelids. They were both getting old. "It's not just you."

Anita glanced back over her shoulder, to where Solomon was holding court. She only had to raise her eyebrows. "How?"

"Mas said..." Brita shook her head. "I don't know. I think Dad's up to something."

"So working together again is going about as well as expected." Anita rolled her eyes, then froze in the middle of sipping her drink. "He's not here, is he?"

"No. Well, not yet." Inwardly, Brita groaned. She hadn't even thought. Anita and her father hadn't gotten on at the best of times, but since the takeover...

"So that's why the invite came from Mas and not you." Anita nodded to herself, as if little puzzle pieces were just falling into place. "She doesn't know, does she."

"Why would she?" Brita sighed.

"Well, I promise to behave myself." Anita unleashed a mischievous grin. "For at least as long as he does."

Brita wanted so much to return her friend's enthusiasm, but she couldn't quite manage it. If Mariska was to be believed, her father had gone behind her back to bring Solomon into the tent. Then Mas had done the exact same thing with Anita. *And now, I'm being just as untruthful, allowing Anita to think that it was my father that didn't want her here, not me.*

It wasn't too late to back out. It would be embarrassing, sure, having to lie to her guests. To tell them they'd been brought here under false pretences, but that's all it would be. Gateway would be safe. She just had to call her father and...

Tell him what? That Solomon had arrived, just as he'd planned? That Mariska had gone behind her back too, and she was pulling the plug at the first wrinkle in the plan? She knew what that translated into. That she was scared. That she didn't have the nerve to pull this off. That her father had been right to doubt her.

And what had really gone wrong? Her pool of billionaires had grown from four to five, that's all. If she couldn't handle that, then perhaps her father was right. She faced the fork in the road: safety or legacy. There was only one choice to make, and Anita was waiting.

She gripped her drink and plastered her face with a smile. "So you really like the dress?"

"Brita. Would I lie to you?"

"Probably. But I appreciate it either way," Brita managed, her throat constricting. She could only put on a brave face. They met one another's gaze, and Brita crossed her fingers behind her back. The little superstitions were all she had. "You should go mingle. Sato has barely stopped looking at you this whole time. Don't keep him waiting."

She pushed Anita towards the young Japanese billionaire with a genuine laugh, but by the time Anita was two steps away, it had turned bitter on her tongue. Mariska cocked her head to check all was well, but she waved her off. If Mas came over now, Brita wasn't sure she'd be able to maintain her composure.

She steeled herself and drained her glass, taking strength from the bittersweet tang and using it to try and bury her doubts. Last one for the evening.

She had just crossed the line, and there was no going back.

19

Solomon was bored.

Sure, the food had been good. And sure, the bar was open. But he'd been expecting fireworks. A private room, stacked with billionaires. An uninvited guest (or two, as it had turned out). The founder of an ailing empire and his daughter, his ouster, spending the whole night duelling for power. He'd been so looking forward to it.

Then Stanley had called, telling him that Hugo would not be in attendance. That he'd stopped by Brita's house for less than a minute, handed over a duffel bag, and then been whisked off to Heathrow, where he'd disappeared behind an impenetrable layer of security. Stanley had no idea where he'd gone.

And so he was stuck with Anita Kingston, regaling the table with stories dredged from her and Brita's college days. Stories that Brita endured with a gracious good humour, that Ming-Xia and the Japanese kid lapped up, and that just about bored him to tears. He fingered his shot glass, one eye on an unidentifiable Chinese spirit the little chef had plonked on the table along with the dessert, the other mesmerised by the trickling water feature that dominated the centre of the table, and wondered where the hell Hugo had flown off to at the last moment. Why Mariska was here in his place.

"Christ," Solomon said to the empty air. "What am ah doin' here?"

"An excellent question, Mr Solomon," Sandeep muttered from his left, a scowl settling across his heavy brow. Probably because Mariska had just wriggled from his clutches and started collecting dinner plates. "A most excellent question."

"Evenin's not quite livin' up to what you had in mind?"

The diminutive Indian shipping magnate shook his head.

"Yeah, me neither."

Solomon stole one more glance at Brita and caught her dropping her hand down to the phone in her lap. He'd seen her do it a half dozen times, and with increasing frequency now that dinner was over. What was she waiting for? Some kind of signal? But then back up it came, empty, without even a twitch of her features to betray what might be going on inside. If not for the compulsive movement of that hand, Solomon would have thought she was actually enjoying herself. That tonight had no ulterior motive.

"Y'know what? Fuck it." Solomon snatched the Chinese liquor from the table and lined his shot glass next to Sandeep's. "No point sittin' here feelin' sorry for ourselves. This is meant to be a party. Bottoms up!"

The clear spirit hit the back of his throat hard, like a twisted, herbal moonshine. He savoured the burn beneath his tongue before sucking it down with a grimace. It was meant to be a digestif; might as well let it do its work.

"My god." Sandeep coughed, slamming the shot glass back on the table. "Is that alcohol or poison?"

"Is there a difference?" Solomon chuckled, pouring out another for them both. "So how did she coax you here this evenin' anyhow?"

"With outlandish promises and much intrigue, Mr Solomon." Tentatively, Sandeep brought the shot glass back up to his lips, only to scrunch up his nose in disgust. "Ugh, no. I don't think I can. It's so...*regional*."

Solomon, however, found he had no such qualms. It was, in fact, doing wonders for his stomach. As if the fuzz induced by the deliberately long dinner was receding minute by minute. "Why, whaddya drink back home in Kolkata?"

"Me? Single malt. The older the better. The locals though, they drink Bangla. Horrid stuff, even worse than this." He waved a hand at his half-empty shot glass. "Very cheap."

"Wasn't that long ago that hooch was all you could get, where ah'm from anyway."

"It is still like this in Gujarat and Bihar. Not Kolkata, though, thank god."

"Really?" Solomon raised an eyebrow. Across the table, Brita's hand did another of its disappearing acts. Another twitch. And was there a quiver in her lips? A knowing glance to her underling? He would never know, for at that moment Mariska leaned across him, reaching for his plate. And for that moment his entire world was the shimmering gold of her gown and the bronze of her skin. Her perfume filled his nostrils, and Solomon got an answer to his question.

Mariska's role thus far tonight had become suddenly, blindingly clear: distraction. And if she worked on him, she would have turned a man like Phil Greenberg into putty in her hands. She pulled back, and, laden with plates, she slid gracefully away. By his side, Sandeep tracked every swish of her hips as she made her way back to the kitchen. Solomon couldn't help a roguish grin. His new friend was just as besotted as poor Phil would have been, had he not so graciously given up his invitation for this evening. She was exactly his type, and Solomon had the footage to prove it.

Poor Phil. Or more to the point, poor Phil's wife.

It took Solomon a good three seconds to realise that while Mariska had been the focus of his attention, Brita had pushed herself to her feet. With an ounce less grace than would have been ideal, Solomon did the same. There was no way he'd be stuck, sat on his ass while whatever Brita had planned finally eventuated. He slapped Sandeep on the shoulder, shaking him from his Mariska-induced stupor.

"Come on, bud. Ah'll pour you somethin' more to your likin' while ah still can."

Sandeep glanced up, and they both watched Brita too disappear into the kitchen. Then, shaking his head, he checked his watch. "Honestly, Mr Solomon—"

"Call me Rich."

Sandeep smiled. "Rich. If it wasn't for the opportunity to spend a couple of hours with your good self, I fear this evening would have been a total waste of time."

"You reckon so?"

"I'm afraid I do. Thank you for your kind offer, but I think I will cut my losses," Sandeep said, plucking his napkin from his lap and dumping it on the table. Solomon laid a hand on his shoulder as he stood.

"If you don't mind me askin', what were you expectin' tonight to be?"

He watched the Indian billionaire's eyes as he asked the question. They flicked across to the kitchen once more, just for a second, and his dark scowl sank even deeper onto his brow. "I haven't the faintest idea." Sandeep pulled his phone from his pocket, fingers poised above the number for his driver. The finger never reached the screen. "What about you? You're the last person I'd expected to see here tonight, after…"

"It ain't obvious?" Solomon asked, gently guiding him across to the bar. Sandeep shook his head. "You saw her tantrum, right? With that hack journalist?"

"What do you think I did the moment I hung up from Mariska's first phone call? The press in this country, I tell you. It really was spectacular. It's half the reason I accepted the invite." Sandeep rolled his eyes. "But that still doesn't explain why she'd have sent one to you."

Solomon simply grinned and touched his finger to his nose, as if he were Paul Newman in *The Sting*.

Sandeep's eyes widened, and a grin tugged at the corner of his lips, lending his expression a suddenly nasty glint. "Ah. I see."

"Damn right you see," Solomon said.

"And she just let you in?"

"She did, and ah don't know if that's a good sign or an awful one." Solomon reached for an unopened bottle of single malt. "Now, how about ah pour you that scotch, and you fill me in on this new microchip manufacturin' hub you're settin' up?"

At the mention of his new baby, a fire burst into life behind Sandeep's eyes. Solomon poured, and Sandeep blathered. AI, Taiwan, security of global supply, blah, blah, blah. Then, as their tumblers clinked together, Brita emerged from the kitchen with the little chef in tow. She stopped by the table, her hands pressed together, and waited for everyone's attention. Solomon was only too happy to give it to her.

"Cho Shi, on behalf of everyone here, I'd like to thank you for a wonderful evening. The meal you have provided has been an absolute highlight."

"Hear, hear!" Solomon echoed, dumping the scotch he didn't really want on the bar so he could bring his hands together. Cho Shi beamed and bowed deeply to a smattering of applause.

"An honour and a pleasure, ladies and gentlemen. If you enjoyed and are visiting London, I have a restaurant in Farringdon, and it would be my honour and privilege to host you again." With the slightest of nods from Brita, he bowed once more, then turned and made his way to the exit.

The majority of the room turned to watch Cho Shi's exit, but not Solomon. Suddenly, despite the food, the wine, the boredom, and the spirits, his mind was clear. He leaned back onto the bar and kept his eyes on Brita. She waited, hands still clasped, until the sounds of the street outside were silenced and the front door had clicked shut. Only then did she nod in Mariska's direction. Solomon turned and saw that Sandeep's reason for staying stood in the corner with a heavy metal box in her hands. He could still smell her perfume. She met his gaze and matched his raised eyebrow with her own.

Finally. Fireworks.

Brita cleared her throat.

"Firstly, I want to thank you all, sincerely, for coming tonight. I see from your empty plates and your moderately glazed eyes that you've enjoyed the evening thus far." This elicited a soft chuckle or two, but not from him. He was too on edge.

"But now, it's time for me to lift the veil. I know you've all been wondering..."

"And about time, too!" Sandeep heckled from his shoulder, and, at the table, Anita almost spat out her drink with laughter. Solomon's teeth ground together as he fought to keep his sudden, nervous tension from showing. Let them joke, think this was all a game. That just played into his hands. *Besides*, he thought, catching the ruthless glint in Brita's eye, *they'll sober up soon enough*.

While the titter died down, Brita pulled her phone from her pocket and made one deliberate tap. Behind them, something thudded home.

"I've just locked the front door. Now, don't worry..." She held up her phone and tapped it again. Solomon grinned at the shocked and bemused expressions that fell across everyone's faces. He couldn't help it. "I've opened it again. You can still leave if you want. But be warned—there will come a point soon where that door will be locked. With what I'm about to show you, I'm sure you'll understand why."

For the first time since his own entrance, the room was silent.

"To that end, I'd very much appreciate it if you could pass all of your phones, your smartwatches, Fitbits, and other Bluetooth gadgets to Mariska, please." At Brita's direction, Mariska dutifully stepped forward, holding out the empty box. "The box is lead lined, soundproofed, and lockable. No funny business, I promise. We'll place the box on the table so you can see it at all times. But I need you all to know we are not playing games. What you are about to see is for your eyes only. Nobody else's."

Solomon cleared his throat. "And, what, is there a non-disclosure agreement you'll be needin' us to sign too? To keep us from talkin'?"

"No, that won't be necessary." Brita shrugged. "No one would believe you if you did."

An uncomfortable silence infiltrated the dining room.

"Ah don't know about everybody else, but ah'm not a fan of this cloak-and-dagger horseshit."

"And that's perfectly fine, Richard. We all know you have a hard-earned reputation for honesty and transparency," Brita smiled with her lips, but not her eyes. Behind her, Mariska fought to keep a straight face. "If you're uncomfortable with this arrangement in any way, you know how to find the door."

Brita clasped her hands and held them, politely, in front of her stomach. She seemed quite happy to wait him out. *And of course she is. She wouldn't care one iota if ah were to pull up sticks and walk out that door right now. She doesn't want me here.*

The room's eyes were on him, he knew it. Waiting to see which way he would go. He took a mental poll of his fellow guests. Sandeep? Sandeep would follow him, he was 90 percent sure. And Ming-Xia... She wasn't stupid, nor was she one for sticking her neck out when she didn't need to. If he walked out now, she would most likely follow. He could ruin the whole night, and it would serve her right.

He swallowed. Sato would follow Anita, and Anita was basically an insider. Christ, it was a miracle she hadn't dumped her phone in the box already. Sweat prickled on the back of his neck, the only outward sign of the furious calculus whirring away in the back of his mind.

Walking out would hurt Brita. But what would it gain him? So much effort had gone into getting him into this room for this very moment. Hundreds of man-hours watching Hugo like a hawk. Favours. Leverage. Precious, hard-earned leverage. And all of it would be for naught if he did what Brita wanted and walked away.

The seconds stretched out, like an elastic band approaching its breaking point. He wanted desperately to turn around so he could see the other faces, judge the balance of the room, but he was stuck at the bar, and all he could see was Brita. Solid as a rock. As a woman who knew she had the upper hand.

Solomon cracked.

"Aww, hell," he muttered, turning and dropping his phone into the felt-lined box. He was right where he'd paid good money to be, within minutes of finding out what on earth was going on here. That was worth a little fuckery. "You sure know how to twist a feller's arm."

Brita smiled, and the tension was broken. Air and colour and life seeped back into the room as the rest of the guests followed suit. Brita even had the audacity to mouth a thank-you at him, when nobody else was looking.

At a nod from Mariska, Brita cleared a space on the table, closed the lid, and locked it. The key was placed safely in her bra. Then, when they were all looking her way once more, she held up her phone for all to see.

"From the outside, this looks like the latest Stora mobile phone. A bog-standard Vasen 24. Looks like most other smartphones on the market, doesn't it? But, as we all know, it's what's under the hood that counts."

Solomon, in fact all of the invitees, were arrayed between the dining table and Brita. He stood with his arms crossed, one snakeskin boot kicked out to the side, and waited for the pitch. Mariska sidled up next to her boss, and the pair of them shared a knowing smile.

"Because this isn't just any phone." She held it towards them, swiped it open, so they could all see that she had her father's name highlighted. Then, she pressed dial. "This isn't even the next generation. It's a brand-new species."

The ringtone echoed through the dining room's high ceilings once, twice, three times before Hugo answered with a click.

Solomon wasn't entirely sure what happened next. With that click, the light and the atmosphere in the room subtly changed. Just an instant beforehand, the wall at Brita's back was plain, uninterrupted white. But now, suddenly, there was a door-sized rectangle of a nighttime vista, glittering lights peeking through a hole that had very much not been there before.

Solomon blinked, and a warm, impossible breeze wafted into the dining room, carrying with it just as impossible hints of the desert. He glanced accusingly at the bar, at the untouched tumbler of scotch, and then to his fellow guests, hoping for... he didn't know what. Proof that he wasn't the only one that didn't quite believe what he was seeing?

A gruff voice filled the stunned silence. "We call it the Gateway. A product I've been working on for a very long time."

Solomon knew that voice. He'd listened to Stan's recording of their late-night meeting half a dozen times, trying and failing to glean an insight into the reclusive founder's motives. He knew it, just as he knew he couldn't be hearing it. That voice had flown out of Heathrow more than six hours ago.

A towering form appeared in the doorway, dressed in a crisp white tuxedo. He stepped forward, and the light from the dining room's chandelier lit his face. Hugo Gundersson, eyes twinkling.

"Please, let me show you," he said, beckoning them through. And then he was gone.

"Come with us." Brita stepped forward, into the darkness. Then she turned, waving them to follow. "Please. It's perfectly safe."

Solomon grunted, his determination not to show fear trumping his shock and his confusion. He snapped his jaw shut and forced his legs to take that first, crucial step. Beyond the threshold, a balcony emerged from the darkness, tiled with terracotta and fenced with sculpted wrought iron. It expanded as he approached, as if the hole was just an ordinary door, and this nighttime balcony was simply on the other side of the wall.

But it couldn't be. He knew it! There should be a bathroom, just around the corner. *Ah took a goddamn piss there not half an hour ago!*

However, this knowledge of what should be faded to nothing before the evidence of his senses. There was a door, right here, where there hadn't been one before. Mutters from behind, words of cautious disbelief, bounced off him as if he were stone.

A door to another world.

There was nothing for it. Eyes closed, fists clenched, he stepped across the threshold...

...and it was just like stepping outside. The breeze was fresh, tinged with cinnamon and smoke and the stench of life. He breathed in, deeply. Nothing like a British, or American, breeze at all.

"What do you think?" Brita whispered, from right by his side.

"I..." Solomon started, then stopped. He'd just opened his eyes, and all the muscles he'd tensed turned slack. If not for Brita, he would have collapsed to the floor. "Tell me they're not the fucking pyramids."

But he knew that they were. From behind, a chorus of gasps, as the others saw what he saw: the Great Pyramid of Giza, rising far above their eyelines and lit from below in a startling blue, its base hidden behind a forest of palm trees and low buildings.

"I'm sorry, Richard, but they are indeed the fucking pyramids." Brita squeezed his hand, then spread her other arm wide, sweeping it across the sprawling cityscape that reached far beyond the famous monuments. "Welcome to Cairo."

20

—·—

"**WHAT IS HE DOING** here?" Hugo hissed, grabbing his daughter by the arm the instant she stepped out onto the balcony and dragging her off to one side.

"Hey—" She shrugged him off, glancing back, making sure they were out of sight. Then she turned on him, a cold fury burning in her eyes. "I could ask you the same goddamn question."

"Me? No. I—you mean you didn't invite him?"

"Of course not! Mas said...Jesus Christ." Brita closed her eyes, massaging her temples with one hand. "How did he even find out?"

Hugo swallowed. It was an excellent question. When Stanley had called him back and told him not to contact him again, he'd almost smashed his phone on his workbench. For two days he'd been anticipating and dreading that call, playing out scenarios over and over in his mind: Solomon telling him he was interested, very interested. That he'd spoken to his lawyers, his accountants, and Hugo—graciously, regretfully letting him know that he'd changed his mind.

He should have been relieved. He'd reached out to Stan in a moment of madness, fuelled by jealousy, by petty anger, and he'd gotten away with it. But all he could think about was that the bastard hadn't even bothered to reject him in person. He'd wanted so badly to rub his smug American face in the opportunity he'd rejected. He would have invited him, out of spite. But Mas had seen right through him. Solomon was the wrong target. He would upset the balance.

And yet, here he was, in wild-eyed silhouette, working up the courage to step through the Gateway portal and out onto the patio.

And I let him in, Hugo thought, before doing what he always did when faced with the consequences of his own actions.

"I bet it was your fucking interview. You just couldn't help running your mouth. You pricked his pride, and now look—"

"No," Brita snapped, cutting him off. "We're not doing this again. They're both here now, so we're going to smile, let them gasp and giggle, and then we're going to smack them between the eyes. All right?"

"Both? What do you mean both?" Hugo asked, but his daughter was gone, off to lend Solomon a steadying hand.

"Tell me they're not the fucking pyramids."

The mix of wonder and terror etched on Solomon's face set Hugo on his heels, flushing his anger and his shame clean away. Richard Solomon was one of the most powerful men on earth, and Gateway had reduced him to quivering with awe. His Gateway.

He was going to change the world.

Behind Solomon, a trio of tentative billionaires approached the threshold, Sandeep Pridha leading the way, with Sato and Ming-Xia close behind. Hugo helped each one of them through, watching them test the ground beneath their feet as if it might disappear at any moment, their eyes flashing between the ancient, unmistakable vista before them and the shockingly normal, brightly lit dining room they'd left behind.

And then the fifth guest stepped across the breach, and Hugo extended his hand. "Anita."

"Hugo." Unlike the others, she briefly met his gaze. "You look old."

"Hah." He barked out a short laugh. Jesus, she hadn't changed a bit. "You too."

"No, I don't. And you fucking know it," Anita said, her eyes leaving his face to take in the view and a mischievous grin breaking across her lips.

Across her shoulder, Mariska stood just on the far side of the threshold. Hugo caught her eye and nodded minutely towards Anita. Mariska shrugged. Later. *She's here now, so deal with it.*

He mouthed *Greenberg* at her, and she shrugged again, though this time her gaze flitted behind him, towards the other. Towards Solomon. Ah. One mystery solved, then. Mariska glanced back and, with a jealous smile, raised Brita's Gateway-enabled phone and hit end. The bright-white portal hissed, fizzled, and was no more.

Behind him, Hugo knew, millennia-old monuments to ancient pharaohs towered over his assembled titans of modern industry, gasping with shock as their link back to reality evaporated. Four seasoned, world-weary men and women, still struggling to comprehend what had just happened. But not Anita.

He let her lead him to the cold iron balustrade. She bent over it and set her elbows down, her hair spilling over her shoulder.

"So you've finally pulled it off, huh? Project Gateway."

"You seem to be taking it in stride."

"It's quite spectacular, I'll admit. But your daughter's been bitching to me about your damnfool ideas for decades. When I heard you'd talked her out of the Solomon deal, I had a bit of an inkling." She pushed herself upright, eyes twinkling in the moonlight. "And now that the big reveal is over, I think you owe us both a thank-you."

"Me? Thanking you?" He snorted. A month ago, he would have raged. "If anything, you owe me an apology."

"An apology? For what? Giving you the free time and maintaining the cashflow that allowed you to work on your little projects? For giving you the motivation, the bitter drive to build what you've built?" She waved a hand in the air, as if to encompass the patio, the Gateway, the pyramids, the last fifteen years. "Face it, Hugo, if Brita and I hadn't done what we'd done, Stora would have folded, and Gateway wouldn't exist."

He gripped the iron railing. *A month ago I would have…* He closed his eyes, not wanting to think about the things he might have done then. That he still might do, if he let his anger get the best of him. It wasn't a month ago. It was now, and they were here for a reason. For Gateway.

He forced himself to breathe. "I can't…"

She put her hand on his arm. "A rage-filled, contemptuous silence seems like an appropriate middle ground for now." She inched a little closer so that he could feel the warmth of her body. They both gazed out at the pyramids, enormous, even against the ink-black sky. "Your daughter wasn't kidding around at all, was she."

"About what?"

"Apple and Samsung. You're going to eat them for fucking breakfast."

Not just them. Hugo thought grimly. "If we make it that far."

"Aha." Anita raised her eyebrows and shot a glance over at the others. They were clustered around his daughter with rapt attention. She held her hands apart, two places, two planes, then folded them together. "How long until the others figure out that's why they're here?"

Hugo shrugged. "Solomon already has. Look at him. His eyes have glazed over. He's already running the numbers."

"Oh!" Anita exclaimed, nudging him with her shoulder. They both watched as Ming-Xia's face changed, the sense of childlike wonder falling away as the reality of the Gateway sank in. Her eyes flicked Hugo's way for just a second, before she interrupted his daughter with what looked like a pointed question.

In the midst of the discussion, Solomon turned their way and, holding up a polite hand, made his way across the terrace.

"Here's trouble," Anita muttered. "Richard! You look like you've just seen a few billion get knocked off your share price."

"Do ah now?" Solomon grinned, as if he knew something Anita didn't. "Ah can't think why that might be."

"Whatever it is, I might leave you two to it," Anita said, all charm, before tossing a final quip over her shoulder. "Hugo, make sure you tell your daughter she owes me a drink for keeping secrets."

Solomon turned and, with one arm on the railing, watched her stride gracefully away. "She sure is somethin'."

"I've known that girl since she was three years old," Hugo growled.

Solomon raised a solitary eyebrow. "Doesn't change the facts, though, does it, Mr Gundersson."

"What are you doing here?"

"Me?" Solomon pressed his hand to his chest as if he were holding his Stetson and praying in a house of worship. "Ah'm beginnin' to understand why your daughter backed out of our deal. Twelve point nine billion would have been a bargain."

"It would have been theft."

"Well, that's a maybe." Solomon grinned. "Ah'm just glad you're willin' to do business." Hugo opened his mouth to protest, but Solomon held up a finger. Off to their right Brita had broken free of their suddenly serious-looking guests and was marching towards them.

"Looks like playtime is over, Hugo. Ah for one cannot wait to see how this shakes out."

21

— · —

With the touch of a screen, Brita dialled her Gateway-enabled phone back in London and crossed her fingers behind her back. It rang once, twice, and then the sliding door that led to the patio flickered and disappeared behind a rectangle of white light.

With a short, nervous breath and a confident smile, she beckoned Anita forward. Let her father wrangle her soon-to-be investors for a moment. She strode across the terracotta without looking back, taking the ten steps to her dining table, 3,500 miles away.

"How did they take it?" Mas whispered. She'd been busy while they'd been away. The plates, bottles, and cutlery had been cleared, with five pens and five contracts in their place. A single sheet of paper each, in duplicate. Five, not four, as they'd planned. As *she'd* planned, anyway.

"Better than you." *Better than me, too.* Brita crossed her arms. She'd been hoping for dazzled investors, so in awe they'd sign without thinking. But Solomon, of course, had nixed that little idea. Not for the first time, Brita found herself sinking into a well of recrimination, at a moment when she could least afford it.

What was done was done. She had—

"What the hell is this?" Ming-Xia demanded, the contract clutched in her manicured fist. Behind them all, the Gateway flickered and died, cutting them off from the last traces of Cairo and the wonder it inspired.

"Looks a heck of a lot like the catch," Solomon drawled, peering over her shoulder.

Brita tossed a glare her father's way and cleared her throat.

"Solomon's not wrong. Not that any of you would expect any less." She eyed each of them in turn, her gut twinging as her gaze passed Anita, scrutinising the simple contract. "Gateway is a wonder, but at the moment that's all it is. To realise its full potential, we need money."

"Money you don't have. And can't get without tippin' your hand," Solomon said, lowering himself onto the back of the closest dining chair. He kicked out his leather

134

boots and looked up at her with knowing eyes. *Christ.* Brita made a conscious effort not to roll her eyes. *All he needs is a strand of wheat between his goddamn teeth.* "How much?"

"Two point five billion pounds. Five hundred million each."

Solomon whistled.

"So that's why we're here." Ming-Xia waved the contract at her peers at the table. "A shakedown."

"I wouldn't go that—"

"What do we get in return?" Sandeep interrupted, arms crossed.

Brita ignored the men. Solomon, for all his attention-seeking dramatics, hadn't even bothered with the paperwork. Ming-Xia and Anita, though: Brita knew first-hand just how hard they'd both fought, how hard they still had to fight, to keep their places atop of the family business. They were the two she needed to convince.

"The sheet of paper in your hand is a promise. 2% of Stora, for each of you, in return for your help getting Gateway off the ground." Brita watched Ming-Xia carrying out the sums in her head, a lump rising in her throat.

It was Solomon, however, who spoke first.

"2%? If ah remember rightly, ah offered you £12.9 billion for the whole kit and caboodle not two months ago. 2% of that is, what, £258 million? You seemed mighty happy with that, too. Before your father so rudely interrupted, of course. To tell you all about this"—he waved a hand at the empty wall where the Gateway to Cairo had just been—"ah assume?"

"What's 2% of Stora worth now? £180 million? £190? Now ah know, ah know, the FTSE's had the wobbles ever since your banker friend got busted financin' Columbian gangsters, and the market don't know about this here...innovation yet. But mah question to you." He looked up at the ceiling and pulled his lips back, as if he were working a seed loose from between his teeth. "What's stoppin' me from approachin' one of your minor shareholders and buying 'em out for 20% more than they're worth, and savin' mahself a few hundred million in the process?"

"Honestly, Richard, I wouldn't even bother with that." Sandeep scowled. "Stora might have been an innovator once, but that was a long time ago. This 'Gateway' is nothing more than a gimmick. A desperate grab for relevance in world that is leaving them behind." Sandeep draped his arms over Ming-Xia's and Sato's shoulders, drawing them in, with complete disregard for the discomfort they both displayed. "This is our world now."

"Now hold on, son. Ah wouldn't be quite so hasty." Solomon smiled, as Ming-Xia wriggled free of Sandeep's unwanted solidarity. "Ah think you might be underselling the Gateway, just a touch. Apple was down at three bucks a share in 2009—"

"And the iPhone never let you walk from London to Cairo in less than a second," Anita chimed in, her first words since her exchange with her father on the balcony. Brita noted a deepening furrow on her brow.

"Damn straight." Solomon smirked. "Now ah'm not sayin' Ms Gundersson ain't offerin' us a good deal. Ah'm just wonderin' what's stoppin' us from walkin' outta here and gettin' a much better one the moment the markets open up on Monday mornin'?"

Solomon sat back and crossed his arms, and for a moment, Brita thought, his eyes had flicked across to her father, and that there had been the barest hint of a nod. *Not now.* Her father and his paranoia could wait.

She made sure to hold Solomon's gaze, but not so long and so hard that it became a staring contest. Solomon might be the squeaky wheel, but there was something in his demeanour that told her he wasn't really worried. He just wanted to be convinced. Sandeep, he was all bluster. Daddy's little boy, convinced he belonged at the adult's table. He would follow Solomon, and Sato would follow Anita.

No. Ming-Xia and Anita still represented the biggest risk. Particularly Ming-Xia. Sandeep's overly familiar embrace had turned her face to stone. *So show her that you know what it's like.* Brita pressed her tongue against the roof of her mouth, the only concession she would allow to the enormity of the moment. *Show her that you want her on the team.*

"The simple answer? Absolutely nothing." She shrugged. "But you'll be leaving billions on the table. Unless, Ming-Xia, you think I just opened *Forbes* to a random page and picked the first five people I could find?"

"Well..." Ming-Xia glanced to one side, towards Sato and Anita, to her father standing impassive behind the bar. Her right hand crept up until her finger rested in the crook of her neck, and for just a second Brita thought she caught a flicker of disdain beneath her father's beard.

Don't worry, old man. I don't need your help.

"My father and I, we don't just want your money. We want a partnership. I want the eight of us here, right now, in this room, to build the Gateway. Together." She was tempted to keep her focus on Ming-Xia, but that would risk excluding the others, pushing them away. So she settled her gaze back on Sandeep, took a demure step forward, and lowered her voice.

"Mr Pridha. I'm going to be honest: I don't trust our current manufacturers. We've had too many competitors come to market with uncomfortably familiar features within weeks of our launches. You control the largest tech-manufacturing hub in India, and we need someone we can trust with the heart of the Gateway: the portal control chip."

Before he could speak, Brita left him behind. "Sato. One of Stora's failings in the past has been an inability to match the network innovations of our competitors. Ask Solomon, he's seen the numbers. We learned the hard way just how difficult it is to sell a phone that can't use YouTube or Google Maps.

"With the Gateway, we actually have a differentiator. A real, marketable edge over Android and iOS. But I don't want to rely on it. We wanted you because you understand the customer experience and network effects in a way we just don't. We want you to create a competitor for Android, with the Gateway as its champion."

Brita was feeling it now, the adrenaline, working its way down her spine, washing all the nerves, all the anxiety away. She knew exactly what she had to say, not just to Ming-Xia but to Solomon and Anita. Exactly how to say it. She spun back to the last of her invitees. Her original team.

"Ming-Xia. You are possibly most important of all. Just think. Tonight, the six of us illegally entered a foreign country. No passports, no visas, no customs. No one would know, or could know, we'd ever been there.

"The time will come when we need to start engaging governments about the release of the Gateway to the general public, and the sudden, complete permeability of sovereign borders will be their primary concern." Brita left the sentiment hanging, waiting for Ming-Xia to make the connection.

"And you want access to my R&D team, so you can present a problem and a solution at the same time?"

"Exactly!"

"All right," Ming-Xia said, slowly tapping her silver nail against her chin. "You've got me intrigued."

Brita floated, her words flying rapid fire, as if she were merely a conduit for the pitch of her life.

"And Richard. Don't think I've forgotten you." She nodded at the table, forlorn in the rear of the room. "Take a look at that centrepiece. See if you can figure it out."

He'd been leaning, elbows perched on the back of his chair, watching her performance with an expression of wry curiosity. Without standing, he swivelled and tipped forwards, bending almost double to inspect the elaborate water sculpture at the table's centre.

The piece was deceptively simple, a stylised crystal spiral wound from a low peak, rough facets reflecting and obfuscating the internal workings. Water trickled softly, silently, from a perforated central spire, cascaded down corrugated stone and rusting metal runnels to collect in a moss-filled tray at the bottom. There were no cables connecting the water feature to a power source, and no batteries.

"Ah." Richard grinned, looking up. "These channels have waterwheels embedded in the corrugations. Look." He pointed one out to Sandeep. "They're powerin' a small Gateway, aren't they. Water pourin' in at the bottom and fallin' out from the matchin' portal at the top."

He shook his head in amazement. "It's genius. Pure genius. You knew that Phi..." Solomon coughed. "That ah've been tryin' to pivot green, and you're offerin' me a license to develop the Gateway into a large-scale, closed-loop hydroelectric powerplant. That doesn't require dammin' or interruptin' the rivers." He ran a hand through his short salt-and-pepper hair, tugging absently at the strands on the back of his neck as he wrapped his thoughts around the implications. "Ah'd be lying if I said ah wasn't impressed."

Brita beamed and turned, at last, to Anita. Why on earth had she thought keeping her on the outside would be keeping her safe? Anita was just as qualified, just as necessary, as any of the others. Of course she should be here, tonight, sharing in her triumph. She owed Mariska an apolo—

"And I suppose you'll be wanting my help smoothing the wrinkles with the EU regulatory bodies? That wedging a foot in the door in Europe will be enough to pressure the US and other markets into following suit?"

Anita's voice was hard and cold, her eyes icy, and Brita's words caught in her throat.

"But that's not the only reason we're all here, is it, Brita?"

The colour drained from her cheeks, and Brita fumbled, searching for her practised response. Of course, this was why she'd not wanted Anita here. Because she was quick. Too quick for her own good.

"No, of course not. You're all good people, investors that focus on creating positive change." She tore herself away from Anita's frosty gaze, knowing that it was useless, but pushing ahead anyway. "We chose each and every one of you because you see the big picture."

"But that's not quite true, is it? I'm not meant to be here. Why not, I wondered? I'm a trusted friend, I have all the right contacts, the capital to help out. Why exclude me?"

Brita's hands curled into fists behind her back, her nails digging into her palms. She felt engulfed, stuck in the inexorable current of a vast river. Mist rising, the thunder of the fall up ahead. There was nothing she could do.

She forced herself to look Anita in the eye. At least she could do that.

"You were protecting me, weren't you. From what you were planning on doing to them." Anita inclined her head in the direction of the others, her eyes never leaving Brita's. "Ming-Xia. Your family's fortune. It's based in hotels, am I right?"

"That's right." A wary undertone had crept back in the Malaysian's voice.

"And Sandeep. You control the subcontinent's international shipping, if I recall. Oil, iron ore, grains, containers?" She spat the question, her stare never wavering. He didn't get a chance to respond.

"Sato is automotive, I am airlines. Richard, despite his stellar performance, isn't meant to be here either. But I can't imagine the wobbliest of the tech giants will fare well when yet more competition emerges from across the pond."

Finally she turned away, granting Brita a moment of respite from her glare. Brita held herself bolt upright, not daring to chance a look at her father, knowing exactly what she'd see.

"Ming-Xia, how do you think your hotels will fare when your customers can simply teleport home to the comfort of their own beds, halfway across the globe?" Anita asked, not waiting for an answer. "About as well as my airlines, Sato-san's cars, and Sandeep's ships, I imagine. Quite a coincidence, isn't it, that the four of us just happen to have tens of billions invested in the industries most vulnerable, most exposed, to the miracle my *friend* has shown us tonight."

"Ah don't believe in coincidences." Solomon still lounged in his chair, but the detached curiosity he'd been projecting was no more. What remained was a grudging respect. Realising that made Brita's stomach churn.

Brita unfurled her fingers with a slow, deliberate motion, using the pain in her knuckles and in her palms to clear her mind. This had always been Mariska and her father's plan, and she'd been naive to think she could navigate her way through such a minefield unscathed.

So be it.

"I don't blame you for being angry." Brita held her friend's gaze, even as the cold anger melted to reveal a regret tinged with betrayal. "But please don't think of this demonstration as a threat. See it as an opportunity, one that no one else will get. The chance to pivot, and the time to plan your exits before the world changes." She turned to address the others. Especially Ming-Xia. "Gateway is at least a year from release. You know what's coming now. Use that time to prepare. You won't regret it."

"And what if I decline? What then?" Ming-Xia asked. "My team did their research. You have a product launch booked for tomorrow evening, in Los Angeles. Another coincidence?" Brita felt her eyes bulge, and a sardonic smile graced Ming-Xia's lips. "I didn't think so."

She slapped the crumpled contract down on the table and held her hand out for a pen. Brita couldn't breathe. Sandeep, suddenly self-conscious, leapt to hand her his, and she scrawled her signature at the bottom of the page.

"If you're going to fuck me, Brita, just do it." Ming-Xia straightened, folded the paper into three, and tossed it at Brita's feet. "All I ask is that, next time, you respect me enough to look me in the eye."

22

The Punchbowl's barman stacked empty pint glasses eight high, each one chinking down into its companion with a brusque impatience.

Jorge ignored him.

He'd packed away his map, and now he sat with his back against the cooling brick wall, his novel carefully curled in his left hand. He'd aligned the book's ageing spine with the stairs down to Brita's front door. The stairs that for four hours had seen no movement. That for four hours had hosted six of the world's richest men and women, one of whom just happened to be Richard Solomon.

Jorge hadn't read a word.

He'd be lying to himself if he'd said he'd been expecting it. Hoping for it, maybe, though he never would have admitted the fact to anyone. Still, that hadn't prepared him for the brief seconds of Solomon's appearance. Right there, in the flesh.

For the first hour or so, tracing and identifying the other guests had been enough to distract him. When he'd matched the last of them, an Asian man in the white tuxedo, to Sato Katsubashi, majority owner of Tsuba Automotive and the genius behind Japan's answer to Instagram, his mind finally got the chance to wander.

That night in Brussels, the moment he'd realised he'd uncovered something grimy. Something real. The conversations with his editors, with legal. The article, draft after draft after draft, only for it to end up spiked. Money trumping integrity. Influence trumping the truth. All this bubbled up from the depths and lingered, staying well beyond their welcome. Hours ticked by.

The memory that just wouldn't leave, though, was the aftermath. Forced to resign. Unable to get another job. Everybody knowing what had happened. Who he'd pissed off. But did it matter? No. He knew what he'd been reduced to. The vapid, meaningless promotional interviews, the humiliation of being the "serious journalist" on the team, whose only role was to lend Roger and his roster of partisan shills a thin veneer of credibility. And then, after all these years, just as he was starting to feel like a real journalist again, the man who had put him there was in his viewfinder once again, not even seventy yards down the lane.

How long had it even been, since he'd last been that close...

The barman returned, whipping a stained tea-towel from the belt of his apron, and Jorge shuddered, grateful to be pulled back from such painful thoughts.

He was young, the barman, no more than twenty-one or twenty-two. He wiped the pint glass rings and slopped beer from the outside tables, his pointed movements broadcasting the unmissable: *Come on, pal. It's late, and you're the last one 'ere.*

That's where you're wrong, Jorge thought. *I've still got five "friends" to see off. At least.* His right hand fell to the camera in his lap. The battery still had charge and the memory card space.

A sliver of light emerged from the sunken entrance, and a glistening black roadster, all gaudy imitation and stylised curves, turned up the hill with an ostentatious purr. A second later Ming-Xia Peng, still draped in her immaculate white gown, her eyes hidden behind oversize sunglasses despite the hour, appeared at the foot of the stairs.

Jorge raised his camera to his eye. Click. The number plate. Click. Her short black hair as it swayed in the streetlight. Click. There was a steely tension driving every step, only evident in the barest hint of mechanical rigidity in her movements. Click. He wished he had a video rolling. The effort she was putting into the control of her movement shouted across the street that the evening had turned sour, and yet it was the kind of small detail that lived between moments. Click. The kind a still image could never capture. Not the ones he took, anyway.

Click. Behind her, the sliver of light reappeared. Click.

A second figure chased her up the stairs.

Anita Kingston.

The British heiress was animated, all gesticulation and frustration. Ming-Xia impassive, listening, then turning her back. Disappearing down into her car. Driving away.

Anita slumped and listless against the wall.

He searched back for the memory of her arrival. He'd been halfway through his second pint, still abuzz from Solomon's arrival twenty minutes earlier, when her taxi had pulled up. She'd stepped out onto the pavement, glamorous in her emerald green gown and draped in a white fur coat. As he'd raised his camera, he'd felt uncomfortably like a paparazzo. She'd walked the dozen or so steps to Brita's stairwell with an easy grace and an excitement that had demanded his attention.

How the picture had changed. Brita's best friend, reduced to tears on the footpath. What could have happened down those stairs, to cause her to break down like this?

He pitied her from afar, in a detached way. It was a familiar sensation, setting his empathy aside, like pulling on an old pair of boots. It was a tool he hadn't needed for such a long time, but one that observers required. Could not survive without.

When he was on the front lines, there was no getting involved, making it personal. It distorted the story. A twinge in the back of his mind told him it might be too late for that, that Solomon's appearance had torn up the rule book, but he pushed it away. He was a professional. He could keep things separate.

He did stop taking pictures, though. There was no need to record every moment of her misery.

He hefted the camera in his hand, watching silently. She pulled herself together, wiped her eyes. Pushed off from the wall and, with a long, regretful glance back at Brita's front door, Anita crossed the thirty or so yards to the main drag, her hand raised to hail a taxi.

There was no grace in this walk. Just a sad woman wanting to go home.

He remained where he was for another thirty minutes, snapping photos as an impassive Sato Katsubashi and then a volcanic Sandeep Pridha made hasty, solitary exits. Four out of five guests, leaving alone. Every single one of them was worth billions, and every single one was rattled.

Except Solomon.

Something had happened behind those doors. Something big. Jorge didn't know what.

But he knew that Richard Solomon was behind it.

23

HUGO FIDGETED, HIS HANDS hidden behind the bar. He rubbed his thumb across the rim of his empty tumbler, back and forth. Back and forth. Mariska busied herself with collecting pens and signed papers, refusing to make eye contact with his daughter or Solomon. They both sat at the empty table. The Texan's lips moved in silence as he read and reread the contract, his pen as far away from it as possible.

The soft bubbling of the Gateway-powered water sculpture was the only sound in the room.

Hugo stared at his daughter's back, stoic and unflinching in the face of Solomon's fastidious stalling. In this mood, waiting out the heat and the anger, for cold reality to rise to the top, she looked just like her mother. He slid the crystal away, sending it clattering into a half-empty bottle of gin. Hugo had never had her patience. Mariska looked up sharply, four signed contracts safe in her grasp.

Neither Brita nor Solomon moved a muscle.

What was the man thinking? If he could just get him alone for thirty seconds... That question he'd asked, the one that had sent the evening into its death spiral: *Ah'm just wonderin' what's stoppin' us from walkin' outta here and getting' a much better deal the moment the markets open on Monday mornin'?* The unmissable implication: *Why did he need me at all?* It had sent Hugo's heart racing just as hard as when the Gateway had fired up for the first time.

Solomon didn't need Brita. And yet here he was. Hugo had to find out what Solomon was planning to do next.

Solomon shifted in his seat, and with an exaggerated sigh, he let the contract fall back onto the table. He glanced briefly across at Hugo, his thoughts hidden beneath his weathered brow, and signed his name on the dotted line.

"Thank you, Richard," his daughter said, as if Solomon's capitulation had been inevitable. Hugo pressed his knuckles into the bar top as she flipped the paper around and added her own signature.

144

"Ha." Solomon's cynical laugh landed somewhere between amused and derisive. He signed the duplicate copy, slid it across to Brita, and folded the original into the inner pocket of his dinner jacket. "It's been a long while since ah've been painted into quite so tight a corner. Ah must say, it's been a pleasure to finally meet the *real* Brita Gundersson."

His daughter stiffened, her hand frozen halfway through her signature.

"Oh, come now. You know what ah meant." Solomon grinned as he pushed himself to his feet, finally meeting Hugo's gaze. "Your daughter spent more sweat and blood tonight, keepin' your Gateway in house for just a little while longer, than she did in the entire three months we stared at one another from across the negotiatin' table."

Hugo took a hurried step forward, determined to intercept Solomon before he made it to the door.

"It's a funny thing, Hugo." Solomon smirked, pausing at the entry to the main hallway, his thumb falling back to its customary place through his belt loop. "The only thing she really dug her heels in over was the goddamn name."

"You wanted to change it?" Hugo asked.

"No. I wanted to keep it. It was all her." He nodded back to the table. "She wanted to kill it."

Kill the name? Kill Stora? How *dare* she! What right did she have? Stora was *his* company. He'd built it from nothing! Hugo's thoughts came thick and fast, trampling one another. He glared at his daughter, his shoulders hunched, his hands curling into fists. She passed the last of the five completed contracts over to Mariska and glared right back.

Hugo snorted, and for a second his anger took over once more. Kill Stora. Maybe having Solomon's attention again wasn't such a bad idea. Maybe she deserved what was coming.

He turned back to Solomon, only to find the space he had occupied suddenly empty. Eyes wide, he lurched into the hallway. The door was already open. Hugo's polished shoes beat a panicked rhythm across the white marble tiles.

"Solomon. We need to—"

Solomon stopped, one foot out the door. He didn't look around. "It's in hand, Hugo."

"I don't—"

"Good. You don't need to." Solomon stepped out into the night. "We'll be in touch."

The door closed with a soft click.

I don't need to? Don't need to what? Hugo ripped his Gateway handset from his jacket pocket and shook it at the empty corridor, the handset squeezed so tight in his grip that the veins on his temples twitched. *Gateway is mine, Solomon. Not yours, not Brita's! I created it, with my own bloody hands. So I'll do the telling, Solomon, thank you very much!* Hugo fumed in furious silence. *This isn't fucking Texas!*

The door mocked him with its implacable refusal to acknowledge his anger. If he were alone, he would have kicked it. Screamed at it, sworn himself hoarse. If he were alone.

But, for the first time in a long time, he wasn't alone. And really, that was a good thing. He could no longer let his anger take charge. Gateway was too important. It wasn't the door's fault that Solomon was a self-important arse, and it wasn't the door's fault that the self-important arse was even at the table.

And it wasn't his daughter's fault, either.

Still. Maybe there was a silver lining to all this. Solomon was a shark. It didn't take much for him to smell blood in the water. The Texan respected his daughter: that was clear enough. *But he sees me as a doddering old fool. A useful idiot. A pawn that he can exploit.*

I can work with that.

He gave the closed door one last withering glare.

"Fucking pillock," he muttered, not quite sure whether he was talking about Solomon or himself.

"Yes, but he's our pillock now," Brita snapped. "Even though we didn't invite him."

She'd been watching him.

Hugo flared his nostrils. He squared his shoulders, cricked his neck, and tried to turn his contempt upon his daughter, only for it to falter almost immediately. She looked so very tired.

"In here." She nodded back to the dining room. "We need to talk."

"Yes. We do."

Mariska was already at the table, her arms folded across her chest. She kept her eyes downcast, meeting neither his nor his daughter's gaze. Guilt. That's what it was. Hugo sniffed. He'd figured she'd be stronger willed than that. *Perhaps that's why she's still a GM and not the boss.*

His daughter kicked her heels off her feet and shoved a chair towards him. Next to Mariska, as if he deserved to be in the doghouse too.

"Why, what did I do?"

"Will you just sit, please?"

"I'm not a fucking dog, Brita." Hugo rammed his hands into his trouser pockets to hide the fact that they'd curled back into fists. "Just who the hell do you think you are? Stora is mine. I birthed it, nurtured it, grew it from nothing. And you have the arrogance to think you could not only sell it out from under me, but kill my legacy as you did! What gives you the right, I ask you? What gives you the right!"

Her hand was back on her forehead, massaging her temple. "God, does it even matter?"

"Does it even—"

"Stop, Dad. Just stop." Brita sagged into a chair of her own, leaving him the only one standing. "We can't go through this again every single time something goes wrong and you feel like you're losing control. Gateway is too big, and things will go wrong. You need to make peace with that."

She looked up at him then, and he saw not the woman who had ousted him for what he knew, deep down, were the right reasons, but his daughter, who'd just betrayed her closest friend for his invention. He didn't have to bite back a furious retort. For once, he didn't have one.

"Thank you." Brita didn't smile; she simply sighed. It had been a long, long night. "Now as for you." His daughter turned to Mariska, still staring morosely down at the pile of contracts on the table. "You went behind my back. And, in the end you were proven right. Anita should have been on the guest list all along. In fact, I should have brought her in from day one. But that doesn't change what you did. If you think I'm making a mistake, then, as Ming-Xia so elegantly put it, I want you to respect me enough to tell me to my face."

Mariska looked up from the table and held her daughter's gaze for one long breath. Then she nodded. "Okay, boss. I can do that."

"Good. Now, is there anything else I need to know? Anything else either of you have been toying with on the side that could bite us in the arse?"

Hugo swallowed, Solomon's last words to him ringing in his ears. *You don't need to, Hugo. It's in hand.* But he didn't confess anything. How could he? What would he even say?

24

AT MIDNIGHT, THE BARMAN cracked, demanding that Jorge leave. Come on, mister. Go home.

Jorge packed his bag, left the man a twenty, and wandered down the hill, his camera slung over his shoulder. His heart rate ratcheted with every step, and a tingle travelled down his arms to the tips of his fingers. He was only ten yards away. Five yards. Two. One.

He paused, strained his ears, but there was nothing to hear. Only the rustle of leaves in the breeze and a cab rattling over cobblestones two blocks over. Most of the guests had departed, the barman had sent him home, but still, no Solomon. Jorge needed to be there to watch his nemesis as he stepped out into the moonlight. Would he be worried? His strategically weathered features creased with concern like the others? No. Somehow he couldn't quite imagine that.

Eleven houses down, on the other side of the street, a terraced apartment building with an entrance the inverse of Brita's: two sets of stairs leading up to the front door, one running away down the hill, and one facing up it. He set his backpack down on the third step from the landing and lay atop it, a buffer between his chest and the hard-edged concrete. He braced his left foot against the wrought iron fence, swung his camera around, and checked the line of sight. Perfect. Only his head and his long focus lens protruded into the open.

Lights flicked on, across the street. A curtain was pulled back, just enough to peer out. Jorge held his breath, his count of his heartbeat reaching thirteen before the blinds fell back and the window went dark. A spot of rain landed on the back of his neck.

He exhaled, and a long, black Mercedes purred past him from behind, rolling into his field of view and stopping at Brita's front door.

The door opened.

Solomon stood framed in the light.

148

He tossed a comment back through into the hall, too quiet for Jorge to pick out the words. The tone, however, was clear. A dismissal, from a busy man with much to do.

Jorge triple checked that his flash was switched off and zoomed in on Solomon's face, silhouetted against the bright light from within. He couldn't see his eyes, but he could read his posture: head high, shoulder's back, energetic. Arrogant even. The bearing of a man accustomed to reducing his competition to furious, futile tears.

He barked three more indistinguishable words into the light and let the door thud shut. Solomon was not a man to wait for a response. Jorge set his camera to rapid fire, not waiting for the sensors to adjust to the lack of light. Solomon clicked his fingers and skipped up the steps two at a time.

The Mercedes swallowed Solomon whole, its windows impermeable as it rolled away up the street. But then, two doors down, it stopped. An apartment door opened, the door directly beneath the briefly lighted window with the watcher's curtain. Jorge rapidly reset his zoom, shooting all the while.

A man darted across the pavement, into the waiting car. Three steps, no more, and then Solomon, his car, and his mysterious friend were gone.

For a long second, Jorge did nothing. He didn't even breathe, until the rushing of blood in his ears forced it on him. He stared long and hard at the window, waiting for he didn't know what. Very slowly he eased his foot out from between the ironwork and let gravity pull him out of sight.

He scrolled back through his photos. The Mercedes reappeared in stop motion, reversing back towards him. Slowing. Stopping. The door opened. A shadowy man lurched out as if tugged by a rope tied around his waist.

A man in a navy blue polo shirt, with a red and blue swirl over his breast pocket.

He flew back a hundred photos. Two hundred. Three hundred, back to when his first beer still sparkled in the sun. The catering van, empty and driving away. Two women, laden with shopping—

There, that was him! Even in the shadows there was no mistaking the logo, the Slavic cheekbones, the watchful eyes.

Jorge extinguished the camera's LCD screen and shrank farther down beneath the landing. He knew, without looking, that he would find that face somewhere in the thousands of photographs he'd taken these last few weeks. And he knew what that meant.

He wasn't the only one watching.

And if I've spotted them...

— • —

Fifteen minutes passed, enough time for the cold of the concrete to seep into Jorge's bones. Had he been seen? Did it matter? They probably had their binoculars and cameras trained on him already, or if they didn't, they would the moment he made a move. The street was empty. A man materialising from behind a stairwell with no door would surely spark their interest.

But they had already seen him. No one pulls a curtain aside to inspect an empty street.

Either they knew he was here and they didn't care, or they didn't and would spot him leaving. Which meant leaving now would do no good, and he would miss the final, auspicious departure: Mariska Farkas. Would she be just as wounded as the others?

As soon as his thoughts turned from being watched back to watching, he knew he'd made his decision. Teeth gritted against the pain he knew would come from movement, Jorge eased himself back to the top of the landing. Blood surged back to his thighs and his elbows where the digging pressure of the stair had released. A welcome distraction from the window up above, and the wide street at his back that he could only hope remained empty.

He adjusted his focus, trained it on the empty door. Ten minutes passed. Twenty. Thirty. His stomach growled, his tongue thick and dry. He forgot for a moment that he was watched, as well as watcher, and his thoughts strayed to Hank Robard, fuming at Jorge's temerity, his nerve, at the thought someone might have a more important story than him. Of Frank Darabont, wheedling with Roger about some imagined slight, Roger massaging his star's ego while he dismissed Jorge's legitimate concerns. Of Solomon, taking two steps at a time with a trail of anxiety and fear in his wake.

He was where he was meant to be.

At 12:56 a.m., the door opened and light spilled out onto the empty street. Jorge blinked, and Mariska emerged. She was resplendent in a shimmering copper gown, someone's dinner jacket drawn about her shoulders. He snapped away, willing her to turn up the steps towards him. Was she elated? Concerned? She looked his way for a brief moment. Worry drew tight lines across her brow.

A second person emerged behind her. Jorge adjusted his focus—

—and almost dropped his camera in shock. For the second time in a month, Hugo Gundersson appeared from somewhere he couldn't possibly be.

Jorge, camera resettled and aperture snapping, ran furiously through the past eleven hours. He'd been on these steps, or perched on his stool at the pub, watching that door the entire time. There was no way Hugo made it through that door unnoticed, and yet somehow, there he was. There must be a servant's entrance, a fire exit. And though he knew Hugo was a reclusive man, Jorge couldn't imagine him skulking about a back alley dressed in a tuxedo and bow-tie.

As quick as they'd appeared they were gone, into a taxi and whisked away up the hill. For a moment, the door stayed open, and Jorge took photo after photo of the thin strip of light that extended out across the pavement, across the road, though there was nothing to see. Not even a shadow.

Then the door closed, the light locked away, the click of the bolt echoing into the night.

Jorge lingered on the step for another hour, camera in hand, unwilling to accept it was over. His camera strayed from Brita's door to the watcher's window, but there was nothing more to see. When he got home, he didn't sleep. How could he? Anita, distraught. Mariska, worried. Ming-Xia, Pridha, Katsubashi, rattled. Solomon energised, watching, playing a double game.

Hugo, for a second time, appearing out of thin air.

And Brita, unsighted behind her door.

Somehow, the break he'd been waiting for had provided precisely zero answers and raised a dozen more questions.

25

— · —

MARISKA PACED THE POORLY lit footpath outside Anita Kingston's apartment. Anxious thoughts fought one another for prominence: *What am I even doing here?* met with Hugo's petrified anger. *I didn't even do anything wrong* sparred against Brita's bitter disappointment. *I should just leave it, go home* was overpowered by the pain on Anita's face as she'd picked apart their plan and laid it bare, as if the heiress had been reading from their planning memo. Her planning memo. The betrayal in her quaking voice would stay with her for a long, long time.

A taxi slowed as it rolled down the empty street, hoping for a fare, and she waved it away with an irritated hand. Light leaked out from behind Anita's heavy curtains. *Just press the button*, she told herself. Her throat closed over, her heart pounding in her chest. God, she hadn't felt so conflicted since her last night in Miskolc, the town she'd grown up in, then outgrown. The night she'd told her mother she was leaving, that she was never coming back.

Ancient memories spurred her into action. She depressed the buzzer and stepped hurriedly back, its harsh buzz and the conspicuous clacking of her heels echoing along the empty street.

It was done. She wrapped Hugo's white jacket about her waist as tight as she could, clamping her fingers down with her elbows. Forced herself not to fidget.

Her heartbeat filled the midnight silence, only to meld, finally, with the thud of approaching, unshod feet. The bolt slid back with a clunk and the door opened. Just a crack.

Anita, hair wrapped in a towel, peered from beyond the threshold. Recognition was instant, and unpleasant. With an almost imperceptible shiver she closed the door. The urge to slap her palm against it, to force it open, was strong, but Mariska was stronger.

Anita's front door closed again with a soft click.

Mariska was alone in the empty street. She listened. No footsteps. In her mind's eye, Anita was slumped with her back against the door. Head back, eyes closed. Torn

152

between just waiting for her to leave and calling in her security guards. Mariska knew which of the two options she would have chosen. She closed the distance between them, rested her forehead against the doorframe.

"I know I'm not the person you wanted to see at your door, but I wanted..." She held her breath but could hear no movement from across the divide. No encouragement, but no direction to stop either. "I wanted you to know that tonight was my plan. Mine and Hugo's, not Brita's. She wanted to find a better way."

The rattle of the catch sliding and releasing from its track pushed her back to the middle of the footpath. Anita stood framed in the pale hallway light, draped in a soft white bathrobe. She wore no makeup and her hair was loose, but her eyes smouldered. "So, what, I suppose you run Stora now?"

Mariska blinked. Shook her head.

"I didn't think so." The older woman sighed. "Let me guess, you're going to tell me she tried milking the usual suspects for seed capital, but when Britannia imploded, they all got cold feet and you swept in with a way to save the day. You wanted me involved from the beginning, but Brita said no. No way. And you couldn't figure out why, could you? Anita would be perfect!" Anita spoke with an imitation smile, ticking traits off on her fingers. "She's vulnerable, loyal, rich. A bit frivolous..."

"I don't think you're frivolous." *At least, not anymore. Not after tonight.* Where had this Anita come from? Until this evening, she'd seen only the woman Anita had wanted her to see. Effervescent, brash, the life of the party. Entertaining, but not threatening. No wonder Anita had succeeded where so many women had failed. She'd used Mariska's own tactics against her, and she hadn't even noticed.

"No?" Anita crossed her arms with a sceptical frown and leaned against the doorjamb. "Then why? Why go behind Brita's back?"

"Because..." Mariska paused. Months of frustrations threatened to boil over, spill from her lips, and she couldn't afford that. She had to be calm. Rational. "Because she excluded you for the wrong reasons. Without you there, she could pretend what we did tonight was 'just business.' But you saw Gateway, what it is. What it will do. There are trillions of pounds just waiting for us to take them." *Trillions that I want my share of.* "We can't afford to pretend there won't be consequences."

"You don't see what you did tonight, extorting millions of dollars from me, from Ming-Xia, from Sato and Sandeep, even Solomon, as wrong?"

Mariska shrugged. "Do you?" She looked Anita up and down, free of her gown, her makeup, rugged up in a luxurious dressing gown, and saw her as she really was. A tycoon who knew how to make the tough calls. "No, I didn't think so. You would have done the exact same thing, only wouldn't have tried to dress it up as a gift, an opportunity. You wouldn't have pretended it was anything other than what it was, because you would have let self-interest carry the day."

Anita crossed her arms. "You don't think Brita is ruthless enough."

"I don't have Daddy's money to fall back on. I need Gateway to be a success, which means I can't afford for Brita to try to be some fucking saviour, as if Gateway is some sort of gift for the world that can be made real by good intentions alone." Mariska hesitated, casting her eyes up to the streetlight, but there was no point stopping now. "I had to show her that there was no getting through this without her getting her hands dirty."

Mariska shifted her weight, unsure what to do with her hands. Now that the words were out there, she heard how they sounded. Anita regarded her with a look somewhere between curiosity and pity, and the weariness that Mariska had been holding at bay hit her like a flood. It had been a long, long night.

"Go home, Mariska. Get some sleep," Anita said, as if there was nothing more to say. She turned away and moved to close the door, reinstate the barrier between them. Then she stopped. "No, hold on. Let me get this straight. You went behind your boss's back and undermined her authority on one of the most important nights of her career, because you don't think she's taking Gateway seriously? Because you think she needs to be more ruthless? Brita Gundersson, the woman who ousted her own father to save the company?"

Anita's words were a verbal slap to the face. "That was ten years ago. Not now—"

"No. Don't speak. You've done more than enough of that. And for what? To prove some sort of juvenile point?" Anita's quiet rage filled the empty street. "I'll admit, I have a certain grudging respect for the trap you laid for us tonight. But Brita is a grown fucking woman and doesn't need you here fighting her battles like some self-appointed hero."

The crunch of tires scraping to a halt in the gutter cut Anita short. Mariska saw her eyes widen, and then, in time with the slamming of a car door, a nasty smile twist her lips.

"I *am* a grown fucking woman, and I can apologise just fine on my own."

Brita. Mariska closed her eyes, her bottom lip jammed between her teeth. The timing could not have been worse. Mortified, she forced herself to turn and meet her boss's gaze. Brita looked straight past her, directing all her attention at Anita.

"I'd like to come inside, if you'll have me," Brita asked, with caution. Anita nodded but didn't move from the door. Mariska's gaze flitted from face to determined face, neither of which paid her any attention at all. The implication was crystal clear.

"I'll, um..." Mariska mumbled, squeezing herself past Brita towards the open pavement. Her boss grabbed her shoulder.

"A quick word before you go, Mas."

Mariska followed Brita's eyes back to Anita. She mouthed something and Anita grunted, disappeared into her hall, leaving the door open. Brita rested her shoulder on the doorjamb, and Mariska followed suit, the open doorway a chasm between them.

"What are you doing here?"

"I wanted to..." She looked up at the streetlights, searching for the right words. Something close enough to the truth. "To stick up for you. Make up for going behind your back."

Brita laughed gently, sadly. "By doing it again?" Mariska could only purse her lips. "I can fight my own battles. Anita is my friend, and I'm the one who hurt her."

She kept her face neutral, slightly apologetic, but inside she wanted to scream: *Only because you didn't listen!* If she hadn't invited Anita, the night might have gone very differently. Sandeep and Ming-Xia were already on the fence. Add in Solomon's surprise appearance and, shit. They might well have swung the other way, and then where would they be? Absolutely fucking nowhere.

"I keep thinking that while tonight was your idea, it was my decision, and I'm the one that has to live with the consequences." Brita let out a heavy sigh, her gaze lost in the middle distance. "But how true that actually is, I don't know. With the surprise appearances of both Solomon and Anita, almost half the room was out of my hands. I could have stopped, I guess, pulled the plug. But that wasn't really a choice, was it? No, it was too late.

"Which brings me back to you." Brita's focus snapped back onto Mariska, and suddenly she wished she were able to slip the cracks in the pavement. Brita's disappointment was palpable, and it burned her wherever it made contact.

"There will be enough surprises coming at us from the outside. I can't afford them coming from the inside as well." Brita pushed herself upright so that she was free of the wall. Standing on her own two feet. "I think you need to take some time. Get your he—"

"What?" The exclamation burst forth out of shock, beyond any rational control. She couldn't be serious! "No, I can't. Not when there's so much to do. There are contracts to sort out, briefings for the new investors, we need to start hiring..."

Brita closed her eyes, took a deep breath, only reopening them once she was finished. "This is not a negotiation, Mas."

Her mouth snapped shut, as the first hints of what was happening began to filter through. "How long?"

"Honestly? That's entirely up to you." Brita turned inside Anita's hallway and, without looking back, closed the door in her face.

"Fuck!" Mariska hissed, a sudden, impotent, spitting, fist-clenching, vein-popping fury sending her spinning away from the door and out onto the street. That didn't just happen. It couldn't have. "Fuck," she said again, her anger giving way to realisation, to the beginnings of despondency. The riches, the opportunity, the power that Gateway would unlock, they'd been the foundation upon which she'd built every thought and every action these last two months. And now, they were slipping away.

"I'd be happy to drive you back home, Ms Farkas. Reckon they'll be in there for a while."

Mariska whirled around to find Henry, Brita's driver, holding open the rear door to her boss's Mercedes. Just the thought of sitting sent a shiver down her thighs. It was so tempting...

"Thank you, Henry, but no." Mariska shook her head. She kicked her heels off, set her bare feet against the ground. If she was out of the tent, she had to figure out what that meant. "I need the walk. Time to think."

26

THE FIRST TIME JORGE had walked into his new newsroom, it had been bustling with quiet activity. He felt like he returning home after years lost in an absurd, surrealistic wilderness. Today, though, it was quiet. Most of his new colleagues were out in the field, or, more likely, out to lunch.

It was just Jorge and his friend, now partner, Gabrielle. They were working the continuing fallout from the Britannia Bank raid. The story they'd broken together had inspired at least four separate data leaks from within the company walls. Gigabytes of data: account numbers, balances, transactions, customer databases, emails. So much they could only divide and conquer. She crunched the numbers; he investigated the characters. The pairing suited their strengths: Gabrielle was methodical and scrupulous, almost painfully thorough. Perfect for traipsing through files, records, and emails, filtering out the dross to uncover the gems. Gems that pointed him towards the difficult questions that needed to be asked and the people that needed to answer them.

Together, they wrote the copy.

They worked back to back, Gabrielle scanning account ledgers and company registers, while Jorge reviewed transcripts of past press conferences, investor briefings, and interviews featuring their next, familiar target: one Hank Robard. And hadn't Jorge been shocked, just so disappointed, to find the Hollywood star's name peppered throughout the leaked documentation. And yet...

The quiet babble of the spacious newsroom—conversations, phones buzzing on particle board desks, the constant clickety-clack of fingers and nails on keyboards, the sound of his colleagues chasing down the next scoop—it helped him keep his focus. Without it, even the prospect of Hank Robard sweating under the grill couldn't stop his thoughts from wandering back to his other story. His own, private investigation.

It had been a fortnight since the dinner party, and he felt himself losing touch. After the conspiracy had incubated within the confines of Hugo's palatial lodgings in Knightsbridge, and a one-night expansion to Brita's apartment in Mayfair, this story had exploded internationally. There were developments to be followed in Kuala Lumpur and Kolkata, Tokyo and Texas. Brita, Hugo, and Anita were all overseas. The few contacts he still had were in the wrong places, and he was but one man. He didn't even know where to start.

He looked away from his screen. He'd been staring at the same transcript for fifteen minutes, taking none of it in. When he looked again, the scanned words blurred into one another.

He needed a break.

A notification sidled into the bottom corner of his screen. There were two kinds of emails here: the kind that gave him another month's worth of work (without extending the deadline, of course), and the kind that gave him an excuse to stretch his legs. He glanced down with trepidation.

Thank Christ.

He heaved himself from his chair.

"I've got a package at reception, be back in five."

Gabrielle grunted in response, not bothering to turn around.

He approached the front desk warily. The receptionist, he'd found, could be more than a little intimidating. Maybe it was just because he was new, while Jacquie had been around for so long, she was part of the furniture. And how did one make small talk with a receptionist anyway? It was all they did, all day, every day—surely it must get tiresome.

"Jacquie, you have a parcel for me?"

She held up a solitary, manicured finger, finishing whatever she was typing before looking up. There was no recognition in her clear blue eyes.

"Sorry, your name?" she asked with pursed lips, her northern accent jarring.

"Jorge," he said, before anxiety drove him to add, "Elorza, I just joined the economic news team." He pointed back over his shoulder with his thumb, a superfluous gesture he regretted immediately.

"Ah. Sure."

He had no idea why he was so flustered. She reached under her desk without breaking eye contact and extracted an A4-size brown envelope, his name scrawled across the top with black marker. How curious.

"You didn't happen to see who dropped it off?"

"No," she said, already onto the next task.

"That's a shame." He didn't know what he meant by that, so he stood there, drumming his fingers against the paper. "Thanks anyway," he offered, before cutting his losses and heading back to his desk.

The envelope was coarse to the touch, thick and heavy. It had the uneven heft of a stack of paper, or maybe printed photographs. His pulse quickened as he imagined its contents. Few things excited him more than an unexpected delivery of documentation.

He hustled back to his desk. Gabrielle had barely moved, her face hidden behind a cascade of brown curls and her left hand still tracing down a column of account details from top to bottom, her right flipping the page to start the process over once more. He plopped into his chair, dropping the envelope onto his desk with a satisfying thud.

It would be so easy to just rip it open, but long experience had taught there was a certain order to these things. He grabbed his camera from a drawer and started snapping away, carefully recording both sides of the package, with several close-up photographs of his name. You never knew what might be important. Only once this was done did he take to the tape holding the envelope closed and pull the contents onto his desktop.

A simple manila folder with no identifying monograms, front or back. Through the lens of his camera, he focused on the small details—grubby marks on the edge of the cover, the dog-eared bottom corner. He checked the envelope once more to make sure there was nothing left inside.

He glanced over his shoulder. Gabrielle was oblivious, scribbling notes with her left finger planted around a third of the way down the open page of the ledger. With a combination of nerves and excitement, and just a hint of embarrassment at just how much he was enjoying this, he straightened the folder in front of him and flipped it open.

It was a photograph—no, a stack of photographs. Photographs that looked disturbingly familiar. Photos of him: sitting huddled on a park bench, six houses down from Hugo's apartment. He flipped it over with a shaking hand, revealing another of him sitting at the same park bench but wearing a different jacket. And another. And another. All of them taken from across the road, from on the footpath. Right under his nose.

He kept flipping. A photograph of him perched on a barstool in the corner of the Punchbowl's outdoor bar, this one taken with a telephoto lens, looking down, as he was adjusting his camera. *From that apartment window.* It had to be. The angle was just right.

Another, in the harsh negative grey of infrared vision, his body splayed on the far side of the set of stairs, camera at the ready. And one more—

He slammed the folder closed and pressed his fist to his lips. *Jesus, Mary, and Joseph*, he thought, every muscle in his body suddenly as tight as a snare drum. *They've been to my house!*

Gabrielle finally looked up from her work, jumping at the violence with which he slapped the folder shut. She peered across her shoulder. "Your package contain a nasty surprise?"

He composed himself and reopened the file, his knuckles popping at the release of tension. He teased the final photo out from beneath the pile, as if to prove to himself that it had really been taken: a close-up of him sitting at his computer, in his living room. Taken through his kitchen window.

"You could say that." An understatement. What else could he say?

"Shit, Jorge." She'd wheeled herself over now and started flipping through the photos. "Has someone got you under surveillance?"

Jorge squirmed. "Sort of."

"What do you mean, sort of? You didn't take these photos of yourself."

"I mean, I was the one doing the watching. At the time. And..." He floundered. How could he explain it all? The interview, the cryptic hints, the clandestine meetings? Harvey and his illegal back door into the city's surveillance network? The sudden, unexpected reappearance of his old nemesis?

"Jorge, this one's at your house. This is..." Gabrielle's voice was serious, her manner alarmed, until it wasn't. She stared at the final photo, her finger tapping on the blurry face of the air-conditioning repair man that just happened to have filled his screen at the moment his tormentor had snapped the picture. "I've seen this guy before."

Jorge blanched, his thoughts suffering from whiplash at this sudden turn of events. "Wait, you have?"

Gabrielle nodded. "Have you got that photo still?"

"Uh, yeah, sure." Jorge fished about in his pocket for his phone and started swiping, back past teary exits, back past uncertain entrances. He stopped at the air-con technician, his mystery follower, and zoomed in on his face. He handed his phone over to his friend.

"Thanks." She bit her lip and stared intently at the man who'd been watching the same people as him. "I'm sure I saw his photo just the other day." Her eyes glazed over. Absentmindedly, she grabbed a pencil and started munching on it, delving into her memory. Jorge sat back, curiosity overriding his sense of shock, any thought that he might be in danger. He'd not worked with Gabrielle for a long time, but he hadn't forgotten this. It wouldn't be a long wait.

After ten or fifteen seconds of intense silence, she lurched back into action, dropping his phone onto the carpet and lunging for her mouse and her keyboard. Within seconds she'd brought up a folder filled with hundreds of photos and was clicking through thumbnails as fast as they would load.

"We only got these the other day. Photos of prominent Hepburn Grisdale clients. You know, Britannia's preferred shell company guys." Jorge nodded impatiently, as if they hadn't been trawling through Panamanian shell companies and client lists together all week. She could get like this at times, so eager to explain that she started from scratch.

"You can skip the background, Gab."

"Right. Sorry." She kept flipping, dozens of men in suits, a few women as well, flickering into view only to disappear again just as quickly. Then she stopped, pointing triumphantly at the final photo. "This was taken just a few days ago."

The slightly overexposed image showed his air-con repairman in yet another uniform, this time dressed as a wealthy man with money to hide. Slicked-back hair, conspicuous gold chains, aviator sunglasses, and the top buttons of his linen shirt open against the obvious heat. She clicked forwards in time, and he closed the door of a BMW, burnished silver shining through from beneath the dust. A second man stepped from the car's far side. Indian, or Sri Lankan maybe. He carried himself with an air of self-importance, wearing a pointed, carefully trimmed beard, a gold necklace around his neck and rings on every one of his fingers.

Just from that one photo, Jorge would have laid salivating odds that his stalker's Indian friend was on Sandeep Pridha's payroll.

"Have we got names for these two?" he asked.

"Nope, not yet. Just JG16 and JG17," Gabrielle said, pointing to Solomon's actual and Sandeep's alleged henchmen in turn.

"JG?"

"Jerry's guest." She grinned and kept rolling.

JG16 looked back over his shoulder; he squinted into the sun, patted the car on the roof; watched it drive away; fell in a step ahead of his partner; made his way towards an ostentatious, stuccoed entrance way. The entrance to a large private villa. An ornate water feature protruded in the foreground, with two security guards, dark sunglasses and close-cropped hair, loitering on either side of a doorway. A man appeared, extended his hand; JGs 16 and 17 were welcomed inside.

"That's Grisdale?" Jorge asked, clicking back two photos and pointing to the balding host, impeccably dressed in a wide-shouldered suit, a gold cross prominent in a tangle of greying chest hair.

"Yep. That's him. Jerry Grisdale. Looks like he's having the time of his life, doesn't he?"

Jorge rolled his eyes. They always did, until they didn't. "Hepburn ever show up in these?"

"Uh-uh." Gabrielle shook her head. "Lance Hepburn is, from what I've seen thus far, more of a silent partner."

Jorge nodded as he absorbed this new snippet of information, trying to fit it into the puzzle. *So Solomon's muscle does more than just surveillance. He meets with shady lawyers in the Panamanian heat. But why? How does it fit?*

"How did we get this?" Jorge asked, just to say something.

"The photos, you mean? Remember the Panama papers, back in like 2016? Journalists have been tracking the clients of the usual suspects, offshore finance, arms dealers, cartels. You know, trying to put faces to names." God, real journalism! Painstaking effort, collaboration across national borders. He nodded, urging her on. It was so good to be back. "Well, Britannia's collapse has driven a burst of activity. Some bright spark thought to hire a PI to stake out the private bases of the company directors, see what shook out."

"And so you were digging around in their folders..."

"Well, yeah. I'd found a few shell companies on the books here"—she patted her printed ledgers, notes scrawled in the margins—"that I thought might be linked to the Ukrainian mob. They have a pattern with their incorporation titles. I thought it could be another for the laundering file. And then..."

"And then." Jorge sat back, letting his breath whistle out through his teeth, and hoped Gabrielle wouldn't notice just how shaky that breath had been. *The Ukrainian mob.* Funny how a few words could pull you back in time, to empty back streets, to a face in a doorway. To the beginning of an investigation that would ruin his career.

He pulled up his stalker's photo again. His prominent cheekbones, his pale skin, his ice-blue eyes. A face that could easily belong to the Donetskaya Bratva. A face that had disappeared into Solomon's waiting car. A face that had possibly, probably, peered through his kitchen window. His stomach began coiling itself into knots.

"Do you think this guy's connected?"

"I don't have anything solid, but..." Gabrielle turned back to face him, her dark eyes telling him she was just trying to be kind. "Shit, Jorge, what are you going to do?"

What else could he do? He opened his contacts and scrolled down to Harvey Turnbull. "I think I might have to call the police."

— ● —

Jorge slipped into one of the empty interview rooms and closed the door. Phone on the table, he set it to speaker and hit dial. Harvey picked up on the third ring: "Jorge! How's my favourite newshound?"

"Making enemies of the rich and powerful," Jorge said, trying to match Harvey's jovial tone. The joke turned bitter in his mouth.

"You and me both, my friend. You and me both." Harvey chortled, and Jorge wondered who the detective had in mind. Lloyd Hargreaves, perhaps, or maybe his boss, DCI Marlowe. Unsurprisingly, she'd been none too pleased with the DI Turnbull-centric coverage her raid had garnered in the media. Phone calls had been made, but his new editor had held firm. He'd brought them the story after all. "Who've you pissed off this time, then?"

"I've just sent you a couple of photos. We've been combing through shell companies which we think might be linked to the Ukrainian mob, and this feller has popped up a couple of times during our legwork." Did he sound casual enough? Too laid back? "Was hoping you might have something on file."

"Ukrainian mob, hey? Anything we might be interested in?"

"Let's just say my boss is rather keen to make up with your boss, should we turn up something useful. How about that."

Jorge heard a brace of pings from the other end of the line. Harvey whistled. "Mean-looking sort of chap, isn't he?" A rattle of cables and keys being pressed. "You take these?"

Jorge hesitated. He'd rather Harvey didn't know how that first photo had come into his possession, but he knew the kind of software the City of London had access to. If Harvey wanted to dig, he would. "The first one. Not the second."

"I should have known. The second one's actually in focus, ha ha."

Jorge rolled his eyes, a smile fighting is way onto his lips, as Harvey chortled his way through another series of clicks. The detective was clearly in a good mood. He didn't want to admit it, but that attitude was what he needed right now.

"Right. The old girl's thinking, shouldn't take long. Say, this photo you took. You wouldn't have spotted this fellow while you were taking a stroll down a certain street in Knightsbridge, by any chance?"

"Not Knightsbridge, no." Jorge clenched his jaw, smile eradicated by one simple question. This was not a line he wanted to go down, but what choice did he have? "Mayfair."

"Ah. The personal beginning to mix in with the professional, is it?"

"Just following the evidence where it leads, Harvey."

"I bet." Harvey ruminated. Jorge wished he could see his friend's face, judge whether the suspicion in his voice was directed at him, or at the man in the photo. "Though I must say, mixing with the Slavs doesn't really seem Ms Gundersson's style."

"It's not," Jorge said, his mind drifting back to that Mayfair street, the high window with its curtain pulled back. A watcher, secreted inside. "But she's made some new friends of late who might not be so scrupulous."

"Ah." Another ping. "Well, well, well. This new friend of hers. They wouldn't happen to be an old friend of yours as well?"

Jorge swallowed. Harvey was too perceptive by half. "I don't know. Aside from Gabrielle, you're about the only old friend I've got."

"Jorge, I'm touched."

No more clicking, no more typing. The algorithms had clearly done their job, and Harvey's self-satisfied smugness radiated through the phone. Jorge could just imagine him, arms crossed over his round belly and a knowing smile plastered across his ruddy face as he read through whatever it was he'd found.

"Go on then, who is he?"

"What, no lecture on the bankrupt morality of state surveillance? No tokenistic defence of the citizen's right to privacy, of the faceless brutality of algorithmic justice?"

"Harvey…" The longer he stalled, the tighter Jorge's throat pulled and the heavier his late breakfast sat in his stomach. Jorge had little doubt what was coming. Solomon had known Brita was up to something and had tasked his underworld investors with finding out what it was. And Jorge had got himself caught in the middle. Again.

He buried his head in his hands. "He's Donetskaya Bratva, isn't he."

"Bingo. One Yosip Bondarenko, thirty-two years old," Harvey chirped; then, after an uncomfortable pause, his confident patter turned suddenly equivocal. "Well, at least we think so. We don't actually have anything solid."

"No, of course you don't." *How about a photo he took of me through my kitchen window? Would that solid enough for you?* Jorge dragged his fingers down his cheeks, sighing with frustration. He couldn't tell Harvey that. What did it prove? The he was being watched. Warned off. That he was onto something. Something he didn't want Harvey's big City of London Police boots trampling all over. Not yet, anyway. "I bet you don't even know where he is."

"Right now? No. And I'd need a warrant to track him, so don't even ask. But I can tell you this. One of his suspected aliases is booked in at some shitty motel out in Harlesden. But, you'll like this." Harvey paused, and Jorge lifted his head from between his knees. Had Harvey's voice regained a hint of his usual swagger? "Your Slavic pal's face has been spotted in the lobby of the Savoy four times in the last month. Maybe he's hoping for a glimpse of your pal Robard, ha ha."

The Savoy. Jorge grinned. He knew exactly who Yosip would be visiting there, and it wasn't some two-bit movie star.

27

BRITA FOGGED THE LENSES of her safety glasses, then polished them with the inside lining of her borrowed lab coat, a dense black Peng Industries logo emblazoned above the left breast pocket. What protection, if any, they might offer against the unstable collapse of one of the Gateway's wormholes was a mystery to her.

Better than nothing though.

Brita and Ming-Xia stood facing the plate glass window separating the observation room from a cluttered laboratory. On the other side of the glass, two of Ming-Xia's technicians were preparing the first round of tests, pitting Peng Industries' jamming tech against the stability of an active Gateway. Her father had jetted into Malaysia within days of the dinner party, vetting the team Ming-Xia had hand selected for the months of testing that lay ahead, before setting off again for Tokyo. For weeks they'd only spoken by phone, never quite managing to be in the same place at the same time. And as for Mariska…

Brita clasped her hands behind her back, pulling back her shoulders. She'd barely had time to think about her former protégé at all. After the long night at Anita's kitchen table, Henry had driven her straight to the office. She hadn't had a wink of sleep, but she had a plan. Her next ten hours had been spent in back-to-back meetings with Stora's new investors, doing what had to be done to rebuild trust and start mapping out the months ahead. It had been rocky, but at the end of the day, self-interest won out.

Just as Mas had said it would. She bit her lip. What had she been expecting Mariska to do? To call and apologise? To beg for her job back? She was too stubborn. They both were. Mariska knew she was the right person for the job. *And she knows I know it, too. Have I been letting my pride get in the way? Expecting her to cave first?*

The lead technician, a plump Chinese Malaysian woman in her early fifties named Ren, spoke through the intercom, pulling Brita back to the here and now. "Ms Gundersson, Ms Peng. We are ready to commence testing."

Her fellow technician, stocky, with the darker skin of a Bornean native, opened the heavy door and stepped back to allow her through. Ming-Xia had introduced him as Kerubang ("but please, Ms Gundersson, just Keru is fine"). He stepped through, the heavy door thudding shut behind him.

The test rig was not complicated: two Gateway-enabled smartphones set atop a flat metal table in simple clamps, held side-on with the screens facing away from one another, about two metres apart. An actuated arm held a fluorescent tube aloft, ready to drive it through an open portal. Behind sat a portable jamming array, the kind you might find mounted on the back of a Malaysian army jeep. This setup was wired back to a control panel below the window, with Ren standing at the controls.

"Good to go?" Ren asked, looking to her boss. Ming-Xia nodded, without consulting Brita. This was her company, her lab. No permission was required.

"Peng Industries. Gateway—Portal Jamming, Test 1." Ren spoke to the video camera. The tests were being recorded, of course. She checked her watch, "Time is 10:17 a.m., Monday, October thirteen, 2024."

Out of habit Brita did the same, then blinked with confusion. Her watch was two and a half hours behind. Still set to Kolkata time. She unclipped it from her wrist, belatedly bringing her timepiece into line with her current locale.

Before Malaysia, she'd spent three tense days with Sandeep in Kolkata, touring factories and preparing retooling plans for his production lines. It had been a relief when Solomon unexpectedly arrived for the last day of her visit, whisking her away to nearby Bhutan—home to an ageing hydroelectric plant with the potential for conversion to Gateway technology.

Of all the investors, Sandeep had taken the deepest offence to her "coercive tactics." He gave all the signs of having been deeply disrespected, though she knew he was no stranger to strong-arming the competition. She had an uncomfortable sense that it wasn't being outsmarted that had gotten under his skin, so much as having been outsmarted by a woman. If not for Solomon's calming influence, she doubted whether she'd be able to control him at all.

She'd voiced her concerns to Solomon at dinner, on their one night in Thimphu, only to be met with a knowing smile. He would not be drawn, instead changing the topic to the source of the succulent meat with their local hosts. Despite the typically gracious Bhutanese hospitality, weeks of ceaseless travel had only compounded her inability to handle their spicy food. Her stomach churned at the memory of that meal, and she cast a cautious eye Ming-Xia's way, hoping she hadn't heard.

Ren worked the controls, confirming the status of the three systems—mechanical, Gateway, and signal jamming. She narrated her work for posterity, announcing that she was about to establish a Gateway call. With a ghostly flicker, the portals popped into existence.

Brita shifted her weight, unnerved by the businesslike ambivalence displayed by Ming-Xia and her employees in the presence of an operating Gateway. She still felt giddy every time and had to work at keeping her demeanour professional, in line with her new colleagues. *Perhaps they are doing the same, for my benefit.*

She certainly hoped so.

With stability confirmed, Ren initiated the mechanical loop. The fluorescent tube sputtered to life, throwing a square of harsh white light onto the far wall through the open Gateway. A soft whirr as the robotic arm drove it forward. It was an odd sensation, watching an object disappear into nothingness and appear from nothing on the other side of the room. The robotic arm stopped with the lit tube suspended halfway through the two Gateways, the far end floating, held steady as a rock.

"Gateway is established. Triggering the short-wave jamming." From what she had understood of the briefing, they were testing three different variants of Peng's signal-jamming technology this morning. Ming-Xia stood with her arms crossed. Only a tapping left foot betrayed the tension she must have been feeling. Brita allowed herself a minuscule smile. She knew that Ming-Xia was just like her, that she felt the same pressures and anxieties, but it was nice to have it confirmed every once in a while. The four of them watched on in silence.

Ren flicked a switch. She wasn't sure what she'd been expecting—some sort of hum? Instead, nothing. Keru monitored a read-out panel, waiting for a pattern of wavering lines to stabilise, and shot Ren a thumbs-up when they did.

"Short-wave jamming operational." The hovering, bifurcated fluorescent tube shone on unperturbed. "No observable effect. Initiating long-wave jamming." She flicked a second switch, and Keru followed the same routine, for the same result. Ming-Xia's tapping foot increased in urgency, then stopped altogether. A sly glance to the side revealed pursed lips, white at the edges. This was only the first test. Her father had told them both not to expect success. But Brita knew what was going through Ming-Xia's mind. She'd had the same thought a thousand times. *Women like us don't often get to fail more than once.*

"Initiating digital scrambler." The confident, matter-of-fact tone of Ren's voice, however, indicated that she was not inhibited by such doubts. She flicked the final switch, and immediately the surfaces of the two portals flickered, pixels cascading across the screens that sat microns behind the Gateway horizon. The fluorescent tube shattered in a cascade of sparks, shards of darkened glass exploding outwards, rattling the thick Perspex window. The Gateway link had collapsed. Dark smoke twisted from the back of the receiving handset on the right.

"Well..." Brita needed to say something, without really knowing what. She coughed and smoothed down her lab coat. Her hands were shaking. "That was exciting."

"Too exciting." Ming-Xia shook her head in frustration. "We need both handsets to continue testing, and if we've broken it..." She sent a stern look Ren's way, but Brita doubted the two scientists even noticed. They were too busy scrolling through the data and hypothesising in rapid Mandarin. "How quickly can you source a replacement? The evidence would suggest we have a lot of work to do—"

Her terse assessment of the damage was cut off by an excited burst of chatter from the control desk. Brita smiled. "Ren and Keru don't seem to share your pessimism."

"No. They don't." Ming-Xia's brow remained furrowed, and she fired off a sentence in Mandarin with such force that Brita had no need of a translator.

Ren started back in Mandarin, then stopped, her eyes widening as she collapsed into a guilty bow. "Sorry, Ms Gundersson. Ms Peng was just asking us what went wrong."

"It's quite all right, I gathered as much. No need to apologise." Brita wanted to walk up to her and pull her upright, even though she knew it would just end up doing more harm than good. "So what did go wrong?"

Ren straightened, and, despite her obvious reluctance to contradict her boss, she couldn't help beaming. "That's just it. Nothing went wrong! The tests literally could not have gone better!"

Brita raised a sceptical eyebrow at the still-smoking wreck that had once been a Gateway-enabled handset. It certainly didn't look like a success.

"Looks can be deceiving, Ms Gundersson," Keru interjected, reading her mind. He adjusted a couple of settings on the control panel and the extraction system kicked in, clearing the acrid smoke. "We managed to interrupt a Gateway portal with one of our existing systems, no modifications required! I was prepared for a long first couple of months of tweaking and testing just to get to this point. With respect, this is a good outcome."

Brita nodded. Her gaze settled on the blackened shards of glass that littered the metal table, thinking back to that night in Cairo, when her entire body had passed through the portal. Ming-Xia's too. What would have happened if the call had been cut off? Would she have shattered into a million little pieces, or simply been sliced in two? A shiver travelled from her neck down to the base of her spine. The consequences of an interrupted connection weren't even her primary concern. "I see your point, Keru. However, there are only so many Gateway handsets in existence. We can't afford for this testing program to be quite so...destructive."

"No, we can't." Ming-Xia's voice remained stern; however, Brita saw that a mischievous twinkle had returned to her eye. "Though perhaps we should consider this an opportunity. The next Gateway your father builds will take into account the data we've just gained, and will be the more resilient for it."

Brita and Ming-Xia marched in lockstep along a dimly lit corridor, both conspicuous in their lab coats and pencil skirts as they made the trek back to the main office building. They'd left Ren and Keru in the lab, happily dismantling the apparatus and sifting through the data.

"How soon can you get us a new handset?" Ming-Xia asked, her back and neck perfectly straight. Just impeccable posture. Brita uncurled her shoulders in an attempt to match it.

"I'll have to talk to my father," she conceded. "It might be a little while. He's barely been home. Neither of us have."

"Perhaps if you hadn't fired your assistant..."

Brita's step faltered. Not much, but enough to force her into a light jog to keep up. "Mariska's not my assistant, and I didn't fire her. I just—"

"Listen, I don't care about the details. It's not just your money on the line anymore, and I expect to see a significant return on my investment. Our testing can't afford any delays."

"Fair. Very fair." *I'll call her on the flight home,* Brita thought, settling her footsteps back into a rhythm. *Though I'm still not entirely sure what I'm going to say. Or if she'll even answer.*

"For what it's worth, I'd keep her inside the tent. You need someone with her...tenacity." Ming-Xia chuckled. "I wouldn't want to get on her bad side."

"No, perhaps not." Brita shook her head, her voice noncommittal. She knew what tenacity meant. What had she done that made Mariska, and now Ming-Xia, think that she lacked balls? That she needed someone on her team that was willing to get their hands dirty? When her father had been threatening to blow her inheritance on yet another crazy scheme, she hadn't hesitated. And when he'd called out of the blue, her pen millimetres from the dotted line, she'd done what needed to be done..

But, when I had the chance to welcome my best friend into the fold, I balked. And when I got called out on it, I balked again. She thought of the half dozen unfinished emails she'd started writing to Mariska, the half dozen more unsent texts. *I'm still balking.*

In the midst of her self-recriminating, it took Brita a couple of steps to realise that Ming-Xia stopped, right in the middle of the corridor, with a pained look on her face.

"Is everything all right?"

"No, not really. I just realised what I said. I didn't mean...after everything you went through with your father..."

"No, it's fine." Brita stepped forward, laid a hand on Ming-Xia's arm. "More than fine. You were right, and so was Mariska, as it happens. I just didn't want to hear it."

Ming-Xia took a long, calming breath, then a quick glance backwards, as if to confirm they were alone. "It was a stressful night. It's easy to judge in hindsight. Not so easy to act in the uncertainty of the moment." She shrugged. "You make mistakes, you make up for them."

Brita noticed that she looked back in the direction of the lab as she said that and remembered the rapidly tapping foot. The terse questions and the tight, pursed lips. The moment didn't last long, but they shared it together.

"Actually, if you don't mind my asking," Ming-Xia probed tentatively, once they'd started walking again. "How have the others reacted? Poor Sato seemed completely overwhelmed."

It was a question Brita had been mulling herself, and yet another area where she could have used Mariska's insight, only to have erected a needless barrier instead. They were a group of six now, seven if she included her father, staking their fortunes on the Gateway. An exclusive club, with unique pressures. She thought back to an exchange she'd had with Sandeep just a few days ago, discussing his plans to retool one of his microchip factories. He hadn't yelled or screamed, hadn't been thoughtlessly intimidating. Instead, he'd channelled whatever resentments he held against her into an utter determination not to let her prevail on even one point.

But Ming-Xia didn't need to know this. Not yet, anyway. "There are some ruffled feathers still, but nothing I can't handle." Ming-Xia raised an eyebrow, though she restrained herself from suggesting a name. Brita wondered whether she would have gone for Sandeep or Richard Solomon.

"But you're right, Sato was a little out of his depth. Dad's over in Tokyo now helping to set up the software dev team."

"Any troubles?"

"No, not at all. Well"—she let out a smirk—"not in Tokyo. Last time I spoke to him, it looked like he and Sato were having a ball. But..." She left a slight pause, letting Ming-Xia dangle for just a second. The pattern of their conversation had changed, the tension of the tests, of the rough beginnings to their partnership fading into the distance. "There was a curly little issue the day after the dinner."

She leaned in a little closer, as if she was letting Ming-Xia in on a secret. Just as she'd hoped, Ming-Xia did the same. "Go on."

"So Dad was meant to leave his phone in Cairo after the demonstration, but he came back through my apartment with it still in his pocket."

"That doesn't sound like that big a deal."

"Ordinarily no. But with him, and his phone, in London, there was no way of dialling back to the gate we'd built into the hotel wall. And he needed to get back to the hotel so he could dismantle it and bring it back."

Ming-Xia's brow was furrowed, not a hint of understanding showing through. "Couldn't he just fly back?"

"He could, but I doubt he would have got much further than immigration. As far as the Egyptian government was concerned, he was already there!"

A light flicked on, and Ming-Xia's eyes went wide. "So what did you do?" Ming-Xia asked as they turned a corner. They were so close together that their shoulders touched.

"I wish it was more exciting. We had to send his phone via private courier, and get it delivered to his room. We told the concierge to leave it on the dining table if he wasn't there, which of course he wasn't. Once the phone was there, it was easy—the Gateway connected wirelessly, thank god—just a phone call and five steps from my home office to the steps of the pyramids. He flew to Tokyo the next morning."

Ming-Xia nodded, absorbing, strategizing. "So you have a, what did you call it, a gate? You've got one in your office at home?"

"Yep." Brita could guess what was coming next.

"We should all have one set up. It would save a lot of money on flights. And time."

Yes, it would. And keep their meetings well away from prying eyes to boot. "That, Ming-Xia, is a good idea. We'd have to be careful, though. We've already seen how easy it can be to get stuck at one end. And what happens if something goes wrong at an inopportune moment? I'll have to think about it."

The conversation faltered for a moment, Brita recognising in Ming-Xia a familiar faraway look as she followed the chain of possibilities that a fully realised Gateway unlocked. She let her explore just a little longer, whilst mentally checking off her Malaysian to-do list—there was only one item left.

They came to a familiar glass door. Ming-Xia swiped her card, and it swung open, letting them out into the bright, marbled atrium of Peng Industries' downtown Kuala Lumpur HQ. After the cramped, seemingly endless corridors, the wide-open space was a welcome relief. They dropped their coats and glasses with the receptionist, and Brita delved into her briefcase.

"One last thing before I jet off. I've got the equity transfer papers with me, for your review. I thought maybe we could grab a bite to eat and I could take you through them?"

"These?" Ming-Xia plucked them from her hand and rifled through them. "Leave them to my legal team—I'm sure they're fine." She whisked the papers away and handed them to the receptionist, who nodded along to a set of rapid Mandarin instructions.

Brita stood with her hands hanging awkwardly in the air. She'd been expecting more questions. Ming-Xia had grilled her intently last week, demanding details on when and how the transfer would take place. But that was then, before she had a team set up. Before the reality of the Gateway had truly hit home. She'd underestimated, again, just how powerful and distracting the idea of the Gateway was.

"All good?" Ming-Xia asked, and Brita gave a thumbs-up. She was suddenly starving.

"Fantastic. The chef you hired for the dinner party was all right, but he's been out of KL for too long." Ming-Xia ushered her towards the revolving glass door. "Time I showed you some real Malaysian food." She grinned. "I hope you can handle your spice."

Before Brita could respond, Ming-Xia was out the door and down the marble steps. There was nothing for it. She could only follow her out into the humid Kuala Lumpur streets, the smell of chilli and garlic, with a cloying hint of durian, in the air.

28

"So this is the Omniverse, huh?" Mariska asked, gazing out at the very wide, very American flatlands that extended to the horizon in every direction. She could just imagine one of those old cowboys galloping into the sunset, leaving nothing but a trail of dust. The projection from her fancy headset was trying so hard to be reality, but it was just as much a fantasy as Hollywood's idea of the cowboy had been. Solomon's too, for that matter.

She could see why Brita had thought it was just another gimmick.

"It sure is," Solomon said, resting against a virtual fencepost with his virtual hat pulled down against the virtual sun. "Welcome to mah world."

Mariska fought back the temptation to sneer. Was the eye-tracking software good enough to pick that up? To overlay her real expressions onto her avatar's face? She doubted it. But it never hurt to be careful. She hadn't yet been told why she was here. "Thank you for inviting me."

"No trouble. No trouble at all." He pushed himself upright, one thumb hooked through his belt loop, gazing off into the distance with a wistful (or less charitably, glazed) look in his eyes. "Y'know, there was time where ah told mahself the Omniverse was goin' to change the world."

"Oh? What changed your mind?" Mariska asked, the picture of innocence.

He cocked his head to one side, as if to tell her that these sorts of games were beneath her. "Ah think you know."

"Yes, I certainly do. Though you shouldn't complain. You're one of the lucky ones."

"Yeah, ah suppose ah am. Luckier than most." Solomon shot her a look that could only have come from his real eyes. "Luckier than you, maybe. Ah hear you've been on an involuntary vacation."

"I'm not sure where you heard that, Mr Solomon, but I fear you've been misled," Mariska said, batting the unexpected question away. Sure, she and Brita hadn't spoken since that night, out in front of Anita's apartment, but her boss would call soon. She was sure of it.

It was like Solomon said. Brita needed her. The question was, how did he know? And what did he want?

He'd taken a step to one side, looking her up and down. Intellectually, she knew she was standing in the middle of her living room, directing her charm towards the yet to be unpacked moving boxes, stacked in front of the her fireplace. But that's not what she was seeing. Or hearing. The open prairie, the tall grass, swaying in the non-existent breeze. Singing cicadas, the odd howl of a coyote off in the distance. Everything about Solomon's world made her want to move around, as if they were actually sharing the same physical space. She wanted to size him up, just as he was scrutinising her. However, this was his world, not hers. And right now she could not afford to accidentally trip over roll of packing tape..

A cold sweat broke out across the back of her neck. From the grin that had come to dominate Solomon's avatar's face, she understood that her discomfort was by design.

"Misled, you say? Ah thought so too, when ah first heard it. Why would Brita deprive herself of the talents of a crucial resource such as yourself, at such a critical time? It just didn't make sense to me. But then…" He stepped closer, the shadow of his hat covering his eyes. "Your boss always has been afflicted with a strident sense of morality."

And suddenly the mysterious headset that had arrived in the mail, the cryptic handwritten note, this entire awkward exchange: it all made sense. "Is this how you pitch all your prospective employees? Boast about your dishonourable reputation?"

"Ah thought you wanted to make billions of dollars, Mariska."

"Billions? No. Not really."

"No?"

"No." She crossed her arms and locked her knee, kicking her hip out to one side. The move accentuated her chest and her waist, and never failed to make men like Solomon take their eyes off the ball. Then she remembered she was in a simulated reality, that her avatar didn't have curves or bared skin. She dropped her hands back to her side and said it straight. "I want to make trillions."

"And ah'm sure you will," Solomon said in his sleaziest drawl. "Just as long as your boss's conscience doesn't get in the way."

His words, coupled with his avatar's unfocused eyes and too-wide smile, made the skin on the back of her neck pucker and crawl. "Look, Mr Solomon, I appreciate your interest, but…"

"It's more than interest, darlin'. Ah want you on my team, and ah know you'll want to be on mine."

Mariska's phone buzzed in her pocket, and she trembled with relief. She pulled it from her pocket and waved it at him, even though she knew the headset couldn't show him. "I'm sorry, I have to take this. I…I'll be sure to pass your concerns along to Brita."

Solomon stepped back and raised his hand to the brim of his hat. Or, more likely, to the headset he couldn't wait to free himself from. "No, you won't." His avatar gave an awkward, eerie facsimile of a wink. "Ah'll be seein' you, Miss Farkas."

Mariska closed her eyes and ripped the headset from her head, spending a good five seconds working her jaw to free it from the tension of the call. She squeezed the power button for far longer than was necessary and let her phone ring out. For some reason she couldn't quite articulate, she didn't want to answer any calls while the headset was in her hand.

Only when the Omniverse visor was safely buried under a pile of used bubble wrap in the empty spare bedroom did she pull her phone from her pocket. There was one missed call, and one message. Both from Brita.

Brita

> Sorry I haven't called.

> Stubbornness is a blessing we both share, but it can also be a curse. I'll be back in London tomorrow morning.

> We need to talk. Straighten ourselves out.

Mariska slumped onto her couch, Solomon's words, his unspoken offer, still ringing in her ears.

"Yes, Brita," she muttered at the moving boxes, as if she were still in the Omniverse, and two oceans, two entire continents, were no more a barrier to their talking than the walls her boss had put between them had been. "We most certainly do."

——— • ———

Mariska huddled herself into her overcoat against the morning cold and glanced down at the stained fabric seats in the arrivals hall with distaste. Why couldn't Brita fly in a private jet like a normal billionaire? Save *her* having schlub through customs, and save *Mas* having to wait out here with everyone else? She tried not to scowl and failed. Miserably. There would be no need for any of this once Gateway went public.

She pulled out her phone, again. Six a.m. Brita's flight from KL via the United Arab Emirates had landed over half an hour ago. Honestly. How much longer could it take?

"Mariska?"

She jumped at the unexpected sound of Brita's voice. As she stuffed her phone back into her jacket pocket, the shock induced her into greeting her with a shy wave. "Morning, boss, welcome back."

"Morning." Brita fidgeted with the strap on her handbag. "Where's Henry?"

"Sleeping in, I hope." Mariska grinned. All the arguments she'd hashed and re-hashed over the last few weeks melted away. It was good to see her. She reached down and took Brita's luggage from her unsuspecting grip. "Come on, my car's this way."

They exited the main hall, the luggage wheels clicking as they crossed joins in the concrete, slick with early-morning drizzle. Out of the corner of her eye she saw her boss shiver as that first, bracing chill hit her, travelled down her spine. After the humidity of KL, Mariska mused, it would almost be refreshing. A reminder that she was home.

They started onto the pedestrian crossing, just two women out of two dozen. Brita didn't talk, leaving space for Mariska to think. Of Gateway, of her fears and doubts. Of Solomon barging his way through Brita's front door without an invite. Black cabs and buses were lined up bumper to bumper with their headlights shining through the drizzle; Solomon knowing things he shouldn't know. A drab concrete carpark looming in the pre-dawn light; Solomon offering her a job, asking her to betray Brita one more time.

"You know, it always surprises me just how many cars there are in the airport carpark, even this early in the morning," Brita said, finally, as they dodged between a pair of hatchbacks. She stopped, turning back as if to survey the hundreds of cars they'd walked past, and the massive concrete pillars that supported the stories above filled with thousands more. "All this infrastructure, built around this airport. Drop-off points, hotels, freeways. It seems so…unnecessary now. Ming-Xia asked me to set up a Gateway in her office. I think I'm going to do it."

"It's a good idea; you'll be able to avoid the red-eye, at least." Mariska regarded her boss with surprise. What happened to talking? To straightening things out? Or was this it? Back to normal, with no more to be said about it? "You should make the same offer to the others."

Brita nodded. She looked every bit like a woman who'd worked the entire night on the plane and hadn't slept a wink. "No more multi-storey carparks. No more warehouses."

Their eyes met, and Mariska held her gaze for a long moment. Their actions in the coming months would have a profound impact on the world. Deeper and more disruptive than they could possibly imagine....*as long as yer boss's conscience doesn't get in the way...*

Mariska coughed, turned away. Her sleek green Jaguar was only a few bays away. She hefted Brita's suitcase and pulled the key from her pocket. A flash of orange, a mechanical thunk. She dumped the suitcase into the boot, then sat on its open edge, staring wistfully up at the ceiling.

"It is a bit sad, imagining a busy place like this empty and abandoned," Mariska said, deciding to follow her boss's lead. Letting her make the first move for once. Brita joined her on the lip of the boot. Together they eyed the rough lines of the concrete plinths, concrete beams, galvanised steel trusses, and exposed ducting, all brought into sharp relief by the harsh fluorescent lighting. "Though I don't know that anyone will miss this carpark in particular."

"No, perhaps not." Brita fidgeted with her phone, flipping it end over end. "But so much of our daily life is built around getting from place to place. Who knows what we'll miss when that drive, that need, is taken away for good?"

There were talking points for questions like this. Mariska had prepared them months ago. She knew them by heart: Gateway will eliminate the daily commute. Fewer cars means fewer emissions, fewer crashes. But Brita already knew the talking points. Where was this coming from? Solomon's leering eyes swam up from the depths, unbidden.

She pushed him away.

"Brita, you told me to think, and I have. I thought about the Gateway, and about what will change once it's ready. I've lived through drastic change before. The wall fell just after I was born, and 'freedom' came to Hungary. It swallowed my mother and crushed my father. They didn't want it. Weren't ready for it. I only just made it out before it got me too.

"Looking back, seeing what Hungary was, what she is turning back into...I know many people who think that the time of the wolf, my childhood, was a golden era. And who knows, maybe it was. Gateway will be like that, I think. It will be good. But there will be casualties. They just won't be people like you." Very deliberately, Mariska said *you*, not *us*. Billionaires would be fine; they always were.

They both watched on as a mother and daughter, chatting happily, loaded the daughter's ragged backpack into their car and slid a brightly adorned "Welcome Home" placard in behind it. The mother clamped her daughter in the kind of hug that only came from months spent apart. Or years. Decades.

Mariska looked away, pushing Miskolc back to the past, where it belonged.

"Brita, I need you to understand that no matter how pure your intentions are, how clean you try to keep your hands, there will always be casualties. You can't just look away and pretend they don't exist."

The mother and daughter broke apart, hopped into their car. Lights flicked on, the engine revved, and they drove away. Mariska studied her boss's expression, watched it harden as the taillights disappeared into the distance.

"You're right, of course. You usually are. I think I knew it, too, at the time, though I didn't realise it until Ming-Xia told me the exact same thing. Different words, of course, but the message—" Brita was bent over, her elbows pressed into her knees. Out of nowhere, a sardonic twist crept up and overtook her smile. "You know what? She wasn't even the first!"

"She wasn't?"

Brita shook her head. "No. It was Jorge. He called me out on it on live TV. Jesus." She pressed her palms into her cheeks and let out a long, exhausted sigh. "I'm sorry I kept you in the dark for so long. It's been a hectic couple of weeks, and I need your help."

"Thanks," Mariska said, a wave of relief washing over her. She hadn't wanted Solomon to be right. "And for what it's worth, I'm sorry for going behind your back."

"Thank you. I appreciate it. Like I said, I need you calling me out on my bullshit. We're a team—we can't afford for either one of us to go off on our own. We'll have enough trouble keeping my father, and our five new backers, in line as it is.

"So. All our cards, out on the table from now on. No more secret resentments," Brita said, standing up, holding out her hand. "Deal?"

"Deal," Mariska said, gritting her teeth and sealing it with a shake not quite firm enough to dispel the uneasy feeling that lingered in her stomach. That had been the moment to tell Brita about Solomon's approach. His warning. That she knew he was up to something.

But she hadn't. She couldn't.

Because she wasn't like Brita, like Hugo. She had no plan B. If it all went wrong, there would be casualties. And she couldn't afford to be one of them.

29

STANLEY'S WATCHING POST WASN'T exactly secret. Just hidden. He never slouched, never lounged. He listened, and he observed. Four monitors projected a green glow into the dark, making his thin hands seem skeletal. It was a pity no one ever saw him in here. His thinness unnerved people, made them think of a starving man, willing to do anything. What would they imagine was in his heart if he was also tinged with green?

Two rooms over, his boss was meeting with his silent business partner. There were three of them, three dangerous men. Yosip and Gustav had Eastern European muscles, the kind that bulged from within fitted gunmetal grey suits. The third, smaller and older, proved that a reputation could be far more intimidating. Volodymyr Uvorvykishki was listening intently. Leaning forward.

Volodymyr was not the kind of man that leaned forward. He tended between accepting and displeased. Occasionally angry, very rarely violent. Stanley had made sure the footage from that day had been promptly deleted. That kind of leverage was too dangerous.

Of the four screens, two showed internal views of the penthouse apartment—the main dining area and the bedroom. A third showed the hallway leading from the elevator. The final screen gave a view of the hotel lobby and had recently become the focus of Stan's attention.

A sharply dressed man had just taken a seat in the lobby café, given his order, and opened his laptop. Long black hair, a fashionable beard. Stanley looked, then looked again. No, surely not. He couldn't be that stupid.

Stanley pulled his phone from his pocket and scrolled back to the photos Yosip had taken outside the Gundersson daughter's apartment. Jorge Elorza, scruffy, nondescript. Blending into the Mayfair streets in jeans and a rumpled jacket. A far cry from the dapper "businessman" who sat with his legs crossed, sipping his latte. However, there was no mistaking the thick black eyebrows, the strong lip. The overconfidence.

Stanley rolled his eyes at the back of his boss's head. "I told you the warning wasn't enough."

Last time Elorza had interfered, they'd ruined his reputation and left him with an understanding: you come near us again, and you'll lose more than your goddamn career. Stanley shook his head. He was a man who just refused to learn his lesson.

— · —

Solomon's phone vibrated on the oak tabletop, face down. He glanced across with what he hoped looked like mild annoyance. He'd set his phone to do not disturb, and for good reason. This pitch was too important. It buzzed once, twice, then silence. A repeat would mean wrap it up and take the rear exit. And Stanley would only make such a call in an emergency.

"A problem, Richard?" Volodymyr asked. His dull-eyed goons were suddenly alert, and yet worryingly relaxed.

The phone buzzed again: once, then twice. Solomon checked Stanley's message, and a grimace flashed across his features. There was no text, just a photo. It told him everything he needed to know. "Gentlemen, ah'm afraid our favourite member of the press has just arrived downstairs. Prudence would advise we cut this short." But not so short that Solomon couldn't ask the question he'd been building up to this last half hour. This last month. "Might ah suggest you prepare to evacuate via mah private elevator, direct to the carpark?"

"Your Spanish friend?" Volodymyr's eyebrows rose, just barely, in a way that made Solomon's teeth itch. He knew how Volodymyr preferred to deal with journalists that strayed where they weren't welcome. "What an unpleasant coincidence. Perhaps Yosip should invite him up for a little chat, yes?"

Solomon's phone buzzed again. Another screenshot, of Elorza deep in discussion with a young man, a recording device on the table between them. Behind Volodymyr's shoulder, Yosip's right hand had already slipped inside his jacket.

"Ah would advise against chargin' in all guns blazin' right at this juncture." Solomon flicked his tongue briefly between his teeth to moisten his lips. "Mr Elorza is currently interviewin' one of this establishment's less discreet staff members. In full view of the security cameras."

"You control the security cameras, no?"

"Up here, sure. But the lobby?" Solomon shook his head. "Besides, there are witnesses. And he knows it. If he sees Yosip, or Gustav here, advancin' on him with their concrete jaws and bulgin' armpits, he'll holler like a stuck pig."

"I see." Volodymyr looked down his nose at him, as he would any of his underlings when they exposed their vulnerable necks. The fact Solomon was richer than Volodymyr a dozen times over, that he had contacts in the halls of power that Volodymyr could never dream of, meant less than nothing. Volodymyr had the only kind of power that mattered. Knowledge, and the willingness to use it. "You want us to keep low profile, yes? Until Gundersson business is settled?"

"Yessir, I do. Her father spooks easy, and we need them eager until it's too late."

"Then we keep low profile. But in return I need results. I want this 'Gateway' in my hand. And I do not like to wait."

"Who does?" Solomon attempted a placating smile. "And the journalist..."

"Journalist is your problem now, yes?" Volodymyr said with finality. And what could Solomon do? He'd said he wanted a low profile. This was low profile. "Good. Gustav, prepare the exit."

Volodymyr stood to leave. He was a full foot shorter than Solomon, and yet he managed to fill the room with malice. This was not how his moment of freedom had played out in his mind. But it was the only moment he had.

"Before you go, Volodymyr. Ah wanted to ask..." His voice wavered, and he rammed the obstruction rising in his throat right back where it had come from. "When it is done, if we could renegotiate our arrangement..."

"That will be discussed after, not before." Volodymyr's eyes glinted with menace. Then, as quickly as the sun bursting from behind a cloud, his face broke into a beatific smile. He offered his manicured hand over the table. "You give me much to think about, Richard. My doubts, all but forgotten." The smile hardened, and Solomon's fingers were suddenly trapped in a vise. "I can trust you to resolve, yes?"

"As always, Mr Uvorvykishki." Solomon refused to acknowledge the pain, holding Volodymyr's gaze for as long was necessary, and a beat or two longer.

"Good." Volodymyr pulled away. "Gustav?"

"All clear, boss!" Gustav called from the elevator.

"I will see you soon." Volodymyr nodded, then paused, a thoughtful finger on his chin belying the violence that had only moments ago burned in his eyes. "Within a week, if freedom from my friendship is your truest desire."

Solomon held his breath while his earliest, most loyal, and most dangerous investor disappeared around the corner, leaving only the sound of his Italian leather shoes on the polished floorboards. *One week. Jesus Christ.* He didn't breathe again until the elevator doors closed and the lighted indicator spiralled downwards. He stepped across to the window and gazed out over the London cityscape, at the slow, turgid water of the river Thames. Behind him, a door clicked gently closed.

"You heard all that?"

"I did, sir."

"And what do you think?"

A long pause, followed by a cough, which told Solomon all he needed to know. "I think we should deal with one problem at a time."

Elorza. Solomon cursed his smug, self-important existence. "Stanley, why in the heck didn't we eliminate the jerk-off when we had the chance?"

"Because killing a Pulitzer-nominated journalist planning to accuse us of being financed by the Ukrainian mob might indicate that we were, in fact, financed by the Ukrainian mob."

"Hard to argue with logic like that." He winced and swivelled on the spot. Stanley was lurking in the no-man's land between the dining table and his secret alcove. "And you reckon this time he was followin' Brita long before he cottoned on to us?"

"So?"

"So. Do you think he's more interested in us, or in her?"

Stanley's eyes lost focus, then hardened with understanding. When he spoke, it was through a clenched jaw. "What do you want me to do?"

"Wait for him to finish his interview, and then..." And then? Could Elorza actually be useful? No one would ever suspect, not with their history... He grinned; he couldn't help himself. If he could pull this off, he would never have to deal with Volodymyr and his thugs ever again.

"Sir?"

"Invite him up. And don't take no for an answer."

▬ • ▬

Jorge knew his latte glass was empty, but still he raised it to his lips, only to settle it back onto its saucer. It was the nerves. He couldn't help himself.

The security guard that he'd lined up for his "interview" was his friend from the Robard debacle a month or so back. His name was Jonathan, twenty-nine, in the final year of his anthropology PhD and eager to leave hospitality behind for good. He'd started by slapping his palm on the marble tabletop and declaring that what Robard had done was nothing, and then proceeded with dishing the most outrageous gossip. Tales that would have had Roger and his collection of cretins and leeches positively salivating. And yet, Jorge had spent every second of it with half an eye over Jonathan's shoulder, wondering what the hell had gotten into him.

What am I doing here? What am I playing at?

Sitting at his new desk late last night, flicking back and forward between the photographs of Yosip outside Brita's apartment, and Yosip cutting deals in Panama, walking right into Solomon's den, taunting him with his presence, with his refusal to go quietly, had seemed like an excellent idea. He wouldn't dare do anything in his hotel. There were too many cameras.

But then Jonathan had started talking, and he'd noticed the man in the three-piece suit, slate grey, sitting at a table half-obscured by one of the Savoy's thick, sturdy columns. He had a moustache. A cane. And he kept looking this way. Was his position—back to the elevators, perfect view of the entrance and the fire exits—a coincidence? Had he been recognised? Was the man another of Solomon's goons? Another Ukrainian hitman with a lump of cold metal death tucked inside his jacket?

He gripped his empty glass, fighting the urge to take yet another empty sip. Jonathan giggled at his own anecdote, his lightweight prattle barely registering. There had to be a better way. A way that didn't poke the bear, that would allow him to continue his investigation without putting himself at risk.

He had to get out of here.

"Jonathan..."

"Please, Jorge." He smiled, his northern curl somehow negotiating the rolled *r* and breathy *g*. "If I've told you once, I've told you a thousand times. I'm Jon. Now where was I—"

Jorge clasped his hands on the round tabletop. "This is fantastic stuff, great colour, and I'm loath to interrupt while you're in the middle of a yarn, but what time did you have to get back? I don't want to get you into trouble."

"Oh, it's no trouble at all. None at all. I've got at least another..." He rolled his wrist over and checked his watch. "Oh my lord, would you look at that? You're absolutely right. I'd best get moving or Mr Langhorn will have my guts for garters, so he will."

"Though it would make quite a story if he did," Jorge said, forcing a smile as he sprang to his feet, his hands instinctively brushing the crumbs from his lunchtime croissant to the black-and-white tiled floor.

"Hah! No wonder the brass told me to keep my eye on you." Jonathan wagged his finger playfully, and then hunched back down and dropped his voice to a whisper. Well, to a volume that constituted a whisper for him, at any rate. "Now. When should I be keeping an eye on the tellie?"

"Friday night at nine p.m., about three weeks from now," Jorge said. Anything to get rid of him. He started gathering his things: pen, notebook, camera. "Now go on, old Langhorn's waiting."

Finally he sauntered off, and Jorge shot another lightning glance at the slate-grey suit. Was it just him, or had he looked away just then? Averted his gaze? He lifted his satchel to his lap, unzipped it, and—

"Going somewhere?" A hand landed on his shoulder, and Jorge squeaked with surprise. "But Jorge, my friend, you've only just arrived. And we haven't seen one another in such a long time."

The pressure on his shoulder released, and recognition was followed swiftly by dread. He didn't dare move, didn't dare breathe. Instinct, though, allowed him to drop his recorder into his satchel.

Stanley Adams, Solomon's chief fixer, stepped out from behind him and dropped into Jonathan's still-warm chair. Jorge reached for his phone, but Stanley was too quick. With a flick of his wrist, he slipped the battery out of Jorge's phone and placed the pieces flat atop the table.

Jorge swallowed.

Well, you wanted a reaction. Here it fucking is.

He bit the inside of his cheek and forced himself to keep his eyes on Stanley's. Deep set, almost sunken. He knew he wouldn't be able to keep his voice from shaking, but he had to say something. "Been watching long, Stan?"

Stanley's lips twitched slightly when Jorge used the shortened version of his name, and a small chunk of the ice at the base of Jorge's spine began to melt.

"A little while." Stanley was gaunt, a mottled grey goatee concealing a thin chin. When he smiled, you could see all his teeth, his gums stretched far too tight. It was not a pleasant sight. "Long enough to know you've had three coffees, and your friend had the almond croissant. What did he think of it, do you know?"

Jorge laughed, in spite of himself. "He said there was no way it was worth eight pounds, but when a man from the 'tellie' is paying, you don't say no." With every word he felt a little better, a little stronger. This was just another interview. Just another nut to crack. "You look like you could use a croissant or two yourself, actually. You've lost weight, Stan. Solomon working you too hard?"

Stanley, unsurprisingly, ignored him. "My employer invites you upstairs for a conversation." His manner was diplomatic, but his eyes belied a cold menace. Jorge got the impression that Stanley would prefer they took a little drive. A drive to somewhere a mite more secluded.

"Is that so? Now, why would he want to do that?" He stretched, giving himself a chance to eye his recorder. Confirm that yes, it was still rolling. He leaned back in his chair. *What's your game, Stanley Adams?* "The Richard Solomon I know would sooner cut off a finger than invite me up for 'a conversation.'"

"That, *amigo*, is a question for the boss." Stanley stood, grabbed Jonathan's crumpled serviette, and tossed it into the nearby bin. As a display of dexterity, it was impressive. As cover for frustration at being just as in the dark as Jorge, it was not quite so effective.

So, Solomon wants to talk, and Stanley would rather I stayed far away, strongly enough that he's let it slip. Jorge couldn't yet see how to use this to his advantage, but it was useful information nonetheless.

"Come on. The boss doesn't have all day." Stanley started back towards the penthouse lift. Jorge didn't move. What was Stanley going to do? They were, quite purposefully, in full view of the security cameras. A far cry from his bout of nerves not five minutes ago, he even ventured to flash the slate-grey suit a knowing wink.

"I'm quite comfortable here, Stan. Richard is more than welcome to pull up a chair, just as you did, if he wants to talk."

Stanley swivelled on the spot, his black boots sliding soundlessly on the tiled floor. Jorge saw that his lips had slipped into a menacing skeletal grin. The kind of grin that said *Please, keep pushing. Just give me an excuse.*

"I apologise, Jorge, if I didn't make myself clear. Mr Solomon would very much appreciate it if you'd join him upstairs for a *private* conversation." As he spoke, Stanley let his jacket fall open, revealing the butt of a pistol, holstered beneath his left armpit.

The message was crystal clear.

Jorge didn't let his smile falter, but his heart was pounding in his chest. *You're fine,* he told himself. *There are cameras in the lobby, in the lift, in the hallway. The gun is just a threat. They can't actually do anything.* He bowed, as graciously as he could, and rose from his seat. As casually as he could, he swung his satchel over his shoulder, still unzipped, the still-running recorder just visible inside.

"No need to apologise, Stan. I'm more than happy to oblige." Silently, Jorge prayed. Something he hadn't done for a very long time. Then, unexpectedly, he smiled. A long-forgotten memory, flooding back.

Stanley noticed the smile in the mirrored finish of the elevator doors. For some reason it appeared to annoy him. "Did I say something funny, Mr. Elorza?"

"I was just thinking of my mother. She was a devout Catholic, you know. Always at mass, always disappointed that I didn't go with her. Anyway, she was always telling me to be careful with my prayers." He gave Stanley a sidelong glance. "'Jorge,' she said. 'You never show Him the proper respect. You neglect Him. One day, when you need Him most, maybe he neglects you. Maybe he answers your selfish prayers in a way you don't expect.'"

30

Jorge hesitated at the threshold of Solomon's private suite, half expecting to feel cold steel pressed into the small of his back, but unable to stop himself. The ornate handle was cold, a shock against his adrenaline-hot skin. He hadn't, knowingly, been this close to his nemesis for well over a decade.

"Go on through. It's open," Stanley urged, his voice little more than a hiss.

The handle turned far too easily.

Solomon stood with his back turned, gazing across Victoria Embankment to Waterloo Bridge and the Thames Beach beyond. The penthouse apartment was sparsely appointed, and all the more elegant for it. It would bankrupt him to stay here for just one night, let alone book it out permanently on the off chance that he was making a trip to London.

"Ah imagine this is an unexpected turn of events for you," Solomon drawled. He didn't turn around.

"The unexpected tends to follow me around, I find," Jorge said, trying to recapture some of the confidence he'd felt in the lobby. It didn't work. It was one thing, bantering with Stan in public. It was quite another standing halfway between two enemies, one with the power to end his career all over again, and the other with a pistol in his back. The door closed with a soft click, and he flinched. He wished he had eyes in the back of his head.

"And here ah was thinkin' the exact same thing. It's quite a talent, ah suppose, to turn up where you're not wanted."

Jorge continued forward, intending to reach out and shake Solomon's hand. What else could he do? Five steps away the hairs on the back of his neck tingled a warning. This close, but no closer. Jorge listened to his gut.

"Stanley, would you mind organisin' a drink for our guest?" Solomon, finally, deigned to turn and face him. They were no more than ten feet apart.

"Just a glass of water please, Stan," Jorge called over his shoulder. *If Solomon doesn't need to turn, neither do I.* He was in no way sure that annoying Stan was a good idea, but he always followed his hunches, for better or worse. Stanley's footsteps receded behind him. For the moment, there was only one enemy he had to face. "I hope I haven't 'turned up' at an inconvenient time. I didn't interrupt anything, did I?"

"Why don't you take a seat." Solomon's face was as fixed as stone. It wasn't a question.

"I'll stand, thanks. I don't plan on staying," Jorge shot back. He had no option but to play into his persona. If Solomon thought he was worried, he was done for. With a swallow, he set his satchel atop the seat he was offered and stepped forward, joining Solomon at the window. "This is a lovely view." He nodded over to the palace. "Can't come cheap."

"A small price to pay for privacy." Solomon clasped his hands behind his back. They stood shoulder to shoulder. Man to man. "Now what is it, ah wonder, that brings you to mah doorstep? You were warned, quite clearly if ah recall, what would happen if ah caught you stickin' your nose in where it doesn't belong."

Solomon let the words hang between them, a reminder. As if he'd forgotten.

"Your doorstep? I was just conducting an interview, when Skeletor over there bailed me up and 'encouraged' me into the elevator. I didn't even know you were in London. Trust me, I've no desire to do any further digging around the skeletons in *your* closet."

"Is that so? Your...nocturnal exploits would suggest otherwise."

"Ah," Jorge said, thinking fast. He only had so many cards, and he had no time to decide what to show, and what to hold in reserve. "Well, yes, I can see how that might have given you a certain impression, but I can assure you I was just as surprised to see you there as you must have been to see me." He was rambling. *Wrap it up, Jorge.* "I was just following the story."

"A coincidence, you say?" Solomon raised an eyebrow. "Well, don't leave me hangin', boy. What's the story?"

He gulped, buying time as he chose his partial truth. A punt trundled along the water below, pushing valiantly upriver, against the wind. "A follow-up to my interview with Brita Gundersson. I'm sure you saw it." He risked a glance at his adversary, but Solomon's profile was unreadable. "I'd heard rumours of a private dinner, that she and her estranged father had suddenly gotten back together, that they had something to wow new investors. The timing seemed suspicious." He shrugged, as if lying in wait outside a billionaire's house was just a part of the job. "I wanted to see what shook out."

"Plausible." Solomon turned away from the view, a vicious gleam in his eyes. "But that doesn't explain why you're here right now."

Jorge floundered. He couldn't tell Solomon what he knew about Yosip. About Panama. The silence stretched, only to be broken by a clatter from behind. Jorge whipped his head around a little too fast to see Stan place a serving tray on the polished teak dining table. Two glasses, cloudy with condensation, accompanied by a bottle of Perrier.

"Thank you, Stanley."

The rest of the sentence, that Stanley's presence was no longer required, remained unsaid. With a snarl, he backed away. Jorge didn't exhale until they were alone once more.

Neither of them moved. He knew that both glasses would remain untouched. The tension in his spine returned, as if it had never left. Solomon radiated the icy calm of a man in charge. His heartbeat thumped in his ear canals so loudly he was sure Solomon could hear it. They both knew who would break first.

"We're following up on the Britannia leaks—"

"We?" Another raised eyebrow, another deadly smile. "Ah thought you'd found your calling in 'entertainment news'? If you can even call it news, that is. It suited you."

"I got a new gig. Back in the bullpen."

"Is that so." Solomon nodded, as if he didn't already know. As if he hadn't been having him followed. Hadn't already sent him a warning, to his office. "Lucky."

"Lucky? Why lucky?" Something in Solomon's voice, his demeanour, made Jorge turn from the window. Since Stanley had strong-armed him through the door, since he'd sat down in the over-plush lobby chairs with Jonathan, he'd been thinking, *Why am I here?* Now the question carried a slight, but significant, twist. *Why has he brought me here?*

A smile spread across Solomon's lips, one that did not reach his eyes. Jorge fought every instinct in his body that wanted to glance back at the recorder, silently listening in his satchel. He nodded.

"You're goin' to write a story for me."

"Am I now?" Jorge raised his eyebrows. Ten years ago, Solomon had killed his stories. And his career. "That would be quite the reversal of fortunes."

"Yeah, well. You did say that the unexpected follows you around."

"I did, didn't I. But I don't write on spec." Jorge's tongue was dry. He glanced over at the table, at the dripping glasses of water just sitting there untouched. But to admit that he needed to drink it would be to concede defeat. He stood with his back to the unoccupied corner of the room. He couldn't afford have Stanley sneak up on him. Or Yosip, for that matter. "Not for crooks like you, anyway."

"Ah see." Solomon shrugged. "Then it seems Stanley will finally get his wish..."

Jorge swallowed. "Though I suppose it wouldn't hurt to hear you out."

"That's more like it. It's right up yer alley, too. Insider tradin'. Fraud." Solomon allowed himself a dramatic pause. "Blackmail."

Jorge kept his expression neutral, but he remembered the succession of guests leaving Brita's apartment in various states of shock. "I assume you're talking about Brita. About the dinner party."

"Ah am."

"It hardly seems her style." He remembered Richard Solomon, last one to leave, practically dancing up the steps in the moonlight. Whatever she'd tried on him, it hadn't worked. He stole a glance at Solomon, studied his expression. Slightly strained, as if he'd been forced into this position. Something had changed. Had Brita turned the tables? Or had Solomon's Ukrainian financier started making demands? "I hope you've got some evidence to back it up."

Without a word, Solomon drew a folded sheaf of paper from his breast pocket. He hesitated. "You know who ah'm friends with. What they'd normally do with an...inconvenience like you."

"Is that a threat?" Jorge stayed firm, refusing to recoil. In his mind his fingers were crossed so tight that his hand actually hurt as he prayed that his recorder could hear every word.

"It's a reminder of what ah saved you from, last time our paths crossed," Solomon said, and a shudder rolled slowly down Jorge's spine. "But, as it so happens, today we have a common interest."

Solomon extended his hand; the papers were within Jorge's reach. Evidence of whatever it was that had gone on behind Brita's door. Evidence that he'd yearned for, that would form the centrepiece of the story that would get him back in the big leagues. And yet, he couldn't take it. Not from him. How could he trust it?

"Why me? I've read the latest little puff pieces. Sure, you're a little banged up right now, but there are plenty of sycophants out there, willing to write anything you want. I bet they don't even cost that much."

Solomon's eyes narrowed, crow's feet crawling out across his temple. "Jorge fuckin' Elorza. Always askin' questions. You're a stubborn SOB, you know that?" There was a tension underneath his frustration that Jorge couldn't quite place. "Why you? Because if you write it, no one will think it came from me.

"Sure, ah took you down, but that was a long time ago, and it was just business. Well, so's this." Solomon waved the paperwork in his face. "This, right here, is your ticket out of the bullpen. Everything you need to expose her. Ah know you want to break this fuckin' story. Hell, you don't camp outside an old man's house for weeks on end for fun. So do it." A fleck of spittle escaped Solomon's lips, and it seemed to ground him, pull him back. He jerked his shoulders and cricked his neck, shaking his jacket back into place. "The minute you do, Jorge, the *Times*, the *Post*—they'll be beating down your door. Ah guarantee it."

Jorge caught himself edging away from the window, using the ferocity of Solomon's desperation as an excuse. "The *Post*? You mean the newspaper you own?"

"Name a paper. Ah don't care which one, it's yours. Ah just need you to put the bitch back in her place."

Jorge had reached the chair that held his satchel, his recorder. Solomon had followed him, thrusting the papers in his face. "So that's your angle? Revenge?" Jorge said, knowing there was so much more to it than that, but not wanting to tip Solomon off. "I could work with that. Secret meetings, billionaire investors, and, according to you, criminal activity. It's a story that needs to be told."

"Here then, take it." Solomon pressed the papers against his chest.

Jorge brushed them aside and pulled his briefcase in close. "But it's a story that needs to be told *whole*. No convenient omissions. You're too important a character to leave out." He backed away. "I don't take shortcuts anymore, Solomon. I learned that lesson the hard way."

He turned on his heel, striding towards the exit, the slightly too rapid steps betraying the panic exploding through his every muscle. He didn't know where he would go, what he would do next, but that was a problem for five seconds' time. Right now, he just had to make it to the door.

"Stanley," Richard called out, and a dark shape materialised from the shadows by the door. A dark shape holding a gun, the midnight hole of its barrel aimed directly at his chest. "Ah think our guest needs a little extra encouragement."

Jorge froze. His breath came in short, sharp bursts. The gun didn't waver. He stared longingly at the door handle, just out of reach. He had only one card to play.

"Stan, I'm going to reach, very slowly, into this front pocket here. And then you're going to put the gun down and let me go."

"I don't think so." Stanley jutted his chin, his eyes ablaze, unwilling to give up this unexpected chance for payback.

"You will, because I've been recording the entire time." Jorge raised his voice, no longer worried at his quaking tremor. As he pulled the recorder out, he flicked the Bluetooth switch, and a steady blue light joined the blinking red. His gaze never left Stan's eyes. He raised the recorder above his head, making sure that both lights were visible to all. A bead of sweat trickled down his cheek, ending in a burst of salt on the corner of his lips. He tapped the blue light with his thumb. "Every word, every threat, every admission, uploaded direct to the cloud. Where anyone on my team can access it."

Suddenly uncertain, Stanley flicked a questioning glance over Jorge's shoulder. "He's lying."

"I'm not, but you don't know that, do you? Not for sure." He saw Stanley's gaze jerk upwards, to the recorder. To the blue light that, as far as they knew, was his salvation. "Best case, you're right. You shoot me and that's the end of it—I mean, apart from having to explain why Stan was the last person to see me alive. Worst case?" The moment stretched, Jorge's nerves fraying by the millisecond. He stared at the gun barrel and tried to imagine it was a camera lens. All he was doing was talking to his audience. "You've just broadcast my murder to some of the best journalists in the world."

"What's uploaded can be deleted." Solomon spoke from behind, his voice ice cold.

"You know that's not true." Jorge's mouth was dry, but it was all or nothing. "Data's a funny thing. It never really disappears, does it. Especially in the cloud. I mean, you would know, right? Stockpiling data's your game."

He strained his ears, listening out for the smallest of sounds, anything to indicate whether his gambit had worked. Stan, rage contorting his gaunt features, looked askance at his boss. He didn't dare blink, and his vision narrowed to Stan's eyes, the gun, and the door-handle. For a fraught second, he saw Stan consider shooting him anyway, consequences be damned.

The tiniest rustle from behind, by the window, so small that Jorge would never have heard it but for the adrenaline coursing through his veins. A signal. Stanley cursed and stepped to one side, his features pure malice. A look that said *This is far from over*.

But in that moment, Jorge didn't care. Graceless, barely holding it together, Jorge bolted through the door and out into the empty corridor. Solomon's door shut behind him with a sinister click.

31

A TIRED AIR CONDITIONER rattled away against the wall of the Pridha Laboratories security hut, valiantly failing to cool the small room even one degree. Sweat seeped from Mariska's every pore. Her blouse was damp on her back; her skirt had suctioned onto her thighs. To make matters worse, she was squeezed in beside Hugo on a plastic bench seat not quite big enough for two people. Hugo ran a finger between his neck and his starched collar, and Mariska shuddered. At least she didn't have to wear a suit and tie.

A fly buzzed from surface to surface, unthreatened by the security guard's laconic swipes. There was no conversation; it was just too hot. Not that Mariska minded. She'd expected Hugo to be on her side, given the work they'd put into planning his Gateway's private debut, given how rapid progress had been since that night. Instead he was even more standoffish than usual. More paranoid.

And in the back of her mind, Solomon's offer, and his warning, festered.

Hugo was probably right to be paranoid.

The security guard glanced up—out of habit, Mariska guessed, rather than by design. His eyes bulged, and he leapt to attention while sliding his phone out of sight under a haphazard stack of papers. His chair teetered on its back legs before toppling over. He ignored it, instead stuffing his sweat-stained shirt into his belt.

She followed his gaze to find Sandeep Pridha striding across the tarmac towards the tiny shelter. *About bloody time.*

"Finally," Hugo muttered under his breath. The bench seat lurched as he struggled upright, mopping his brow with a pristine handkerchief. Not that it did much good. His new wardrobe, a stark contrast to the dishevelled loner he'd presented as a mere two months ago, just wasn't suited to the Kolkata climate.

She smoothed out the wrinkles in her skirt, standing as Sandeep slid open the glass door, ramming it against the stopper. He hurled a flurry of Bengali at the security guard, a reprimand most likely, and turned to them with an agitated smile.

"My sincerest apologies for the wait. Welcome to Kolkata." He slapped his left hand down onto the security guard's desk and shook the fly's remains from his fingertips with disgust. Mariska stepped forward, offering her hand in greeting. He ignored it, brushing right by to shake Hugo's instead.

"A pleasure, Mr Pridha, I can assure you." Hugo dodged the handshake, instead clapping him on the shoulder. "I'm sure you remember Ms Farkas. She's leading our delegation until my daughter arrives."

Sandeep's eyes flicked from Hugo's ruddy, smiling face to hers. His gaze travelled down her body, then back up. Trying to reconcile her sweaty, slightly flustered countenance with the shimmering golden goddess he'd been unable to take his eyes off that night in Cairo, perhaps? A fraction too late, he broke out his best charming grin. "Of course, Mariska. How could I forget?"

She accepted his hand with gritted teeth. "Kolkata is a beautiful city, if a little warmer than we are accustomed to."

A prim smile, and a turn back to Hugo. To the man. "We get that a lot. Is your esteemed daughter far away?"

"She was held up in London. Nothing serious, but she ended up having to take a later flight." Mariska could see the question in Sandeep's mind before he asked it. "She doesn't believe in private aircraft." Mariska shrugged. She couldn't understand it either, not with so much on the line.

"A problem that will no longer exist, if our work here is successful."

"Exactly right, young man. Exactly," Hugo said, and, with a heavy arm across Sandeep's shoulders, directed him towards the facility. "Shall we?"

Sandeep nodded graciously—well, as graciously as he could under Hugo's determination to get indoors—and waved them onwards. Mariska mouthed Hugo her thanks before following him out into the harsh morning sun. The modest office building obscured the vast research and production facilities operating beyond. Now that they were out in the open, the hum of extraction fans, of heavy machinery, was obvious.

As they followed a manicured garden path, the difference between the security hut and the office was stark—crisp lines, muted blue and white tones. Cool air. Mariska shivered as she crossed the threshold into the climate-controlled environment, her sweat-soaked blouse suddenly chilly on her back. Past reception with a swipe of a security card, they were among scores of young, well-dressed workers, spaced out across an open-plan office. The dull roar of machinery was no longer audible. This was a quiet place, where serious, industrious, diligent work was done.

"Please, this way." Sandeep guided them into a long corridor. "This is our design hub. I've collected some of the best and brightest Indian minds. Some I even poached back from Omni. Don't tell Mr Solomon." He flashed an overly cheerful grin.

"Divya and her team have been working round the clock to get the prototype rig up and running."

"We certainly appreciate the effort, Sandeep. It's progressed much quicker than even I had anticipated." Mariska glanced across at Hugo. Their argument over bringing in Sandeep for his vulnerability and ambition, or one of the Taiwanese chip manufacturers for their track record and expertise, had been the most heated. And yet again she'd been proven right. Sometimes it felt like she was the only one who actually wanted the Gateway to succeed. "We are very much looking forward to meeting Divya; she's done a remarkable job."

"Yes. I'm rather keen to discover just how she's managed to solve the stability problems with the updated microchip design," Hugo said.

Sandeep wrung his hands, "I'm afraid Divya is unavailable. A flu of some kind." Something uncertain flashed across his features. "You'll have to put up with me filling in as your tour guide."

"That's a shame. Please convey our thanks, and our hope that she recovers soon," Mariska said. Was that flash something more? Or just nerves at having to speak on matters Sandeep knew Hugo understood better than he. Mariska pursed her lips. It would explain why they'd been left waiting in that tin hut for so damn long. "I hope you're ready for a barrage of questions—I've never known Hugo to hold back."

"I'll do what I can." He didn't look confident, but still. The question lingered in the back of Mariska's mind, like so many had since her conversation with Solomon. Doubts that just wouldn't go away.

Sandeep guided them to a small anteroom, adjacent to what looked like the main entrance to the factory floor. "Please, take a seat."

Slim grey lockers lined three of the windowless walls, and brushed stainless steel benches formed an island in the centre. Along the fourth wall, racks carried rows of sterile white overalls. The room had an uncomfortable feel, as if it were both a locker room and an operating theatre. The skin on the back of Mariska's thighs puckered as her damp skirt touched the cold steel benchtop.

"With your daughter's delay, and Divya's unplanned absence, I've taken the liberty of adjusting this morning's schedule. Just through this door is our principal microchip production facility. We've both got a lot on the line with the Gateway project, so while we're waiting, I'd like to show you what we can do."

She watched him as he spoke. Sandeep's lips twitched minutely, and was he avoiding her gaze? Or just focusing on Hugo because they were both men? Because they were both technical people, and she was not?

"What that means, of course, is that we'll need somewhat of a costume change. The entire factory floor is a clean room—no dust. And that's where these come in." He patted the closest rack, the overalls swaying from side to side at his touch.

Ah, Mariska realised. He just didn't want to get caught thinking about her taking her clothes off.

"Fantastic," Hugo said, oblivious to the subtext, as always. "It's been years since I've inspected a microchip plant, and from what I've seen over the last few weeks—my old suppliers are a little behind the cutting edge. I'm intrigued to see the advancements you've made." He grinned across at her. "This'll be just like the old days."

"I wasn't around in the old days, Hugo."

"True, true," Hugo said, his voice trailing off. Perhaps wondering just what the old days would have been like if she had.

"We pack just over a billion transistors per chip these days. How much bigger did they used to be?"

Hugo raised an eyebrow in her direction. "Sandeep, I started in radio manufacturing in the sixties. If you were good with a soldering iron, you might have been able to fit two or maybe three onto one of your chips."

Sandeep, it seemed, didn't know what to say. Hugo pulled his phone and wallet from his pocket, bringing the discussion back to the present. "I assume it's an empty-pockets policy on the shop floor?"

"Yes, that's right, you can use one of the spare lockers to store your belongings for the duration." He opened a cabinet beside the overalls rack and pulled out a drawer. "I've got booties, gloves, glasses, masks, and hairnets for when you're ready."

"I'd better let Brita know where we'll be," Mariska said, before she put her phone into the locker.

"Oh, no, don't do that."

She looked up from her half-typed text. Sandeep's voice was oddly insistent. "I mean there's no need. I've organised a driver to pick her up from the airport and bring her straight here. She can meet us mid-tour."

Sandeep had already turned his focus back to the hairnets and safety glasses as he finished speaking, and Mariska stared at his back. She was unable to get a read on Sandeep this morning. At Brita's dining table he'd been like an open book, all unbridled attention and agitation, but today he was confused, even haphazard. If he'd already sent for a driver, why did he ask how far away she was? Surely Divya didn't carry so much responsibility here that her absence would throw him so off kilter.

Or perhaps she did. Brita had said her father had been very impressed with her work. With a shrug Mariska slipped her phone back into her handbag and packed it away with the others. The locker closed with a clang. She followed Hugo's lead and grabbed a set of overalls from the rack. They all seemed to be the same size.

The white suits, made from what felt like a high-tech raincoat material, were surprisingly comfortable. Velcro straps tight across the ankles, wrists, and the lower half of their faces. The masks, custom designed to match the suits. With the whole ensemble fitted, she felt as if she was about to enter a quarantine zone.

Satisfied, she turned to Hugo and stifled a laugh.

"What?"

"Have you seen yourself?" She giggled. His beard was barely contained, sprouting around the edges of his face mask.

"Oh, and I suppose you think you look quite fetching?"

She struck a pose, kicking her hip out to one side, and turned to Sandeep. *Let's see how he reacts to this.* "What do you think, Mr Pridha?"

"Mostly right. Though your hair is falling out the back of your net." Sandeep, uncharacteristically, seemed focused on technicalities.

She adjusted her hairnet with a performative pout and clomped out into the hallway. She tried to mentally review each of their little encounters this morning, to discern a pattern, but the suit made it hard. She wanted to swing her arms and legs out wide, like a cowboy. Like she was wandering the vast, virtual plains of Solomon's Omniverse ranch. By the time Sandeep had inspected them both and waved them towards what could only be described as an airlock, her suspicions had been cleansed from her mind, just as bursts of air cleansed their bodies.

"To remove any traces of dust!" Sandeep called out over the noise, his voice muffled by his face mask. He might as well have said to remove any traces of doubt.

32

—·—

BRITA SAT BACK AND sipped her coffee. Freshly brewed, flat white, soy milk. She pursed her lips and pressed her tongue against the roof of her mouth. It was a little weak. However, the hum of the jet engines was barely perceptible; she still had a mountain of work to do, a private cubicle all to herself, and a half hour until landing. She could make do with a weak coffee.

Her phone vibrated in her pocket, and she rolled her eyes. Not that long ago, midair connectivity had felt like a novelty. And before that... how nice it had seemed, with the benefit of hindsight, to be able to switch off for a few hours. To disconnect from the world.

And it was all about to change. Again.

She pulled out her phone and it rumbled in her hand: a number she didn't recognise. Whoever it was could probably wait, she thought, as the seat belt sign illuminated. Her overnighter to Kolkata was preparing to start its descent. With a defeated sigh, she pushed her laptop to one side.

"Hello?"

"Brita? Thank god. Listen, I've got—"

"I'm sorry, who is this?"

"What? Shit, sorry. This is Jorge. Jorge Elorza. We met at..."

Brita pulled herself upright, finally recognising the gruff accent. She pulled the phone from her ear and prepared to kill the call, but something held her back. Had there been a hint of weary relief in his voice? Memories of the interview flooded back, his smug smile, his insulting tone, and his incessant questions, the kind that cut far too close to her own anxieties for comfort.

What was he doing, calling her right now? She checked her watch. Five a.m., London time. *I should just hang up.* She bit her lip. A nosy reporter was the last thing she needed, and yet...

"'Met' is doing a lot of heavy lifting there."

197

"You would prefer set up, maybe? Or ambushed?" He paused, and she imagined his cheesy, disarming grin. It didn't work that well in person and was even less effective over the phone. Brita held her tongue. He'd called her; let him do the talking. "Listen, I'm sorry about all that, what I said about you and your father…If it helps, I don't work at O2 anymore. It's not the kind of reporting I ever wanted to do."

Brita clenched her teeth. Where was this going? "You didn't just call me to apologise, though."

"No. No, I didn't." There it was again, a world-weary exhaustion. "Listen, I've been digging through the Britannia Bank fallout, and I've uncovered something that I know from experience you'll want to hear."

She eyed the cubicle door. This was highly unusual. Normally with reporters, information only flowed one way. And what did he mean, 'from experience'? "If you're expecting comment, you can forget it. Why don't you just run it, and let me hear about it on the nightly news with everyone else?"

"It's…not that kind of story."

"Of course it isn't. Jesus. I don't know why I didn't hang up the instant I recognised your voice."

"It's about one of your investors. Your *new* investors."

Brita's breath caught in her throat. There was only one thing the phrase 'new investors' could mean. But how could he possibly know? It was all she could do to stammer: "This would be all off the record?"

"One hundred percent."

Breathe in, breathe out. She couldn't let him know he'd got her rattled.

"All right, go on then. I'm listening," she said, thanking all that was holy he couldn't see her face.

"Not over the phone. We need to meet, so I can tell you in person."

"Jorge, I'm on a plane, about to land. I won't be back in London for days."

"Shit." A fraught edge had crept into his voice. She wasn't the only one fighting off panic. But what did he have to panic about? "But you're free now?"

"As long as you make it quick."

"OK. OK." A pause as he collected his thoughts. "I want to make one thing clear, up front. Despite what you think of me, I know you stand by your principles, and I respect that. It's one of the reasons I am talking to you at all."

She rolled her eyes. For a reporter with a reputation for bluntness, he was certainly taking his time getting to the point. "All right, that's one reason. The others?"

"I've been in the position you're about to be in. It…wasn't pleasant."

An announcement from the captain rang out over the loudspeakers, but she shut it out. She had an uneasy feeling she knew where this was going. She remembered

Mariska briefing her about his history. It was one of the reasons they'd agreed to that damned interview in the first place. A mistake that continued to haunt her.

"You're talking about Solomon, aren't you."

"I am."

She shuddered, from the tips of her ears to the base of her spine. But when she spoke, her voice carried an icy calm. "And what does Solomon have to do with me?"

"I spoke with him, yesterday morning. He wants me to write a follow-up story. About you."

Her eyes darted around the cubicle, though she knew she was alone. Her laptop sat forgotten on her fold-out desk. "Is that so? Did he have an angle in mind? A think piece? Human interest, maybe?"

"He told me about a dinner party and made some very serious allegations. Insider trading, fraud. Even extortion."

The tips of her fingers fell limp and, if not for her clammy palms, her phone would have slipped to the floor. Her throat was suddenly dry, her mind blank. He knew everything.

"The thing is, I know Richard, probably far better than you do. If you knew what I did, there is no way you would have even considered him as an investor. So when Solomon asks me for a favour, it sends up a giant red flag. I did some digging..."

Only half of Jorge's words made any impression. Each breath was coming faster, shallower. She grabbed her water bottle and gulped, spilling half of it down her chest. The cold water shocked her into a semblance of clarity. *If you knew what I knew...*

I didn't even want the arsehole involved! But he'd found out, somehow. And sure, she'd toyed with pulling the pin when he'd walked through that door, protecting Gateway from his intrusion. But she hadn't. She'd held firm, and it had proved to be the right decision. Without Solomon in the room that night, the whole thing might have collapsed.

Solomon wasn't a risk to the Gateway.

But Jorge was.

"Are you seriously telling me that Richard Solomon came to you, specifically you, Jorge Elorza, the reporter with a vendetta so unhinged that it almost cost you your career? And that he dangled some cock-and-bull story? For what? To discredit me? To tank my share price, maybe buy a few percentage points in my company?" Her throat tightened as the threat Solomon had made that night found itself spilling from her lips. "Solomon is in the middle of a battle with Congress, dealing with a horror product rollout, and fending off a group of activist shareholders. I think he's got more important things to do with his time. You're just fishing, hoping I'll bite." She spat the last sentence, her anger boiling over, spurred by the seed of doubt that had taken root in her mind.

"He's not the man the world thinks he is. He's ruthless."

"Anyone who's sat across the negotiating table from him knows that." Brita scoffed. She'd spent more time there than most.

"Please, Brita, tell me you're not this naive? You know what he did to me, right?" He was pleading, desperate. She should end the call. Just hang up. Every logical neuron, every instinct honed over decades at the top, was screaming at her that he was a journalist, a hack, that he'd been hounding her for months. It was all a con, an attempt to manipulate her into giving up some hint about the dinner party. About Gateway. She knew all this was true, but the knot in her gut, the part of her that feared he wasn't lying, knew Solomon was more dangerous than he let on.

She stayed on the line. She listened.

"He threatened me, but I didn't back down. Why would I? I had him, dead to rights. I knew it went all the way back to his IPO. For a while there, Omni looked like being a bigger flop than anything from the dotcom boom. But then along comes an angel investor, spending big to prop up the share price while Solomon got his house in order.

"You know who that investor was?" Jorge asked, even though of course she didn't know. And of course he was going to tell her. "Volodymyr Uvorvykishki, moneyman for the Donetskaya Bratva, the most cold-blooded branch of the Ukrainian mob. And you know why he sank so much money into Omni? Because Solomon cut him a deal: Volodymyr would keep Solomon afloat, and Solomon would give Volodymyr a back door into the private data of anyone he wanted. Rivals? Journalists? Politicians? Volodymyr just had to say the word, and Solomon would offer them up on a platter.

"And the best part? Volodymyr had had it planned from the start. A handful of subtle threats, a rumour or two of mismanagement; it didn't take much to make Omni start to smell. Then Solomon got the call. He practically bit Volodymyr's hand off."

A knock on the door, one of the cabin crew, asking her to pack away her laptop, her desk. She nodded brusquely and focused on tidying up her things. It was easier than thinking about what Jorge was saying.

"And I could prove all of it. Every single compromising detail. I had the account numbers, the shell companies. So you know what he did? He threatened my newspaper. Gave them an ultimatum. They had two choices: spike the story and fire me, or he would block them from Omni. Just blank them from his algorithm. They laughed. He tweaked his magic formula, and their readership collapsed within a day. I was gone the next. Untouchable. A pariah.

"That's the man you've gotten into bed with, Brita."

"I don't believe you."

"If that was true, you would have hung up five minutes ago. But you know there's something off about him, don't you. So you stayed on the line, and you listened."

"Why did I let that man back through my door," she muttered and slumped into her chair, totally drained. He was right. She'd known. Of course she'd known. Mariska's report on how he'd discovered their plans, forced his way in, it should have only confirmed things. Only she'd needed to not look scared, not look like she'd balk at the first sign of trouble. And so she'd let the fox into the henhouse and left him unchecked.

There was only one thing left to do. Limit the damage.

"What did he tell you?"

"He didn't tell me anything much. Just what I said, you know: fraud, blackmail. I don't even know why he's so bloody keen." Brita closed her eyes. Maybe he didn't know *everything*. There was still hope of keeping this contained. "Everything I've got from there I figured out for myself. In the four weeks since your dinner party, dozens, no, *hundreds*, of shell companies have been floated, all tied to Richard Solomon and Omni through Volodymyr's money man. And every single one of them has started buying up Stora shares. I can send you the data. He's planning something. And I think Sandeep might be in on it."

Through the floor of the cabin, Brita felt the landing gear extend, and her eyes snapped back open. "Sandeep?"

"Maybe. It could be one of the others, though I doubt it."

"The others?" Brita's head was spinning. How much did he know?

"Ming-Xia, Sato. Anita—"

She stabbed the disconnect symbol as if it were a physical threat and stared at her phone in disbelief. How could he—She let her phone fall. By the time it clattered to the floor, her hands were balled into fists. She pounded the table, her seat, her knees, none of it doing any good.

He could only know because he was told. About the meeting, about the Gateway, and about her stupid, stupid plan. And if he knew that...She forced herself to breathe, in and out, in and out. There would be time for self-flagellation later. Right now, she had to act. She uncurled her fingers, one hand at a time, and laid them atop her thighs, silencing her tremors through force of will alone. The plane jolted, angled sidewards, and her empty water bottle toppled to the floor, coming to rest next to her phone.

She snatched it up and called Mariska. No answer. She tried again, her fingers tearing at the frayed edge of her seat as the call rang out. She left a message: *Call me back. It's urgent. We've been betrayed. Gateway is at stake.*

Her finger hesitated over her father's number, remembering his reaction last time the Gateway was threatened. He would be no help. Just another wildcard she couldn't control.

The intercom sounded: The plane was in the final stages of its descent, could passengers please switch off their mobile devices. She let the phone drop to her lap and pulled her knees up to her chest. She stared out the window, chewing her lip.

Kolkata loomed through the parting clouds, sparkling from above in the early-morning light. Mechanically, she gathered her things and prepared to disembark. She could think of nothing else to do. Her phone pinged, but it was an email from Jorge, with a spreadsheet attached. Proof she didn't need. She tried Mariska again, but again there was no answer.

The second the aircraft door opened, she was moving, brushing past the bubbly flight crew. She emerged from the jet bridge listless, like a boat that had somehow survived passage through a torrent of whitewater and felt lost in the sudden calm. She should call Anita. Or Ming-Xia. Even Garfield—

"Mrs Gundersson?" She turned slowly, searching vaguely, distracted. She didn't recognise the voice. "Over here! Welcome back to Kolkata. My name is Stanley. I'll be your driver today."

33

Mariska stumbled into Sandeep's back. He'd paused in the middle of the corridor, in the middle of a sentence, an uncertain answer to yet another of Hugo's questions. He ignored her apology and opened a Velcro patch on his wrist, exposing a smartwatch. His lips became a thin, tight line.

"Bad news?" She asked.

"What? No. Just that Brita has arrived. She's getting changed." He closed the flap and scanned the hallway. It was empty of workers. "It is good timing, actually. We'll meet her at the newly installed processing plant for the Gateway's microchips. Come, this way."

He set off at a brisk pace, weaving across the factory floor. She recognised sections they'd already visited—the silicon processing line, the etching baths, the autoclaves. The facility's vastness had been compounded by Hugo's never-ending stream of obscure technical questions, making the tour seem far longer than the roughly two hours she'd been strapped inside her uncomfortable white suit. She pitied the poor factory workers, stuck in them for ten or twelve hours a day.

Sandeep turned up a flight of stairs, and she groaned. Her heels were not designed for this sort of activity.

They crossed a steel walkway suspended between two internal buildings, crossing a pathway populated by hurried workers pushing trolleys and carts below. At the end of the walkway their route was blocked by a double-glazed security door. A few strokes on the keypad from Sandeep and the door unlocked, sliding open with a thunk-hiss.

Via a short corridor, walls gleaming white like all the rest, the room opened into a small warehouse. The space was dominated by a taut silver tarpaulin with a large, blocky mass roughly the size of a shipping container huddled underneath. It sat in a depression in the floor—the platform on which she stood extended out at approximately one and a half metres above the floor, providing access to whatever was underneath the tarp. On the opposite wall was a large roller door.

Hugo stepped forward, curious. Before she could ask Sandeep what was under the covers, though, a door on the lower level opened, letting in two more white-clad figures. The first directed the other to a short flight of stairs. Mariska recognised Brita's long legs, her slightly hunched shoulders, and hurried across the platform, her weariness forgotten. Even under the coveralls and face mask, Mariska could see that something was wrong.

"Long flight?" she asked, extending a gloved hand to help Brita up the stairs.

"We need to talk. Privately." Brita's voice was barely a croak. Her eyes were blood-shot; the few strands of her fringe that had escaped from her hairnet were stuck fast to her brow from sweat. There was no colour in her cheeks. As she reached the top step, their shoulders touched. With a start, Mariska realised her boss was trembling all over.

She linked arms, supporting her weight, and turned to wave to Hugo. He was already at her side, brow tight with concern. Mariska looked past him, towards their host.

"The heat seems to have gotten to her. Feeling a bit peaky," Hugo shouted through his mask. "Sandeep, can you go get us a chair or something? Maybe a glass of water? There's a good chap." Hugo raised his eyebrows, his eyes not leaving hers the entire time. If Sandeep happened to be out of earshot for a few moments, he seemed to be saying, so much the better.

"What is it?" she asked. "You look awful." Her father took her other arm. They huddled in a small group at the centre of the raised platform.

Brita started speaking rapidly, in incoherent bursts. Something about that hack reporter, Jorge. About shell companies. About Stora being in danger. Then the words came to a sudden halt, and Brita's red eyes bulged. She was staring over Mariska's shoulder.

"Why, how wonderful it is to see y'all again. Welcome." That southern drawl. It made Mariska's skin itch.

She whipped round so fast she almost knocked Brita over. Richard Solomon blocked the exit, leaning casually against the security pedestal. His light-grey suit, rawhide boots, and matching satchel jarred her senses, incongruous in the sterile setting. Sandeep hovered behind his shoulder, a bundle of nervous energy.

So Divya wasn't just sick, and it wasn't just nerves. The realisation of what was happening landed heavily in her gut, dredging up all the doubts she'd harboured since that very first night. The doubts she'd been trying to suppress.

She pushed Brita behind her, adrenaline pumping. Should she crouch? Run? Tell him where to go? A soft click from behind stopped those thoughts in their tracks. It had been a long, long time since her teenage nights on Miskolc's dingy streets, but Mariska hadn't forgotten the sound of a pistol being cocked.

She closed her eyes and raised her hands, very slowly, above her head.

"Well, well, well." Solomon grinned. "Ain't this a touchin' reunion. Though ah must say, Brita. You don't look very happy to see me."

Mariska stumbled as Brita shoved her out of the way. She couldn't have heard the pistol. Or perhaps she had and didn't know what it meant. Mariska watched with a mix of horror and awe as her boss uncurled her shoulders, pulled herself to her full height, and ripped off her mask. Brita had heard, and understood. She just didn't care.

"Whatever you're doing here, Solomon, I want no part of it," she said, her voice far steadier than her legs appeared to be, and the jumbled sentences her boss had uttered before Solomon's arrival coalesced into meaning. Shell companies. This was a takeover. She caught a wry smile in Solomon's eyes. He'd been planning it all along.

And his invitation was still open.

"Ah'm afraid you ain't got a choice." He shoved his satchel into Sandeep's hands. "Cuff 'em."

"What? Cuff us? What the hell is going on here!" Hugo blustered, stepping forward, his confusion quickly morphing into menace. She'd never seen such a look of fury on him before. Not when she'd dropped his Gateway prototype and almost severed his hand, not when Brita had told him that the Gateway, like Stora, was hers as much as it was his.

"Ah wouldn't." Solomon held up a hand and nodded towards his sidekick, his face covered by his mask, who'd edged around so they could see him. And his gun, aimed squarely at Hugo's chest.

His large frame slowed, suddenly uncertain, hovering on the point of no return.

"Stanley here is an excellent shot."

"Dad, don't. It's not worth it," Brita whispered. Mariska saw his neck stiffen at her words. She could just imagine the thoughts racing one another in his head. *Not for you, maybe. You're young. This is my last shot.* They were the same thoughts careening around in hers, only substituting *young* for *rich*, and *last* for *only*.

Her boss's knees buckled as, with gritted teeth, Hugo stepped back. Although Mariska offered her body as support, she couldn't bring herself to look down, in case she accidentally met her gaze.

Solomon sneered over his shoulder to Sandeep. "Hurry up. Ah haven't got all day."

"Turn around. Hands behind your back," Sandeep said, his hands needlessly rough as he jerked Hugo around, his eyes stuck halfway between what he was doing and the barrel of Stanley's gun. Hugo protested, but there was nothing he could do. Sandeep pinned his wrists, wrenched them backwards, and slipped a set of plastic restraints around them. With a short, sharp zip, he wrenched the bindings tight.

"It'll be okay, Dad," Brita whispered, though Mariska could tell she knew her words were hollow the second they left her mouth. She patted Mariska on the shoulder and turned around, offering Sandeep her hands.

"What the hell is going on here?" Hugo whispered. As if it wasn't obvious.

"Jorge called me on the flight, warned me that Solomon is not all that he seems," Brita said, her gaze steady over Mariska's shoulder. The barrel of Stanley's gun was like a magnet. She could feel it between her shoulder blades. Off to their left, Solomon crossed the platform and started unclipping the tarpaulin. "He had a theory, something about buying Stora out from under us. Why Solomon is here right now, though…"

The tarpaulin slithered to the ground with an escalating rustle, revealing a battered six-wheel truck underneath. It was backed right up to the edge of the platform.

"Jesus," Mariska muttered under her breath. At the sight of it, Brita collapsed, landing with her back against her father's shins. Reality must have finally kicked in. Instead of helping, Mariska felt herself edging away. As if her body were no longer her own to control.

"Brita!" Hugo dropped to his knees, futile as the action was with his hands locked behind his back. He peered up at Mariska, helpless. "Why aren't you helping?"

"I'm all right, Dad. I'm all right," Brita mumbled, trying to lever herself upright.

"Christ, boy, help her up and get them into the truck," Solomon said, unhitching the rear door with a clunk. It swung open to reveal an empty metal container, no fittings of any kind.

"What about her?" Sandeep asked, one hand reaching for Mariska's wrist.

"Good question." Solomon stopped, hand clamped around the lever of the other door, and turned his gaze on her. "What about her indeed?"

"Mas?" Brita asked, her back propped up against her father. "What does he mean?"

"What's the end game here, Solomon? You want the Gateway for yourself?" Mariska asked, as if she didn't already know. As if this was a decision she hadn't already made.

"Somethin' like that." Solomon didn't blink. He held a padlock in one hand.

"And this is, what, plan B? I'm guessing plan A didn't involve Jorge blabbing." Mariska jerked her hand free of Sandeep's clutches. "And you need to keep us quiet while it plays out."

Solomon straightened, eyeing her carefully. *So I'm not far off, then.* Brita was staring up at her, her mouth moving. She was pleading. Mariska didn't hear a word. All her focus was on the plastic restraints dangling menacingly from Sandeep's hands.

"What happens next?" she asked, taking a small step forward, knowing what it meant. *If I do this, what happens to them? To me? When it's all over?*

"Once ah've won, ah'll let them go. Ah'm not a monster." He slid the padlock through the handle and let it hang there, menacing. "Though there'll have to be an understandin' as to the consequences of lettin' out our little secret, of course."

She took another step forward. Brita, Hugo, everyone was watching. "And after that? Who is going to run things? Sandeep?" She was close to him now, barely a step away. They'd been this close before, in the Omniverse, but she could see in his eyes that this was different. This was the real world. Real decisions were being made. With real consequences. "You need someone who knows the product, knows the people, and knows the market. Someone willing to go all the way, to do what needs to be done."

"Mariska!" Hugo bellowed. "If I ever get my hands on you..."

"Shut up, old man. I've been on the losing side too many times in my life. Not this time." She didn't even bother to turn around. She stepped up to Solomon's ear, where only the two of them could hear. "You better know what you're doing."

She backed away and crossed her wrists behind her back for Sandeep. Her eyes never left Solomon's. Never turned towards her friends. Her former friends. Sandeep grabbed her wrists and slipped on the bindings. *Let them think this was spur of the moment,* she prayed. *Let them think I convinced him, not that he convinced me.*

"Stop." Solomon held out a hand. "They won't be necessary. Mariska, why don't you come with me." He waved a dismissive hand at Sandeep, and guided her towards the exit.

Mariska's pulse was racing. Her breath fogged her mask. Behind her, she heard Hugo's furious protestations, Stanley's gruff commands: "On your feet! Into the truck!" Brita, she noticed, hadn't made a sound. The trucks doors slammed shut, the heavy thuds an exclamation point on the choice she'd made. On her betrayal.

Solomon swiped his card and pushed open the door. Outside, the sunlight was blinding. "You made the right choice. And trust me, ah know what ah'm doing."

Mariska set her jaw, nodded, and stepped across the threshold, as if she was just as confident as he. But inside, a thread of doubt remained: *You know what you're doing. But do I?*

— · —

With a hand low on her back, Solomon ushered Mariska into the back seat of his waiting Mercedes. The crisp white clean-suit hissed as she shuffled across to the far side. He slipped in behind her, reached over the front passenger seat, fetched a small carry bag, and handed it to her. "Your phone should be in there."

The bag held three phones. She pulled hers out and handed Hugo's and Brita's phones straight back. No hesitation, because she'd made the right choice. The only choice. Solomon fished them out anyway.

"Now are these..." He turned Hugo's handset over and over in his hand, looking for something that wasn't there.

"No. We don't just carry Gateway around in our pockets. It's too valuable." *Too high a risk of it falling into the wrong hands*, she thought, *though it might be too late for that.*

"Sensible." Solomon shrugged and stuck his head out the still-open door. "Sandeep. Dispose of these. And ah want these destroyed. Not just tossed away, y'hear? Gone for good."

"Of course, Mr Solomon," Sandeep said, his words almost drowned out by the escalating rasp of the roller door sliding open and the rumble of the truck engine thunking into gear.

"Good." He slammed the door shut, cutting the sound of the revving truck to nothing. Mariska knew that if she just turned her head, looked out the back window, she'd see the truck nosing its way out onto the maintenance road, diesel smoke belching from its exhaust as it drove away. She didn't look. Thinking of Hugo, of Brita, huddled in a dark corner of that container would do her absolutely no good. She had to look forward. There was no going back.

She swiped open her phone. The most recent message flashed up on the lock screen.

Brita

Do not trust Solomon.

Attempting hostile takeover.

Call me.

With a flick of her finger, the message disappeared. If only Brita's face, distraught, disbelieving, unable to look away as Mariska left her behind could be erased so easily.

Solomon lifted his phone to his lips. "Set destination: Netaji Subhash Chandra Bose International Airport."

The engine purred. *Destination confirmed: Netaji Subhash Chandra Bose International Airport.* Mariska grabbed the back of the empty driver's chair and peered at the centre console. The gear indicator shifted from Park, to Neutral, and into Drive. Then the car was moving. Slowly, deliberately, Mariska moved her hand across to the armrest and braced herself.

"Solomon. Tell me you're not serious."

"Ah'm always serious." His head was buried in his phone, his fingers flying across the keyboard. She knew she should be wondering what he was writing, and who he was writing to, but she couldn't take her eyes of the steering wheel, turning of its own accord.

Estimated time to destination: thirty-seven minutes.

"This car's been tested?"

"Thoroughly."

"On the ranch back home? Or on roads with tuk-tuks?" Mariska winced as they slid smoothly by a stack of pallets laden with boxes and turned towards the compound's side entrance. "Wait, does it know they drive on the left-hand side here?"

"D'you think ah shipped this all the way from Texas, just so ah could commit a felony in comfort?" He patted the driver's-side headrest. "This is Sandeep's baby, not mine."

"Ah," Mariska conceded, though she maintained her tight grip on the armrest as the car slowed for the compound's boom gate. "As long as it works better than your Omniverse headsets, I guess we'll survive."

From the corner of her eye, Mariska caught Solomon scowl. "Surely you've got calls to be makin'? Emails to be sendin'?"

The steering wheel spun of its own accord, and they turned out into the street. She relaxed her grip.

"About what? I don't know what you're planning. Honestly, it seems to me that the less I know, the better." She shrugged and looked away, at the industrial landscape whizzing by. "For now at least."

"True, true. Besides." He hit send and slid his phone back inside his jacket. "The calls'll start comin' through soon enough."

"You've tipped off the media."

"A friendly journalist or two, nothin' more'n that."

Mariska clicked her phone open and brought up the London Stock Exchange. It was approaching midday in Kolkata. The exchange was just over half an hour from opening, and Stora's pre-trade stock price was stable. For the moment.

"It's quite a drastic step. Kidnapping, I mean." She refreshed the page, waiting for the moment the news dropped and the ticker dived. Solomon would have already sent word to his buyers. They would be ready to pounce.

"Ah had to accelerate mah plans somewhat."

"Jorge?"

He turned away, hands folded in his lap. He didn't acknowledge the question one way or another.

"What will you do with him? It's not like you can ruin his career again."

"It's like you said. There're some things you're better off not knowin'." She saw in his reflection in the window that he'd given himself a self-satisfied little smirk.

She turned away too. They were on the freeway now, sitting steady in the middle lane, the drivers on either side oblivious to the fact they were next to a car with no one at the wheel. She hoped it wasn't an omen, a sign of things to come. Solomon was a man used to being in control of his own destiny. She could tell, however, sitting so close to him as he brooded over what he'd just set in motion, and what was sure to come, that by pushing Brita and Hugo into the back of that truck, he'd stepped well outside of his comfort zone. Had perhaps been pushed himself.

And he didn't like it. One little bit.

She shifted in her seat, her clean-suit rustling, the seams chafing against her neck. Despite the heavily tinted windows and the climate control, she was still sweating. It was high time the bloody thing came off. She ripped at the Velcro and shrugged her shoulders free.

"It's not so drastic, anyway. Just a little scare, for the market. Ah won't need long."

Mariska pursed her lips. It sounded like he was trying to convince himself.

"So, what do I say when these calls come?" She arched her back as she slipped the clean-suit down to her waist, knowing that he'd take notice. Not even really knowing why she did it, other than that she always had, and that it had always worked with men like him. Had always lowered their guard in some crucial way. "When did I last see them? Where were they off to?" She paused, her hands and the clean-suit bunched just below her hips. "What's the scenario?"

"The bare minimum." His eyes traced the contours of her back, and he grinned, as if he knew what she was doing and that he might as well let her. "What is it you Brits say? Play a flat bat?"

Mariska fought the temptation to roll her eyes. "I can't just stonewall my way through questions like 'when was my last contact with Brita? With Hugo?' You know she called us, right? To warn us?"

"About what?"

"About you."

Solomon's eyes narrowed, suddenly serious. "No, ah did not."

"Now that you do, do you think Hugo and I are the only people she called?" She glanced down at her phone in her lap. It was just after midday. 7:40 a.m. London time. If Brita had called Garfield...no, she wouldn't have done that. He didn't know about Gateway, and he was the kind of snake you kept out of the tent as long as possible. But she might have called Anita. And Anita lunched with the LSE chairman and played tennis with his wife. "The market opens in twenty minutes. All it takes is one phone call, a timely trading halt, and your plan is toast."

"Our plan," Solomon corrected her.

This time she let herself roll her eyes, as if to say *Really? Right now?*

Her phone buzzed in her lap, Garfield's sweaty, bloated face popping onto her screen. "Perfect timing." Solomon leaned forward, opened his mouth, but she held up a finger. "Uh-uh. You made this mess. The best thing you can do is watch while I clean it up." She winked. "And who knows, you might learn something."

She considered letting Garfield's call ring out. It's what she'd normally do. Pass him off to Luan or Sunil, unless it was critical. But not today. Too risky. He might bypass her completely. She flicked the green icon and lifted her phone to her ear, giving her hair an irritated flick just to get into character.

"I've got two minutes, Garfield. What is it?"

"Have you seen Brita?" A jowelly quiver to his voice. A slightly panicked tightness.

"Not yet. She had to change flights, and I've been in meetings..." She heard Solomon shifting uneasily in his seat. Let him squirm. She looked resolutely out the window, to the dry, dusty construction sites whizzing by, and gave off an exasperated sigh, just as she did whenever Garfield came to her with some bullshit problem he should have been able to solve himself. "Listen, can't Anna help you with this? I've got—"

"For Christ's sake, Mas! This is not the time for your churlish games! Have you seen her?"

"No, I haven't! And if you'd bother to listen—"

"Oh god. Oh god..."

She let herself realise that something was wrong. "Garfield? What's going on?"

"...oh god, oh lord..."

"Garfield, if you don't tell me what's going on, I can't help." She softened, playing the part he needed her to play, ignoring how demeaning it was, to have to pretend to be his mother just to get him to do his goddamn job. "Why do you need to know where Brita is?"

"Mariska, she's been kidnapped!"

She bit her lip. "Kidnapped? That's ridiculous. Here, I have a message from her, less than two hours ago. Listen." She dropped her phone from her ear, as if she was actually reading from it. "Just landed. Heading straight to the hotel, need to freshen up. See you after lunch." She put her phone back to her ear. "See? She's fine. She's probably just having a nap—"

"No, you don't understand. They *called*, Mas. They called, and they said—"

"Who called you, Garfield?"

"Roger. Roger Nielson."

Mariska's eyebrows shot up, and she risked a quick glance Solomon's way. He'd buried his head in his phone and was once again furiously typing away. Developing contingency plans? With who? She shivered. *I don't want to know.*

"The editor at O2 News? That Roger Nielson?"

Garfield sniffled his assent.

"What did he say, exactly? I need you to tell me his exact words."

"He told me they had multiple reports that Brita's been kidnapped..." A pathetic, choked sigh. "In Kolkata..."

He didn't want it to be true. He wanted to be told everything was okay. She could work with that. "Multiple reports? Or multiple *confirmed* reports?"

"I don't..."

"It doesn't matter. An outfit like O2 will run whatever they want, no matter what you or I say. Listen, you stonewall, all right? Give them nothing. I'll put off my meetings, head back to the hotel, and check on her, okay? You just sit tight." She waited, listened. "Garfield?"

"But what if they run the story..."

"Then we'll get Brita on camera and get a little revenge for their hit job a couple of months back." She clenched her jaw. 7:50. Cutting it fine. "I've got to go. I'll call you as soon as I know more, okay?"

"All ri—"

She hung up, turned to Solomon. "Redirect this thing to my hotel."

"What then? You can't tell them she checked in, you can't get her on camera..."

In answer, she showed him her phone. The news had broken, and Stora's pre-market stock price was diving. "The markets open in ten minutes. All I'm doing is buying you time."

34

JORGE'S EYES SNAPPED OPEN and he lurched upright, at once alert and totally disoriented. He didn't know where he was, or how he came to be there. Just that he had his phone in his fist, and someone's hand was on his shoulder.

"You pull an all-nighter?" Gabrielle plopped down beside him and cast her eye across a mess of paperwork. "What did you find?"

"What did I find?" Jorge blinked in an attempt to get his eyes to focus. He glanced down at his desk, at the ledgers and spreadsheets encroaching into Gabrielle's territory, and the events of the past twenty-four hours came rushing back. His frantic jabbing at the button for the lobby, only to collapse to his knees the instant the lift doors closed. His fraught taxi ride away from the Savoy, hunkered down in the back seat, imagining gun barrels behind every blacked-out window they drove past. He couldn't go home. They knew where he lived. But the Broadsheet's offices had security guards. Cameras. Checkpoints. So he'd come to work, and he hadn't left.

He ran a hand across his bearded chin, found his right cheek slick with drool, and wiped it with his forearm. "You wouldn't believe me if I told you."

"Oh yeah?" She crossed her arms and leaned back in her chair. "Try me."

So he did. He started with the interview, how Brita had wanted to brag, though she wouldn't say about what. Then Hugo, that same night, meeting with Stanley Adams. The dinner party, the billionaires, Hugo again appearing where he couldn't possibly be, and all of it under the surveillance of the Ukrainian mob. Solomon's offer, and then his discoveries. Shell company after shell company, buying up Stora shares.

"That's...that's a lot," Gabrielle said, puffing out her cheeks. "And these Ukrainians, they know what you look like?"

"Yeah." He glanced around at the empty office. It was just shy of eight a.m. They were the only ones in. "That's why I'm here."

She bent over the ledgers he'd been combing last night, a stack of which had toppled over and now covered her keyboard. He'd highlighted dozens and dozens in green, all following the same Ukrainian pattern. "You reckon these are all buying Stora shares?"

"Hundred percent. I've got the market data right here."

Her phone buzzed in her pocket, and she fished it out without looking up. Gabrielle in focus mode, dialled in to the details. Her painted fingernail, navy blue, traced each column, and she nodded at each of his selections. "You missed one. SRSA Holdings. Can you check if it matches the pattern?"

He woke his laptop, his screen flickering to life, and tabbed through his open applications looking for the London Stock Exchange data he'd pulled. "SRSA Holdings, you said?"

No answer.

"Gabrielle?"

"Holy shit."

He spun around. She held her phone with both hands, and her eyebrows had shot towards the sky. "What? What's happened?"

"Turn the TV on."

"Gabrielle?"

"The TV, Jorge, Christ!"

He leapt from his chair, mind racing back to the times in his life he'd scrambled for the TV remote like this. The Berlin Wall. The train bombings in Madrid. He stabbed the power button and glanced back at Gabrielle. She was biting her lip.

The picture resolved to the BBC news desk, and with his heart in his mouth, he waited.

Nothing.

Well, not nothing. Far-right politicians winning state elections in Germany, accusations of vote rigging in Hungary, the never-ending conflicts in Ukraine, in Palestine, in Yemen. But nothing explosive. Nothing new. He turned back to Gabrielle, palms open. What was going on?

"O2 TV," she whispered. He clenched his jaw tight but rolled through the channels anyway.

"This had better be worth it."

"—ws just in." Stacy Winthrop, breakfast news anchor, Roger's star protégé (who was not-so-secretly fucking Frank Darabont on the side) pressed her finger to her earpiece and nodded along to whatever Roger was saying. "We have a breaking story in Kolkata, India, with reports that Brita Gundersson, CEO of Stora Telecom, has been kidnapped. She was last seen leaving Chandra Bose airport at ten a.m. local time. She is reported to have been in Kolkata for a business meeting with the shipping magnate Sandeep Pridha—"

Jorge let the remote clatter to the floor. He'd turned Solomon down, so the bastard had switched to plan B. Leaking the story to his old station had just been another twist of the knife. He bent over his laptop and signed into Harvey's secure portal. Solomon wasn't doing this for fun. He wanted whatever Brita and her father were working on, and that was in London. Not Kolkata.

"You think this is Solomon?" Gabrielle scooched her chair up behind him. He nodded. "But why? It's so drastic. It doesn't seem his style."

"Because I called her this morning. To warn her that something was coming."

"But kidnapping?" she asked.

He opened a new search window, typed in *Stora LSE* and hit enter. A graph filled his screen, with a precipitous red drop. The pre-trade data had already priced Brita's disappearance in.

"How many shell companies did you say?"

"Hundreds."

"Jorge, this is huge. We have to bring Eddie in on this—wait, is that what I think it is?" He'd flicked back to Harvey's secure portal and opened the security feed from outside Brita's house in Mayfair. Already there was a media scrum outside her front doorstep. "Where did you get this?"

"I did a friend a favour." He changed cameras. He'd seen all he needed to there.

"Another one? Is that Kensington? Hugo's too? Jorge, this is..." She was just winding up to admonish him, tell him that spying on private citizens was not only illegal, but immoral too, when a pair of labourers appeared on screen. They sidled, nonchalant, up to Hugo's front door. One stooped at a nearby communications cabinet and removed the access plate while his companion dropped a trio of collapsible high-visibility safety cones ahead and behind. After less than twenty seconds' work, he gave his colleague a nod, who slipped something long and slender from the folds of his jacket and put his shoulder into the door. With a single, swift jerk, he was inside. Ten seconds later, the communications cabinet was whole, the cones had been retrieved, and Hugo's door swung shut.

"Who were those men?"

"I don't know, but I can guess," Jorge said, slamming his laptop shut and fetching his camera from beneath a stack of paperwork. He couldn't guess what they were after, though. It was the one thing he still didn't understand. It was high time he found out just what Brita and Hugo had been working so hard to protect, and what had made Solomon this desperate.

35

IT WAS IMPOSSIBLE TO tell how much time had passed in the din and the dark. The growl of the engine, the roar of the heavy tires, the rattle and clang of loose doors and fittings had numbed Hugo's mind. If only he could say the same for his body. Every jarring bump, every pothole, every juddering corrugation sent fresh spasms across his shoulder and down his spine.

They'd quickly realised that the front of the container, closest to the cabin, offered the least uncomfortable ride. The rear of the truck, unburdened by cargo, bucked and weaved with each hump or dip in the road. He and Brita sat back to back, legs braced against the side walls in an attempt to hold one another in place, their shoulders twisted to ease the pressure on their tightly bound wrists.

At some point, the frequent, sudden braking of city traffic, which had slammed their shoulders into the wall, gave way to the calmer rhythm of country roads. His eyes adjusted to the darkness. Oil and grime streaked the once-pristine white overalls. His booties were now covered in dust.

There hadn't been a turn or a surge for a while now. Minutes, maybe. They must be on a freeway. Against the protests of his too-old joints, he released his brace and edged back, until he and Brita were side by side. He gritted his teeth and raised his arms behind him.

"Drop your head a bit!" he yelled, through his mask.

"What?"

"I said drop your head!"

She flopped down on one elbow, and he managed to get a grip on her hairnet and her hood. The truck bucked and weaved, sending them both sprawling as he pulled her coverings away so that least her head was free. He levered himself back upright with a grimace and prostrated himself so that she could return the favour. The hot stale air was like a cool breeze against his cheeks, the back of his neck. He mouthed his thanks so he didn't have to shout over the clamour.

He lay panting, flat on his back, for as long as he dared, then hauled himself upright. With a shared sigh, they shuffled to the front of the truck and settled into their positions. He leaned his head back, until it touched hers.

"You don't seem worried," Hugo shouted.

"Neither do you. Which is strange, considering..."

"Considering what?" That they were tied up in a truck, being driven who knew where? That two of their investors, at least, had betrayed them? That Mariska had too? That Gateway, after so much work, was slipping from his grasp? He gritted his teeth, partly against the pain in his wrists, but more so against the dawning realisation that if he hadn't been so quick to panic that first night, maybe none of this would have happened.

"Considering your history of calm and rational behaviour when Gateway has been"—the truck jerked; they both grunted—"threatened."

"This is different."

"How?"

"Well, it's not under threat, is it? It's fucking gone."

And there was only one person he could blame.

Brita shifted so that her left shoulder pressed into the gap between his shoulder blades. She rested her head back, nestled into his neck. He did the same. Beneath the dirt and the pain and the exhaustion, it was actually kind of nice. Her hair tickled his ear.

"I don't buy it."

A knot of guilt twisted in his gut. She'd always been smarter than he was. More perceptive. "Buy what?"

"I dunno. This." She shrugged. "You've been a lot of things, Dad. But meek was never one of them."

"It's not that, it's..." The truck veered left, crossing onto a rumble strip. The vibrations started at his butt and travelled all the way up his spine. "It's regret. All this is because of me."

"What?"

Hugo closed his eyes. He'd hoped it would never come to this, but of course, it had. How could it not? "I called him. Solomon."

Brita pushed herself upright, the intimate moment over. "When?"

"That first night, with you and Mariska."

She didn't speak, leaving him to sit with the grunt and rattle of the rusty truck that his temper had pushed them into. "We hadn't spoken for so long, and then to have you surge back in and take control...I'm sorry. The red mist descended."

"Dad, what are you saying?"

"I'm saying I called him and offered him Stora if he'd help me, you know…" He trailed off. Now that it came time to say it, he realised all over again just how petty he'd been. How childish.

"No, Dad. I don't."

"If he'd help me get rid of you and install me in your place."

"You're not serious."

"I'm sorry." He wished he could see her face. Or even feel her shoulder against his so he could judge how much he'd hurt her. He swivelled around on his arse, but it didn't help. She was just a dirty shadow in the far corner. "He said no, by the way. Until he walked through the Gateway onto that balcony in Cairo, I thought I'd gotten away with it."

"Obviously not." Brita snorted.

"No."

Another silence. He winced, the plastic restraints digging at his wrists. He lay his head against the container wall, hoping the deafening hum might drown out his thoughts, but even that wasn't enough. He'd blown it. Again. Maybe for good.

"Did you know?"

He looked up. Brita knelt in front of him. He'd never seen such gravity settled on her shoulders, not even when…He blinked, looked away. He couldn't take it.

"You did, didn't you."

"Not this." He was back at her front door, Solomon halfway through it. *It's in hand, Hugo.* How furious he'd been, at Solomon. At his daughter. At anyone but himself. "But I knew he was up to something."

"And you didn't tell me. No, don't speak. I already know what you're going to say. Gateway was yours, Solomon was your mess, and you wanted to clean it up yourself. Well, you can't do this by yourself, Dad. You need help. We all do. We all did, anyway."

Hugo wished he were that selfish. If he was honest with himself (and locked in the back of a truck somewhere outside Kolkata, it was hard not to be), he knew he'd ignored it and hoped it would go away on its own. And what had he wasted his time on instead? Nights on the town with Sato. Policy sessions with Anita. And tinkering, always bloody tinkering—

"Hey, help me get these booties off."

"What?" Brita recoiled. "Get your own booties off. I need to…I need some space."

"How about some peace and quiet?" He pushed himself to his knees, damn his screaming joints. This was too damn important. "Far away from here?"

"Dad, what the hell are you talking about?"

The excitement, the exasperation got the better of him, and he started scraping at the bootie that covered his left shoe with his right. "Now you'll need to be quick. There is only enough power for about ten seconds."

"Ten seconds? Ten seconds of what?"

"I have an emergency Gateway in my shoe!" He bashed his partially freed foot against the wall. "Sato's idea. He's a good egg, that one—"

"You mean you've had that the whole time, and you're just bringing it up now?" She glared at him, incredulous, but at least she was talking to him. He could see her mind whirring already, assessing the possibilities, the next steps. He lay down on his back, feet up in the air facing the car container wall. He beckoned her over with the only free limb he had: his head.

"Come here, lie down by my side."

She shuffled across, her face carrying a mixture of puzzlement, frustration, determination, and lingering disappointment. "Don't mistake this for me forgiving you."

"That's fine. Saving Gateway is more important." He edged across so they were shoulder to shoulder, relishing the touch one last time. "This will take you to my workshop. Be ready, you won't have long."

"Wait, wait, wait. What about you?"

"No time."

"I'm not leaving you here."

"Brita, I can barely walk as it is. It has to be you."

"But you'll be all on your own. And Solomon—"

"I can look after myself. But I can't get the Gateway back off Solomon. Only you can do that."

The truck bucked and lurched, and they slid a foot one way, then a foot the other. The movement trapped his hands beneath the small of his back. He gritted his teeth against the pain.

"You ready?"

"No," she said. But she nodded. It was time to go.

He waited for a smooth stretch of road, then, with the sole of his left shoe facing the wall at a distance of about half a yard, tapped his heels together three times. His heel blew with a blinding flash, and the copper-and-plastic ring, tethered to the power pack buried between his toes, splattered against the wall. At the moment of impact, the dusty metal wall within its bounds shimmered out of existence. In its place was a portal into her father's workshop. Her childhood bedroom. Dark. Deserted. So close she could smell the lingering scent of flux, and bounded by an oval less than a foot above the floor.

"Go! Go! Go!" he shouted, wedging his shoulder beneath hers, urging her to her knees.

She pushed off the steel with her fists, aiming her feet towards the Gateway. First her feet, then her legs up to her knees. In his head he was counting down. *Eight...seven...six...*He braced against her back and prepared to push—

The truck reared wildly, and for a second gravity fell away. He slammed into the wall, and it all came rushing back. Where was she? He craned his neck and saw his daughter, outlined against the low light of his workshop, one leg hooked through the portal. She was scrabbling for purchase, flat on her back. And almost out of time.

Instinct took over. Pure adrenaline. He screamed as he flung himself towards her, caught her square in the back with his shoulder. He heaved.

She toppled.

The portal winked out of existence, and his head smashed into the container wall.

As he lay on his back, the pain didn't matter. Nor did the noise, the ringing in his ears. The grime, the dirt, the self-remorse. She'd made it.

Like it had been for the last decade, it was up to her now.

36

BRITA BOUNCED OFF THE edge of her father's metal workbench and tumbled onto the floor. Her father had thudded into her back so hard, shoving her through the Gateway at the last possible second, that she couldn't breathe.

Her ears rang with the sudden silence.

Breath, when it finally came, came hard, face down on the grit-covered floorboards. Her bindings traced a line of hot, white fire about her wrists. Her ribs ached, the inside of her knee burned where it had hooked onto the rim of the Gateway portal and then slammed into the floor. Even the thought of trying to stand made her moan with pain.

But she did it anyway. Solomon had taken her father, corrupted her friend, and was trying to steal her company. She didn't have time to be lying down.

Brita brought up one clean-suited knee and then, levering her chest up off the floor with her chin, forced herself upright. The spiked copper ring tacked to the wall above the bench hung empty. The only evidence that a portal between the clanking, rattling truck and safety had ever existed was a scrap of paper hairnet, cleanly sliced, with a sweaty tuft of her father's hair inside.

A spasm travelled down her leg, right where the copper ring had scraped at her skin. Right where her leg would have been severed if her father hadn't... She looked away. That had been far too close.

The workshop was dark, the only light bleeding through scratches in the blacked-out windows. She cast around for a pair of scissors, pliers, even a knife. Something she could use to free her hands—

CRACK!

Brita froze, bent over her father's tool-chest. Very slowly, she turned her ear towards the stairs. The front door creaked open, and a voice whispered, hushed and urgent.

"Who could..." Brita cocked her head to one side, puzzled, before realisation sank in. "Shit. Shit, shit, shit." Of course, Solomon wouldn't just be content with a kidnapping. He'd want everything her father had been working on in his hot little hands as soon as possible.

She seized the closest tool on the workbench and darted towards the stairs—

"Vas khtos bachyv?" A male voice, heavy. Slavic.

"Nemaye. Bse yasno." Lighter, higher pitched. Still male though, which made it two men against... against her. With her hands tied behind her back. "Shchos?"

"Shche ni." The front door creaked again as one of them swung it closed, pressing it into what could only be the ruined doorjamb with a crunch. Still rooted to the spot in the middle of the workshop, she heard soft footsteps, receding into downstairs rooms.

Her heart pounded in her chest, adrenaline swamping her aches and pains. Stairs? No, they'd hear her. And where would she hide? Aside from a single drink in her father's kitchen, two months ago, she hadn't been up those stairs in over a decade.

But she couldn't stay here, could she? This was the room they were most likely to search, and where would she hide? No, upstairs was the only way she could—

"Porozhniy?"

"Porozhniy."

Shit. She'd taken too long. She spun on her bootied heels, but there was nothing. Only racks of equipment, and the workbench with more tools and appliances, shelves and spare parts cluttering up the space. There was nothing—

The cabinet!

Tall and slender, painted a dull grey, it sat huddled in the corner, one door hanging lazily open. Wincing at every rustle of her clean-suited legs, she darted across to it. Eased the door fully open. Stepped inside. The metal was cold against her back, creaking softly in protest against the unfamiliar load. She took the internal latch between her teeth and pulled the door closed.

Just then the first intruder reached the top of the stairs. "Isus. Shcho za smitnyk."

"Tikho." The second intruder joined him. "Vy perevirte tsey riven, ya pidu nahoru."

Brita sat frozen inside the cabinet, jaw clenched tight to prevent her teeth from chattering. What had Jorge said about Solomon's first investors? Russian mobsters? Did it even matter if they found her? She tracked footsteps: starting over by the far window, following the workbench all the way along. Coming closer with every step.

Her fingers trembled, the pair of pliers she'd snatched from the workbench quivering with them. She clamped down and pressed her knuckles against the cabinet's back panel. She couldn't afford to have the pliers rattle against it. Not now.

The footsteps stopped, and her imagination ran wild. He'd heard her, seen the glint in her eye, trying to catch a glimpse of him through the crack in the door. His gun, held casually in one hand, swung up. Aimed right at her head—

Then the footsteps started again, just as before.

Breathe, Brita. Just breathe. He doesn't know you're here. No one does.

He was ten feet away. Eight. Six.

He stopped. His jacket rustled. Something clanked as he dropped it on the ground…no. On the workbench. She squeezed her eyes tight. He was looking right at her, she knew it. She could feel his gaze, his attention. She knew, with every fibre of her being, that the next creak of metal, the next rasp of breath, the next pump of her heart would give her away, and it would all have been for nothing. His hand reaching for the door, a dark sneer twisting his lips—

And then he was walking away. Sharp footsteps, no longer careful. Purposeful. Halfway across the room. Beyond the equipment racks. Up the stairs.

He was gone. She'd survived.

For now.

Brita blinked, suddenly aware of the pain in her knees and her calves, forced into an awkward, unsustainable crouch. Even though she was alone, aching, trembling with relief, she couldn't bring herself to move.

But he'll be back. They both will. They're here to take whatever they can.

I can't stay here.

The pliers. She shifted her weight, flipped the pliers around in her grip, froze at the creaking metal. One heartbeat, two, three. Nothing. *They didn't hear. There are three more floors to clear. You have time.* Telling herself these things made them easier to believe. Made it easier to do what she had to do.

She held the pliers by one handle and braced the other into the corner of the cabinet. If she could just get her bindings between the teeth—

Pain, slicing at her wrists. She hissed, her fingers spasmed. The pliers, dangling. Almost falling. Almost, but not quite.

One more, Brita. Just one more.

She was expecting the pain this time. She pulled with her shoulders, clenched her jaw, forced a gap between restraint and red, raw skin. Felt the cold metal of the pliers slide in. Leaned back, put her whole body against the handle, and heard a single, sharp click.

Release. Like a cool summer breeze, chased by clap of thunder. Her hands sprang apart, and hours of tension became pain in an instant. She swallowed a scream whole and let the pliers slip down into her lap.

Her fingers were swollen, tingling with renewed blood flow. Just a second, that's all she needed. A second to catch her breath, to let her body adjust. Then she'd go. Make a break for it, while they were still distracted. But she just needed another second—

"Porozhniy?"

The call echoed down the stairwell, and Brita bit her lip, pressed her back against the cabinet wall. She knew she'd missed her chance.

"Tak. Verkhniy poverkh rokamy pustuvav. Nichoho, krim pylu."

Footsteps, traipsing back down the stairs. Back to the workshop, to find the Gateway. *To find me.*

Sorry, Dad, but it's over. I tried, I really did.

She sagged down from her haunches, her right foot kicking out to the other side of the cabinet. Knocking against something heavy. Long. Metallic. She reached out a trembling hand, and her fingers, just regaining their feeling, closed around the barrel of her father's hunting rifle.

She felt her father's hand on her shoulder, his voice in her heart.

Not fucking yet it's not.

She pushed herself back upright. Ears pricked. Muscles taut. Ready.

A pair of feet landed on the creaking, exposed floorboards. Upstairs, cupboard doors smacked against walls, drawers slammed open. Cutlery rattled. Down here, with her, footsteps approached, and the same pattern repeated. Hands rifled through equipment racks, opened drawers, rummaged through tool-chests.

She counted down the distance, just like before. Only this time she wanted him to get closer. Four feet. Two feet. Her hand slipped down to the trigger guard, and her finger slipped inside. She wanted him to reach out, open the cabinet door—

The instant his hand touched the handle, she kicked.

Clang!

"Aaaa! Shcho za—"

He was lying his back, blood streaming from his nose, leaking between his fingers. At the sight of her, still crouched in the bottom of the cabinet, rifle pointed at his chest, his jaw dropped.

"Serhiy? Ty v poryadku?"

She looked him in the eye, shook her head. He didn't move.

"Serhiy?"

Footsteps, hurrying down the stairs. She stepped out of the cabinet, rifle trained on Serhiy's chest, shocked at how steady she was able to keep it. She edged to the right, keeping Serhiy, still prone, between her and the stairs.

The other thug, the older one, burst into view, then skidded to a halt. "Bozhe chortove! Serhiy? Xto vona?"

"Vona bula v shafi," Serhiy blubbered.

"Don't move," Brita croaked, her voice cracking under the strain. "Not one more step."

Now that they were both here, that she was outnumbered, the reality of where she was, what she was doing, sank in. These men were both hardened criminals. Professionals. Her father had security, and they'd bypassed it as if it wasn't even there.

She was outnumbered. She'd had the element of surprise, and she'd used it. Now what? She didn't even know if her father's rifle was loaded. The barrel began to waver.

And the thug in charge noticed.

"Okay. Okay." He raised his hands, squared himself off against her. "We are calm. Very calm, yes?"

"Very calm, Toli," Serhiy answered.

"Good. That's good."

Brita's breath was coming ragged again. Her head spinning. She backed herself against the workbench. *This is just like any other negotiation,* she told herself, as if it were remotely true.

"Very calm." Toli took a small step forward. "Because we are friends, yes? Good friends?"

"Stop that." Her eyes darted from Toli, to Serhiy, back to Toli. Toli didn't stop. "I said stop!"

"Or what? You will pull trigger? Kill me, unarmed man?" Toli smiled and shrugged, as if it were just a sad fact of life. Somewhere down below, the wind pushed the busted front door open with a crunch. "But I am wondering, is gun even loaded?"

He thinks I'm just some girl, in the wrong place at the wrong time. He doesn't know who I am. Why I'm here. What I want.

Why I want it.

This was a negotiation, and she had all the leverage. The information edge. The motivation.

Crucially, she also had the only weapon.

She raised it, aimed it directly at Toli's nose. "My father's been taking me pheasant shooting since I was ten years old. So when I say don't move, I mean it." Toli stopped. She dropped her aim back down to Serhiy. "You, flat on your back. And hands behind your head. Both of you."

They complied.

"Good. Now, how much do I have to pay you to walk away and tell whoever sent you that you couldn't find what they were after?"

Serhiy glanced back at Toli. Toli peered down at Serhiy. Toli shrugged. "It is not so simple."

Brita's confidence wavered. If she'd been at a real negotiating table, flanked by her lawyers, well rested, well fed, she would have never let it show. She'd miscalculated. She knew it, and then Toli knew it too.

"One hundred thousand pounds." She blurted it out. A panic move.

Toli almost laughed. The rifle stock was sweaty, heavy in her grip. "The boss does not forgive, yes? Does not forget."

The balance was shifting. She didn't know what to do. There was only one option left; her finger trembled against the trigger. But she couldn't pull it, and that's what it came down to. She wasn't willing to go all the way.

Toli had been right all along. Mariska too. She was never going to shoot.

He shifted his weight. Just a small movement. A testing of the waters. Her mouth was dry, her knees weak. There was nothing she could do to st—

Movement on the stairs, a head. Coming up from below. The blood drained from her face. Toli grinned.

Jorge Elorza stared at her, stunned, for a full second. Then he held his finger to his lips.

She snapped her focus back to Toli, ignoring her unexpected ally. Willing Toli and Serhiy to do the same. If she could just buy him some time. A few seconds.

"Five million."

"Money is not enough." He shook his head. Took a step. Jorge loomed behind him.

"Ten million. Cash, shares, whatever you want. Even the deed to this house—"

On the ground between them, Serhiy tensed. He thought he knew what was coming. Jorge rose up from behind, camera held by its sling. Toli flicked his wrist, Brita flinched—

A double crack echoed in the expanse of her father's lab.

When Brita opened her eyes, Toli was on the ground, Jorge's knee in his back. Half of his camera lay on the ground. He'd already unclipped the other half from the sling and was using the sling to tie Toli's hands. She glanced behind. A black iron pry bar was embedded in the wall behind her head.

"Shcho za! Ty khto?" Serhiy had rolled up onto one elbow. "Shcho vy robyly z Anatoli—"

"Serhiy!" Brita jerked back into action, rattling the rifle in his eye line. "Back down, on your stomach!"

"Tak, tak…"

Holding the rifle up with one hand, she scrabbled behind her on the benchtop until she found what she was looking for. A bundle of wire, coated in black. She tossed it to Jorge. "Here." He caught it and set to applying it around Toli's wrists. Blood had begun to pool from beneath his neck. "Is he…"

"Arggghh!" Toli bucked, kicked out, but Jorge had him bound tight.

"He seems fine to me." Jorge grunted, shimmying down Toli's body and holding his legs so he could bind them too. "Seems like I arrived just in time."

"You did, though I don't…" Brita trailed off. "What are you doing here?"

Jorge twisted his wire bindings off, and Toli stopped flailing. There was no longer any point. "I could ask you the same question." Jorge glanced up, the leftover wire bundled in his fist. "You have any pliers?"

"I've got another bundle of wire, will that do?" She tossed a second bundle, this one striped green and yellow, and nodded to Serhiy, still lying on the floor with his hands behind his head.

Jorge caught it and stood from Toli's back. "What did you say his name was? Serhiy?" She nodded. "Hands behind your back, please, Serhiy. The less you struggle, the gentler I'll be." He glanced back up at her, his hands busy with their work. "You still haven't answered my question."

"What do you mean? This is my father's house. Why shouldn't I be here?"

"You don't know?" He scrunched his face up with confusion, then seemed to understand something. "But then, why would you..." He dropped Serhiy's tied hands and pulled his phone from his pocket. He tossed it to her. "Here, look yourself up."

She fumbled the phone, catching it against her stomach with her wrist.

"You can put the gun down now, by the way."

"Oh, yeah. Right." She placed it gently on the benchtop and pulled up Jorge's web browser. What didn't she know? It seemed like so much had happened already. How could there possibly be more? She didn't even have to wait for the first headline to pop up. The auto-filled search suggestion told her everything she needed to know: Brita Gundersson Kidnapped.

She whistled.

"Now look at your share price," he suggested, standing up. "Pliers?"

"In the cabinet." She slapped the phone down on the metal benchtop. She didn't need to look. She knew what would be happening. "So this was Solomon's plan B, huh?"

Jorge bent down to look into the bottom of the cabinet and turned to face her with the mangled cable tie bindings she'd only recently freed herself from. She held up her wrists, showing off the raw, bleeding rips they'd cut into her skin.

"So you really were..."

"Yep, my father and me."

"Hugo too?" He frowned, as if another puzzle piece had landed in his lap, and it still didn't fit. "Wait, then how are you here?"

"That's a long story." Brita picked up his phone. There were so many calls she needed to make. So much she needed to do—"Wait, you haven't answered my question. What are you doing here?"

"Another long story." He grinned and set about cutting and tying off Toli and Serhiy's bindings. "One that I'm hoping will finally win me that Pulitzer." He dropped the pliers on the workbench and gently took the phone from her hand. "We need to get you somewhere safe."

Her immediate instinct was to stay here, but there were two men lying on the floor. Two men who had broken in as if her father's fortress was a kid's cubby-house. She needed somewhere they would not think to look.

"Anita's. Besides, I'll need her help."

"You two have patched things up? That's good."

"Yes, we have—how do you know about that?"

Jorge merely waggled his eyebrows and raised his phone to his ear. "Harvey? Jorge. I've got a tip for you. Burglary at Hugo Gundersson's house in Knightsbridge. How do you think I know. Yes, they're still there. If you hurry, they might even still be there when you roll up." A pause, a wink. "Don't ask me that, either." He flashed her a roguish grin. "Also, you might want to run your eye over who's buying Stora shares this morning. Yes. Yes. No. Look, I've got to go, Harvey. This is a live one. I'll be in touch."

Brita shivered. Her hands were shaking. The adrenaline was fading, and the shock of everything that had happened these last few hours was beginning to sink in. She stumbled, fell back against the workbench. Jorge caught her arm.

"Come on, let's get you out of here." He walked her towards the stairs. "Is there a back way out? Be good to avoid the camera in the street, if we could."

"Yes. Through the courtyard, into an alley." She pulled herself upright, pushed his hand away. She didn't want to rely on his help, as much as she appreciated it. What a day it had been. Solomon, Mariska arrayed against her. And now Jorge was her friend.

"Fantastic. I can pick up my drone on the way."

37

THERE WAS NO BEGINNING or end, to anything. Not the pain, not the noise, not the guilt. They all churned together, ceaselessly tumbled, until he simply gave up and let it happen. Fighting had only made it worse. The rumble and roar were his constants, along with just a single spark of pride: he had spared Brita from the worst of the damage.

The vibration shifted. Tires, rasping on gravel, coming to a juddering halt. The sudden silence was incomprehensible. A gift. The driver's door slammed, and moments later the smell of diesel, overpowering.

Hugo lay back, his head against the floor. Basking in the moment of respite, his mind, very slowly, turning over. Idly wondering: Where were they going? What would happen when they got there? How would they react when they swung open those doors and found him all on his own?

His eyes flicked open. Stared into the darkness.

I have to give Brita as long as possible. It wasn't much, but it was the only advantage she had.

With that thought in his mind, the silence, punctuated only by the ticking of the cooling engine and the churn of the diesel pump, felt empty. Oppressive.

Suspicious.

Hugo moaned. Low, feeble. But not so injured as to attract the wrong sort of attention. Then, in a high, tight voice: "Dad, are you okay?"

"Yeah, I'm...I'm all right. I just..." He rolled over, made an audible show of struggling to sit up.

"Here, let me help." A grunting, wholly unconvincing impersonation of his daughter's voice. Lame, pointless, that anyone who knew her would see through within a second. But Solomon's lackey didn't know her from a bar of soap.

"I said I'm fine, Christ—"

Thud. Thud. Thud.

Fist against metal, reverberating. "Hey. Keep it down, you two. Remember I can hit the brakes whenever I goddamn please."

Hugo smiled, and muttered the vilest, most abusive insults he could muster. Shushed himself. Let his head fall back with an audible bump. Rubbed his synthetically overalled legs against the metal floor. The diesel pump clicked, fell silent, the nozzle rattled back into the rack, and boots on gravel receded into the distance.

Hugo signed off his performance with an imagined bow.

"There you go, Brita. I've done all I can." He lay back, panting from the effort. He shuffled himself, trying to find a comfortable angle for his hips. There wasn't one, but it didn't matter. He would live with the pain for as long as it took.

— • —

1:00 p.m. here. 8:30 a.m. there. The London Stock Exchange had been open for half an hour.

Solomon's driverless sedan had dropped Mariska half a block from the front of Brita's hotel. She'd hopped out, pried the back cover off her phone, pulled out the battery and the SIM card, dumped the whole lot in a bin, and hopped right back in again. If anyone looked, they'd assume she'd been snatched right off the street, just like her boss.

They'd been circling the industrial roads behind Kolkata airport ever since, and without her phone Mariska didn't know what to do with her hands. So she sat on them and stared out the window at the same few warehouses and hangars as the last loop they'd driven, the same stacks of pallets, the same lines of lorries parked, waiting to be filled. She clenched her jaw and tried to ignore Solomon's increasingly anxious swiping at his phone.

Tried, but failed. It was impossible not to watch him in the reflection of the window. Impossible not to notice as, three loops ago, he'd stopped typing orders, sending commands. Two loops ago, when he'd settled into a rhythm of swapping between two different apps with an aggressive swipe and grinding his teeth. One loop ago, when he'd given up obsessively checking his watch, unfastened it, and rested it on his knee.

He swiped. Swiped. Pressed his white knuckles to his lips. Swiped once more, and let his fist fall softly to the armrest.

Mariska tensed. He knew something had gone wrong.

With barely contained volatility, he raised the phone to his ear. "Stan." He shook his head. "No. Plan B." A pause. "Ah'll see you in eighteen hours." Eighteen hours. Plan B. Wasn't this already plan B? He scrolled, scowled, made another call. "Fire her up, Yevgenii. It's time to leave."

Solomon killed the call and dropped his phone in disgust. For a moment he sat still, seething in private. Then he barked an order at the car, and the pattern broke. The sedan turned, set on its new course to a private airfield, just around the corner.

For the entire remainder of their journey, not once did Solomon look her way.

⸺ • ⸺

The footsteps returned, approaching the rear of the truck. Hugo held his breath, his heart pounding, the pumping blood accentuating the pain in his wrists, his shoulders, his neck. He closed his eyes, willing the footsteps to continue, straight on. *Go on. Be a bastard. Don't check on us, we don't fucking need it.*

The footsteps turned, slid away. The driver's-side door opened, then slammed shut. Hugo braced for the squeal of the engine starting, the end of his precious silence. The confirmation that his subterfuge had worked, for now. Instead, a panel slid open at the front of the container. A square of blinding light.

A plastic thump, followed by another. The panel slid shut. Then, before he could catch his breath, the engine was rolling, the tires crunching gravel once more. Gravity, and then centripetal force, pulled him tight into his corner, and a plastic bottle of water rolled into his hip.

He couldn't help but laugh. What in god's name was he going to do with a bottle of water with his hands tied behind his back? If Brita had been here to help him, maybe. But she wasn't. She was off doing what needed to be done.

Somehow, the noise, the pain, they didn't seem quite so overwhelming anymore. They were external now. A duty to be endured. He'd broken through an impenetrable barrier and found purpose on the other side. He rested his head against the back of the truck, gathered the water bottle between his knees, and closed his eyes.

It took a while for Hugo to realise that something had changed. The rumble of the engine, the roar of tires on bitumen, the rattle of suspension as the truck juddered over potholes and against curbs, that all seemed normal now. But slowly, almost imperceptibly, he realised he was finding it harder and harder to brace himself into his corner.

The truck lurched, kicked, angled. Hugo's grip failed, and he slid all the way from the cabin to the rear. Gravity had pulled him.

The truck had started driving uphill.

38

—·—

HOT WATER RAINED DOWN from above and jetted into her from both sides, gently massaging Brita's scalp, her ribs, and her back. She clutched her welted, swollen wrists to her chest to protect them from the spray. The steam, the all-encompassing rush should have felt comforting, but all it did was leave her free to dwell on everything that had happened.

About Mariska, her friend. Her closest confidante. Deserting her without a second thought. She leaned her head back and let the water smother her face, rivulets running down her neck, the hot spray scraping across her wounds, driving everything that wasn't pain to the fringes. No thoughts meant no regrets. For a few seconds anyway.

But she couldn't stay in the shower forever. She hadn't fought her way back here just to hide away. No. What she needed was a plan.

She scrawled on the fogged glass, mapping out her resources. What she knew, and what she needed. As fast as she wrote, the details faded, fresh spray and fog wiping out any progress she might have made. How could she mount a rescue when she didn't know where he was? How could she stop Solomon when she couldn't let anyone know she was here, when any public appearance would raise uncomfortable questions about just how she'd gotten from Kolkata to London impossibly fast?

Her thoughts strayed back to the dark, jolting truck. To an emergency Gateway, tucked into the sole of a shoe. Where had that even come from? And to a confession, another betrayal. If her father could hide a portal in his shoes, what more was he—

"Hey!" The glass rattled, a firm hand banging on the outside. "Hurry up, woman, you'll shrivel like a prune!"

Brita wiped away the steam, revealing Anita, a forced cheerfulness twisting her smile.

"Did you get through? Is it done?" she shouted, over the roar of her friend's ridiculous shower.

"It's done. Finally. Trading halted at eight forty-six."

"How bad is it?"

Anita paused, looked away. "There's clothes on the bench. Bandages, antiseptic. And food outside, when you're ready."

"That bad?" Brita asked. Anita nodded. "Fucking Garfield. I should have…" She shook her head, her sodden hair flicking out, slapping back. She lashed out with a fist, slamming the tap off. The last of the water gurgled as it spiralled down the drain.

"Don't be too hard on him." Anita held out a towel as she opened the door. The rest of the bathroom was just as ostentatiously luxurious as the shower: pristine white marble, enormous mirror shrouded with steam, and rose gold fittings for the dual sinks as well as the swimming pool–sized bath along the far wall. Brita snatched the towel away and smothered her face.

"Why not?" she muttered, voice muffled. "All he's done his entire bloody career is obstruct, obstruct, obstruct."

"He spoke to Mas. She told him you were fine. That you'd checked into your hotel and were probably just sleeping."

She scrunched the towel tight. Bit into it, pressed it into her face, so hard that a bright cascade of colour burst behind her eyes. "She told him that?"

"She told him to wait, said she was going to check on you. Just in case."

Delaying the trading halt, for just long enough. She released her towel and wrapped it beneath her armpits. In the fogged-up mirror, both Anita and she were little more than indistinct blobs. "Let me guess. She never called him back." Anita's blob shook her head, and Brita found herself, inexplicably, laughing. "Jesus Christ."

"What? What's funny?" Anita asked.

Brita turned, faced her friend. Ran her hand back through her sodden hair, unable to wipe the unwelcome smile from her face. "Nothing. There's nothing funny about this. I just realised that I'm not even surprised."

"You shouldn't be. I'm not."

Brita raised a solitary eyebrow, inviting Anita to continue.

"She invited me to your dinner party because she wanted to force you to be ruthless. She wanted an alpha to follow. Now she's got one."

Brita pulled another towel from the rack, bowed, and dipped her head so that she could wrap it around her hair. As she twisted the towel into a tail, she considered the implication between Anita's words. That she didn't have what it took to bring Gateway to life. Or, at least, that's what Solomon and Mariska thought. She wrung the towel tightly, until water dripped between her fingers, and flipped it over her shoulder as she stood upright.

"You think she'd try to flip if I could manage to take Gateway back?"

Anita snorted. "Maybe. Would you want her to?"

Brita shrugged. Probably not. But getting the chance to turn her down... It was morbid to think about, darkly pleasing. Not productive, though. She forced her mind to the half-baked ideas she'd scrawled on the misting glass, not a one of which had been any good. "God, Anita. What am I going to do?"

"What about..." Anita nodded back through the door, waggled her immaculately plucked eyebrows.

"What, Jorge?" Brita shrugged again and stayed away from the mirror, suddenly aware of a rising flush. Self-conscious of the fact she was wearing nothing but a towel. "He doesn't know anything."

"About Gateway, maybe," Anita said, just a hint of mirth in her voice, indicating she knew exactly why Brita had turned away. "But he knows just about everything else. And he knows Solomon, better than the rest of us."

The rest of us... The thought snapped Brita upright. "We need to call Ming-Xia. Let her know what's going on."

"Yes." Anita rapped her knuckles on the marble benchtop. "Gather the brain trust. I like it." She plucked a pile of clothes from behind her and dumped them into Brita's arms. The tube of antiseptic cream clattered on the wet marble floor. "You get yourself respectable. I'll do the rest."

"Respectable? In these?" Brita said, unfolding a truly hideous pair of faded pink tracksuit pants with matching top, but Anita had already skipped out into the hall.

— • —

With a pair of deep breaths, Brita braced herself. She pulled her sleeves down, covering the fresh bandages on her wrists as best she could, feeling totally ridiculous. Honestly, pink? It was as if Anita had selected the most obnoxious outfit she owned, on purpose. And the underwear...she fidgeted with her bra straps, but there was no getting away from the fact they were just too small.

The indignity of it all.

What else was there to do? Push on. There was no other choice. She turned the handle, her cheeks flushed to match Anita's horrid velvet sweater, and stepped out into the corridor.

She emerged out into Anita's spacious, tastefully understated lounge area to find it barely occupied. Anita was nowhere to be seen, and Jorge was pressed up against the wall in the far corner, peering surreptitiously through the curtains and out onto the busy street below. She stopped, loitering behind one of Anita's custom Japanese lounges, tried not to think about the awful colour clash, and observed.

How different he seemed from the slick presenter of two months ago, just waiting to spring his ambush under the bright studio lights. Or the savvy street journalist, easing her away from the confusion at the police barricade at the foot of the Britannia Bank steps. His black hair, streaked with grey, was unkempt, a visit to the barber long overdue. Half a week's worth of stubble. A drab suit that bore all the hallmarks of a long, sleepless night, and the remains of his camera poking from his jacket pocket.

He looked just as tired as she felt.

"Like what you see?" Brita jumped at his unexpected question, and he flicked her his familiar, charming grin. His gaze lingered, eyebrows raised, as he took in the styling Anita had foisted upon her. "I was going to say you look better after a shower, but…"

"I feel better, at least." Brita shrugged, ignoring the scratch of an overtight strap beneath her armpits, and started across the room. "See anything out there?"

Jorge allowed himself one last glance up and down, keeping his features neutral, though he was unable to hide his amusement from his eyes. "Nothing out of the ordinary, no—"

The instant he turned back to the window, his demeanour changed, the colour draining from his face. By the time he waved at her to stay back, she'd already frozen, her shins pressed up against Anita's genuine Noguchi coffee table.

"What is it?"

"Stay back."

"Jorge?" Brita crouched down, one hand on the glass tabletop, the other on the floor. "Who's out there?"

"I don't know. I thought I saw a face…"

Visions of Slavic thugs lurking beneath lampposts swam to the surface. Of Serhiy and Toli, having escaped Jorge's police friend, having ransacked her father's house, now moving on to hers, to Anita's. Of Mariska, whispering in Solomon's ear, telling him just where to look.

"Got some visitors, do we?" Anita's bright voice sliced right through her spiralling panic.

But not Jorge's. He maintained his vigilance at the window, his brow creased with concern. "I…maybe." He ducked a little, changed his angle, then turned back to the room shaking his head. "But I could just be being paranoid."

"Paranoid? After everything that's happened? Sounds like you're taking appropriate precautions to me. And speaking of…" Anita turned her focus to Brita and twitched her head in the direction from which she'd come, speaking with a suggestively raised brow. "Just got off the blower with Ming-Xia…"

Brita stood. "How is she?"

"Relieved to hear that you're safe. Concerned about your father." Anita glanced back towards the window, the threats waiting beyond. "She suggested that perhaps we might like to make a strategic withdrawal, just for the time being?"

"You've got a secret back door too?" Jorge rolled his eyes, a wry grin flashing across his lips. "Of course you do. Why am I not surprised."

"I wouldn't count those chickens just yet, Jorge." Anita laughed, a mischievous glint in her eye. "Should we warn him?"

Brita's gaze flicked from Anita to Jorge and back again. He wore an uncertain, slightly worried, very curious frown. She could see the gears turning, trying to figure out just what she meant, though she knew he would never guess. A part of her wanted to put him out of his misery; he had warned her about Solomon *and* saved her from his goons. But he'd also ambushed her, questioned her integrity. Spied on her...

She smiled, shook her head. "No, I don't think we should. Do you?"

Anita too shook her head, her sweet smile never leaving her lips. Perhaps it was a small act of vengeance, keeping Jorge in the dark. Perhaps, after such a turbulent morning, they both just needed a laugh. His frown deepened. He opened his mouth, then shut it again. There was no point asking: the decision had been made.

Brita gave the windows a final glance before turning her back on them. As long as whatever was out there stayed out there, and she stayed in, she wouldn't get hurt. And her father would stay kidnapped, her company, and Gateway, in limbo. She would have to make a move, and soon. Hopefully, with Ming-Xia's help, she'd know the right move to make.

"Come on," she said, beckoning Jorge to follow. "This way. You won't want to miss this."

— · —

Anita's private office was as pristine and opulent as ever, the ostentatious display of wealth designed to both impress and overwhelm whoever was unfortunate enough to be caught on the other side of her desk. *The complete opposite of mine*, Brita thought. As always. She honestly could not imagine how her friend got anything done in here.

Jorge stopped at the threshold, one hand resting on the doorjamb. He peered cautiously within.

"Nothing to see, I'm afraid. Not yet, anyway." Anita tossed her hair back and pulled her desk phone across red leather and polished mahogany. She offered it to Brita. "Would you care to do the honours?"

"Is this it? The big reveal?" Jorge asked.

Mock bravado. It wouldn't last long, Brita knew. She took the phone and pressed the button marked *M* with relish. It rang once, twice. She watched Jorge's eyes.

Behind her, a Gateway fissured Anita's wall, and a rectangle of Malaysian afternoon sunlight spilled out onto the carpet. Jorge's eyes bulged, his jaw falling slack.

"Jorge, may I introduce Ming-Xia Peng and Project Gateway." Brita stepped back, making sure Jorge had an uninterrupted view. "Have you visited Kuala Lumpur before?"

He swallowed, hesitated. "This is, uhh…" He crept forward, his eyes on the portal's rim, on the seemingly impossible thinness of it. There was no plaster or timber, no brick or aluminium doorway, just a hole in space that connected Anita's office to Ming-Xia's, with nothing in between. He extended a curious finger, as if to touch the shimmering interface, then thought better of it. "Well, this fills in a gap or two."

"Such as how Brita is here, when your tabloids are reporting she's been kidnapped in Kolkata?" Ming-Xia asked.

"That's one, yes." Jorge gave the Gateway one last appraisal before stepping through and turning his attention to Ming-Xia and her light-filled private office at the top of Peng Industries Tower. "I'm sorry, we haven't met. You must be Ms Peng. Jorge Elorza."

"I understand you've been following us rather closely," Ming-Xia said.

Brita tensed, glancing Anita's way. She'd warned Ming-Xia that Jorge would be coming, hadn't she?

"If I hadn't, Brita would be back in Solomon's hands right now, and the rest of you would be up shit creek, if you'll pardon the language." He turned slightly, so he could speak to all three of them. "You all know Solomon is no friend of mine…" Jorge's eyes widened, his blunt, pragmatic demeanour faltering just for a moment. "Those really are the Petronas Towers over there, aren't they?" He glanced back through the portal, to Anita's office, to Kensington. London. He blinked and ran a hand over his disbelieving eyes and stared up at the ceiling.

"It's a lot to take in, I know…" Brita said.

"It's just…It's starting to make sense, that's all. How you wound up in your father's workshop literally minutes after the press put in you India. How your father walks through your front door just hours after disappearing through the check-in gates at Heathrow…" Jorge turned his gaze back to her, all wonder, all amusement gone. "By bundling you and your father into the back of a truck, Solomon has risked everything. When you first told me, I didn't get it. I almost didn't believe it. Now, though…" He shook his head.

"You didn't think he would be so ruthless?" Ming-Xia asked.

"No, I wouldn't say that. I just didn't know why he'd take such a risk." Jorge's jaw was set, his lips pulled tight. "Now I do."

"Well, I for one am delighted you're beginning to catch up," Anita quipped, making her way to a set of tastefully aged couches, tucked into a secluded corner of Ming-Xia's office, out of sight of the floor-to-ceiling windows. "But we have a serious, serious problem here. It's time to get down to business."

Brita followed gratefully, sinking into the cushions across from Anita with relief. The stresses of the past few hours had begun to take their toll. Ming-Xia took her place beside Anita, her movements graceful and understated in comparison to Anita's flamboyant drama. Jorge, for the time being, appeared unable to tear himself from the Gateway.

"Before we start," Ming-Xia said, her voice lowered. She had both her hands folded in her lap. "When Anita called, I feared the worst. When I heard that not only were you unharmed, but that you'd managed to escape to London..." Ming-Xia's gaze danced up and down, her eyes widening just a little, the corners of her lips curling into the barest hint of a smile. "I have to say, I'd imagined you looking rather more...bedraggled."

Brita felt herself blush, again. She clasped her knees with her hands, shrinking her body as much as she could. "We both have Anita to thank for that."

"Now, now. We couldn't have you getting recognised by our bloodthirsty media—present company excepted of course," Anita said, dismissing her embarrassment and pre-empting Jorge's non-existent indignation with a waving hand. "Not with so much at stake."

"Of course. A...sensible precaution." Ming-Xia let her smile fall away, indicating that the time for levity had passed. Brita, by contrast, felt even more ridiculous, sitting between her peers, dressed like a fool. "Now, Brita. I'd like to hear it from the beginning."

And so Brita told it, forcing her feelings of shame down until even she barely knew they were there. She spoke of her descent into Kolkata, Jorge's warning about Solomon and his plans ringing in her ears. Of the radio silence from her father, from Mariska, of the unbearable ride from the airport, where one minute she'd had her finger over Anita's number, desperate to get her insights, and the next finding Stanley's gun pointed directly at her chest. And as she spoke, as she stepped her accomplices through all that had happened, she noticed a pattern emerging from her narrative.

At every point, her fate had been in someone else's control. Jorge with his warnings, Stanley driving her into a trap. Solomon taking what wasn't his, Mariska following the winning hand without a second thought. Her father stepping up, getting her to safety. Jorge, again, rescuing her from falling back into Solomon's hands. Then Anita, offering her shelter, dealing with Garfield and the market, protecting her from the dangers outside the window. Anita, taking charge. Solving problems, two and three at a time.

But Stora is my company, and Gateway is my legacy. Not Solomon's, not Anita's, not Mariska's. She gritted her teeth, thinking back to her father's confession in the back of the truck. *Not even his.*

It was time she showed everyone she was worthy of it.

Those thoughts had been playing out in her head as she'd finished her telling. Jorge managed to tear himself away from the Gateway at last. Ming-Xia blinked, pursed her lips. Thought for a second, then asked the only question she could. "What have you got planned?"

"Well—" Anita began, but Brita cut her off. Not rudely, not defensively. Anita had practically carried her into the shower. She knew better than anyone how high a toll this morning had taken on her and was just trying to help. But it wasn't the help Brita needed anymore.

"We've got a few things going for us. One: as far as we know, Solomon doesn't know I've escaped. Two: we have Jorge." Brita turned her focus to the Spanish journalist, who raised his eyebrows at his inclusion on her list. "I only know Solomon from across the boardroom table. You know him from the shadows. You can help us predict his next moves."

"I mean..." He vacillated, but Brita couldn't let that slow her down.

"And three: we have Gateway, and he doesn't."

"Counterpoint," Ming-Xia said, raising a slender finger. "He might have control of your company. If so, this is all moot."

"Yes, he might. And he might not." She glanced across at Anita. "If he had the numbers, surely this would all be over, right? What advantage is there in dragging this out?"

Anita shrugged, flicked a glance Ming-Xia's way. "I can't think of any. Can you?"

Ming-Xia shook her head. Jorge frowned, but when she nodded his way, inviting him to speak, he waved her away.

"Good. That gives us time to do some number crunching of our own. Confirm exactly what happened with this morning's trades, or at least a worst-case scenario. Anita, can I leave that with you?"

"Yes, boss. Old Garfield will be sick of the sight of me by the end of the day." Anita grinned.

"Excellent. Ming-Xia." Brita pressed her palms together, her forefingers against her lips. "Solomon doesn't know where I am, and I don't know where he is. I'd like to change that. Is that something..."

"Consider it done," Ming-Xia said with a brusque nod, her phone, like Anita's, already in her hand. Brita had a feeling that Solomon was not the only one with contacts on the shadier side of the law. Ming-Xia stepped away, phone pressed to her ear. Brita looked away. There were some things she just didn't need to know.

"Brita, one question," Jorge asked. "This 'portal' you said your father had in his shoes. Did you know your father was working on such things?"

"No, none. All he told me was that it was Sato's idea." With a jolt, she realised that nobody had called him, and he was part of the team. A vital part of the team. He should be here. "Anita, can you—"

"As soon as I've dealt with Garfield..."

She turned back to Jorge, his question worming its way deeper and deeper. When could he have had the time? "I thought he'd been working just as hard as...as the rest of us had been, getting the project teams into shape." She shrugged. "But who knows? Maybe he was Gating back to his workshop every night to work on it."

"We were both there this morning. Did it look like he'd been hard at work there to you?"

She thought back. Shook her head. "No. It actually looked kind of dusty." Jorge smiled. "Why? What do you know?"

"Me? I don't know anything." He flashed her his TV reporter grin. "But I do have a hunch."

39

The helicopter's harness chafed against Mariska's neck, the small, ovular window just too far away for her to rest her head against it. White-capped peaks and deep, shadowed ravines passed far below, and she watched minuscule cars twisting and turning their way up and down the Himalayas. She reached for her pocket, a reflex, wanting to check a map, to see whether they were still over India or had strayed into Bangladesh, or maybe Nepal. But her pocket was empty, and would remain so for the foreseeable future.

Not that she would have had reception up here anyway.

Her headset protected her against the roar of the rotors above, but not the vibration. Everything rattled, from the clips in her harness to her teeth. When it crackled to life, she could barely make out the words.

"We leave India. Come to Bhutan." The pilot, the Yevgenii that Solomon had spoken to back in Sandeep's car, had a thick accent. It was only the second time he'd spoken. The first time, telling them that they were about to take off, she'd guessed that he was Russian. Now, though, she knew. Ukrainian. She recognised the hard breathiness, the way *come* had almost been spoken with a *ch*.

She'd been observing Solomon since it had all gone pear-shaped. He'd been completely unprepared for the aftermath of his actions. As if he'd acted out of fear. Of desperation. And she'd wondered why. Why was this powerful, influential man so hell bent on taking control of Gateway? Not generally. That much was obvious. But why right now? This morning, and not tomorrow? Or next week?

It could only be because Gateway wasn't what he actually wanted, but a bargaining chip for something he wanted even more. Something he was scared of, or someone he was beholden to. And if it was the Ukrainians, that was not a good sign.

"What's in Bhutan?" she asked, shouting into the microphone at her chin.

"Somewhere quiet." Somehow, even strapped into a military helicopter, he managed to look relaxed. He wasn't, though. He kept checking his phone, every couple of minutes, and then clenching his jaw, his thin lips growing even thinner when he didn't find what he wanted. Brita had been doing the same thing at the dinner party.

"For how long?"

She'd wondered how long Garfield would wait for her call before he acted. Fifty minutes. The trading halt had been called at just after 8:40 a.m., and in those forty minutes of active trading, Stora's share price had been punished. Down twenty-three points, with volume through the roof. Solomon flipped his phone in his hands, dropped his eyes. Grimaced. Put his phone away. He'd said he wouldn't need long. Evidently, forty minutes had not been enough.

"How long?" she asked again.

"How long what?" he snapped.

"Will we be in Bhutan?"

He curled his top lip, like he was growling. "Forty-eight hours. At most." He slapped his knee as if that was the end of it. Job done.

"All right. What then?"

"What then?" He reared back suddenly, breaking out into a raucous leer. "Then ah fuckin' win."

The helicopter was cold, but that wasn't what made her shiver. That gleam in his eyes, it was almost manic. He was not acting like a man about to close a meticulously planned, ruthlessly efficient, very profitable business transaction.

She'd seen it before, that look, a long time ago, in the small town she'd tried so hard to forget.

He looked like a man who was fighting for survival. And losing.

He's going to take me down with him.

"And after you own Stora? Control Gateway? What then?"

"That's why you're here."

"Ah." She leaned forward, gripping her harness straps with both hands. "So you expect me to de-escalate this from a fucking international kidnapping. Just talk Brita down, get her in front of a camera, tell everyone it was a big misunderstanding. Something like that? Just hope everyone ignores that fact that during those forty-eight hours, the ownership of her company, the company her father founded, has changed hands?"

"They won't know. No one will, except the four of us."

Mariska processed each new piece of information, her picture of what was actually happening here forming and reforming. "If you don't need public control of Gateway, then why go to all this effort? Why bother with this at all?"

"Because ah needed them to know who has the power here. That mah preference is to keep them involved, that they can still be the public face of Gateway. They can still become very, very rich. But"—he sneered, leaned forward—"ah can so easily cut them out if they don't do as they're told."

Mariska shook her head. "Hugo will never. You don't understand what this means to him."

"That's where you're wrong. Ah do understand." Solomon flashed her a knowing grin, and the sudden queasiness in the pit of her stomach told her she'd missed something. Some crucial piece of information. "This was his fuckin' idea."

"I'm sorry, what?"

"Yeah, you heard me right."

She sagged back into her seat, the picture in her mind shifting, distorting, previously unrelated facts coming into focus: Hugo storming from his workshop that first night at the very thought of losing an ounce of control, and his complete transformation not four hours later when she'd shown up at his door.

At the time she'd thought he'd just cooled down. Come to his senses, her judgement clouded by the fact he had like her idea. The idea that had turned into the dinner party, Gateway's debut, that Solomon had somehow found out about. *The dinner party that Hugo had wanted to invite him to...*

"Wait, that doesn't make sense. If Hugo was in on it, why did you have to coerce Phil Greenberg into giving up his ticket? And why is he in the truck with Brita..."

"Ah didn't say he was in on it. He was just the...inspiration."

Before she could respond, their headphones crackled. The pilot sliding into the conversation.

"We will commencing our descent." There it was again, that soft *ch*, the idiosyncratic phrasing. *Jesus Christ, Solomon. What are you doing playing with the Ukrainian mob?* The chopper lurched, angled forward, only adding to the nausea she was already feeling. *What am I doing getting stuck in between them?*

The helicopter banked to the left, leaving her dangling from her webbing, barely touching the seat beneath her. For the moment, all she could think about was the thrumming of the engine, the chop chop chop of the rotor blades, the only things holding them aloft. Keeping them alive. Across the cabin, gravity pressed Solomon back against his seat, his harness loose, taking slow, deep breaths. He looked like he was about to be sick. A good thing their positions were not reversed. She'd be right in the firing line.

Through the window behind his head, she picked out a rectangular pattern of lights, clearly man made, bright white and industrial. A stark contrast to the organic layout of the local villages they'd previously overflown, their windows warm with firelight. Just beyond the lights, almost buried in the gloom, she made out an expanse of dark water and a long concrete ridge with four slender concrete tunnels disappearing into the valley below.

A dam. He was taking her to his hydroelectric plant.

The pilot circled the landing site, the rotors kicking up a ring of dust that blew away into the night. The landing, incongruous with the violent power of the chopper's engines, was light as a feather. She didn't even realise it was over until the whine of the turbine began to ramp down, the ever-present vibrations dying away. At the edge of her vision sat what had once been the plant's main admin building. From the sparse, flickering lighting and the overgrown weeds, it must have been deserted for a long, long time.

Solomon tore himself free of his restraints and yanked at the door. By the time she'd unclipped hers and stepped out into the night, he'd already chugged a plastic bottle of water. She stood by his side, resisting the urge to retrieve the crushed bottle he'd just tossed aside. The wind from the still-thrumming helicopter blades caught it, blew it out of sight.

"Welcome to the future of electricity," he yelled, as if the helicopter was still whining at full power. The colour was already returning to his cheeks, his gaze once again completely focused. He was watching her every move. She pointed to the doorway, twenty or so metres away; ducked; and ran out from under the blades. He sauntered over to meet her, perfectly erect. Irrationally confident.

"The perfect hideout," she muttered, eyeing the stark landing area, tufts of hardy mountain grass poking between dust and rubble. It was a foreboding place. "Why here?"

"It's close, it's secluded, and it's mine. Well, almost. Ah've agreed terms with the government. It's with the lawyers now." He placed his hand gently on her back, directing her inside. "Plus, it's a token for your old boss. Show her ah'm still committed to doin' this right once ah've taken over. Come on, ah'll give you the tour."

Behind them the helicopter's rotors spun up once more. With a turbo-powered roar, it took off.

The building was just as barren on the inside, empty rooms with cleaner patches of concrete where furniture and equipment had once been. She kept careful track of their winding path. Fluorescent lights flickered on ahead of them as they walked through. There must have been sensors somewhere, though she couldn't see them.

"Here we are. This is where ah'll put the Gateways." Solomon opened a door out onto an iron gantry overlooking a vast concrete cavern, the weak light from the corridor barely illuminating its depths.

"Wow," Mariska said. And she meant it. The sight of the concrete: blocky, sturdy, utilitarian. "It reminds me a little bit of home."

"That must have been some childhood."

"Huh? Oh, no, not literally. It's the concrete, the shape of the windows. The handrails even." She leaned over the railing, her eyes adjusting to the dim light. On the far wall she could just make out a row of giant holes, six, maybe seven metres in diameter. They were so much larger up close. "I grew up at the tail end of communist rule in Hungary. Take out the entrances to the tunnels in the wall over there—this could be a Soviet concert hall. It's…I won't say it's comforting. But it is bringing up a lot of old memories."

And some not so old. Her and Brita, sitting on the boot of her Jag at Heathrow, lamenting the impending demise of yet another set of utilitarian concrete monoliths. At least this one would get a facelift. A chance at a new life.

"Ah never would have guessed an ambitious young thing like you was born red." Solomon joined her. The creaked beneath their combined weight, and she pulled back, hiding her burgeoning doubts behind her discomfort at the ancient, creaking metal. She'd acted on instinct, letting her ambition drive. Her greed.

I shouldn't be here with him. I should be in that truck. With them.

There had to be a way to undo this, to set things right.

To find it, though, she'd have to keep playing his game.

"We can't help where we're born. Miskolc. A rough little town, closer to Ukraine than Budapest. My dad was even a party member." A party member first, father second. Husband third.

"Ah'm not surprised you saw the light. What did you do when the wall fell?"

"Me? I was only seven or eight at the time. Just a kid." This was getting personal, real quick. "I survived. I've been surviving."

"Ah know your daddy left you. Abandoned you, and your mother, for the Party. For Russia. Ah've done my research." He rolled around, looked her dead in the eyes. "And ah can imagine what that did to you. Makes me wonder if you would really do the same to Brita and Hugo."

She held his gaze, unblinking, heart pounding. There was no way he could know these things. But he did, and she could use that fact against him. Let him think he knew her. "You're right. Dad leaving us changed everything. I swore I'd never get left behind again." Her hands were clasped behind her back, her grip on herself so tight that it hurt. "I'm not in the business of losing, Mr Solomon. The Gateway is my ticket, and I intend to cash it."

His eyes, black in the dim light, burned right through her, burrowing deep to determine the truth of what she'd said. The moment stretched for what seemed like an eternity, so long she had to force herself to breathe. In the silence, drops of water made a rhythmic tinkle.

"Well," he conceded, pulling himself upright. "Ah can certainly respect that. You want somethin', you gotta take it. No one's gonna just hand it to yer, ah can tell you that." He broke into one of his charming smiles and offered her his hand. She had to unclamp her fists from one another to take it. Inside, however, she remembered the manic gleam he'd let slip in the chopper. Just how close to the edge he really was.

She could not afford to do the same.

"That's a lesson I learned a long time ago, Mr Solomon." *From more dangerous men than you.*

"Please, call me Richard." He took one last look around the chamber, then turned towards the beckoning corridor. "Come on, ah'll show you where we're sleeping. Then we can eat."

40

Brita sat with her ankles hooked around the legs of her barstool, her shoulders hunched and her baseball cap pulled down low. She felt like a slob, but at least she'd managed to find something that wasn't Anita's pink tracksuit.

Jorge had ushered her into the dingy little bar, and she'd instinctively taken up a position at the high counters that butted up against the grimy front windows. A seat she could watch from with her back to everyone. Somewhere she could see, without being seen.

Outside, it seemed like just another ordinary day in Waterloo. Cabs and scooters, workers in hi-vis and suits, students and shoppers, all of them just getting on with their days. None of them aware that the kidnapping victim whose face had been plastered across every TV screen and newsfeed in Britain was sitting just on the other side of the glass.

"Here you go."

Jorge plonked a glass in front of her, a lemon lime and bitters, and wrestled his barstool into a comfortable position at her side. She glanced longingly at his tumbler, filled with two fingers of whisky and a single ice block.

God, she wanted one. Her mouth watered, even as Jorge winced at the first sip, and he glanced back at the barman with a look of betrayal. She wanted that drink for the wrong reasons. She bit her lip, swallowed, and wrapped her hands around her own glass. Relished the cold condensation against her palms.

If she started now, she feared she might never stop.

"So, are you going to tell me what we're doing here or not?" Brita asked.

Jorge grimaced through another mouthful, as if determined not to give in, and nodded through the window and across the road. At an underpass, a café, a cluttered and overgrown storage yard.

"What am I looking at?"

"That first night, after our interview—I am sorry about that, by the way—I, uh."

Brita watched him fidget with his glass and, for the first time since she'd known him, he was unable to meet her gaze.

"You what, Jorge?" She considered telling him not to worry, that she'd already forgiven him, but watching him squirm was…revitalising. She took a sip of her drink, and her tongue puckered at the touch of the sweet bubbles. She wondered if this is what it felt like to be Jorge, to sit on the other side of the microphone.

"Well, I had a bit of a crisis of confidence, I guess." He knocked back the last of his whisky and sent the glass skidding away down the faded countertop. "I knew there was a story, right? You knew you'd said too much; so did Mariska. And so did Solomon, as it turned out. But then it kind of hit me, all at once. I hadn't chased a real story in years, not since Solomon torpedoed my career. And then the first sniff that comes my way and he's involved? It was too much."

"And?" Brita looked from Jorge to the street outside, trying and failing to spot the connection. "So what? You obviously got over it."

"I went for a walk, to clear my head, and just about tripped over your father having a midnight coffee with Stanley fucking Adams. Just around the corner from here."

She pursed her lips. So that's how it had all started, that very first night. And Jorge had been there, watching it all go down.

"You didn't know?"

"Not until this morning." She shook her head, took another long pull from her glass. Imagined it was wine, a rich Shiraz maybe. "He confessed in the back of the truck. Right before he got me out of there."

"Interesting timing."

"Mmm," Brita said, non-committal. She could pinpoint the moment she'd gotten over the role Jorge had played in kick-starting this whole mess: the sheer relief she'd experienced as his head had emerged from the stairwell in her father's apartment, at the perfect time, was hard to ignore.

She could not say the same about her father. His admission of guilt still stung, to the point where she'd not mentioned it to Anita or Ming-Xia. A father and daughter walked by the front of the bar, hand in hand. The girl couldn't have been much more than seven or eight, and the look of trust—

Brita turned away, back to Jorge. She didn't have time for such thoughts. "None of that explains what we're doing here, though."

"Ah, well." Jorge raised his eyebrows. "I followed him, you see. Afterwards. Straight here."

"To this depressing little pub?"

"Nope." He pointed out the window, towards the yard. "There. He talked to the receptionist, pulled a key from his pocket, and disappeared inside."

"The self-storage place? That could mean anything—"

"He never left, Brita. When I watched the security footage back—"

"Hang on, security footage?"

"How did you think I knew they'd broken into your father's house this morning?"

"I—" Brita stammered, her mouth flapping in the stale air. She snapped it shut, and he grinned at the look of realisation that must have flashed across her features. "I don't... just get on with the story."

"Right. So I followed your father and sat in this very spot and drank some truly horrid Shiraz and watched an empty door for about three hours before giving up and going home. But, when I watched the security footage from outside your father's house, I saw"—Jorge started counting events off his fingers—"your father storm out at around eleven, you and Mariska leave in your big black CEO car about half an hour later. Mariska came back at about two." He glanced up, as if to check whether she'd reacted to this new revelation. He waited a moment, but she remained impassive. Even impatient. "She waited on the front step for a little while, until two thirty, when your father opened the door and let her inside."

"So?" Brita shrugged. She was beyond caring what Mariska or her father had been getting up to behind her back. All she wanted was to take Solomon down. Get her company back. The rest could wait.

"He never left the storage facility. Not by the door anyway."

Brita looked up at Jorge, then across at the run-down storage facility. So plain, so normal, you could walk past without even knowing it was there.

The perfect hiding spot. Especially if you didn't have to use the front door.

—— ◈ ——

Brita pushed against Stowaway Self Storage's front door, tinkling the little bell suspended above it, and stepped inside. The damp, muddy yard out front belied a neat, dust-free interior. The carpet was clean; the racks of tape and scissors, boxes, and cable ties were pleasingly symmetrical; and a plump woman with short hair and her glasses down on the bottom of her nose sat behind the counter.

"Hi." Brita waved. "I'm..."

"No, don't tell me." The proprietor stood up, her words rolling with a Scottish lilt. Her eyes, which had looked up merely with politeness, took on a gleam of recognition. The woman beamed. "I'd know your face anywhere." Brita felt her face freeze, her smile fixed in place as the little old lady tottered out and took her hand. "You must be Sarah. Graham's daughter. He's told me all about you." The woman turned her attention to Jorge. "Though he never told me you had such a handsome husband."

Try as she might, Brita could not speak. The whole situation was so bizarre. Colour flushed to her cheeks, from embarrassment, from the momentary rush of fear when she thought she'd been recognised by this kindly old woman. Thankfully, Jorge leapt into the breach, putting on his most charming Spanish accent.

"Jorge Elorza. A pleasure to meet you, madam."

"Yes, quite." The little woman blushed, and then jumped, raising her hand to her lips. "Och, where are my manners? Here I am gushing and you don't know me from...anyway, I'm Agatha. It's so nice to finally put a face to all of Graham's stories."

Brita blinked, attempting to regain control of her face. Either Agatha was horribly confused, or...

"How is the old so-and-so? He hasn't been in for a quite a while..." Agatha's voice trailed off, and her cheerful smile vanished. She came forward and took Brita's hand once more, no longer in greeting but commiseration. "You poor dear. I'm so sorry."

Brita glanced across at Jorge to find he was just as stumped as she was. But there was something in his eyes, something about imagining them both standing there with blank, confused looks on their faces. She finally twigged to what must be going on. Agatha had worked here a long time; she must know the patterns. How often must it happen? An old client stopped coming in, only for the children to walk in one day to clear their things out of storage.

"He, uhh..." Brita stared up at the ceiling. Setting up an account here under a pseudonym was just the wrong side of paranoid that he might have done it. But making friends with Agatha, leaning into the role he was playing so far that he told stories about her? Unbidden, tears began to well in the corners of her eyes. He must have been so incredibly lonely.

"You don't have to say another word, dear." Agatha patted her hand. "He was a lovely man. An absolute gentleman, and so, so proud of you. Come, I'll show you."

Agatha tottered back behind to desk to fetch her keys, and Brita took the opportunity to sniff and dab at the corners of her eyes with the cuff of her cardigan.

Jorge put his arm protectively around her shoulder, playing the dutiful husband, and whispered in her ear. "What on earth is going on?"

"I'm getting us into my father's storage unit without the key."

"You think..." Jorge eyed Agatha as she jangled her keys and waved them through to the depths of the building.

Brita nodded.

"I hope you're right."

Me too. Brita thought, and, as Agatha led them down a twisting path lined with white plaster walls and blue roller doors, tried not to let her imagination run wild. The cheerful old woman had recognised her as soon as she'd walked through the door. What could her father have hidden away back here?

"Here we are. Number thirty-eight," Agatha said with a wan smile. She held out the key. "I'll give you two some privacy."

Brita held the key close to her chest, only daring to breathe once Agatha had disappeared around the corner lest that breath turn into laughter. Or tears. *He was an absolute gentleman, and so, so proud of you,* Agatha had said, and when she'd said it, Brita had believed her. Even though she knew her father had gone to Solomon to try to oust her, not two months ago. It was... she didn't know what to think.

She knelt down and slid the key into the lock. "No sense in waiting, I suppose."

"You are, though," Jorge said, and he was right.

Her fingers were shaking, and she didn't know why. *That's not true, though, it is, Brita?* She knew exactly why. She didn't want to turn the key and find that Agatha's Graham was somebody else. Someone other than her father.

"Do you need me to..."

"No, it's fine. I'll do it."

She twisted the key, and the lock fell away. She closed her eyes and stood. With a soft rattle, she raised the roller door all the way up. Beside her, she felt Jorge lean through the opening and flick on the lights.

"Well, well, well," he muttered.

Her stomach climbing up her throat, she opened her eyes. Jorge stood half a step beyond the threshold, hands on his hips, staring. The space was neatly organised, just like her father's workshop. Racks along the wall, stacked with boxes. A workbench, a giant whiteboard, covered in equations, and...

Brita's breath caught. Tears welled once more. Photos of her. Dozens of them. From her childhood, of the three of them together, before her mother left. And after. Sitting up beneath her bedroom window, sunshine rolling in, her nose buried in a book. Dressed up for a concert with Anita. Graduating from college. At the airport, leaving for America, and ten years later, coming home. Newspaper clippings. Articles, puff pieces and take-downs both. Anything with a photo of her, he'd kept it.

Kept it in the safest place he knew.

"Aha!" Jorge exclaimed. He'd started rummaging through the boxes stacked on the storage racks and had one open on the ground. "This is what we're looking for, I assume?"

He held a Gateway unit in his hand.

41

THE MAIN COURTYARD WAS just as dusty and sparse as the mountains that loomed on all sides, jutting into the dark, cloud-obscured sky. Mariska slouched against the concrete fence and gazed down to the concrete tunnels, designed long ago to funnel the water downhill. Had they ever even been filled? Or had they lain empty all these years because other things—money, politics, the egos of the people in charge—got in the way?

Hundreds of metres below, the tunnels disappeared into a dense fog. Mariska shuddered and turned her back.

A faded sign hung above the front entrance. A mixture of pictograms (hard hats, gloves, glasses) and the impressions left behind by letters long since lost to the weather. Its message was now inscrutable. She had some idea where she was: an abandoned hydroelectric plant in the mountains of Bhutan. A five-hour helicopter flight from Kolkata. Enough to feel uneasy. Not enough to be useful.

Solomon had cooked her canned beans and bread. It wasn't much, but at least it was warm. Then, he'd grilled her. Not about release plans, or timelines, or regulatory strategies. He didn't care about those. All he'd wanted were the latest details on jamming and interception from Malaysia. How did it work? At what range? What weaknesses had been uncovered? What defences had they devised?

And with every question, the yawning, uneasy knot of suspicion solidified in Mariska's gut. Solomon wasn't just ruthless, hunting profit by any means necessary. He was corrupt. More than that, he was desperate.

Gateway was not about money.

Far off in the distance, a truck engine coughed, the sound carried to her on the wind and then whisked away down the mountainside. Her heart skipped a beat as she imagined Hugo and Brita, still trapped inside as it wound its way along the winding, potholed roads. She spun back towards the valley, trying to find a bright flash of headlights in the murk, but there was nothing.

Gateway wasn't about money for her either. Not anymore.

At some point during his questioning, she couldn't pinpoint when, she'd started slipping in the odd leading question of her own. Trying to tease out hints at his intentions, at what he actually wanted. Where they were, how long they would be here.

Unconsciously, she'd started playing a double game. Putting herself at risk.

When she realised what she was doing, she'd gone all stiff, her skin puckering and her mouth dry. He'd stopped, mid-question. Stood up. She didn't know where to look, his words from before rising unbidden to her mind: *Ah know everything about you, and what ah know makes me wonder...*

She'd tensed, glanced down, only to feel his jacket slide over her shoulders and his fingers linger against the nape of her neck as he adjusted the collar. She'd smiled politely, nodding her thanks, and tucked that card safely away. Hopefully, she would have no need to play it.

Footsteps crunched on gravel and echoed off the compound's concrete walls. *Speak of the devil.* A slight shiver traversed her spine, but she didn't turn. Solomon leaned back on the fence next to her, one foot raised and pressed against the concrete, just as he had when they'd met in his virtual field. Only this time he stood a little too close. She could feel his body heat, radiating.

"Enjoyin' the clean mountain air?"

"It's helping. You don't have any aspirin stashed away, I suppose?" She touched her temple, lending her spur-of-the-moment excuse for being out here, in the cold, a touch of veracity.

"Ha, no ma'am." He twisted around, resting his elbows on the concrete barrier. He offered a plastic bottle of water. "Best I can do."

"Thanks." It was better than nothing. At least she could rinse out her mouth. She swilled a mouthful and tried to imagine her distaste, her regret mingling with the water. She spat it to the gravel at her feet.

"It doesn't look like much now, but this place is gorgeous in the light of day," Solomon said. The moon broke out from behind a cloud and pierced the fog, revealed another harsh, utilitarian building at the foot of the slope, hundreds of metres below. The dammed river glistened above it with a dark menace. He dangled his bottle over the edge with one hand, staring off into the depths.

She studied his profile. He seemed so relaxed, though she didn't understand how. Not when so much had gone wrong. And yet, the wrinkles didn't seem as deep, the line of his jaw not quite as tight. *A part of the puzzle must have fallen into place. One I don't know about.*

"How long has this place been out of action?" she asked, for something to say.

"Oh, it was mothballed a couple of decades ago, ah s'pose. Was never even finished. The generators are still sittin' in their crates down at the bottom of the hill. Fundin' disappeared when the wall fell, I heard, and Bhutan, well, they just plain didn't need the electricity. But with India on the rise and just around the corner…Once ah get this place up and runnin', ah plan on connectin' into the Indian grid. And with Gateway, ah can even go about deconstructin' that dam and restorin' the original river table for the lowland farmers. It'll be a good project."

He offered a weak smile, as if in consolation.

"Are you trying to make me feel better?" she asked.

"Not just you, ah think."

"Then why…" she started but broke off at the sound of a truck crunching its gears. Much closer this time. Solomon checked his watch. Frowned.

"Expecting someone?"

"No." He shook his head and dropped his empty water bottle over the edge, letting it clatter down the cliffside, out of sight. The engine growled, and a brief flash of headlights lit up the mountainside just across the valley. "No ah am not."

Mariska looked again, and the ease of five minutes ago was gone. Now, his jaw was set, his lips tightly drawn. If he didn't know who was in that truck, he certainly had his suspicions. He took a few steps out into the open space and stood full chested, fists clamped on his hips. She pulled his jacket tighter around her shoulders. It was tempting to ease herself behind him, to let him shield her, but she resisted it. She took up position right by his side, butterflies in her stomach.

The rough grumble of the engine echoed across the plateau. It grew louder and louder, until it felt as if the truck was right on top of them, long before the headlights and the dark-green canopy rounded the final bend. Even though knew it was too soon, she'd held out hope that it might be Brita and Hugo's truck. But their truck had had a container on the back, with wide doors for loading cargo. This truck was canvas lined, designed for carrying soldiers, not cargo. The unsecured tail flapped in its wake and smoke belched from its stack, disappearing into the night sky. It juddered to a halt in the courtyard, about five metres from where she stood.

She held her breath and stood tall as a mountain of a man stepped down from the cabin. He had a broad Slavic brow and square jaw, sandwiching his wide nose and clear blue eyes, and a mean black rifle slung from his shoulders. It glistened in the floodlights. She watched with a mix of awe and horror as six more men, from an eerily similar mould, jumped from the back of the truck and took up position behind their driver.

"This place, it is difficult to find."

Mariska's throat tightened as she heard that same, harsh breathiness. Ukrainian mercenaries, here in Bhutan. She stared straight ahead, not trusting herself to look them in the eye while she wondered what kind of men they could be if they were here, at Solomon's beck and call, while their homeland was under siege.

The mercenary leader twisted to look behind him at the road they had just traversed, the only one in and out. *Difficult to find*, she thought, *and impossible to escape.*

"That's the idea," Solomon said, his voice tight.

"I was told to expect only you." The mercenary shrugged his rifle from his shoulder and took it in a loose, easy grip. She could tell he was studying her closely, although his face was now bathed in shadow. She decided it was time to meet his gaze.

"Ah was not expecting you at all."

"No?" A raised eyebrow. "Change of plan."

"On whose orders? Ah don't need you here—"

The mercenary glared and gripped his rifle just a little tighter. Solomon's protests died in his throat.

"No? You have taken how many hostages in Texas?" he sneered, and Mariska shivered. "I fix your mistake. You fix Volodymyr's money."

"I'm handlin' it," Solomon snarled. She could tell he was not used to being dictated to.

The mercenary raised his eyebrow once more. "Volodymyr does not agree."

"Well, you can tell Volodymyr to—"

"Who is she?"

Solomon paused, and she thought she saw him swallow. "She's part of the team."

"Mariska." This was the moment. She stepped forward. She was not afraid.

She was ignored.

"She has been vetted?"

"She doesn't need to be, Yosip. Ah'm vouchin' for her." The hard edge returned to Solomon's voice. "You manage hostages. Ah fix takeover, yes?"

So his name was Yosip. He towered over her, his glare impassive. "Yes."

"Good. Ah need her, then. So back off."

"Okay." He relaxed his grip on his rifle. "No phones, yes?"

She shook her head, wondering whether the police had fished it from the bin outside Brita's hotel yet. Yosip barked a short set of commands in Ukrainian. She picked up bits and pieces, something about a perimeter. She'd not heard it spoken since she was a teenager. She pulled Solomon's jacket tight against the cold, long-forgotten encounters on the streets of Miskolc flooding back. She didn't know how Solomon got involved with this mob, but his real motivation for stealing the Gateway, the reason he was so desperate, was now crystal clear.

A flurry of activity from the back of the truck as the mercenaries began unloading packs and crates. She edged back over to Solomon, and Yosip joined them. "I want look inside. Show me." She wondered if he'd ever smiled in his life.

"Sure thing." They started back towards the compound. "Listen, I mentioned to Volodymyr an opportunity to use his influence with his brothers in Tokyo..."

"No." Yosip cut him off, glanced back at Mariska. "No more questions."

"Ah see." They walked in a tense silence. "Listen, Mas, why don't you set up our bunks while ah show Yosip around?" He glanced up at the Ukrainian, who gave his blessing with a curt nod. A pair of soldiers bustled past with a pile of canvas sacks, dumping them into the room as directed.

"You two, in here." Yosip didn't share where his men might be sleeping, although a second set of packs was dumped in the room across the hall, and a third outside, facing the courtyard. "Let's go."

Yosip and Solomon disappeared around a corner, and she was alone. Thirty minutes ago she would have felt ill at the prospect of sharing a room with Solomon, but now... The rough laughter of the soldiers echoed across the courtyard. No. Sharing with Solomon was the only option she had.

— • —

Mariska lay in the almost total darkness, unable to sleep. Not from anxiety, or guilt, though those emotions were certainly there, but anger. A silent, futile, seething rage. At herself, for her own selfishness. For putting herself in this position. At Yosip and his soldiers, set up down the corridor, guarding the entrance. At the pervasive, choking stench of their cheap cigarettes. At their words: their idiotic, brutish yakking and grunting. At Solomon, for fucking everything up.

She tried to imagine what it must be like to be Solomon. He had not meant for things to go as far as they had, but now his ersatz kidnapping had become real. Had been taken over by his... his what? Volodymyr. She'd heard him use the name, and Yosip's hard, burning stare had been enough to tell her she shouldn't have heard it at all. Who was he? Solomon's shady backer? His secret, criminal puppet master? So much had gone wrong, had slipped out of his control, and yet somehow he could sleep.

A harsh, brutal laugh echoed down the corridor, and Mariska clenched so tight that she shook. Unlike Solomon, sleeping peacefully just a metre away, she could understand the cruel things spilling from his soldier's mouths. She knew what they were saying. They were talking about her. About her body, about how she compared to the girls back home. Real or imaginary, she wasn't even sure that it mattered. Then one of them had a revelation. "Mariska—that's a fucking Magyar name, isn't it? Yeah, it is. Shit, it's right there—those wide cheeks and fucking slanty eyes. Fucking *Bozgor*."

That had made her blood boil, despite the cold. Bozgor. Street rat. An insult from her long-forgotten past. A past that she'd thought she'd left well and truly behind. She tried to shut it out, but there was no way. She heard it all, every word: what they should do with the filthy Magyar street rat. Before and after they slit her throat.

She rolled away from the door, clamping her makeshift pillow across her ears, trying to drown them out. But it did nothing, their words repeating over and over, their grunting laughter above it all, like a hand at her throat. She could barely breathe. She wanted to run right up to them. She wanted to scream, to tell them she could hear every fucking word they were saying. To show them just what this dirty rat whore could really do…

Something buzzed. A light chatter of metal against metal. Then it stopped. She listened, the thugs and their taunts that she was never meant to understand fading into nothing. She knew that sound. That was a phone, Solomon's phone, going off.

No phones, Yosip had said. To her, not to Solomon. Worried about what she might do. About who she might contact, and what she might say.

Rightly fucking so.

The only sound, the only one that mattered, was Solomon snoring. Tense, she rolled back towards the door, towards the smoke and the malicious, taunting voices. She maintained a silent vigil for what seemed like an age, eagle eyes surveying the oily, velvet darkness. Finally, just as she was about to give up, it happened again. The staccato hum of his phone, vibrating against one of the aluminium bed poles. The one closest to her, she thought. The notification light blinked, faint grey on the inside of his trouser pocket, just poking out from beneath his woollen blanket.

She held the phone's position in her mind's eye, focusing hard as she reached out. Solomon's cot was, just, within arm's reach. Her own cot trembled as she overloaded one side, her fingertips making contact with his cot's canvas lining, stretched taut over the aluminium frame. That finger traced along it, inch by inch, as she prayed to all that was holy that her own bed might, just this once, refrain from creaking.

Her arm approached the limit of its reach, and she twisted, the tips of her fingers searching in vain like the foot at the bottom of a ladder, yearning for safe ground. Nothing. She edged down her bed, wincing at every rustle, every scratch, listening for even the slightest shift in Solomon's snoring, ready to snatch her hand back. It remained stable, in and out, in and out.

She was safe, for now.

Her finger resumed its journey, smooth metal giving way to stitched canvas and back again. Surely this was the one…Yes! There it was, the smooth cold glass of a phone screen. She poked, gently wiggled it. Confirmed that it was loose. She wedged it between her index and middle fingers, her thumb just out of reach, and gave the softest of tugs. It moved, edging along the taut canvas without a sound. She tugged once more, careful not to let it slip.

A burst of laughter from the thugs outside. Raucous. Loud. She froze, holding her breath. Solomon snorted and rolled away, leaving his phone behind, dangling between her fingernails and the slippery railing. Sliding, slipping to one side. Falling.

She tensed, ready for the weight.

Gravity took hold. It flipped over as it fell, but she clung on, pulse racing, neck straining. Gently, gently, she lowered it the fifteen centimetres to the ground, only daring to breathe once it touched the concrete and she could safely adjust her grip.

To obscure the light she hid it, and herself, under her blanket, only to be faced with a flashing red warning—fingerprint not recognised. Shit.

She lifted her thumb from the sensor—she could not afford to lock herself out. Facing the screen outwards, through a sliver of blanket, she touched the power button. In the cold grey glow, less than two seconds' worth, Solomon was just visible. He lay on his back, his left arm draped across his eyes, right flopped over the edge, palm hanging down with the back of his thumb, the one that she needed, resting against the railing.

Two deep breaths, no movement, outside the room or within. Two more, giving her eyes time to adjust back to the dark. It was now or never.

Mariska snaked her hand from the relative safety of the blanket, clutching the top of the phone to present the fingerprint scanner at where she thought his hand was. Nothing.

She squinted. Adjusted. Met nothing but air.

There was no other option. She pressed the power button, basking his fingers with that sickly, electric light. A second, not more. Enough time to guide the phone between his fingers and wince at the shadows she cast across his face and the wall behind.

Darkness fell once more and she angled the screen, trying not to tickle his fingertips. She brushed his little finger with hers. His entire hand twitched and she jerked back, taking the phone briefly out of range.

Hand trembling, just slightly, she raised it again. Clean this time. Easy. It touched his thumb. Buzzed. The screen flashed, and she imagined, hoped, that the pulse of light was grey, not red.

Back beneath the covers, she sighed with relief. She was in. She opened maps, extracted their GPS location. Composed a lightning email:

> *Anita—Mariska. Kidnapping is real. Solomon behind it. Repeat, kidnapping is real. Solomon making takeover play, with armed criminal backing. Repeat armed. At hydro plant in Bhutan: GPS 27°03*

'40.4"N, 89°33'45.4"E. Send Help. Do not, under any circumstances, reply.

And for what it's worth, I'm sorry.

She copied in both Anita's personal and work accounts, and her finger hovered over the send arrow, her thoughts dragged back to the night after the Gateway's disastrous debut. To her grovelling apology that Anita had, rightfully, flung back in her face. *Anita probably doesn't even know what part I played in all this.*

She deleted the last sentence and, with a beating heart, hit send.

The little wheel spun, each revolution feeding her anxiety. Would the message even get through? Then, with an animated whoosh, it was gone. She closed her eyes and, under the protection of her blanket, allowed herself to sag, flushed and sweating despite the cold.

She deleted the email from his sent folder, closed both apps she'd used, and clicked the power button once more. The screen went dark. She regretted it immediately—she should have had a look around, to see what else she could find. Briefly, she considered attempting a second unlock, but now that she had stepped over the line, the violence laughing and joking just outside her door felt that much closer, that much more real.

Carefully, she slid the phone back onto the edge of Solomon's bed, under his hip. Then she rolled back, buried her head into her pillow, and hoped that what she'd done was enough.

42

—·—

Brita hefted her duffel bags, one in each hand. Jorge did the same.

"You ready?" he asked.

Their bags were jammed full with Gateway tech, prototypes her father had never even mentioned, let alone shown her. Including a plain case with a micro-SD card with the words *last resort* scrawled on the back. She thought back to the tail end of that first night, her and Mariska sitting at his kitchen table, drinking his whisky, laughing at his paranoia, what it might drive him to do if pushed to the limit, while he tried to sell Stora, and Gateway, out from beneath her feet.

She allowed herself one last look at the collage of her past that he'd pasted above his workspace. The fear that must have driven him to keep it hidden from her, from everyone. Was there anything they could do to rebuild what they'd once had? Un-burn those bridges?

She nodded, tight-lipped. Those were problems for another day, another place.

Jorge hit dial with his knuckle. The phone buzzed five times before the connection was made. A rectangle of concrete wall rippled and disappeared, revealing Anita's curious face peering across from behind her desk. Jorge shook his head in wonder. When she caught his eye, he couldn't hide his smile.

"Still can't quite believe it's real?" Brita asked.

"I just hope it doesn't get old."

"Are you two going to just keep staring at the hole in my wall, or might you actually step through it sometime today?" Anita heckled.

Brita shooed him through, as best as she could with both hands weighed down, but Jorge stepped back and waved her forward.

Anita raised her eyebrows as Brita dumped her duffel bags in the corner of the room. "Who would have thought he'd been holding out on us all along."

"I wouldn't go quite that far." Of course Anita thought the worst. They'd always butted heads, even before she'd helped Brita save Stora. But she hadn't been in the back of the truck, hadn't felt his panic, his fear as he shoved her through the Gateway

260

at the very last second. And the photos he'd kept, despite everything…"Leaning into his paranoia perhaps. Justifiably so, too."

"Mmm."

"Hey, if it wasn't for Dad's pathological need for secrecy, Solomon would have won by now. I'd have been whisked away to who knows where, his goons would have stolen the majority of the working Gateway prototypes, and Garfield would have dithered on the trading halt for so long that Solomon could have bought and sold us three times over, instead of just the one."

Anita arched a single plucked eyebrow and tapped a fingernail against the edge of her keyboard, as if she was tossing up whether to push back or let the fact that Brita had just sided with her father go. Then, decision made, her gaze slid back to her laptop. "Three times over might be a bit of a stretch."

"Oh?" Brita set herself down on the armrest of one of Anita's exorbitantly expensive Scandinavian office chairs, unable to read her friend's face. For most of the last hour she'd been digging through her father's things, finding answers to questions she hadn't asked. Anita, as always, dragged her back to reality. To practical matters. But did she mean Solomon's plan had failed? Or had it merely been delayed?

Before she could ask, however, Anita flashed Jorge a wan smile. "I'm sorry, but would you mind…"

"You're not sorry, but that's fine." Jorge winked at both of them. "I'll go check if the coast is clear; we wouldn't want our friend Agatha to start asking awkward questions."

They both watched him disappear through the Gateway set against Anita's wall. Brita didn't turn back until she'd heard the roller door roll up and back down again.

"So, what's the damage?" she asked.

Free from Jorge's always watchful eye, Anita grimaced. "Look, forty-six minutes is a long time. It could have been worse."

Brita leaned forward. Anita squinted at her screen, sucked her teeth.

"You have to remember this is just an estimate. Even with Jorge's list of Solomon's shell companies, there's only so much we can surmise…"

"Anita, Jesus Christ. Just spit it out." Brita's stomach coiled and twisted, but she fought to keep her exterior calm. "How much of my company does Solomon own?"

"25%."

"Jesus." Brita slid down from the armrest and into the belly of the chair, a roll-call of her investors racing through her thoughts, one after another. "Who jumped ship?"

Anita took half a breath, swallowing whatever it was she was about to say. "We think there's about 4% still in the wind, split pretty much even between retail and institutional investors…"

"Anita," Brita interrupted. "Who did we lose?"

Finally, her friend met her gaze. Brita's heart sank. "HSBC. Vector Group. RBS…"

"RBS? How?" Brita stared down at her empty hands, her bandaged wrists, looking for answers and finding none. "Andrew's been with us since I was a kid. They didn't just offload us on a whim, surely."

"Garfield spoke to them. He asked Andrew that very question, and they all said the same thing." Anita made a strange noise, as if her words were choking her. Brita looked back up, dread in the pit of her stomach. "They all spoke to Mariska, and suddenly they got cold feet."

Brita sagged back, her head in her hands.

"I'm sorry. I know that's not what you wanted to hear, but it's not as bad as it looks. You and your father still hold 51%—"

"41%."

"What?"

Brita elbowed her way upright. "We sold each of you 2% to fund Gateway, remember? Which means Solomon already had 2%. Add Sandeep's 2%, plus this morning's gains, and that puts him at 29%. More than me. More than dad."

"And what can he do with 29%? It's not like he can flip Britannia's 20%—their holdings have been frozen ever since Lloyd got busted with his snout in the Columbian trough. And even that's not enough, he'd need the trading halt lifted so he can get at that last 4% sitting on the market, or one of us to go with him…"

"Anita, he has my father tied up in the back of a truck. We can't just assume he's going to play by the rules."

The metallic rasp of the storage unit's roller door rising, then slamming to the ground, cut Anita off before she could respond. Brita whipped around just in time to see Jorge free the Gateway handset from the storage unit wall and slip through the portal, dragging the connecting cable behind him.

"Kill it," he hissed, chopping his hand at his neck and staring anxiously behind him. "Cut the connection."

Behind her, Anita hit the button on her desk phone, and the portal fizzled out of existence. Jorge stood staring at a blank wall, the handset still clutched tight in his fist. The black cable that had only a second before helped to sustain the portal across London now dangled limp, permanently severed.

There would be no going back.

"*Gracias.*" Jorge panted, waving his hand around in exhausted gratitude. "They must have followed us. I don't know how, but…" He looked down at the Gateway unit, the truncated cable, and shivered. "We're not safe here. We should jump back to Malaysia. Right now."

Brita gripped her chair's armrests, as if she were trying to rip the timber free of its joints. She was sick of running, sick of hiding, sick of letting Solomon and his hired thugs dictate her every action. "Why? What can they do to us here that they can't in Malaysia? We've got to start fighting back."

"How? With what?" Jorge glanced back at the wall, at where the threat had just been. "You don't know him like I do. All you have is in those bags in the corner—"

"Brita—" Anita tried to interrupt, but Brita was standing now, the chair pushed back, a steely fire coursing through her.

"Gateway is not nothing. And Solomon doesn't understand it like I do. Like my father does. He doesn't know what it can do."

"But Mariska does, doesn't she," Jorge snapped. "He bought her to take away your one advantage. This is what he does, Brita."

She wanted to scream. Of course Jorge wasn't getting it: he was scared. He'd been burned before, was getting burned again, right now. But it wasn't his friend Solomon had corrupted, his legacy Solomon was trying to steal. He hadn't been the one tied up and bundled into the back of a truck. She snatched the handset and its severed cable from his hand.

"Brita, Jorge—"

"Mariska can't tell Solomon what she doesn't know. If Ming-Xia can find out where he's taken them—"

"Brita, for fuck's sake!" Anita shouted.

She jerked, snapped around. Anita had come from behind her desk. She held her phone facing outwards and looked ready to shove it right under Brita's nose.

"Thank you." Anita rolled her eyes, just slightly, and handed her the phone. "Here. Read this."

Brita took Anita's phone from her hand, and then almost dropped it.

It was an email.

From Mariska.

— • —

The Kuala Lumpur skyline glittered through the window in the pre-dawn darkness. Ming-Xia had left a trio of security passes on the desk in her office. Brita and Jorge each held two duffel bags, while Anita carried only her laptop. A private lift whisked them down to the carpark where a chunky Rolls Royce, polished black, waited with open doors.

Ming-Xia's driver offered to take her bags, but Brita politely declined. She would not let Gateway out of her sight. Jorge, following her lead, did the same.

Brita sank back into the plush leather seats and watched the tight, winding Malaysian streets fly by. Across from her, Jorge and Anita whispered over practicalities, why Solomon had chosen his Bhutanese hydroplant, what his plans might be. How they could exploit them.

Brita let it all flutter by her. Her thoughts were dominated by Mariska. By the message itself. No admission of guilt. No remorse for the part she had played. But the fear...*Armed criminal backing. Do not, under any circumstances, reply.* Fear trembled beneath every word. Brita imagined her friend—despite everything, she still thought of Mariska as her friend—lying awake, staring into the darkness. Listening to Solomon argue and scheme with his cronies. Wondering how she'd gotten herself into such a mess. She imagined her father doing the same.

At the same time, though, she knew exactly how. Mariska's ambition. Her father's paranoia.

Her own indecisiveness underlying it all.

She hugged the duffel bags, filled to the brim with batteries, cables, and Gateway prototypes. Pulled it tight to her chest.

It was up to her to get them out of there. Bring them home.

The car slowed. Tall steel gates, set deep in a whitewashed stone wall overgrown with creeping vines, opened at their approach and welcomed them along a narrow, fern-lined driveway. Within five metres it was as if there had never been a city, only Ming-Xia's private forest. Remnants of the night's rain dripped from the leaves onto the car windows as they rolled to a stop beneath the grand entrance.

The Rolls' headlights illuminated a pulsating marble fountain and paired with the light spilling from the open doors, casting Ming-Xia's silhouette across the glistening paving stones.

"Come in, come in, let's get you out of the rain." Ming-Xia stepped back and swept a robed arm towards her cavernous, gleaming entrance hall. Brita led Anita and Jorge across the threshold. "Noor can take your bags."

"No," Brita blurted, jerking the duffel bag away from Noor's outstretched hand. She blushed as Noor glanced uncertainly back at her boss. "Thank you, but these don't leave my sight."

Ming-Xia nodded, and Noor retreated wordlessly. "Jorge's hunch played out, then?"

"More than we'd hoped," Jorge jumped in, eyes eager and watchful as he took in the opulence of Ming-Xia's private home. He raised one of the duffel bags for inspection. "Hugo has been a very busy man."

"I wish I had such good news to impart," Ming-Xia said, leading them into a small dining room dominated by an intricately carved table, its patterns obscured by rolls and rolls of maps. "I can confirm that Solomon and your, uhh... Mariska left Kolkata by helicopter, just after one p.m., local time. But after that..." She slid a map of Southeast Asia in front of herself. It had a series of hand-drawn circles centred on Kolkata, on nearby international hubs, extending from Goa to Delhi, all the way through to Tibet and Hanoi. "I'm afraid I just don't know."

"We might have a lead there," Anita said, passing Ming-Xia her phone, just as she had for Brita. And just like Brita's, Ming-Xia's eyes went wide, and then wider, as she read and then absorbed.

Brita pulled the map towards her, grabbed the pen, and circled the hydroplant. A small black marker, buried deep in the Himalayas. "That's where they are. The question is: What do we do now?"

And just like in the back of Ming-Xia's Rolls Royce, the discussion quickly devolved into an argument about logistics. About what to tell the authorities, whether they could do anything, whether they could even be trusted. About how quickly they could get boots on the ground, the relative merits of local mercenaries who knew the area versus a more experienced, international crew that both Ming-Xia and Anita had worked with before.

Brita tore her gaze away from the map and glanced up at Jorge, but he was just part of the conversation, as if engaging mercenaries was just something that her friends did whenever they had a curly problem that needed solving.

It was ridiculous. The whole thing was ridiculous. Brita decided that she'd had enough.

"I'm going."

Across the other side of the table, the conversation stopped. Anita's jaw fell open. Behind her, Jorge smiled.

"I'm sorry, what?" Ming-Xia sputtered.

Brita crossed her arms across her chest, burrowing her fists into her ribs. "You heard me."

"But you can't! Solomon has armed mercenaries—"

"Ukrainian mobsters, actually," Jorge interjected with a grin.

"Yes, exactly." Ming-Xia waved her arms with exasperation. "We don't even know how many—he might have an entire platoon of them for all we know."

"Mariska has risked her life to get us this information. Hell, my father almost got himself killed just getting me out of that truck..."

"That's right, and he did that to *get you out*."

Brita recognised the unspoken part of that sentence, the unsaid concern that lay beneath Ming-Xia's protestations. Solomon had two cards: 29% of Stora, and her father. It wasn't enough, and by going, Brita risked giving him both herself, and any Gateway technology she took with her. Ming-Xia had invested in Stora, in *her*, and she wasn't about to let that money get thrown away on a whim.

But it wasn't Ming-Xia's decision to make.

"He's my father, and Gateway is mine to protect. Nobody else's."

"Brita, it's too dangerous," Anita said, without conviction. She could see in her friend's eyes that she knew there was no changing her mind. She was only making a token effort, for appearance's sake. Silently, Brita thanked her friend for the opening.

"Too dangerous? What other option do we have? We tell the police and Gateway is gone forever. And if we hire mercenaries, as the both of you were so keen to do? For one, it makes us no different than Solomon, willing to spend the lives of others for a healthy profit. And I don't know about you, but I wouldn't trust hired killers with something as valuable as the Gateway. Do you think Blackwater or G4S would just let us have it, once they knew it existed?"

Brita glared across the table, and she could see that Anita knew she was right.

"I didn't think so."

"Jorge." Ming-Xia turned to him, a note of desperation in his voice. "Back me up here. This is madness!"

Slowly, deliberately, Jorge shrugged. "Actually, I think she's right. I mean, they'll never expect it. And with some of the gadgets Hugo's been working on, we could be in and out before they even know we were there."

"You just want the fucking story," Ming-Xia scoffed.

"There's no story, Jorge," Anita said, jabbing her finger down onto the table. "This stays between us."

"Actually, no. I don't think that's right," Brita said, catching Ming-Xia's eye, her mind racing. "We need Solomon to come out looking like a lunatic. If Jorge is willing to break the story with a focus on Solomon's behaviour, and leave the reason he wanted to buy us out vague, what can he do? Claim that we invented teleportation? If he even tries, he'll be crucified."

Ming-Xia huffed, chewed her lip, but she didn't respond. Brita turned to Jorge, not willing to give her any longer to come up with a retort.

"So how about it? You want to help me take Solomon down for good?"

Jorge's grin could not have been wider. "I thought you'd never ask."

"Anita? Are you in?"

Brita held her friend's gaze. Anita held hers in return. "God, I hope you know what you're doing."

Brita turned to Ming-Xia. After what seemed an age, with the only sound in the room the ticking of a clock against the far wall, their host muttered, "I don't know how we're going to get you to Bhutan..."

She exhaled and waved the concern away. She smiled, knowing that the battle she'd just won was going to be the first of many. She doubted any of those to come would be quite so easy.

"That's just logistics. I trust the two of you to handle that. Now, let's get down to business."

43

Mariska stretched out, her feet easily extending beyond the confines of her camp cot, a dusty light filtering through the unfinished door, little more than a hole in the concrete wall. She squeezed her eyes against the temptation of just falling back asleep, yawned, and pulled her head left and then right, teasing out the crick the had developed at the base of her neck. The inevitable result of using her white overalls, rolled into a ball, as a flimsy pillow.

Given the circumstances, she was amazed she'd gotten any sleep at all.

There was no noise in the still air. She cast a surreptitious eye in Solomon's direction, but his cot was empty. Thank heaven for small mercies, for a moment of privacy.

She swung her legs around and sat up, adjusted herself, and considered her situation. It had been hours since she sent her message. Five at least. So far, it seemed, her little rebellion had gone unnoticed.

Which meant nothing had changed. Which meant she had to act like nothing had changed. Act like this was where she wanted to be, that she was here to help Solomon implement his plan, whatever the fuck it was.

She wondered if even he knew. The idea of Solomon no longer being in control, of Yosip and his band of killers taking charge, was not one she had any desire to contemplate.

She ran both her hands through her hair and, while doing so, caught a whiff of her armpits. What she wouldn't give for a mirror and a toothbrush. But they were all in the same boat. And perhaps that was a good thing. The more haggard she looked, the less temptation for a bored, lonely mercenary.

With that unpleasant reality foremost in her mind, she hunched her shoulders, slipped into the corridor and out into the courtyard, stripping a bottle of water from a pack as she passed. Bright morning sun blazed down the valley, and it, in combination with the bracing mountain air, knocked the last of the comfort of sleep from her body.

267

Two piles of muscle guarded the entrance. Both were lazing in the shade of a gnarled and bristled tree—one leaning against the trunk, picking his teeth, the other in a camp chair with his feet up on a chunk of busted concrete. She watched their hands. They'd moved to the triggers of their oily black weapons as soon as she'd entered their field of view. She shuffled right on past, knowing they were enjoying every second. And worse, knowing she could do nothing about it.

She walked to the edge of the railing, as far away from them as possible, and bent over it. Keen to see the water tunnels in the daylight. To think about anything else.

The view didn't disappoint. Giant concrete worms plunged down the mountainside into the heavy morning mist. The silence was eerie. No wind, no movement. Not even birdsong.

Mariska hoped that wasn't an omen. That far away, beyond the mountains, her message had set things in motion. That something was being done.

She took a swig of water, washed her mouth out. Let it spray over the edge and down into the chasm below. Judging by the height of the sun above the plateau, she'd been in limbo for just over six hours. She'd spent most of it asleep, and still it felt like an age. Twenty hours since they'd been bundled into the back of that truck. And she'd had a bed, her arms free of bindings. Been given food to eat and water to drink.

A wave of nausea washed over her as she struggled to suppress the imagined horrors of their journey. Her stiff neck and the unwanted attention of Yosip's men seemed inconsequential in comparison. And all she'd managed to do with her freedom was send one short email.

She took another sip of water, her thirst winning out over her desire to remain in the dark about the lavatory arrangements here. That was a battle that could not be won. Besides, there were more important battles that she would need to fight—

The crunch of gears not quite meshing echoed up the mountain side, shattering the silence. Mariska's whole body tensed. Finally. There was no doubt in her mind. She knew that sound, and what it would bring.

God, she hoped they were all right.

Behind her, a radio squawked. The truck must have passed through their perimeter. Heavy boots crunched the gravel, and Yosip was there beside her, assault rifle held casually in one enormous hand. This was the closest they'd stood to one another, and she was surprised to discover he wasn't that much taller than she. Last night he'd seemed so much larger. Looming. Intimidating.

He, on the other hand, didn't acknowledge her at all. His focus was trained in the same direction as hers, his eyes hidden behind reflective glasses.

She saw the smoke first, a hazy plume in the air. The truck followed, breaching the road's horizon, the container poking into view, then the cabin. The truck was exactly as she remembered. Its night on the road had made no impact to its permanently grimy exterior. It was almost at the compound entrance when Solomon burst into the courtyard.

"Was anyone goin' to warn me?" he yelled, indignantly shaking his phone in the air. He looked just as dishevelled as she felt: crinkled suit, dusty shoes. He was lucky he had short-cropped hair, or that would have been all over the place too. "Yosip? You know what ah'm tryin' to do here. Every minute is goddamn critical."

Yosip made no response. Mariska, for her part, was not surprised. It was still the middle of the night in London. It would be six hours, at least, until the markets opened again. Right now, there was nothing he could do but wait. And if she knew it, Yosip must have know it too.

He called out to his underlings, issuing orders in Ukrainian. Two heavies detached themselves from the shade in the lee of the building—she'd not even known they were there—and took up position on either side of the approaching truck. It skidded to a halt on the gravel, and Solomon's lackey stuck his head out the window. He peered down at the Ukrainian mercenary that had stepped up to his door and caught Solomon's eye with a raised brow.

"A helpin' hand from our mutual friend, that's all," Solomon said, trying and failing to play down the unexpected presence of Yosip and his team. "How are they?"

The driver smirked. "You got a hose?"

"What?" Solomon asked, as if he didn't understand. Mariska thought she did, however, and her stomach churned.

"A hose. Water. It fucking stinks back there. It's been almost an entire day."

"You mean you haven't stopped? Not even for a toilet break?" She launched herself from the rail towards the truck, an unfamiliar anger rising in her throat. "Have they had anything to eat or drink? Do you even know if they're still alive?"

The driver—she couldn't remember his name and frankly didn't care at this point—ignored her. "Boss?"

Solomon turned to intercept her with an open hand, but his focus was directed over her shoulder. "Yosip, can you get one of your men to fetch us up a hose, or a bucket of water? Lord knows there's more than enough of that around here."

She ignored him and burst past, her rage focused on the two thugs standing at the back, watching the entire scene unfold with cocky smiles.

"What the fuck are you looking at?" she yelled, getting right up in the closest one's face. She drew herself up to her full height. It wasn't much higher than his chin, but it was enough. He couldn't have been much older than twenty, his neck and his knuckles were spattered with washed-out tattoos. His grey eyes flashed with uncertainty. *Just you wait*, she thought.

In her harshest, ugliest Ukrainian, she barked at him to open the fucking door, and he stumbled back a half step, obviously shocked to hear her spit his own language from her *bozgor* mouth. He glanced across at his partner, and she knew that she had him.

She grabbed him by the collar and dragged him over to the container door. "Right fucking now!"

— ● —

Stillness. No engine, no swerves, no bumps, no jolts. That the truck had stopped took a long time to worm its way into a conscious realisation. By the time it did, there was yelling in a language Hugo didn't understand. To his battered, exhausted ears, it sounded so far away.

A clunk reverberated through the container door and into his skull, and he opened his eyes to the gloom. He croaked, tried to speak, forgetting for a moment that he was alone. It didn't matter; his voice was gone. A second thunk, and he jammed his lids closed again, blinded by the sliver of light that burned through the fresh opening.

He could feel himself slipping and didn't fight it. The door swung wide open under his weight, and he flopped. There was a rush of cool air, then another crash. Just another change of direction, another corner, another pothole.

But no.

There was no sound. Fresh air. His face was in the dirt, there was sun on the back of his neck. The yelling started again. Rough hands grabbed hold, and his shoulders squealed in protest as he was hoisted to his feet.

Another voice joined the chorus, English this time. There was shock and panic. Recriminations. They're not going to find her. A smile spread across his lips in the brief moment before the rush of blood to his legs brought a wave of pain and everything went black.

— ● —

"Solomon, she's not fucking there. But Hugo is, and he's unconscious..." She trailed off, seething. They weren't listening, still shining their torches into the truck's vacant corners.

Mariska was torn between elation and white-hot fury. Brita had escaped! She didn't know how, and perhaps that was just as well. She could never have imagined Solomon would be so cruel. Hugo had been dumped to one side, and Yosip had ordered all but one of his goons off, spouting some bullshit about re-checking the perimeter, as if Brita had jumped out of the truck just on the other side of the bend.

Just one mercenary remained, the kid she'd dressed down just moments ago, eyeing her suspiciously, his finger hovering menacingly over his trigger.

Hugo lay at his feet, dried blood caking the side of his face. Piss and shit dribbled from the elastic bands that held the hems of his once-pristine clean suit tight to his ankles. His hands were still bound behind his back.

"Give me your knife," she ordered, Ukrainian again. He flinched, at her accent, at the anger in her voice, she didn't know. Perhaps he was wondering if she'd understood what he and his mates had said about her last night. She hoped so. "Just give it. Come on, he's in his seventies. He's not going to run away."

He didn't move, but he avoided her gaze. Then, his finger slid carefully away from the trigger, finding a resting place on the grip instead. She scowled and unhooked the knife from his belt. With one quick swipe, Hugo's wrists sprang free. She rolled him onto his side. At least this way if he threw up, he wouldn't choke. He was shivering despite the sun's warmth.

"Go get me some water. And a couple of blankets." She didn't bother to turn around; she knew he'd go.

"Hey, Hugo, it's me. Mas." She caressed his face, feeling the cold sweat on her fingers. He responded to her touch, the hint of a smile coming to his lips. He opened an eye, just for a moment. "What the hell happened?"

He mouthed something she couldn't hear. She leaned in closer, right up to his mouth, but it was unintelligible. His head was suddenly heavy. She placed two fingers to his neck, relieved to find a strong pulse. Say what you like, the old bastard was tough. A shadow fell over them both. The young muscle, back with bottles of water and a pile of blankets bundled in his arms.

"You got a name?" she asked, slipping back into Ukrainian.

He crouched beside her, folding a blanket to place underneath Hugo's head. "Aleks."

"You know first aid, Aleks?" She took a bottle of water and held it to Hugo's lips. "Tak."

"Good. You're in charge. Get him cleaned up. Fresh clothes, a bed. Food." She stood. She had to get back to Solomon and Yosip. Any longer and Yosip would get suspicious. More suspicious. She wiped her eyes as she stepped away.

A heavy crunch, boots on gravel, just as she rounded the back of the truck. Yosip had just jumped from the container, brandishing a familiar tangle of copper wires. It was all Mariska could do to stop herself from smiling.

"What is this?" he demanded, standing over her.

"Huh, very clever. May I?" she said, taking the cables without waiting for Yosip's permission. They were thinner than the original version, and the power pack was tiny. But there was no mistaking it. *Hugo, you sneaky little...*

"Solomon, why does she smile?" Yosip snatched the copper mess back. Solomon had eased his way back to level ground and was searching for somewhere to wipe his hands. She ignored Yosip's accusation, slipping past him.

"Solomon, does he know?"

"Know what?" Solomon barked, having settled for the truck's rear tires, distaste evident as he brushed his now-muddy hands on the legs of his only trousers.

"About the Gateway?"

"No, of course not."

Yosip's hand engulfed her shoulder and wrenched her backwards, her head clattering into the side of the truck. His thumb hooked into her collarbone and locked her in place. "What in fuck is 'Gateway'?" He brandished the mysterious coil, shaking it in her face.

"Woah, okay, Yosip. Hold yer horses." Solomon hunched slightly, raising his hands. She could only stare, sweat prickling on her brow, her back. *Is he making himself seem small on purpose?*

"No. No horses." Yosip's face was so close to hers that their noses almost touched. He squeezed, hard. She moaned, felt her knees buckle, but his grip held her aloft. "Talk."

"Jesus, it's their tech, Yosip. The old man, he invented it. The one who's missin', it's her company ah'm taking over." Yosip's grip relaxed, just enough that she could breathe. He spun her around, pressing her chest against the tail of the truck. Wet filth seeped through her top.

"Where she go?"

"I don't know, I don't!" Her voice was so high she didn't recognise it. "The Gateway, it's...it's like a portal." She scrambled, frantically trying to remember the Ukrainian. "Dvernyy otvir. Understand? Connected to her phone. She dials a place, and away she goes. Gone." She mimed a phone call, then blew through her fingers, like a puff of magic dust, to make him understand. His eyes widened and he dropped the snarled mass of wires, as if he'd discovered it was actually a writhing, coiling snake. He backed away, from it and her, as if they were magic.

"Shit. She could've been gone for..." Solomon cursed. She watched his eyes, saw them harden with realisation. The trading halt had been Brita's doing. For almost a day he'd thought Brita was safely locked away in the back of this truck, and yet she'd been free, doing who knew what. It was better than she could possibly have hoped.

"Stanley!"

"Yes, boss." She jumped. Stanley, that was his name. She'd had no idea he was still in the truck until he was right behind her.

"Ah want you to reacquaint yourself with our guest. Ah want to know exactly what happened here, and when. And take her with you—make her prove her fuckin' worth."

He stalked over to Yosip, not giving her a second glance. "Reset your perimeter. And keep this to yourself."

"Volodymyr…"

"Volodymyr will know when he needs to know, and not a goddamn second earlier, you got that, boy?" Solomon snapped, his agitation lending him a sense of command. Yosip, in contrast, was the picture of uncertainty. His eyes were still on the remnants of the Gateway and the empty truck. Mariska sensed that the balance of power had shifted. "This stays between us until ah know what's what."

She felt Stan's hot breath on the back of her neck. "You'd better tell the old man to make this easy." She shivered. He jumped down to the ground, with two arch-shaped pieces of rubber clutched in his fist, worn from heavy use. An image flashed in her mind: empty cavities in the soles of Hugo's boots.

The imprint of Yosip's thumb, deep in her neck, rested heavy on her mind. He would follow orders—Solomon's or this mysterious Volodymyr's. She had to keep herself useful, for as long as possible.

44

—·—

THEY DUMPED HUGO IN a huge holding chamber and tossed a pair of canvas rucksacks after him. The floor was muddy and damp. Pools of water had collected in the dips in the undulating floor. Rust-covered sheets of metal and concrete rubble lay in piles in the far corner. Up above, accessible only by a metal staircase, the door slammed shut with a clang that reverberated off the high ceilings. Ghostly echoes floated from the monstrous circular holes in the far wall, full seconds after the door had been sealed.

He was alone.

Weary, aching, and shivering, he pushed himself to his knees. He made a couple of attempts at undoing the straps atop the closest sack, but only succeeded in tipping it over. Lifting his arms was almost impossible, his shoulders stiff from so many hours locked into position in the back of the truck, but at least his hands were free. With the straps at a more manageable level, the bag's contents spilled out onto the floor: fresh clothes, bottles of water. A packet of ration bars.

He'd already scarfed two before the thought that he should perhaps be protecting his empty, exhaustion-sensitised stomach entered his foggy head. At about the same time, his digestive system rejected the sudden and unexpected food, sending him retching into the corner. Panting, he crawled back on all fours, washed his mouth out, and took a few careful sips.

Using the second sack to prop himself up, he inspected the contents further: aluminium poles with a canvas lining. A camp bed. So Solomon wasn't a complete barbarian.

He took another swig, wary of his now-roiling stomach, and fumbled his way towards an assembled resting place. He grabbed a ration bar and eased his protesting body up the almost impossible twenty-centimetre cliff and ate his reward lying down, much slower this time. His eyelids drooped in the relative luxury of canvas...

A screech of metal against metal shocked him awake, his half-eaten ration bar falling from his cheek and onto the floor. How long had he been asleep? A few seconds? An hour? It didn't matter. Two shadowy figures stomped along the gantry and down the stairs. He only had time to mash the rest of his ration bar into his mouth and wash it down with a mouthful of water before they yanked him to his feet.

The wide gloom of his prison was replaced by close corridor walls. The corroded metal door swung closed with finality. One of his chaperones let go of his arm to drop a bar across the doorway, even though it was empty.

A message: there will be no escape for you.

"Where are we going?" No response. He tried again, in Russian this time, an educated guess based on prominent cheekbones and angular jaws. Again no answer, but a shared glance told him he was on the right track.

The corridors became a maze as they hauled him along. Any delusions he may have had about keeping track of his route quickly faded. His head was getting clearer, but that only meant he could feel every one of his aches and pains, bruises and lacerations.

At least, he thought, when he realised that his captors were also labouring, he wasn't the only one struggling. The one on his left's breathing was becoming ragged, and he could feel their heartbeats where his shoulders were pressed into their armpits, though their vise-like grips never slackened. He made himself as heavy as he could. Better their effort than his. And besides, he would need all his strength for what was surely coming next.

Abruptly they turned and shoved him into a small room. Without their hands beneath his arms, he collapsed to the floor.

"Pick him up, put him in the chair."

It was Stanley who spoke, his words echoing in the windowless room. Hands reappeared beneath his armpits and hauled him into a sitting position. He listed, blinked. Hands on his shoulders prevented him from toppling back down to the ground.

Stanley was sitting across from him, and beside him was another of his Eastern European grunts, though this one had the air of being in charge. Behind them both he caught sight of Mariska, off to one side, cleaning her fingernails as if this was the most normal thing in the world. Curses and accusations fought one another at the back of his throat, then died away. He was too tired to care. When a blinding white light flicked on, shining directly in his face just like the movies, all he did was close his eyes.

"Your friend has been quite forthcoming." Solomon's rat was doing the talking then. He couldn't imagine the soldier having such a reedy voice. Or an American accent, for that matter.

"Friend? She's not my friend." Hugo squinted, hoping to catch a glimpse of Mariska's face, but the light overwhelmed all else. "What did she tell you?"

"How did your daughter escape?"

"She didn't say?" He couldn't bring himself to say her name.

"I'd like to hear it from you."

He had a decision to make. Was there any value in holding out, keeping mum? Brita had been gone for hours, maybe days. He couldn't see what use they'd be able to make of any information he could provide. All the same, he wanted to make them work for it.

"There are many ways to skin a cat, as they say, Mr Gundersson. If you won't divulge willingly..." The rat let the sentence linger. A chair scraped against the ground, and a shadow fell across his face. He opened his eyes to find the soldier, grinning, a pair of pliers in his hands.

Right. Decision made.

"All right, all right, no need to resort to violence. You want to know how Brita got away?"

"Please."

"You would have found the wires on the truck wall?" A pause, no denial, and a soft shuffling of feet over by the wall. His hearing was coming back. "And she told you what they were?"

"Indulge me."

If his eyes had been open, he would have rolled them. Nevertheless, he launched into the whole story—his sulking in the corner, his confession, everything. He omitted nothing. What did he care if they knew how much he hated himself for what he'd done?

"Where do you think she went?"

"Where? My apartment in Knightsbridge. Second floor, next to the workbench, if that helps." A pencil scratched on paper. "I'd tell you the address, but I'm sure you already know it."

The rat ignored him, instead holding a muttered conversation at the back of the room. Hugo only caught snippets: *that must be how...* and *she's just one woman...*Hugo grinned, trying to catch whoever he was talking to behind the light.

"That you, Solomon? I hope Brita's leaving didn't scupper any of your plans."

Silence. He probably shouldn't have been enjoying himself this much, but he couldn't help it.

"How long into your journey did this happen?" Stanley asked. He must have been standing now; the direction of his voice had changed.

"Our *journey*?" Hugo snorted. "Hard to judge, I'm afraid—time flies when you're having fun."

"Please, Mr Gundersson. My compadre here is growing impatient."

"All right, all right." Best not to push it, although, why not give that search party something to chase? "The road was uphill, winding. And there was no light coming through the cracks in the doors, hadn't been for hours. After midnight, I'd say. So what's that—twelve, fourteen hours in?"

More scribbling. "So let me get this straight. You had an escape mechanism—a magic door back home—but you waited twelve to fourteen hours to use it? And why just her, why not both of you?"

"Well, the second part is easy. The 'magic door,' as you call it, was only open for a short time. Seconds. And, sad to say, I'm not as spry as I used to be." He held up his hands, showing them the lacerations that encircled his wrists. "Plus, fourteen hours bouncing around in the back of a truck with our hands tied behind our backs..."

"And the first?"

Yes, the first. "Honestly? It's because I was sulking."

A shuffling of bums in seats, a stir of interest. "Sulking?"

"Yes, and understandably so, I might add. You stole my life's work, after all. After the first half an hour, Brita had quite given up on getting anything out of me."

"You're saying she didn't know that you had a Gateway stashed away in the soles of your shoes, for just such an emergency as this? And you didn't think to tell her?"

"That's exactly what I'm saying."

"What was it that brought you two around?" That was Mariska's voice. His lips tightened. He didn't trust himself to speak, not to her. He kept his mouth resolutely shut.

"Answer the question, please, Mr Gundersson."

"I will not answer questions from her."

"You're not in a position to be picky, I'm afraid."

"I don't want to hear her voice again." There was no comment, no discussion. He listened, thinking he could hear her squirming in the background, though he may have been imagining it. He was tiring again, the effort of sitting upright and talking, choosing his words. The adrenaline was wearing off.

"Brita was talking to herself, trying to come up with ways out of this mess. What our people back in London might be able to do, if she could somehow let them know. It was all daydreaming, though, nothing more than that."

"Daydreaming? I thought you said it was nighttime?"

"It's a figure of speech, for Christ's sake. How about fantasising, is that better? Jesus." He gritted his teeth, re-adjusting his posture, trying and failing to find a comfortable angle for his aching back. "Regardless, I must have started listening, over the noise of the engine and the road. Suddenly I remembered which pair of shoes I was wearing and I realised I could send her back to London. That I could have done it hours before..." He shook his head. He didn't have to dig that deep to find something to hate himself for.

"You look angry, Mr Gundersson. It must have been aggravating, to have had such an escape route all along, during so much unnecessary suffering."

"You know what?" He raised his hand to shield his eyes despite his protesting muscles, despite the fatigue. "All of that unnecessary suffering *was* aggravating, you little rat. But it wasn't me that put us into the back of that truck. It wasn't me that tied my hands behind my back. And it wasn't me that bailed at the first sign of trouble, abandoning her friends. How did *you* enjoy *your* journey to this hole in the mountainside, Mariska?"

He lets his anger take over, spittle flying from his lips. It gave him energy, enough to stand, despite his guard's hands on his shoulders, despite the pain, the exhaustion. All of his self-loathing came bubbling to the surface, and he realised he wasn't yelling at them. He was yelling at himself, at the Hugo Gundersson of two months ago, sipping his coffee across the table from Solomon's rat, at how he'd let his fear and paranoia take over and drag everyone into the hole with him.

"Fuck you! Fuck all of you. I'm done with your stupid questions. Brita's gone. You can't get her now. She'll know what to do, my daughter, and when she does, you'll all...you'll all..."

He swayed on his feet, lurched, and crashed to the floor. The haze was back, the room swirled, and he was floating. He reached out for a familiar face.

He wanted to apologise. He felt like he'd said the wrong thing.

He was sorry, so sorry.

It all went black.

— • —

Mariska watched on, biting her lip, as Aleks and Yosip carried Hugo from the interrogation room. She was half a step off the back wall, hiding in the shadows. Who from, she didn't know. Herself maybe.

"So, should we believe him?" Stanley asked, still scribbling notes.

"Believe what? You saw the wires, and you were driving the truck. When else could she have gotten away?"

"Oh, there's no disputing that. I mean that bullshit story about clamming up, forgetting about the escape route hidden in his shoes."

She thought back to that night at Hugo's. His face, bright red, as he slammed the cabinet shut and stormed off into the night. And that had been over what, Brita challenging him on just how difficult it would be to bring Gateway to the reality he imagined?

Two corridors away, she heard the metal screech of the door, opening onto to the chamber where Hugo was being held, and Yosip flashed back into her mind. Sitting there, toying with the pliers, just waiting for an opportunity to use them. What would a man like him do with the ability to cross national borders with nothing but a phone call? Drugs, guns, women... she shuddered.

Brita had been right, all those months ago. Gateway would be dangerous if it got into the wrong hands, and that was exactly what had happened. And what stood between Solomon and total control?

Not much at all.

But if she could just convince them to underestimate Brita, give her time to...to what? She didn't know. That was up to Brita. Mariska could only play her small part.

"You haven't worked with Hugo. I have," she said, emerging from the shadows, putting her neck on the line. "When he loses control..." She exhaled slowly, letting her face sell the message. "Being loaded into the back of a truck, with his legacy ripped away from him? I can imagine him just about shutting down. Ceasing to function."

"Oh, I'm well aware of how...volatile Hugo can be, Miss Farkas," Stanley said, looking down on her with a sinister smile. "But let's play devil's advocate, just for the moment, and imagine Hugo—hands bound, betrayed, positively catatonic. What could have inspired such a turnaround then, do you think?"

"Who knows?" She fought the sudden urge to fidget, refusing to find a channel for her rapidly building nervous energy. "Faith in his daughter, perhaps."

He raised his eyebrow, as if he knew something about Brita, about Hugo, that she didn't. "Should we be worried?"

"About Brita?" Stanley's gaunt face was tightly drawn, deep purple ringing his eyes. He mustn't have slept in almost thirty hours, and yet he glared at her like a puma, stalking its prey. She steeled herself and told him what she hoped he wanted to hear. "I didn't jump ship on a whim. With Brita in charge, that ship was only going in one direction. Your arrival has only accelerated it."

"Our arrival...yes, I suppose you're right. About that, at least. But you're wrong about this." He waved a vague hand over at the Gateway cables, which had been dumped carelessly in the corner of the room. "Brita was gone before we left Kolkata, I think, and he's covering. It would explain the trading halt, though I suppose your friend Garfield might have come to his senses of his own accord."

Mariska scoffed, involuntarily. Garfield was just about incapable of independent thought. If he called the trading halt, it was because someone like Anita had gotten a hold of him and brow-beaten him into line. Or Brita, though how she would have explained away the kidnapping stories, or her sudden re-appearance in London when she was meant to be in Kolkata...

"Look, all of this speculation is pointless," she said, launching herself upright in an exaggerated show of exasperation. "What can she do that she hasn't already done? If she was going to come out in the press, she would have done it already. The fact that she hasn't means she doesn't want to expose Gateway. Solomon and I have been here for what, twelve hours? And what have we done?"

Stanley faltered, because of course he didn't know. He only knew snippets, whatever he'd been able to glean on the road. She decided to fill him in.

"Nothing but wait, and, after your friend Yosip and his goons arrived, glower at one another from shadowy corners." She crossed her arms and kicked her hip out to one side, a pose that accentuated her curves, designed to distract at just the right time. "Brita has made her move. It's high time we made ours, if anyone can tell me what in God's name it might be. Or even who's in charge, here."

Stanley's tired eyes flicked down and back up.

"Well?" she demanded.

Her defiance seemed to resettle him. His gaze hardened, and he was back to the impenetrable, shadowy servant. "Solomon's the boss. Yours and mine. You want to know what he's planning, you'd better ask him."

45

—·—

THE FLIGHT FROM KUALA Lumpur to Thimphu was short, barely four hours. But after twenty-four hours that had included waking at his desk to news of Brita's kidnapping in India, interrupting a burglary only to find Brita quivering in the middle of her father's apartment with a rifle pointed straight at the burglar's chest, being followed by the Ukrainian mob, learning that real, honest-to-god teleportation existed and that Solomon was in the middle of stealing it, a four-hour flight to sit and reflect felt like an aberration.

An undeserved luxury.

Jorge relaxed back into the plush leather of his chair and tried to enjoy the silence and privacy afforded by Ming-Xia's family jet, without thinking too hard about just how many poor migrants she'd exploited to be able to afford it.

Brita was laid out opposite him, already fast asleep, a marvel that right now he could not comprehend. They'd barely even left the ground. He'd awoken with the first light and felt so amped that he couldn't imagine sleeping ever again. And he was the one who'd spent his youth trekking through war zones, while she'd what? Drunk too much when she was meant to be studying? Gotten a job from her father, and spent too long in front of her computer? She had no right being this calm.

He shook his head and sipped his water, ice cold, in a crystal tumbler. Crystal, on an aeroplane—*No, Jorge.* That line of thought would only distract him. He returned his attention to the maps spread across the table between them.

The plan, concocted by Brita and Anita while he'd been attempting to sleep, was as simple as it was insane. Ming-Xia had dug up detailed schematics of the hydroelectric plant where Solomon was holding Hugo hostage, as well as maps of the surrounding area. She'd marked out the key points of their approach, possible entrances and exits highlighted, and, thanks to Hugo and his apparently ever-present paranoia, a means of escape. The only unknown was where exactly he was being held. That, and how many goons Solomon had rustled up to protect him. How many guns they might have. How ruthless they might be. Just what part Brita's friend Mariska would decide to play. And, he was certain, as many problems again that they'd not even considered. That they'd just have to figure out on the ground.

He laughed at himself, from nerves, but also at the ludicrousness of that phrase. *Figure it out on the ground.* God, he sounded like a character from one of his mother's spy novels. It was too simple. Of course, Brita and Anita had recognised this. They didn't know what they were doing, and trying to make it any more complicated would only make the inevitable screw-up more likely. They probably still would, anyway. Despite the khaki trousers, thick socks, hiking boots, and well-equipped backpack at his feet, despite how familiar it all felt, he knew, deep down, that he was just pretending.

He wasn't that man anymore. He wasn't certain he ever had been.

He found himself scratching at the tiny wire taped to his chest: the second part of the plan. Rescuing Hugo was only one scuffle in the fight for the Gateway, and a minor one at that.

Solomon would not give up, not after having so drastically exposed himself. He'd gone all in, and so had his underworld backers.

Hence the microphone strapped neatly just below his throat, and the go-pro clipped to the cross strap of his pack. Brita was sporting the same arrangement. If they managed to get back unscathed, he would have all the evidence he'd need to shut Solomon down for good.

He could practically smell the Pulitzer committee falling over themselves to welcome him back into the fold.

Observe. Tell the story. That was his job. He was no hero.

All he had to do was get out of this alive.

46

Mariska heard Solomon before she saw him. He was holed up in the office at the far end of the southern wing. It was the only room in the entire abandoned building with a window. Well, a space where a window might have one day been installed. Solomon stood before it, leaning with his knuckles pressed into the weathered concrete and looking out over the dam's tranquil waters.

She slowed as she approached the doorway and realised that the view was incidental. Solomon was wearing one of his awful Omni headsets. He was literally in another world. She placed her feet carefully and listened:

"—no, thank you. Ah'm sorry no one thought to contact you earlier and let you know what was goin' on." He chuckled to himself, nodding and grinning at no one, his eyes and his brow swallowed by the slick white visor. "Ah only wish I could be bringing you better news."

Mariska cast about. There was a pack in the corner, with a second gleaming headset just waiting to be worn.

"Ah totally agree. Very poor form on their part. A total lack of respect, for the both of us."

She bit her lip. It would be so easy to just slip it on, find out who he was talking to.

"Ah know, ah know. Mah bankers are askin' the same damn questions and ah just don't know what to tell 'em."

Mariska snorted. This was excruciating. Her fingers twitched just thinking about who might be on the other end of that phone call.

"Is that so? That's such rotten timin'." Solomon pressed a disingenuous hand to his chest. "Katsubashi-san, if there's anything ah can do to help, just ask. Heck, ah reckon ah could even buy you out, if yer that desperate for cash."

An uneasy feeling bubbled at the pit of Mariska's stomach. Something about the way Solomon had said *rotten timing*. She thought back to last night, just after Yosip's thugs had arrived and taken over. What was it he'd said? An opportunity for the

283

mysterious Volodymyr to use his influence, in Tokyo? She dug her hands into her pockets. All of a sudden she had no desire to listen in as Solomon extorted poor Sato out of his 2% stake in Gateway.

She dropped down into the gravel—this room was dirtier even than the main corridor, probably because of the window—and ran the numbers in her head. Her stalling with Garfield had bought Solomon forty-six minutes of trading, during which his shell companies and dodgy accountants had managed to accumulate 10.6% of Stora's shares from the open market, and another 14% she'd scared out of Brita's institutional investors. Add to that his and Sandeep's buy-in, from that night at Brita's apartment, and he controlled 28.6% of the company. And now he'd flipped Sato, too.

30.6%.

Significant. But far from enough.

And there were only two people who could give him what he needed. Well, three, but Lloyd didn't count. His assets would be so tied up by the City of London Police as to be practically inaccessible. Which left Brita, who wasn't here. Who needed time to gather the authorities, to marshal her resources and mount her defence.

And Hugo, who was just downstairs. Who just happened to be the most stubborn, hardheaded, intractable old man she'd ever met. She shielded her eyes from the glare of the sun and looked up at Solomon as he pulled his head free of the Omniverse headset, the beginnings of a plan forming in her mind.

"What does Sato think of your little gadget?" she asked.

Solomon turned slowly, as if he'd known she was there the whole time. "Katsubashi-san has always been an early adopter."

"But he's getting cold feet with Gateway, though."

He clenched his jaw and rubbed his hand over his hair, trying to tamp down the tufts that the headset straps had raised. She could see him wondering just how much she'd heard.

"Which, I'm guessing, means your pal Volodymyr came through with the goods?"

The skin around Solomon's eyes tightened. "That's a topic ah'd steer well clear of, if ah were you."

Mariska batted the warning away. She needed him off balance. "He's the one pulling the strings, though, isn't he. And for a long time, I imagine, given how long ago you burned that reporter for sniffing around." She pushed herself to her feet. "What's he got on you?"

He opened his mouth as if to speak, then thought better of it and made to brush past her. She stepped across and held her hand mere inches in front of his chest.

"Uh-uh, I don't care how important you think you are; you don't get to just walk away from this conversation. You owe me some answers."

"Ah don't owe you a goddamn thing." He sneered, but he stopped all the same.

"I betrayed Brita for you. Without me you'd have, what, 15%? At most?"

"You did it for the money, not me."

"Damn straight I did. But the more I see, the more I hear, I get the feeling I'm the only one."

Solomon started. She could see his mind whirring behind his eyes. When he spoke, it was through clenched teeth. "If yer goin' to say somethin', just say it."

"You don't want Gateway for the money. You want it to pay off a bad debt."

"You don't know what yer talkin' about—"

"Yes I do, and I want my cut."

"Yer cut?"

"My cut. If Volodymyr gets Gateway, and you get your freedom, I want my cut." She steeled herself, held her breath. The entire duration of this conversation, numbers had been bouncing about in her head, and now the moment was here. She took the plunge. "One billion."

Solomon's sneer began a slow transition into wolfish grin, as if she'd flubbed her lines. "You've got nerve, ah'll give you that—"

"You'll give me my money. Or I'll tell Volodymyr how you had the chance to turn 31% to 51% and blew it because you refused to pay the price."

Solomon's smile faltered.

"You wanted me on board for a reason. This is it."

She held his gaze, and he broke it, pulling away to stare above her head and run a hand through his hair. By the time he turned back, she knew she had him. "One billion. It'll take time."

"You know people, or Volodymyr does. I'm sure, between the two of you, you'll figure it out."

"You speak as if you know him, but you don't."

"Solomon," Mariska said, stepping back, letting her eyes take in the Soviet-era concrete box in which they stood, bolted to the mountainside. "You're forgetting where I grew up. The kind of people I grew up with. Now. Do we have a deal?"

She stuck out her hand, knowing that it wouldn't betray even a hint of the emotion that was broiling inside her. He hesitated, but only momentarily. As his hand slapped into hers, just one thought dominated her mind: *Come on, Brita. I'm counting on you. We both are.*

"Boss? You down here?"

"Yeah," Solomon shouted, answering Stanley's call. He tried to pull his hand away, but she clung on.

"I need to hear you say it."

"Say it?"

"Say it."

He squeezed, hard, but Mariska refused to flinch. She would not be dominated.

"Fine. We have a deal," he growled. "Now where am ah goin' to get my last 20%?"

Mariska nodded back down the corridor.

"That old coot? He'll never flip, not with his daughter on the outside."

"You don't know him like I do. And you certainly can't push his buttons like I can."

"So that's the deal? You tell me how to flip Hugo Gundersson on his own company, and ah give you a billion dollars?"

He still had her hand gripped tight in his, but she dared not pull away now. She'd pricked Solomon's ego just enough to make him want to prove he could defeat even Hugo, but that relied on his being unable to defeat her, right now.

"Take it or leave it—"

"There you are." Stanley burst into the room, his phone in his hand. "I've got Marlowe on the line—"

"Good. Deal with her," Solomon said, finally releasing her hand. "Mariska here is going to tell me how to break Hugo Gundersson."

47

— · —

THE GPS IN THEIR four-wheeler, a rickety old Mahindra Legend that Jorge had bought for cash outside Thimphu airport, chimed and flashed. 27°03′40.4″N, 89° 33′45.4″E, just as Mariska had said.

He pulled onto the side of the road, just across from a walking track that should lead to a cliff face overlooking the abandoned hydroelectric plant in the valley below.

"You ready?" Jorge asked.

"I feel like a Swiss army knife," Brita said with forced levity, adjusting her straps, tweaking the route of the microphone tucked beneath the underwire of her bra. She repositioned a half dozen other items too, secreted away in case of emergencies. "All I'm missing is the corkscrew."

Jorge turned the car off, and the engine fell ominously silent. "And maybe a bottle of wine. For when we get back."

Brita put her hand on the door handle. It shook. *When we get back...*She forced her doubts out of her mind and put on a smile. It was far too late to be having second thoughts. "We're going to need something a little harder than wine."

"We'll be fine. Solomon has no idea that we're coming."

And we have no idea what we're walking into—No. She couldn't afford to think like that. She and Jorge had the advantage. Surprise. Mobility. Sheer audacity. And they were in the right. She tensed her shoulders, the angular shapes of Gateway handsets and battery packs digging through her backpack's padding. Reminding her what was at stake. Her father's life. Her company. Her legacy.

She tugged on the handle and stepped outside.

The afternoon sun was ahead of her, shining down weakly through the thin mountain air. Jorge was already a dozen paces ahead of her, but she didn't rush. She pulled her sunglasses from her pocket and gave the four-wheeler an affectionate pat on the bonnet. It had done its job and would remain here until some lucky farmer came looking and found the keys Jorge had left on the front seat.

"You coming or what?"

Brita sighed. Jorge had only known Anita for what, twenty-four hours, and already he spoke just like her. That abrupt impatience. She stepped away from the car, ducked beneath the errant branches of a drab green bush, and followed Jorge down the track.

The trek was not a long one. They breached the top of the rise in less than ten minutes, and the valley fell away before them. Triple peaks rose in the hazy distance, framing the sinking sun and the high clouds, tinged apricot and peach. The shrubs clinging to the dry and dusty hillside were a muted grey, the victims of a long, hot dry season.

She crouched down at the cliff's rocky lip, mapping the aerial photos and schematics they'd studied on Ming-Xia's table, and on the plane, to what lay before her. Just a couple hundred metres below, sunlight shimmered and sparkled off the surface of a vast, man-made lake. On the far side, a concrete box was just visible. She and Jorge pulled their binoculars to their eyes, and she traced the water tunnels, rolling down the slope into the deepest part of the valley.

"Brita, tell me what you see just in front of the building. In the courtyard."

She trained her binoculars across and adjusted the focus. There were two trucks, not much more than green blocks in the distance. And movement behind them, but the detail was lost in the dusky haze.

"One of the trucks looks familiar, I think. I only saw it for a moment though, before we were shoved inside." She squinted, but it was no help.

Jorge nodded, packed his binoculars away. "Looks like they have guards set up too. Time to get moving."

She took one last look, straining to catch a glimpse. Of Solomon maybe, or Mariska, but the shadows were too long, and growing deeper with every minute. Again, Jorge had taken off without her, picking his way across a rocky outcrop to their left like a natural. He turned, crouching, and offered her his hand. The rumpled khakis, mirrored sunglasses, and salt-and-pepper beard suited him. He was much closer to the young war correspondent she'd seen photos of than the slick TV reporter she'd met under the lights of the studio.

"Thanks," she said, her cheeks flushing. Next to him she felt clumsy, out of place. Like she was playing at commando. "You've missed this, haven't you?"

"What, climbing rocks?" He was already scaling the next shelf.

"No, chasing stories. Putting yourself where people like Solomon don't want you." She waved his hand away, grabbed a crevice with her fingers, and heaved herself gracelessly over the ledge with a rolling flop. She propped herself up on her elbow. "This is you. The real you. Just a camera, a microphone, a notebook, and your wits."

He shrugged, but his face broke out into a roguish grin. Then he turned and scrambled up the hillside without a word. She followed, shaking out her fingers. She shouldn't be tiring already, surely? Jorge's precarious path led them around the curve of mountainside, and they were no longer visible from the lookout. If the satellite photos were accurate, there should be one more ledge and a small plateau. She heard the scrape of his boots against rock as she rounded the bend and there it was, a flat rocky plinth, out of sight of prying eyes, with Jorge standing atop it.

She accepted his help this time, and within seconds they were settled on the edge, overlooking the valley below, growing ever more beautiful in the gathering dusk. But that beauty was deceiving. They had to make the most of the failing light. Jorge ripped open his backpack and pulled out his drone aircraft—gunmetal grey with a sharply angled body and modified with one of her father's new prototypes: a remotely deployable Gateway module, mounted securely to its belly.

Brita scooted back from the edge while Jorge set up his drone and shrugged her backpack from her shoulders. She focused on simple movements, one thing at a time, and tried not to think about the bigger picture. Zips open, unfold her schematics, pressed flat into the rocks. Orient the drawings, and herself, with the real building across the valley. In this way she could scan with her binoculars, mark out access routes and landing zones without her fear for her father, for Mariska, taking over.

She marked two possibilities on her map, double-checked her work, and handed the binoculars across to Jorge.

"There." She pointed to two outcroppings, one to the north and a second a hundred metres or so farther east, both a short scramble from where the hydro-plant's flat concrete roof met the mountainside. Jorge followed her line, checked the maps, and nodded. "That one." He tapped the second marking on her map. "It's a little further back from that courtyard. Better hidden."

He passed her a laser pointer and a tripod from the drone's case.

She set the tripod well back from the cliff edge and clipped the laser into place. With one eye closed, she lined up the chosen plateau manually. Small goals, small wins. Releasing her breath, she pressed the switch and waved her hand across the beam to confirm the little red dot was actually there.

Bringing the binoculars back up, she zoomed in on the rocky outcrops, scanning in a methodical, expanding pattern for the telltale pinpoint of light. And there it was—she had it pretty level but was about twenty metres off target to the east. As she adjusted the laser gently with her free hand and tracked its progress through her polished lenses, she wondered if twenty metres was good or bad for a first timer.

"Ready?"

She dropped the binoculars at his question. He sat with his legs crossed, elbows on his knees, touchpad controls clasped in his hands. The drone was perched before him, waiting silently for its first command.

"Just a second." She controlled her slightly trembling fingers, edging the pointer ever so slightly to the right. She'd directed them to the lookout. Followed Jorge up the side of the mountain. Selected a landing point. Directed the laser right where it needed to go. She'd done all this, and would do the next task too. And the next, until the whole thing was done. "Yep, got it. We're good to go."

She sat back from the laser, watching Jorge work the controls. At the touch of an icon, the drone buzzed to life. The blades, one at each corner of its moulded body, disappeared in a blur, and it leapt into the air. Its movement was so sudden that by the time she'd jerked in surprise, it had already paused, hovering a foot above the rock, as steady as if it was sitting on solid ground.

"You sure you know how to drive that thing?" she asked.

"I've dabbled."

She could hear the smirk in his voice, and his arrogance made her want to remind him that he'd fished it out of her father's overgrown courtyard only thirty-six hours ago. But that line of thinking only opened herself up to the bigger picture again, to the possibility that things might go wrong, so she held her tongue. With another light touch the drone zoomed up into the air. She craned her neck, but it was gone. Out of sight, out of hearing.

"How high is it?"

"About one hundred and sixty metres," Jorge said, squinting, taking a readout from his screen.

"Let's keep it that way. The less chance we give the guards the better."

"Roger that."

She watched over his shoulder. He switched on the camera, and the darkening valley sprang to life on the screen—the two of them huddled on their little patch of rock, minute in the steep valleys of rock and scrub. He worked silently, setting the drone to homing mode—now it was its turn to scan for the laser. The view oscillated for a few seconds, circling the valley, and locked on to the red point of light. Another string of keystrokes and the drone was off—gliding across the gloomy valley slopes.

"I've locked the altitude for now. Give it a few seconds, and it should come to a rest right above our outcrop. There."

He changed views, and the image began to zoom in. No, that wasn't quite right. The drone was dropping, right into place.

"Incredible. Great flying." She squeezed his shoulder and he shrugged, as if to say he'd hardly done a thing. She didn't argue; it was time for her to get moving. She crawled over to her bag and pulled out a much larger tripod. This one, though, was a little different, set up more like an easel, with a spiked copper frame unfolding on its face. There was a bracket on the back leg for her to connect her phone. Carefully, she folded her schematics and slipped them into her breast pocket. The backpack, now much lighter, slid easily over her shoulders.

"Drone is in position."

"Are you all packed up?"

"Yep." He patted his pockets and swung his pack onto his shoulder—tablet held loosely in his other hand. With a grin, he pointed the camera on his shoulder strap right at her. "Want to say anything for posterity, Brita?"

"Oh, put that away. Save it for Solomon." She turned her back to hide her agitation. *Small steps, Brita, small steps.*

She pulled her phone from her pocket, her hands trembling again, much worse than before. She closed her eyes, balled her fists but it didn't help. The reality she'd been trying to keep at bay had come flooding back. She was a CEO, for Christ's sake, a software engineer, not a soldier! What was she doing crawling around on a mountainside in combat boots? Walking towards armed guards! *It's too big. I can't do this, I can't...*

Jorge appeared in front of her, his strong hands gripping her shoulders. "Hey, Brita. Look at me. I want you to look at me, okay?" He took her hands in his. His fingers were surprisingly rough for a man who'd spent the last decade in a TV studio. "I may be the one that is used to skulking about in dangerous places I definitely shouldn't be, but I want you to remember—that is your father down there."

She nods, focusing on his eyes. How could she forget.

"It's your technology they're trying to steal, and this Gateway, it is your trump card. I don't know it like you do, and neither do they. It's your way in and your escape route. You got away from them once, you can do it again—and this time..." He cracked that roguish grin again, all teeth and crinkles in the corners of his eyes. "This time you have me by your side, okay?"

He let her go. She was gripping the phone tight, but her hands no longer shook. A deep breath, and another. She nodded. She would be all right.

She smiled, a crazy, or maybe crazed, smile. She was really going to do this. More, she *wanted* to do it. She glanced over his shoulder. The sun had sunk below the far mountains, and the valley below rested in deepening shadow. She was the only one who *could* do it.

She plugged her phone into the easel while Jorge reactivated the drone's control screen. On her mark he triggered the Gateway module. There was no indication that anything had happened, other than a small flurry of motion at the edge of the video feed. She navigated to the pre-saved number and dialled. In the gathering darkness there was no sign that the Gateway had made a successful connection—no telltale shimmer to give it away. One second, it was just a black aluminium easel set on a rocky mountain, the next it was a doorway across the valley—shifting just slightly as the drone hovered and adjusted to the soft breeze.

She ran her eyes over their ledge—none of the objects strewn about were things they would need. With a nod from Jorge, she switched off the laser.

"Right, let's go. And thanks," she said, without looking back, and stepped through to the other side, ducking to keep her hair away from the drone's blades. As soon as she was clear, she dropped into a crouch. Jorge was right behind, taking up position behind one of the larger rocks, staying out of sight.

She shuffled across to the open portal and reached through to grab her phone. The cable came away easily, and she pulled it through to her side before ending the connection. A brief spark from the severed cable was the only evidence of the Gateway flickering away into nothing, permanently cutting them off from their entry route. The cord dangled limp from the port on her phone.

She reached up and took a gentle grip on the underside of the drone. With a stroke from Jorge, the rotors died and the hum faded, leaving only silence. They both crouched in the shadows, listening. No curious whispers, no alarm. There was nothing. She waited another ten seconds, listening intently between the thumps of her heart, pounding in her ear.

"I think we're good," she whispered. Jorge held up a finger and brought it to his lips. He nodded over his shoulder. She listened. Very faintly, she could hear voices, though she couldn't make out any of the words. From the patterns, it just sounded like a normal conversation.

Jorge pointed up at the sky. It took her a second, but she got there. She unclipped the Gateway module from the drone's belly and rested it gently on the large flat rock at her side. She held the drone out on the flat of her hand, and the buzz was back—it vibrated with life in her palm and disappeared up into the purpling sky.

She dropped to her chest and crawled across to the edge of their new outcrop. Not far below, the concrete roof was visible through the gloom—a harsh, man-made scar jutting from the side of the mountain. She scanned it intently, and yes! There in the far corner, just as the schematics had shown.

A hatch.

She turned back to signal to Jorge the good news. He was huddled, silent, eyes glued to the screen. He caught her watching and held up three fingers before beckoning her over.

"Hatch is right where it should be," she whispered, craning her neck so that she could see the live feed from above. His eyes bulged as he mimed at her to zip it, jabbing a finger at the screen. Feeling cocky, only the panicked tension behind his eyes gave her pause. She twisted to his side, as quietly as she could manage, to get a better look.

It took her half a second to orient herself. She found the concrete roof, the access hatch, and worked her way back to her and Jorge, crouched in the shadows.

She recognised the front entrance from the schematics, still safely stashed away in her top pocket. She patted them, just to make sure. Light spilled out through the main entrance and she tensed, having taken way too long to understand that the long shadows were being cast by two guards, stationed off to one side.

Jorge deftly double tapped the bottom left corner of the screen, a section of the compound roof barely fifty metres away. Right next to the other landing zone, one they'd very nearly used. The feed zoomed down to what felt like almost their level, and she ducked, looking up instinctively. No telltale buzz. The magnification must be digital.

Her train of thought was cut short by movement in the frame. A third guard, on the roof, heavily armed and only metres away. A chill ran down her spine. Jorge's eyes blazed a warning, but her mouth was so dry she doubted she could talk even if she wanted to.

If they'd sent the drone to her first choice rather than her second...

If she'd angled the laser just a little farther to the east...

But she hadn't, and they'd spotted him, before he'd spotted them. She was amazed at her ability to focus, to not panic. To not fixate on his heavy black weapon and instead move onto the next small task. To focus on the next question: What should they do now?

She caught Jorge's gaze and raised a solitary eyebrow. The mercenary just beyond the ridge was blocking their planned access route. Jorge thought for a second, brows furrowed. He switched off the tablet screen and placed it gingerly against the boulder, their shelter, their protection. He pulled out his phone and motioned for her to do the same.

She double-checked that her phone was on silent as Jorge typed, dimming her screen to its lowest setting. The brief flash of the notification light was the only indication of the arrival of Jorge's message.

Jorge

I have an idea

Get the Gateway from the drone set up against the rock

No

He nodded his head at the large, flat-faced shelf of limestone just behind them. It was the perfect size. She knew what was coming next, was already typing furiously.

It's too dangerous.

She shook her head as she hit send, pleading silently.

I'll be fine

I'll draw our friend away

He smiled at her, his face lit dimly by the glow of his screen. The sunlight was almost completely gone.

I may not look it, but I can run fast when I have to

Plus, I'll set up my escape route beforehand

He patted a bulging pocket, the one she knew contained his emergency Gateway and power pack. He could key it specifically for the portal lying in a crumpled mess at her feet.

I don't like this

She closed her eyes as she hit send, resigned, knowing it was futile. The guard was too close. There was no other way. She grabbed Jorge's hand, gripping it hard.

—·—

Jorge crouched behind the canvas-topped transport truck, his heart pounding. It was parked in the courtyard about seventy metres from the main entrance and the two guards stationed outside it. Their laughter echoed through the courtyard, loud and obnoxious. He didn't need to understand a word they were saying. He'd known enough soldiers, knew the way they spoke. The tone, the cadence, told him everything he needed.

It had taken him just under thirty minutes to pick his way across the rough terrain in the near dark. Without the light from the stars, and the ability to watch himself from above, he wouldn't have made it. Now he used both to map out an escape route. There was a steep ravine, just behind the first turn of the access road. The Gateway was set up, hanging from a mangled tree just behind that corner. He checked his camera and microphone—both were recording—and whipped out his phone.

He waited for a response, his breathing rapid, wondering again why he was even here, what he'd gotten himself involved in. The guffawing jarheads over there, the ones he was planning on luring into a chase, were armed to the teeth, enough to kill him a dozen different ways. He squeezed his eyes shut against the bubbling images, thankful for the distraction as his phone flashed in his hand.

He wasn't sure what he'd been expecting. More resistance perhaps. But the quick-to-anger CEO he'd first met across the other side of his studio desk had receded farther and farther from view the closer they had gotten to Solomon and his hydro-plant. To her father. To her game-changing, legacy-defining product. The quiet determination he'd sensed beneath the surface that night had fully taken over.

So all he got was a good luck.

He stashed his phone safely away. No more time for thinking. He clambered up on the truck's passenger-side doorstep, swinging the door open wide, and fumbled around under the bench seat, looking for something, anything he could "accidentally" drop with a clatter. His fingers came to rest on cold metal, a familiar handle grip with a smooth, machined barrel. He hefted the pistol. It was heavy, fully loaded. He tucked it away for later. You never knew when a gun might come in handy.

He returned to his search and came upon a metal cylinder. Dragging it out into the faint light, he discovered, to his surprise, a fire extinguisher. Maybe these thugs were legit. Or at least very well organised. Ready for an emergency.

He wiped his hands, all of a sudden sweaty, and flicked the fire extinguisher onto the gravel. The heavy cylinder rattled across the ground, and he jumped down behind it. If he thought his heart had been pounding before, when he peered around the open door, it felt as if it was trying to leap right out of his mouth. His breath came in short, sharp bursts.

The laughter had stopped, abruptly. One of the very large meatheads was standing, shining a torch in his direction. The beam played across the front of the truck. He planted his feet, holding his trembling limbs fixed in place, letting the light track across his face and off into the night, then swing back with a jerk.

There was yelling, footsteps. He couldn't wait any longer, slamming the door behind him to make sure they heard. He bolted, legs pounding, darting behind the cover of the two trucks. Torch beams flirted at the edges of his vision, but did not find him.

He was halfway there. Gravel crunched underfoot. The torches lit his path now, shone on his back. He couldn't hear the yelling, though he knew it must have been there. Just his blood. His breathing. The cold steel of the pistol pressing into the small of his back with each tearing step. He rounded the corner and ran his thumb across the fingerprint scanner on his phone. It almost slipped from his hand.

The Gateway hung from the tree, right where he'd left it. There were shouts, thumping footsteps, nearing the bend. He slipped, sending a trail of rocks down the slope. Torch beams re-appeared in his peripheral vision, playing wildly, over his head.

He dialled the Gateway. Dove out of cover. A shout, a tumble, a blinding light. He landed on his shoulder, crunching hard against the boulder. He rolled away from the light, holding his phone above the ground. He stabbed at the red 'end call' icon and the light flickered, went dark. Only his ragged breath and his hammering heart remained.

— · —

Good luck

There was so much more she wanted to say, but couldn't find the right words. *Don't do anything stupid. Don't put yourself at risk.*

Don't do exactly what we've come here to do.

She watched the dimmed screen, looking up only at the sound of yelling in the distance. Something was happening, though she could only hope that was Jorge doing what he did best. Throwing cats amongst the pigeons.

A call came through a radio, not far away, bathed in static. She couldn't make out the language, let alone the message. A curt acknowledgement, then a few seconds later, a shadow passed beneath her. More yelling, beams of light flashing across the mountainside.

The coast was clear, for her at least.

She waited until the shadow was well and truly gone, until it slipped silently over the rooftop edge. She did her best to emulate its powerful grace, sliding as quietly as she could down the short slope to the concrete rooftop. She stumbled as she met solid ground, her cheeks flushing as she pushed herself upright and scurried across to the hatch.

It opened with a rusty squeal. She winced, but no one came running. A soft light emanated from inside. A lit hallway, filtering upwards from an empty room. She dangled her legs inside and took a last look up at their outcrop, their hideout.

There was a crunch of gravel, a scrabble and a flash of light, quickly snuffed out. She hoped it was Jorge, returned to safety, but she didn't wait to find out. There was nothing she could do if she was wrong. She brought the hatch down so that it was resting on her head, lowered herself through the hole, and dropped to the floor.

The hatch slid shut, as if it had never been opened at all.

48

HUGO FOUGHT TO KEEP his head up. He'd barely collapsed onto his camp bed before they were hauling him back up the stairs for round two. Round three.

"Money talks, Hugo." Solomon bent down, maintaining eye contact. "You know it does, and ah have more of it than you can imagine."

"Not to my daughter it doesn't. She's not like you."

Solomon had turned the light off, sent his muscle-bound thugs away, and was sitting across from him. Mano a mano, as if he wanted to be the one that finally broke him. Solomon clearly thought he was being relentless, but Hugo had suffered through worse. The back of the truck, tossing him from side to side with every corner. That had been relentless.

"You don't think so? It spoke loud enough for her to oust you from your own company, didn't it? And again, when ah approached her to buy it outright."

"Only until I called her," Hugo wheezed. The prick could say what he liked. Do what he liked, for as long as he liked. He could take it. The longer he held out, the longer Solomon wasted baiting him, the more time he gave Brita to...to...

"And what was that call, Hugo? Forget Gateway, forget family. You offered her a better deal, nothin' more. Don't kid yourself. Anyone in her position would've done the same. Ah've made the same offer to you both, straight up. Twenty billion dollars, in cash. How long are you willin' to wait for her to take it?"

Hugo snickered. "You don't even know where she is—"

A shout echoed down the hallway. Then another. She wouldn't take the deal, no way. He knew his daughter. She would never deal with a thug like him. From a distance he thought he heard a car door slam, the sound of boots on gravel.

Solomon's chair scraped. Hugo forced open his swollen eyes, but there was nothing in front of him.

"Stanley, wake up," Solomon hissed. "Stanley, now. Something's going down."

Hugo cocked his head to one side. There was panic now. Men running.

"You stay here," Stanley commanded. A sharp, metallic click—a breech being checked. "You, get him out of here."

Hugo smiled. Rough hands grabbed him, dragged him to his feet. He dangled, a deadweight. Let them do the work. He'd done his part. Stalled as long as he could.

He just hoped it had been long enough.

— • —

Brita landed with knees bent, arms out. Not even a wobble. Her and Anita's childhood gymnastics instructor would have been proud.

She was proud of herself.

She took in the room. Stark concrete, layer upon layer of dust. No furniture, not even any finishing around the doorway—just an opening out into a dingy corridor. She tucked herself into the darkest corner, out of sight. Before she could do anything else, she had to know. She pulled her phone out of her pocket, and—

She stopped mid-message. She wanted to know that Jorge was all right, but what if he wasn't? What if he'd been caught? Or injured? What if Solomon was holding his phone right now?

Sending that message was too great a risk. He was either fine, or he wasn't. He was out of her control.

She focused instead on the next task on her list. The folded sheets in her top pocket, her pen, that's what she needed. The rustle of the paper seemed explosive in the destitute, echoing silence, and she cursed herself for bringing a pen she needed to click. But she couldn't afford to take ten breaths between each movement—the longer she was here, the more chances she gave them to catch her. Wincing at the noise, but soldiering on, she opened the layout she'd sketched up on the plane, spread it out over her knee, and put herself in Solomon's shoes. If she were an egomaniac, where would she keep her hostages?

She stared at the map, ears pricked, senses straining. She'd hoped that it would be different once she was here, that being within these walls would tell her something, but it was no use. She couldn't think like him, not even for a moment. She'd have to check each room, one by one.

The compound had only the one level, and she mapped a route to take her past each room, a red line snaking through the maze. She crossed out the room with the hatch, her starting point. One down, thirty-one to go.

She slid her pen into her pocket, careful not to click it closed. She only wanted to do that once. The map stayed clutched in her left hand. Boots pounded on gravel, and harsh, shouted words echoed down the corridor. Her breath caught. Were they angry? Celebratory? Coming closer or still far away?

She just couldn't tell—

Her phone vibrated in her pocket. She slumped against the wall, eyes closed, relief draining the pent-up energy from her neck, her shoulders.

Made it back

No problems

She exhaled and huddled herself deeper into the shadows.

I heard you land back at the outcropping

I was worried

I had to give them something to chase :)

Did it work?

Are you in?

I'm in

With a start, she realised she hadn't activated her mike, or her camera. She pressed the button on the cable tucked neatly within the lining of her bra.

Ready and rolling

I'll be here if you need me

Stay out of sight

That rooftop guard won't be gone for long

She returned the phone to her pocket and took one last look at the map in her hand, at the route she'd traced. Left, left, then a right. Stay low, stay vigilant. Move fast.

She knew what she had to do.

—— ◆ ——

"What in fuck is this?" Yosip roared, storming into the empty interrogation room. Mariska barely had time to register the coil of spiked wires he'd flung at her feet before he was on her. He smashed her up against the solid wall, knocking the breath from her lungs. Her feet no longer touched the ground. The mercenary had the lapels of the jacket Solomon had lent her bunched tight in his fists.

"Yos—" She couldn't speak. Could barely breathe.

"Yosip, put her down," Solomon drawled. Yosip merely tightened his grip. "She's been here the whole damn time, fer Christ's sake."

"My men see a man. They chase him. A villager, they are thinking. Then he disappears, and they find this wire, this magic 'Gateway.'" He pressed the knuckles of his left hand into her chest, just below her collarbone, so he could release her with his right and wave at the cables coiled on the floor. She moaned. Her vision blurred. He was so strong. "How this man know we are here?"

Solomon's answers were muffled. She could no longer make out faces, pick out people from the concrete walls. The lights blared up at her from the corner. She felt weightless, and also heavy, so heavy...

—— ◆ ——

Brita slipped through an open doorway and pressed her back into the corner, below the lip of the ragged concrete. She marked two more rooms off her map: almost a third down and no sightings, of any kind. She'd ruled out the entire southern wing and was just around the corner from the main corridor.

She'd heard footsteps, shouted conversations, but so far had seen no one. She bobbed quickly on her toes, peeking over an unfinished wall. Empty. Keep moving. With a lightning look back at where she'd just been, she darted across the corridor in a crouch.

From her new vantage point there were two more rooms visible—both unoccupied, though only one was empty. The other housed a stack of weathered cardboard boxes and a scattering of rubbish—plastic bottles and discarded food wrappings. She crossed both off her map and adjusted her position so she could get a better look down the long corridor.

Poking her head out, just enough, she could see all the way along, almost to the front doors. A weapon emerged from a doorway, maybe five doors down, closely followed by its uniformed, shaved-headed owner. She recoiled, back to the shadows, eyes closed, heart pounding. That had been close. He'd come out of nowhere.

She sat back on her haunches, thinking. If there were guards, they must be guarding something. So, how to get them out of the way for a while? She risked another glance—there were two now, sauntering towards her. Her heart raced. She knew she was deep in shadow and couldn't be seen. At least she hoped she was. The temptation to burrow deeper was overwhelming. But no, moving now would only make her more likely to be seen. And if she was to figure out a way past them, she needed to know how the guards were moving.

They were both huge, heavily armed, and shockingly young. The one on the left was barely old enough to shave. They swung past her position, chatting quietly. She shuffled across behind them, into the junk room.

They took up position either side of a wide, rusty metal door. One pulled out a packet of cigarettes, and they both lit up. Their rifles slung casually over their shoulders. They looked bored.

She watched them for thirty seconds, then pulled back and listened. Their conversation picked up the pattern of bored teenagers everywhere. She didn't need to understand to be able to guess what they were discussing. They didn't look like they planned on moving anytime soon.

She took a quick look at her sketch—it didn't extend beyond that door. Adjusting her feet, her back against the wall, she pulled out the larger schematic and settled down to wait.

— · —

Water.

Mariska snapped awake, chest and neck aching. She wanted to wipe her face dry, but her hands wouldn't move. She blinked. Looked down. Through the fuzz, she saw black plastic strapping about her wrists.

She felt them then, too, bright, throbbing.

"Welcome back."

The low, gloating voice belonged to Stanley. She kept her head hung low as the lamp snapped on. Whatever she did, she couldn't panic.

"Stanley, what the fuck is this? We're partners. Your boss came to me, remember?"

Defiance. It felt good. She tried to control her rapid breathing and ignored the brightness of the light. Once she locked onto Stanley's eyes, she could not afford to look away. Not for a second.

"Don't bother. It'll only get ugly." He crouched down, one hand on her knee. "You think we don't know it was you who gave us away? Come on."

She jerked her knee, trying to knock him off balance, but his grip was like iron. He smiled, as if her resistance was nothing more than the petulance of a child who'd been caught with their hands in the cookie jar. But he was wrong. Lying. He had to be. They couldn't know. She'd covered her tracks. And the second set of Gateway coils...

She didn't want to think about those.

"Gave us away? Fuck, Stanley. I'm all in with you guys, for better or worse. There's no going back." Her voice cracked, went high pitched. She couldn't control it. Her eyes darted, trying to see past the light, into in the back of the room. "Tell him, Solomon, call him off!"

Stanley let her go with a bitter laugh. She pulled back, shook her head, trying to shield her eyes from the light with her dripping hair. "Solomon's not going to save you, is he, Yosip."

A shadow came forward. The hulking mercenary sergeant. "No. He will not." He spoke in Ukrainian; the satisfaction in his voice was crushing. She didn't dare look down at his hands.

"Is this how you treat your new partners?"

"No."

Smack.

Her head snapped back, left cheek stinging. She hadn't even seen the blow coming. "We trust our partners. You are mistake."

"How can I make you trust me?" she asked, hot tears tracing a painful line across the rising welt on her cheek. She couldn't focus. Any semblance of strategy was out the window. She just wanted out, of this chair, of this room, of this awful place. She'd sworn she'd never let herself be put in this position again, and yet... There was almost nothing she wouldn't say to make it happen.

Almost.

"How can she earn our trust, she asks?" Yosip laughed, cold and empty. Stanley sat back down, pulling his chair up to hers so that their knees touched. He wanted her to recoil, and she did. She told herself that she did it to please him, but deep down she knew it had been involuntary. Instinct.

"You can start by telling us who is outside, and how they came to be there."

49

THE LURKING MERCENARY HAD retaken his position less than ten metres beneath Jorge's rocky hiding spot. Jorge had heard him coming, fourteen minutes after Brita had disappeared inside the compound. He'd held the pistol so tight that his entire arm shook, counting every step. He'd been ready to pull the trigger, just waiting for that dark shape to sneak into view. But it never did. Instead he'd heard a stuffed utility belt clatter against the concrete roof as the soldier sat down, followed by a string of incomprehensible mutterings. Thirty seconds later he was engulfed in the foul stench of a cheap Eastern European cigarette.

And for every minute since then, Jorge had waited, tense and anxious, with one eye on his phone and the other scanning for movement. He'd forgotten how much waiting there had been, back in his youth, and how difficult it had been to endure even then.

Now, with his shadow friend just metres away, he barely dared breathe.

His phone vibrated in his hand, and he grunted from surprise.

He couldn't help it. It had been inevitable. And surely, surely, he'd been heard.

He chewed his lip and listened for movement over the sound of his own blood rushing in his ears. There was none. Not even an interruption to the steady curl of smoke wafting up from below. He exhaled, carefully, and allowed himself to check his phone.

Brita

> I think I've found him

> Two guards, posted outside the main water chamber

The main water chamber. That wasn't in the search plan. Luck was with them. He prayed that it would hold just a little longer.

What's your plan?

He hit send, and begged her to tell him she had one, that it was under control. He didn't know how much more of this he could take.

I don't have one, yet

I'm waiting to see what happens, just for a little bit

Damn.

He surveyed their resources. His drone had been up in the air for almost an hour now. In the mad scramble of his distraction, he'd forgotten all about it. He couldn't bring it down now, not with his companion so close. Not here, anyway.

He winced at the bright light of the drone controller's screen. A red exclamation mark flashed urgently in the top right corner. The battery was dangerously low. And when the battery was low... he checked the settings and switched off auto-homing mode. At least it wouldn't betray him in its final moments.

He glanced across at the concrete roof to its very edge, to the precipitous drop over the edge of the dam. Perhaps he could turn this to his and Brita's advantage. He worked quickly, setting the drone to hover just on the far edge of the compound roof.

Low Battery Warning! Ignore.

Auto-Homing Mode Disabled! Ignore.

He waited. A minute later, the video feed juddered and dipped, then went dark.

He counted down the seconds: five, four, three, two, one...

The drone crunched into concrete, and Jorge thought he saw a flash, a few sparks maybe, before the drone was swallowed by the darkness. All that remained was a diminishing rattle as the wreck tumbled down the mountainside.

A surly curse and a scrape of boots told Jorge that the drone's sacrifice had worked. He waited until the dark shadow, distinguished by the single red dot of the cigarette dangling from his mouth, was halfway across the roof. He followed the same path he'd taken before, across the mountain and down into the other side of the main courtyard.

He heard a muffled radio call, well behind him, but he didn't stop, didn't look back.

— · —

Brita had been hunched in the same corner for too long. She was getting stiff, and she needed to pee. Such domestic considerations never seemed to come up in the movies, and for a moment she was able to forget where she was. Just how much danger she'd put herself in. But it was only a moment. The two guards, and her father, were far too close.

There had been a brief, static-filled conversation over the radio, maybe fifteen minutes prior. Her two companions, unaware of their companionship, had glanced at one other, at the door they were guarding, and back again. Their conversation thereafter was muted, and their guns made their way back into their hands.

Is everything ok?

No response. She didn't dare send another, and tried not to think about why another message was such a risk. She kept her focus on the job at hand, running through what she'd do, the moment she got a chance.

Jorge paused, panting, behind a patch of scrub. He was back at the edge of the courtyard, about six metres up the escarpment and hidden from the guards posted by the door. He scanned the scene carefully, acutely aware of how much less he knew without his drone up above.

There were still two men at the entrance, illuminated only by the glow in the door, though they were no longer lounging or laughing. Their rifles rested uneasily in their grip. Brita had said there were two more guards inside, as well as their friend on the roof. How many more could there be?

Just how much was this story, was Solomon's downfall at his hands, actually worth?

No need to decide yet. He retrieved the pistol, felt the reassuring weight in his hand. Covering the mechanism with his free hand to muffle the sound, he confirmed there was a round in the chamber and unlocked the safety.

Taking a last look at the two guards, assuring himself that they were looking elsewhere, he picked his way across the steep incline, back towards the little alcove with the gnarled and leafless tree. If he was going to attempt anything, he needed to make sure he still had an escape route.

Aside from the two boys, smoking and chatting, very little sound had made it all the way back here. The odd shout, a scrape of metal against the concrete floor, and one muffled scream that had echoed down the long corridor before being abruptly cut off.

Had that been Mariska? She couldn't know, but it had sounded female, and she couldn't think of another woman who had any cause to be here. That line of thought brought anxiety, an emotion she could ill afford, so she blocked it out. Raise the bar, open the door, slide the door closed, and let the bar fall back in place. Find her father, find Mas, get them out.

It was her mantra now. Find them, and get them out.

A gunshot, sharp and clear, like a single beat on the tightest snare drum. It echoed down the hallway, leaving a trance-like stillness in its wake, only broken by a frantic radio call. The corridor devolved into chaos: filled with sounds of people, of action. Yelling, into the radio, at each other.

The two guards took one look at the barred door and darted down the corridor. This was it. She rocked back on her heels, pushed herself forwards. Peered out after them. The corridor was empty. There was movement and noise, shadows and echoes of the commotion outside. Somewhere, deep down, she knew that Jorge was the centre of that commotion, but right now Jorge's fate was out of her control. She could influence only what lay in front of her.

Raise the bar. She sprang upwards, pins and needles jolting her too-long-immobile legs, almost sending her sprawling. She clung to the doorframe for support. She couldn't let Jorge's bravery...*No. Not now.* Raise the bar, open the door. Nothing else mattered.

Brita stumbled out into the corridor, not bothering to look back. She was already beyond the point of no return. She hefted the bar with one hand, opening the door with the other. She slipped through the gap and was left holding the wooden rail with one hand stuck through the door, unable to close it. Panic rose, but she fought it down. She was inside. That was what mattered. She let the bar fall to the floor; it landed with a soft thud. She closed the door behind her and turned around.

She found herself standing on a rusted metal gantry overlooking a massive, dingy concrete cavern. There was a light in the far corner. Beside it, a bed, and a figure huddled beneath a green army blanket.

She rushed down the metal steps, no longer caring about the noise, and splashed through the puddles and rusted scrap. It had to be him.

"Dad? Dad?"

Movement, beneath the blanket. A familiar head of white hair poked out from within. "Brita?"

She skidded to a halt, bringing her hands up to her mouth. "Jesus, Dad. You look…" She'd been with him only yesterday morning. He was gaunt, skin hanging loosely from his cheekbones. Dried blood caked the side of his face. She crumpled on top of him, drawing him into a hug as best she could. "I'm so sorry."

"Sorry, why are you…" He pushed her away, blinking, incredulous. "What the fuck are you doing here?"

She sat back on her haunches, ignoring his outburst. He was tired, hurt, but she'd found him. Her mantra circled back, helping her drive her emotions away, out of sight.

"I'm here to get you out."

"Get me out?" He shook his head, as if he couldn't believe his eyes.

Beaming with pride, Brita pulled her emergency Gateway from her backpack. She ripped open the pouch as she stood and plastered the wire frame on the wall at head height, a plastic tab at each corner holding it in place. The spiked copper loop dangled in a rough square, the power-pack nestled down in the mud. She checked the settings on her phone. It was synced back to Ming-Xia's office. They were good to go.

She turned back to her father, Gateway in her hand, ready to dial, but he hadn't moved. "Dad, what are you doing? We haven't got much time…"

"Haven't got much time? I gave you as much time as you could possibly want, and you've fucking wasted it!"

She stared, unbelieving, for a full second, before she realised how exhausted he must have been. How poorly he'd been treated. It had been too much. She approached, intending to ease a hand beneath his armpit, an uneasy eye on the metal platform and the chaos that was surely raging beyond the door. "I'll tell you everything, I promise, but first I've got to get you home."

"No, uh-uh. I've been manhandled more than enough for one day!" He pushed her away, again, and stood, shakily, on his own two feet. "Of all the hare-brained schemes…"

"I'm sorry, are you *annoyed* that I've come to rescue you?" Brita scoffed. She couldn't believe her ears.

"Of course I bloody am!" He wobbled, arms waving, spittle glistening in the corners of his mouth. "I didn't push you out of that truck so you could play Harriet the fucking spy. You're meant to be saving Gateway!"

"Jesus, what do you think I'm doing?" This was not the reception she'd expected. Through gritted teeth, she reminded herself just how much her father had been through. Twenty minutes in the back of the truck had been bad enough. "Look, we can fight about this later. Let's just get moving, shall we?"

"But Solomon, and Mariska—"

"I know, Dad. We're handling it."

She grabbed his hand and threw his arm over her shoulder. Together they moved across to the Gateway on the wall, one step at a time.

"We? Who's we?"

"Anita. Ming-Xia. The usual crew." She pulled out her phone. "Come on, we're nearly there."

"How did you even know where to come?" he asked, just as she was about to hit dial. She tensed, and she could tell he felt it. "Christ. It was Mariska, wasn't it." She nodded. "You'd better go back for her."

She nodded again. Anything to get him moving.

"Good," he said, as if he would have expected nothing less. "Now dial that thing and get me the fuck out of here, before it's too late."

Brita had never been so relieved to do as she was told. Before their eyes, the damp, rust-stained concrete shimmered and disappeared, replaced with the blindingly bright interior of Ming-Xia's top story office. It was dark out, and the Kuala Lumpur skyline glittered invitingly from across the room.

"Shit! Brita! I thought you were going to warn me!" Ming-Xia sprang from the couch and hurried across to the threshold.

"Sorry, Ming-Xia, no time. Dad's been argumentative." She hefted him, taking the final steps towards the portal. "Here, can you give me—"

Crash!

The metal door slammed into the wall above, shattering the silence, echoes bouncing from floor to ceiling, floor to ceiling. She twisted, swinging her father behind her. Solomon stared back. He had a gun in his right hand, pressed against the chest of a bedraggled, slumped figure, propped up with his left.

Brita gasped. "Mariska!"

Solomon sneered, dropping Mariska to the floor. Her head bounced sickeningly off the railing, and she hit the grating with a wet slap. He brought the gun round until it was pointed directly between her eyes. "Hold it. Right fuckin' there."

Her feet were rooted to the spot. She wouldn't have been able to move, even if she'd wanted to. She felt her father's arm slither from her shoulders, and she turned, trying to catch him, but he wasn't falling. Her father had thrown himself at the Gateway for a second time, her collar tight in his grip, and she was falling backwards, flying towards the portal.

She saw Ming-Xia's mouth, open with shock, Gateway handset in her hand. A single shot rang out, the deafening echo crashing through her eardrums again and again. Metal. Concrete. Shattering glass. Shimmering water.

She clutched her hands to her head and thudded into the wall.

50

"Hands where ah can see 'em. Higher."

Brita pushed herself to her knees, her ears ringing. Solomon shouted down his commands from the gantry, but he might as well have been on another continent for the amount of attention she paid. She'd been out, and she'd willingly put herself back within reach. She'd gambled her company, her legacy, maybe even her life, and she'd lost.

She'd lost, which meant Solomon had won.

Her hand found a cold wetness spreading down her side, and she knew that the pain would soon follow, that if she looked down, she would find her hands covered in blood.

She was wrong.

Brita opened her eyes to find only damp, only mud.

"Brita, get the fuck up. On yer feet."

She stood, unfeeling, unthinking, alone and on the fringe of this giant room, trying to keep two men in her field of view at once. At the cavern's centre her father stood, arms above his head crooked and swaying. She caught his gaze for just a second and looked away. Up above, at the other end of the gun barrel, Solomon raved. Her worst nightmare come to life.

"Stanley! Ah'm gonna need restraints!" He bent to one knee, grabbed Mariska by the jacket, and muttered something Brita had no hope of hearing as he hauled her to her feet. She hadn't thought it possible, but Mariska was in even worse shape than her father. Her clothes were drenched, one side of her blouse stained with red. Her friend stumbled, and then, from the corner of her eye, she saw her father fall to one knee as if from sympathy.

"Keep those fuckin' hands up!"

"He's exhausted, Solomon, leave him be." Her voice wavered. They needed her to be strong, now more than ever, but what could she do? She didn't understand what had happened, what had gone wrong. The Gateway had been there, and then, in the

310

flash of a muzzle, her escape route, her way out, had disappeared. Where had it gone? Where had that solitary bullet landed? And what had shattered? The wall, the floor, her body and her father's, all were totally unmarked.

She looked back at her father, guilt and shame fighting a losing battle. He looked so, so tired. His back bowed as he struggled to stay upright. She shook her head. There was no need for him to fight so hard, not right now. He needed to save his strength.

"We both know he's not going anywhere."

"That's what ah thought last time." Solomon shoved Mariska towards the stairs with disgust and leaned back through the open door. "Stanley!"

Brita bit down on her feelings, lest Mariska's pain, oh so evident with each of her trudging, hesitant steps, overwhelm her. Mariska relied heavily on the railing, barely managing to stay upright. She left elongated red handprints in her wake. Brita clenched her jaw, her fists. Her entire body shook. Mariska had always been so strong, and look what he'd done to her.

But she had no recourse. She could only glare, her feet rooted to the spot, her arms high in the air, and swear she would not give in. She ignored the barrel of the gun, stared straight past it.

He would not beat her.

Solomon returned her glare, for a second, before relaxing over the railing, letting the gun dangle loosely over the side.

"You've gone down swingin', ah'll give you that. You should've stayed put, though. You were never goin' to win."

Mariska reached the bottom of the stairs and steadied herself, looking up at Brita for the first time. Brita gasped, in spite of herself. Mariska's face was puffy and swollen, blotches of purple and deep red already showing. If it wasn't for her familiar clothes, and the cold anger in her eyes, Brita would never have recognised her. But Mariska was still in there, holding on tight. She even managed a smile before slumping to the ground.

Brita took half a step, then stopped as Solomon straightened, shaking his head. The gun was up, once more pointed in anger. She remembered the camera, the microphone. She dropped her hands from her head, instead clasping her fingers across her mouth, pointed upwards, as if she was holding something back rather than trying to hide her defiance. She made sure she faced Mariska front on before turning and arching back, so that Solomon was centre of the frame.

"You got somethin' you want to say?" He waved the gun as if it were a cigar, and not a deadly weapon.

"Whatever you think she did, she didn't deserve this."

"This? This was you, Brita. Your meddlin'. Your interference. Anythin' we did, you brought upon her."

Stanley burst through the door before she could respond, coming to a halt alongside his boss on the gantry. His eyes darted, narrowing only when they settled on her. "Well, well, well. Where did she come from?"

"You got the restraints?" Solomon demanded, keeping the gun steady. Stanley brandished a handful of cable ties. Brita's wrists throbbed at the sight. "Good. Cuff 'em."

"Gladly." He started down the stairs, eyes locked on hers, a grim smile spreading across his lips. "We caught up with your friend, by the way." Brita tensed. She didn't dare glance across at her father, in case she gave something away. "My man Yosip is softening him up as we speak."

"Who?" Solomon interrupted. Stanley paused midstep, glowering.

"Your buddy, the fucking reporter." He spat the last word, still looking straight at her. "And Aleks will live, not that you care."

So Jorge had been captured, and he'd put up a fight. Brita couldn't imagine how he'd managed to injure one of Solomon's thugs, but at least he was alive. That was something. She watched Solomon, hoping to see something in his face. She was not disappointed. At just the mention of Jorge's presence, here, within his grasp, Solomon's face lit up like winter fire.

Stanley started down the steps again. He collected Mariska from her spot on the floor and dragged her roughly through puddles and muddy residue, dumping her on her back in the middle of the room. He kneeled down and started strapping her hands together.

"You still haven't answered my question, Solomon—where did she come from?" His eyes jumped across to her father, to the spiked copper wires tacked out on the far wall.

"Ah've no idea how she got in, but they almost got away, look." He waved the gun at the Gateway loop stuck to the wall. "Ah caught them red handed."

"Lucky." A wicked grin spread across Stanley's skull-like face. He grabbed Mariska by the hair, pulling her head up off the floor. "You hear that, you two-faced bitch? Your boss here, she was gonna leave you behind." Brita merely bit her lip, letting the camera, the microphone, drink it all in. "What's that? Got nothing to say, huh?"

"Why bother? She knows it's not true," Brita said, pretending a confidence she didn't feel. Unconsciously, she stepped forward, wanting to pry Mariska free from his grip.

"Woah, back up there." In a flash Stanley was standing, his pistol whipped from its holster and pointed at her chest. "That's far enough."

She stopped, heart pounding, and slowly raised her hands back up above her head. Mariska lay prone between his legs. It was time to shut her mouth. Showing defiance would do none of them any good.

"Bring those hands out in front," Stanley demanded, sliding his pistol back into its holster and preparing the second set of restraints.

"Take your backpack off first," Solomon called down from the platform. "And pat her down. I don't want any more surprises."

Dutifully, she shrugged her backpack to the floor, dropping it in such a way as to obscure the camera on the left-hand strap, but still allow it a limited field of view. Stanley kicked it aside and grabbed her wrists, slipping the bands over her hands and tightening the straps. It stung, but her bandages offered some protection. At least they were out in front this time.

"Up," he said, tugging her bound hands upwards, over her head. He crouched and started at her hips, patting down each leg. She bit her lip as he groped and prodded, refusing to acknowledge the lascivious glint in his eye. He knew exactly what he was doing. She couldn't let it rattle her.

"What do you want me to do with this?" he pulled the phone from her pocket.

"Toss it up here." Solomon fumbled the catch and the phone clattered onto the platform. Her father, silent for so long, snickered like a little boy. Even now, after everything, he still had the energy to prod and jab at Solomon's weaknesses. To probe for a chink in his armour.

Brita winced as Stanley tossed her pen, her knife, her maps, down onto the floor. The second Gateway, wrapped and stuffed in her thigh pocket drew a skeletal wink, then followed the others down into the mud.

She gritted her teeth as his hands worked her hips, her stomach, under her armpits, his fingers lingering, his hot breath on the back of her neck. Her father seethed, wanting to intervene. She could feel him raging against the impotence that Solomon and his unwavering handgun imposed. She looked resolutely ahead, blocking them all out as best as she could. She couldn't afford to react, at all, in case she gave away the microphone that was wound around the underwire of her bra, recording everything. Or the razor blade secreted beneath the hooks at the back, just waiting for them to be left alone.

Finally, Stanley's fingers fell away, and she allowed a shiver of disgust to travel down her spine. He'd turned to her backpack. He smiled for the camera and crushed it with his foot. She groaned, as if the camera was her last secret, but it didn't stop him from turning her pack inside out, dumping every last piece of equipment onto the floor.

"Don't forget her shoes," Solomon ordered, and Brita bit her lip. It had been too much to hope they'd make the same mistake twice.

"Aha," Solomon gloated, smug pride dripping from his lips. Her expression must have given it away.

Stanley forced her down, seating her on the cold, wet ground. He tugged off her shoes, and she looked away. Towards Mariska. She watched for the rise and fall of her chest. It was shallow, infrequent, but it was there. One foot, then then other, landed in the cold damp. Her socks immediately soaking through.

Heavy footsteps on metal jerked Brita's focus back to Solomon. He was descending to her level, and he held his hand out for her boots.

"Ah reckon a little demonstration is in order, don't you?" He took both shoes from Stanley, barely acknowledging him. "Don't forget the old man, either."

Solomon studied the boots carefully, turning them over, taking in every detail. "They really are quite good. If ah didn't know, ah wouldn't be able to tell." He pressed the eyelets, each of them in turn. Nothing. Yanked the laces, squeezed the heels. Still nothing.

"Done, boss." Stanley stood and trekked over to the wall, ripped the copper Gateway frame down from it, and tossed it onto the pile.

"Excellent. Go make sure that Yosip hasn't killed our favourite reporter."

"What do you want me to do with all this?" He was standing over the pile of Brita's equipment. Her lifeline.

"Ah don't know, Stanley, just get rid of it." Solomon nodded at one of the massive holes in the wall, the entrances to the water tunnels, falling away down the mountainside. "Toss it down one of them for all ah care."

Stanley shrugged, bundled all her gear together, and heaved it into the closest of the dark openings. The clatters and scrapes echoed up the pipe, their only hope of escape sliding down into the gloom. Stanley listened until the echoes died away completely, before turning on his heels and stalking back up the staircase. At the top, just before he reached the door, he locked eyes with her one last time.

"I'll tell Jorge you said hi." He winked and was gone.

Just Solomon, alone with the three of them, and the last functioning Gateway in his hands.

He shook the boots violently, bashing the soles together. "How do you make these damn things work?"

"Careful!" she cautioned. "It could go anywhere."

"Tell me how," he demanded, brandishing the boots at her. If she wasn't tied up, his prisoner in the middle of nowhere, it would be ridiculous.

Brita shivered, the sensation of Stanley's hands pressing, prodding, refused to fade away. Solomon watching on, almost as if he'd been enjoying it. An idea had popped into her head, and she fought to keep it hidden. But could she really, when push came to shove? She looked across at her father, now sitting, his eyes closed, shoulders sagging. At Mariska, head drooped and on her side, each breath a little moan. Brita's lips tightened, her heart hardened, and she decided that she could.

"Go up to the wall, about a metre away is fine, and hold the boots together, soles facing the wall. Right, that's it. Now swing the toes out, keeping the heels together, and tap the toes three times."

Solomon looked back at her, sceptical. "No place like home, hmmm?"

"That's it."

Solomon did as instructed. On the third tap, the coiled copper exploded with a puff of smoke and splattered onto the wall in front of him. The force, or maybe his shock at its suddenness, pushed him back. The instant the coil hit the wall, the wall disappeared, the black night and pale white boulders of her and Jorge's outcropping shimmering into view.

"Incredible." Solomon dropped the shoes to the ground and stepped forward. "It really is a shame. You were right, that night on Jorge's show. Apple and Samsung wouldn't have known what hit 'em."

Brita's heart pounded. She watched, waited, counted down the seconds. He examined the copper frame, traced it with his fingers. *Come on, step through. Let your curiosity get the better of you.*

Movement caught the corner of her eye, but she refused to let her focus lapse.

"That's where Jorge and I staged our incursion. Just up the mountain, out of sight." A grunt, from her father's direction. Just a few seconds more. "Go on, take a look."

"Brita," her father hissed. He'd levered himself off the floor, eyes wide with concern. *Don't. Don't do this,* he mouthed. *We'll beat him another way.*

Behind him, Solomon eased his upper body through the Gateway and turned to look up at the stars. This time there was no trigger to pull, no Ukrainian mobster eyeing her like a predator. All she had to do was stay silent, and the battery would run dry. The Gateway would die, and so would Solomon.

She glanced at Mariska's pummelled, bruised face, remembered her anger, her bloody hands on the railing, just barely holding on. Her father's gaunt exhaustion. Imagined Jorge, strung up against a wall with a gleeful Stanley just barely keeping him alive.

Toli, advancing on her, taunting her. *You won't pull trigger. Not on me, unarmed man.* Solomon leering down at her, Stanley's hands between her thighs—

"Solomon, get back!" her father shouted.

Solomon turned, hesitated, snapped his head back just in time.

The portal disappeared, and it was just a wall again, as if it had never been broken.

51

For a fraught moment, no one moved. Solomon looked down at his hands, at the shoe that the Gateway had sliced clean in half. No smoke, no singes. When he lifted his gaze, met Brita eye to eye, she saw that he knew. That she could so easily have killed him, and if not for her father's intervention, she would have.

"Well, shit. Ah didn't think y'had it in you."

"Until I saw her," Brita snarled, flicking her elbow out towards Mariska, "I didn't either. But you would have deserved it. You would have brought it on yourself—"

Brita almost choked on her words as they tumbled from her lips. Because they weren't her words. They were Solomon's.

Her blinding anger turned to ash on her tongue.

"Y'know what? Ah'd think so, if ah were in your shoes." Implausibly, Solomon chuckled, perhaps mistaking her disgust at herself for futile, choking rage. He tossed her half shoe up in the air. "Ah tell you what, though, Volodymyr is goin' to like this way too much."

Brita gritted her teeth, telling herself she would never let her emotions take control ever again. He was acting as if this was normal. As if she hadn't, very nearly, committed murder. His murder. And what had she expected? That Solomon's brush with death might give him pause? Trigger a realisation that Gateway was more powerful than any of them realised? That trading it to the Ukrainian mob for his freedom would be a terrible, terrible mistake?

Of course it hadn't. Solomon was all in. Had been from the moment Stanley had picked her up from Kolkata airport and shoved a gun in her face. Reason, morality, the common good. None of these things mattered to a man like him. He responded to only one driver: self-interest. She was entirely within his power, and she had only one asset left to offer.

Up above, a mercenary appeared at the cavern door, the light from the corridor casting him in shadow. Tattoos covered his exposed forearms, his neck, even encroaching onto his cheeks and his temples. He gripped his rifle, and a wordless exchange passed between boss and underling. Solomon shoved his pistol down into his waistband and waved the mercenary away.

Solomon was back in control, and he wanted her to know it.

He ripped the Gateway cabling from the wall, coiled it tightly about the one and half boots he had at hand, and tossed it down one of the tunnels. The bounces echoed, echoed, and fell away. Brita saw her father sag, and she knew what he was thinking. That perhaps he should have kept his mouth shut. That if he had, maybe Solomon wouldn't have just tossed their last hope of escape beyond their reach.

She couldn't let herself think that way. Not yet, not while she was still standing. Not while Mariska was lying there bleeding, and Jorge was in their hands. Not while there was a chance she could extract Gateway from his clutches, free it from his corrupting influence.

She would not let Solomon win.

"Brita, ah offered your father a deal. Ah'll offer the same deal to you. Ah need twenty percent. Ah don't give a shit where it comes from: you, yer father, Anita, Ming-Xia. Heck, split it four ways for all ah care. Ah'll pay twice what you asked for back in April, three times what they're actually worth."

"Even after..." Brita asked, nodding towards the empty wall.

Solomon shrugged. "Why not? We'll all make more money if ah work with you, rather than against you—"

"Never," her father said, butting in, as if Solomon cared what he had to say. "Not in a million years."

"Dad, just shut it, for fuck's sake. Haven't you said enough?" Her gut told her that division was what Solomon wanted, so she glared across at him. Did whatever she could to make Solomon think her father was the sole focus of her anger. That her anger was impotent. She turned back to her captor, looked up at him. Feigned resignation. "What if I refuse?"

Solomon merely glanced down at Mariska, prone at his feet.

"Do your worst, you son of a bitch," her father spat, his anger driving his exhausted body to the edge of collapse. "We're not signing a goddamn thing!"

Solomon rolled his eyes, and a glimmer of hope smouldered in Brita's chest. She risked a glance at the mercenary. Bored, looking back through the door, down the corridor. If she could string Solomon along, buy them a tiny sliver of time...

"Don't think of what ah'll do to you if you resist. Think of how much you gain by playin' along." He followed her gaze, up to the gantry. To the tattooed mercenary. "Tell you what, ah'll even throw in a sweetener. Sign right now, and Volodymyr will forget your names for good."

Brita squirmed and nodded towards Mariska. "Hers too?"

Solomon nodded.

"Brita—" her father exclaimed, but she silenced him with a look, a shake of her head. She knew what she was doing. Up on the gantry, the guard turned his back on them and stepped away, leaving them alone. Brita pushed the ember down, smothered it, lest the hope it kindled reach the surface where Solomon might see it.

"And Jorge?"

Solomon's nostrils flared, and Brita felt a familiar flutter in her chest. The thrill of putting her opponent, across the negotiating table, under pressure. He wanted Jorge. Wanted him bad.

"He knows too much."

"So do I. So does she."

Solomon vacillated.

Brita pushed. "Do you want Gateway or not?"

She could see him thinking, trying to read her. Could he hold out? Could he break her down, keep Jorge out of the deal? He knew that he could, but at what cost? She'd only been missing for thirty-six hours. She was uninjured, but if this were to drag on, if she reappeared a week from now, battered and bruised, fingernails and teeth missing, questions would be asked. Questions he couldn't answer. He knew this; he knew she knew it. She glanced across at the wall, as the spot where his body would be lying, if it had been left up to her.

"Is that a yes or a no?" she asked.

His eyes narrowed, as if he smelled a rat. She was counting on whatever was driving him—fear, greed, lust for power, she didn't even care—to override his natural suspicions, and the longer he hesitated…

"Jesus Christ, yer like a dog with a fuckin' bone. All right, you win. You sign and all four of you walk away. You happy?"

Brita let herself fall back on her haunches. She let exhaustion creep into her voice, as if all she wanted was to go home. "Just get me the fucking paperwork."

"Good. About time." He stalked up the stairs, his footsteps ringing out across the heavy silence left by his words. His actions. Her apparent capitulation. He paused at the door, looking back one final time. "Now don't you go disappearin' on me again."

He winked, and then the door slammed shut. The bar thunked into place, and they were alone.

Brita didn't waste a second. She shuffled across to Mariska on her hands and knees.

"Brita, what the fuck was that? You can't—"

"She needs water, Dad. Water and a blanket."

"Brita—"

"God, Dad, I'm not signing anything. I just needed to get him out of here, give the arsehole something to think about that wasn't us," Brita hissed, cradling Mariska's battered face in her cable-tied hands. "Now will you get her some water, please?"

Mariska moaned, and the anger and confusion that had contorted her father's face melted away. He nodded and let himself be ordered around.

Brita brushed the hair from Mariska's eyes. She was shivering uncontrollably.

She glanced back at a rattling scrape and saw her father on his knees, dragging over his camp bed, laden with blankets, water, and food.

"How is she?"

"Not good." She checked her friend's body for damage, as best she could with her hands bound, one side at a time, feeling for wounds, for broken bones. Mariska was drenched, whether from sweat or water she couldn't tell. But, it could have been worse. Mariska whimpered with pain as Brita pressed against her ribcage. Brita pulled back. "We'll get you out of here. I promise."

Mariska coughed, liquid gurgling in her throat. Red dribbled from the corner of her mouth. Brita pulled her knee forward so she could roll Mariska onto her side. She winced in sympathy at the pain she knew she was inflicting. "I know it hurts, I know, but it's for your own good."

"God, look at her." Her father was close enough to get a glimpse at her face. His anger returned, bright red, his fists balled up, his knuckles white, muscles bulging around the edges of the cable ties that bound his wrists together. That first night, the three of them together, when he'd shown Mariska the Gateway and she'd told him how dangerous it could be, he'd been mad. The day, eleven years ago, when she'd told him she was taking over as CEO, that he was out, he'd been furious.

But she'd never seen him anything close to this.

"I can't believe Solomon...and I...I'm the one who..." He stopped, pressing his fists against his eyes. "Sorry, that's not helping anyone." He pulled the bed up alongside Mariska's prone body. "How do you want to do this?"

Brita sat back, taking in both the camp bed and her friend, barely conscious on the muddy floor. Her father, fighting to regain his composure, to hold his guilt in check, just enough that he could function. She took in herself. How was it that she was so calm, after everything that had happened? After everything that had been done to her, to her friends? How was it that even with her hands bound, again, she could—

She started, stared down at her wrists. "We can't do anything like this." She turned her back to her father and bent over, doing her best to hoick up the back of her shirt. "Dad, can you..."

"Brita, what are you doing?"

"There's a razor blade under my bra strap. Under the clips, in a plastic sheath."

"Ah." She didn't need to see his cheeks to know they'd flushed crimson. His calloused fingers fumbled gently with the elastic strap. Unexpectedly, her father's kind clumsiness started washing the crawling remnants of Stanley's violations away. Tears prickled, unbidden, in the corners of her eyes, and a sob threatened to interrupt her breathing. She fought it down, but her father must have sensed it all the same. His hands fell still on her exposed back.

"Are you all right?"

"I'm fine, I'm fine," Brita said, wiping her tears with an unaccountable smile, glad to know there were emotions tucked away in there, after all. "Have you got it?"

"Almost." Her bra strap flicked, and the razor blade sprang free. "There we go."

"Great, now hurry up and cut me loose." She shrugged her shirt down, turned around, and held out her bindings. Her father slipped the razor from its sheath and held it carefully between thumb and forefinger. He took her hand in his for stability and... hesitated.

"What?" She looked up to see tears streaming down his cheeks. "Dad, what's wrong?"

"I am." He sniffed. "You've put your life on the line to come and get me out of here, even after everything I've done, and what do I do? Fucking yell at you. Instead of thanking you, I spend so long arguing that..." He choked up, wiped his nose on his sleeve. "And even then you don't lose your cool. Even with that creep's hands all over you, you're still thinking about how you can turn the situation to our advantage." He pulled his hands away and showed her the razor blade, the evidence of her levelheadedness, his sniffles turning into a soggy chuckle. "And then you had Solomon right where you wanted him and I..."

A bright flush rose on Brita's cheeks. "Dad, don't you ever apologise for that. I don't know what I was thinking."

"I do. I've seen you like this before."

She glanced down at her hands, bound, fists clenched in front of her. The fists of a woman angry enough to kill if given the chance. "I don't think you have."

"No, I mean focused. Task oriented. Ruthless. Doing what needed to be done."

"When?"

"When you kicked me out. Took over. Saved Stora."

Brita had never heard her father talk like this. She didn't know where to look.

"I hated you for it, and my pride wouldn't let me acknowledge it, but deep down I knew. You were exactly what Stora needed. You still are."

In a rush, her father's words took her back to those frantic, chaotic days. Emergency meetings, panicked phone calls, press conferences, strategies, compromises. Jobs and friends cut loose, because it had to be done. And she recognised that same pattern of thought: head down, the big picture was too big. If she'd looked at it, let it overwhelm her, she'd known she was done for, and Stora with it. So she'd focused down on what had to be done right now, what had to happen next, and nothing else—whether that had been assuring Lloyd that his money was safe with her, that they could ride the wave together and come out the other side, or having security escort her father from the company he had built, never to return.

Whether it was sending Jorge off to distract Solomon's mercenaries so she could slip inside the compound undetected, or letting Stanley get his kicks without giving anything away. All of that she'd managed on her own, but she'd needed her father by her side to pull her back from the brink. From crossing the uncrossable line.

Brita coughed, wiped her jaw. She met her father's gaze. "We found your storage unit."

"You did? And you saw…" A wave radiated from him, which may have started as embarrassment but turned into relief, a burden lifted from his shoulders. He glanced across a the gaping mouths of the water tunnels, at the Gateways that had disappeared into their depths. "Of course you did. I'm…I'm glad."

And for a handful of heartbeats, neither of them moved. Even amidst the muck and Solomon's crazed violence, there was space for a moment of peace—

"Could you…huggh…could you untie. My fucking hands. Please?"

Brita jumped. Behind her, Mariska had opened her eyes. "Jesus, yes, of course. We didn't…" She shoved her hands back towards her father. "Dad, can you…"

He took her hands with a purposeful nod and readjusted his grip on the razor blade. With just two carefully placed slices she was free. Shaking out her wrists, she took the razor from her father and returned the favour. She turned to Mariska.

"Go on. Take your time." Mariska tried to smile but could only grimace. "It's not like I'm in that much pain."

Brita took Mariska's hands, gently. She didn't know if there were breaks or torn fingernails. Just that they were bloody. "That's a bold line to take, for a woman who abandoned us to the back of a truck."

Mariska groaned as Brita freed her wrists. Her shoulders collapsed without the bindings holding her arms in place. She sank down onto one cheek. "I guess. That's fair." She was only able to get two or three words out between heavy breaths. "I got. You here. Didn't I?"

"Yeah. You did," Brita said. She set the razor to one side, turned to her father. "Come on, let's get her up out of the mud."

"No. I can…" Mariska wheezed, dissolved into a hacking cough, her eyes squeezed shut against the pain. "I can do it."

Brita could only hover as Mariska, grunting with determination, hauled herself out of the mud and onto the camp bed. Only once she'd settled onto the canvas did she allow herself to whimper, to acknowledge her pain.

Hugo wrapped her in both blankets, uncapped a bottle of water, and held it to her lips. Mariska snaked a trembling hand up from under the covers—unwilling to let herself be cared for. Her father let her take the bottle from him, and she took the smallest of sips. Then, she levered her head over to the edge of the camp bed and spat a bloody mouthful onto the floor.

"Thank you." It was barely a whisper. Mariska took another sip and, holding the bottle out for her father to take, sank back down. Her eyes closed, and as far as Brita could tell, she was already asleep.

How much had pulling herself up onto the camp bed cost her? How much had Solomon, Stanley, and their thugs taken from her? Brita's bottom lip began to wobble, and she clamped her hand over it, determined to hold it in. If Mariska would not be bowed, then neither would she. Her father took her in his arms and led her away to a pile of abandoned construction refuse, where they could sit.

"She's a tough kid. She'll be okay."

Brita leaned onto his shoulder. She hoped he was right.

"Now, how about you fill an old man in on everything he's missed. Starting with who the heck is Volodymyr?"

— · —

Stanley strode eagerly along the main corridor, spurred on by the shouts, grunts, and wet thuds emanating from the interrogation room.

"Yosip, buddy. Ease up, hey? Leave some for the rest of us," he said, as he skipped through the door. The powerful Ukrainian pulled back, but not before landing a final blow to Jorge's ribs.

The reporter was shirtless, arms bound behind him to the aluminium chair. Blood dripped from his nose, mingling with the saliva that oozed from his puffy lips. One eye was swollen shut, and he hunched over, coughing. At the sound of his voice, though, Jorge raised his head, his good eye burning white hot. He spat a globule of claret-stained spit in Stanley's direction and curled his lip.

"You're going to have to hit me harder than that."

Good. Stan grinned. He hadn't broken him yet.

This was going to be fun.

"How are prisoners?" Yosip wiped Jorge's blood and sweat from his knuckles with a mangy rag.

"We've gained one, actually." Yosip raised an eyebrow. *Jorge looks as if he would have, if he could.* "We caught the old man with his daughter, just as they were about to escape."

Yosip reached for his radio, already halfway to the door. Stanley rolled his eyes "Don't bother. It's under control." Yosip kept his hand, and his radio, up to his face as his gaze flitted across to the untidy coil of black wires, shoved into the far corner.

322

"No one else lurking? We are sure?" Stanley shook his head. Brita had fired her shot, and fucking missed. Yosip flexed his neck muscles, trying and failing to hide his discomfort. "I do not like this magic wires."

So the mighty Ukrainian was superstitious, and spooked. Stanley snickered and turned his gaze back to Jorge in order to hide it. "What did our friend have on him when you caught him?" He asked Yosip, nodding to the torn, camel coloured shirt crumpled in the corner, beside the tangled Gateway.

"Another magic wires, like we find on the tree. Knife, phone. Camera." He lifted a go-pro from the pile, "and gun of course." The battered pistol seemed tiny in his hands, but the weapon had a calming effect on it's holder.

Stanley picked up the camera, turning it over in his hands. He wandered back to Jorge, relishing his hard, impotent glare. "You two, you've got style. Sneaking into our hideout, camera's rolling. She very nearly got away, you know." He dropped the camera to the floor and crushed it underfoot, just as he had the girl's. "I wonder if she would have come back?"

"Solomon shouldn't have invited you up. And I should never have let you leave." He swiped at Jorge's face with the back of his hand, catching him across the cheekbones. He held his hand rigid despite the pain. Jorge's head snapped back, but his fiery glare was undiminished. "You won't get a third chance."

"I want to neutralise him in Mayfair." Yosip interjected.

"That would have been better. But he's here now." He crouched down to Jorge's eye level, so close their foreheads almost touched. Jorge seethed, but what could he do? Stanley studied the sinews in Jorge's neck, straining and glistening with beads of sweat. "So let's enjoy it, while we've got the chance."

"Yosip. Yer guys, they got any paper?" Solomon's rapid, excited drawl pulled Stanley's head around. His boss was leaning through the doorway, a manic glean in his eye.

"Yes. In truck."

Solomon nodded, patted himself down. "And a pen?"

"I've got one, boss." Stanley said, fishing one out of his jacket pocket. "Whaddya need it for?"

"Brita's cracked. She took one look at what ah did to her friend and collapsed like a shanty town in tornado season." *What you did to her?* Stanley rolled his eyes. As if his boss ever got his fuckin' hands dirty. "Ah need to draft up a contract. Then, Yosip mah friend, you can call Volodymyr, and tell him Gateway is all his. And he can leave me the fuck alone."

Stanley grimaced. Even though the reporter was a dead man walking, they shouldn't be doing this in front of him. But it was too late for that. "Can't you just write something up in *Omni*? Get her to sign it virtual-like?"

"Ah want to hand it to her. Watch her sign it with mah own eyes. Ah want him to watch," Solomon pointed behind Stanley, to Jorge, still strapped to his chair and trying to look like he wasn't listening. "And Hugo. The bitch too. Ah want to be able to hold that piece of paper in mah own two hands." He clenched his fist, as if it was already tight around Brita's throat. He leered over at Yosip. "In yer truck?"

"*Tak*. Under front seat."

"Thankin' you." His boss just could not stop grinning. "Stan, ah'll need you to give it a once over, before, y'know..."

"Sure boss. Let me know when you're ready."

"Will do." And with that, the doorway was empty. They turned back to Jorge.

"You didn't hear a word of that, now, did you?" Stanley sneered.

The reporter nodded, defiant. It was clear that every movement he made caused him pain. He couldn't speak, but he mouthed his answer all the same. *Every. Fucking. Word.*

"I do not understand your Solomon." Yosip said, stepping up, towering over him. "Nosy reporter, snooping around Volodymyr? He dies."

Whack. Yosip grunted with effort, landing a meaty blow to Jorge's ribs. Stanley stayed up close, watching as Jorge sucked in a ragged breath through gritted teeth. The reporter refused to cry out. For now.

"That is an excellent policy, Yosip. Solomon thinks he's clever though. Always has. It's how we got tangled up with your boss in the first place. No offence." Stanley cocked his head, enjoying the grimace that threatened to overtake Jorge's features, that the reporter just kept in check. "And how this fucker got tangled up with us too."

"*Tak?*"

Whack.

Something cracked. Jorge grunted and his eyes bulged. He cut off a moan with bared teeth, eyes squeezed tight. Better. They were getting somewhere.

"Yessiree. Invited him right up into his apartment in London, offered him an olive branch. Not 10 minutes after selling this Gateway shit to your boss." He pulled back. He was probably speaking out of turn, but right now he didn't care. "And you'll never guess what our snivelling friend did next."

"Nemaye."

Whack.

"He turned on his heels and ran, straight to that blond bitch, telling tales."

"That was not smart decision."

Whack.

Jorge hunched at the impact of Yosip's latest blow, breathing fast, short, suppressing a scream. His good eye, however, remained trained on Stanley, unblinking.

"No, no it really wasn't, on either part. Alas—here we are. We make the best with what we have."

Yosip shaped to strike once more, waiting to see Jorge flinch away. He didn't. Gotta respect that. The reporter was tough.

"You want ask questions yet? More softening required, I think."

Whack.

Yosip landed another the blow. Tears streamed down Jorge's cheeks, but still he didn't make a sound.

"I don't have any questions." Stanley pulled up a chair and rocked back, putting his hands on his head. "What is there to ask? You heard the boss. They've already lost. I'm just here to enjoy the show."

—— · ——

Brita eyed the empty platform, the closed door. The guard she knew was posted just the other side. She and her father had tallied their resources—four bottles of water, four blankets (standard issue), half a packet of rations, two camp beds and the canvas bags they came in. A razor blade. The clothes on their backs, and their wits.

It wasn't much.

She stepped out from her damp little corner. Mariska was resting fitfully a few metres away—twitching and moaning in her cot. It was hard to watch, harder still to suppress the thought that Mariska had put herself in this position and gotten herself burned. She hated herself for even thinking it, but still, she did. She'd come through in the end. That was what mattered. She hovered over her, watching, and poured a much needed mouthful of water through her friend's lips.

"Let her rest, Brita. It's the best thing we can do right now." Her father whispered.

"I thought you were asleep."

"As if I could sleep with you pacing about."

"I don't know how you can sit still. Aren't you angry?"

"I'm furious, believe me. But I've also spent the better part of the last 36 hours sliding about in the back of a truck."

"Fair." She said, sheepish. With Mariska so badly hurt, it was easy to forget just how much her father had been through. And he was an old man now. Had been for a long time. She shook her head, pushing away yet another set of unwelcome thoughts, about the part he'd played in bringing them all here. It didn't matter, none of it did. She just had to get them home. Stop Solomon, any way she could.

"There's got to be something..." She muttered to herself, peering into the dark corners on the other side of the cavern, "Maybe there's something in those piles of junk."

She struck out across the muddy floor, careful where she placed her bare feet. Concrete & iron construction refuse was piled untidily along the far wall of the cavern. Steel reinforcement stabbed upwards from half-finished columns. Plate metal leaned against the wall, while torn plastic sheeting exposed sodden plasterboard with swollen joinery stacked on top.

She climbed gingerly up onto a smooth slab, steadying herself by gripping the edge of a steel plate. She surveyed the scraps and leftovers, disappointed. There was nothing of use here—just a pile of internal furnishings that were never installed.

She turned to climb back down, mind churning on their limited options, when a shape caught her eye; a stack of roundels, covered in black plastic shrink wrap, hidden deep behind the stacked plate metal lean-to. She stopped and stepped across the gap, her feet sinking unpleasantly into the mushy stack of rotting plaster. On hands and knees, she dragged the top roundel out into the open.

"Did you find something?" Her father called out. She waved her hand, exhorting him to silence as his voice echoed around the chamber. Fishing the razor from her pocket, she sliced the plastic free and dropped onto her haunches. Electrical cables. Three roundels. Her gaze flitted over to the gaping holes in the far wall, leading down into the depths. There had to be, what, 300 metres? That could be enough.

She dragged the other two roundels out and set them rolling across the cavern. She followed along behind, hauling the third roll onto her shoulder. Her father stood, watching with grave interest. One of the roundels came to a stop at his feet, flopping onto its side with a soft splash.

"Is there enough?" They both eyed the dark chasms, just metres from where they stood, ominous in their almost total darkness. They both knew what Solomon had disposed of down there, thinking it unreachable.

"I don't know. My schematics are down there with everything else. The tunnels looked pretty long from up on the mountainside. And very steep."

Her father crouched down, fiddling with the frame of his camp bed. He held out the two long aluminium poles. "You can use these as an anchor. I'll keep watch."

"Oh, so I'm going down, am I?" She arched an eyebrow, but he didn't rise to her bait.

"As my only daughter, and the only person in this godforsaken concrete mausoleum capable of standing upright for more than two minutes—I have complete faith." He grinned. "Here, roll me one. I'll start tying them off."

He made quick work of the knots—a relic of his navy days. She split the plastic on the other two rolls. Within minutes they were ready. She took the aluminium anchor and laid it on the ground, along the bottom of the opening. The cable, tied securely in the middle of the pole, lined up where the bottom edge of the hole met the cavern floor. She gave it a tug, and the anchor held firm. Only twenty centimetres or so were unsupported. The length of the anchor pole fit snugly in the concrete cornice.

Her father gathered the spools of loose cable in his arms and stepped up to the threshold. He was about to toss them over and down the hole. "You ready?"

A hoarse croak from behind stopped him, just in time. They turned from the tunnel opening to see Mariska struggling to right herself. Brita scurried over, "Woah hey, don't hurt yourself..."

"That's the wrong..."—a deep breath, a desperate sip of water from a trembling hand—"hole."

Brita twisted on her heels, back to the opening with the anchor stretched across its base. "Are you sure?"

"Boots only. Useless." Mariska grimaced, levering herself into a sitting position, and Brita's chest ached in sympathy. She just would not quit. Mariska pointed at the opening on the left. "Backpack. That one."

Brita thought back, straining to remember. She'd been standing right there, her father kneeling a yard or two further along. Mariska had been huddled on the floor right here, where they'd set up her bed. She stood in the same position, closed her eyes, imagining Stanley rummaging through her backpack, running his hands up and down her thighs—She shivered, urging her eyes back open.

"She's right." She said, to both of them, and to no-one.

"I know." Mariska coughed, hacking up blood. "Food?"

"Yeah, of course. Dad, do you mind..." Brita asked, and her father nodded, looking more than a little relieved. Much easier to fetch a ration bar than to haul hundreds of metres of cable back up the wrong tunnel. She swapped the anchor over to the correct tunnel entrance and tossed the bundled cable back down it only after receiving a thumbs up from Mariska.

If there was any sound of it hitting the bottom, she didn't hear it.

"How are you feeling?" She asked, back at Mariska's side. Mariska gave her a look, bloodshot eyes rolled back.

"Shithouse."

Brita felt her face crease with concern. "I can't believe he did this to you..."

"Don't." Mariska raised her croaking voice. "My choices. Not yours."

"Whatever you did, you don't deserve this."

"Just get. Gateway. Away from him. And Yosip." Breathing was becoming harder for her, exhaustion written in the strain on her face. Brita held her hand, supporting her as she lay down once more. She tucked her friend back under her blanket.

"I promise." Brita said, more to herself, than to Mariska, who as far as she could tell had already fallen back asleep. She stood, and conferred with her father. "She'll never make it down the hole in that condition. And if that's any indication of what they're doing to Jorge, neither will he. I'll have to bring the Gateway components back up."

"Do you think you'll be able to?"

She didn't know if she'd even make it down, if her makeshift rope was even long enough. If there was even anything to find, wherever the bottom was. "I'm going to have to, aren't I?" She shrugged. There was no other option.

She grabbed a couple of ration bars for herself. The wrapper was plain, black with grey Cyrillic lettering. They could have been a week old or a decade. She wolfed one down anyway, washing it back with half a bottle of water, and slipped the other bar into a pocket. Her father stood around, looking useless.

"I'll be fine, dad. Don't worry."

"I just want you to know that I'm..."

"Dad, come on. You don't need to apologise."

"Apologise? I was just going to say that I believe in you." He pulled her into a bear hug, lifting her off the ground. As he put her back down, her toes squelching in the mud, she wondered where he'd found the strength. He looked down at her feet, and promptly sat, untying his shoelaces. "You'll need these more than me."

She accepted them and, despite their uncomfortable warmth, slid her smaller feet into the too-big boots.

"They're a bit loose. But better than going barefoot." She tightened the straps and stood, ready. "Actually, can I grab those socks as well?"

She clomped over to the tunnel opening, their last hope of escape, and stood at the threshold. It ran level for a metre or two before dropping down at a forty-five-degree angle, at least. She peered down. The white cable disappeared into the darkness below.

She slipped her father's sweaty socks onto her hands. In lieu of gloves, they'd have to do. Especially if she was ever going to make it back up again. She picked up the white plastic sheathed cable and swung it over her head. Her father stood with his bare feet holding the anchor in place. Once she'd descended a few metres, her body weight would take over. For now, though, he stood watch.

She set the cable around her waist, settling it into the belaying position with her improvised gloves. The sensation of the rope tight around her waist, gave her flashbacks to the high ropes courses she'd endured at high school camp. A very long time ago. She leaned back, testing her grip. Hopefully it hadn't been too long.

"Good luck," Mariska whispered from her bed.

"I'll need it." She muttered. She was not confident, but it didn't matter. It was the next task on the list, so it had to be done.

"You'll do fine." Her father said.

She looked away, tested the rope one more time. "See you on the other side."

Brita stepped over the edge and descended into the dark.

52

SOLOMON RUMMAGED AROUND BENEATH the front seat of Yosip's truck. He found a fire extinguisher, a duffel bag filled with bullets, leather holsters, sheathed knives, balaclavas. In his head, he was already drafting the contract: *I, Brita Gundersson, being of sound mind and of my own free will...* He unearthed a stockpile of discarded ration bar wrappers, two more pens, and a greasy rag.

But no paper.

"Jesus fuckin' Christ." He slammed the door as hard as he could.

Across the courtyard, one of the sentries stepped forwards at the noise, squinting, his assault rifle at the ready. God, they were jumpy. You'd think they'd never been in a firefight before. And the way Yosip avoided looking at the Gateway coils, like they were cursed. He snorted. Yosip had better get used to them, and fast. Volodymyr was not a patient man.

Gravel crunched beneath his boots as Solomon stalked the courtyard and realised that the guard, standing to attention, was the kid that had gotten shot. The way Yosip had carried on... Yeah, the kid had a bandage on his calf, and favoured his other leg, but still. He was standing.

"Hey! Kid!" Solomon was close enough now that he could see their eyes, their nerves. Jesus, all because of Jorge. "You got any paper? Paper?"

The kid and his buddy, sitting but no less tense, stared back at him, blank expressions on their simple, Slavic faces. Suddenly, he remembered Brita's boot, sliced clean in half. His face in that moment had probably looked just like theirs did right now, his head less than a second away from having been separated from his neck.

You just had to look at these kids to know. They'd never be able to deal with Gateway portals. Not the way Volodymyr would use them. They were superstitious peasants, born of a radioactive wasteland and paid in vodka.

He stopped at the edge of the light spilling from the open entranceway and wondered if these kids could even read or write. "Paper?" He mimed writing, flipping sheets from a notepad. Anything. "You know, paper?"

"Vin khoche papir?"

"Ya tak dumayu," the younger one said, the one still sitting, with his gun laid across his knees. He cocked his head to one side, furrowed his brow, as if thinking very hard. "You want papir?"

"Tak. Yes." Solomon took another step forward. The twitchy one mirrored him, as if he needed to protect his young comrade. Through gritted teeth, Solomon said, "Please."

The taller one nodded, and the younger one bent over, careful to keep one hand on his gun at all times. He pulled a battered notepad from beneath his chair. Half of what looked like a letter was scrawled on the front page in illegible, blocky letters. Ukrainian? Whatever, Solomon didn't care. He just wanted the paper. The mercenary glanced down, peeled the front page free, and offered the notepad over.

Solomon snatched the pad from the boy's hand. His injured comrade twitched, and despite himself, Solomon flinched.

"You boys keep an eye out," he said, as if he still had the upper hand. All he got in return were blank stares. He turned on his heels and stalked back inside.

He made for his office, the room with the window. Not long now, and Gateway would be his. Well, his to hand over to Volodymyr. Forcing those peasants to use it would be Yosip's problem. Not his.

Solomon, finally, would be free of the Ukrainian mafia for good.

— · —

Step by step, the light receded. The soft grey glow of the tunnel opening shrank to almost nothing, the round walls enveloping Brita, cutting her off. Before long, all she could see was the white cable as she let it play through her grip. But she was not alone.

Every scuff of boot against concrete, every jerk of the cord that whipped it against the tunnel wall, sent reverberations up and down, up and down. The noise was constant, feeding on itself. It was comforting, in its own way, drowning out her doubts, allowing her to focus on one step at a time.

"You doing okay down there?"

She winced as her father's voice pounded down, echoing and distorting, travelling past her and continuing down into the depths. "I'm good, Dad," she called back.

"See anything?"

"Not yet." Their conversation started to overlap, their words bouncing back and forth, intermingling.

"Yeah, well, hang in there." His chuckle followed his words, multiplying and bombarding her, morphing into something menacing. She tightened her grip. The tunnel was damp and followed the slope of the mountainside. She was leaning back at an uncomfortable angle, parallel to the damp, curved floor, all her weight dangling on a cable that was who knew how old. She shivered at the thought.

"As long as your knots hold on, I will too," she said, letting loose her own chuckle, and climbed farther down as her laughter chased away the last sinister echoes of what had come before.

She'd been tracking along at a steady pace. The first joint in the cable should be coming up soon. Sweat beaded on her brow, but she couldn't wipe it away. It brought back uncomfortable memories, from the last time she was stuck in a dark, cramped space, noise so loud she couldn't hear herself think, unable to get her hands to her face. A drop broke from her hairline, tickling as it trickled down between her brows and along the ridge of her nose.

The drop kept crawling, down, down, until it dangled from the tip her nostril. Until it was all she could think about. She jerked her right shoulder across, dipping her head so she could wipe the drop away on her shoulder—

"Aaah!"

Her foot slipped, and the cord whipped through her hands, tracing a hot line of friction across her back. She scrabbled for grip. Too late.

She was upside down. Sliding on her back.

Squeeze, Brita! She clamped down, twisting the cord around her waist, and it shunted her sideways. She was barely hanging on when the one hundred metre knot slammed through her leading hand and jerked it free of the cord.

She careened upwards, rolling over her shoulder as the knot tore along her back. That knot. It had almost brought her undone, but it was also her last chance of regaining control. She clamped her right hand as it snaked past, and it damn near yanked her arm out of its socket. The change in momentum crunched her knees against the hard concrete. Her yelp of pain echoed and warped.

But she was no longer falling.

She lay still. Panting.

"Brita!"

"I'm...I'm okay!" she yelled. She scrambled with her left hand for the cord and wrapped it tightly around her wrist. She flexed her fingers. They hurt, but they still worked.

That was too close.

"What happened?" Her father's voice was awash with concern, clear even through the echoes.

"I slipped a little, that's all." No need to worry them. She was still panting against the cool concrete curve. "I'm at the first joint in the cable. Your knots are holding up okay." She forced herself to smile, using the knot to lever herself to her knees, making double sure of her footing before standing.

"You sure you're okay?"

"Yeah, I'm sure." What else could she say? She would continue either way. She imagined him on hands and knees, peering down after her. Wanting desperately to drag her back up so he could spare her, do it himself. "It sounded worse than it was, that's all."

She adjusted her grip, ducked under the cable, settled it against her back once more so she could lean, let it take her weight. She took stock—everything seemed to be working still. Just a few more scrapes and bruises to add to the list. She stretched out each leg, wincing as she bent her right knee. It had taken the brunt of the landing.

"I'm going to keep moving." She almost had her breathing under control, but a nagging doubt crept about in the back of her mind. The fall had been so fast. The climb back up would be much more difficult. Letting go of the knot, she took three steps down, until it was just visible at the edge of the gloom.

She stopped and reached back up along the cord with her trailing hand. She gripped it hard, set her feet, and levered herself back up the slope. She managed about twenty centimetres, at most, and reset, holding her weight with her lower hand and reaching up once more. Again and again she reached, hauled, and reset.

It took her ten cycles to regain her grip on the knot, and she was almost completely spent. Her forearms ached from the effort. She twisted the cable around her wrist and let her shoulder carry the weight. She needed to think. With her free hand she wrapped the loose cable about her foot and pushed down until it held her weight. She lay back against the angled floor, gently tapping her head against the damp slick. She was never making it back up this tunnel.

She opened her mouth to call out, let her father, let Mariska know that it was hopeless, but nothing came out. What good would it do, really? They'd just worry. They might even try to follow her down in some stupid act of solidarity. She pictured Mariska slumped, bleeding on the floor, her father kneeling off to one side, barely able to stay upright, Stanley's hands—

No. No sense telling them. They'd get themselves into more trouble trying to help. Trying to make up for their mistakes.

She hauled herself to her feet. It wasn't even about escaping, about saving the Gateway anymore. It was just about not giving in. Not letting him win.

The cable at her back, gripped tightly in her fists, she gazed upwards at the soft glimmer of the tunnel, to her father, her friend, and took the next step.

She was careful with her footing, slow and steady. Even so, she was upon the second knot within minutes. Two hundred metres. The darkness was almost complete, and the frequent shouts of encouragement from up above took longer to reach her, growing more and more garbled by the distance with each step. She negotiated the knot with a resigned ease, watching it fade into the darkness above. It was only her and the echoes down here.

She counted her steps from the second, and final, knot—twelve, thirteen, fourteen. She whipped the cord behind her with her lead hand, and it responded without the sluggishness of all that dangling weight. She was nearing the end. Twenty-eight, twenty-nine. All the way down, for nothing. They were all just as stuck as before, she even more so. Forty-one, forty-two—

She jerked, gripping the cable to halt her descent. Her foot had slammed down on an obstruction.

Gingerly, she lifted her foot and slid it back down the slope, slowly this time. Abruptly, the slope stopped. She slid it farther, as far as she could, and released her grip, letting her other foot follow. She let the cable fall, and she was standing.

Standing!

"I think I've found something!" She crouched down, ripping the socks from her hands so she could feel properly. There was no light down here; her fingertips would have to fill in for her eyes.

"The backpack?" came the echo. It was so distorted now that she couldn't tell who was speaking, could hardly pick out the words. She centred herself on the cable and turned right, ninety degrees. She spread her hands out. The concrete floor was wet and cool, and flat. Not sloping, not curved. She headbutted a wall, ran her hands over it. There was a door.

"Not yet. Just a flat spot, a maintenance access point maybe." She doubted they'd be able to understand her by the time her words reached the top, but it didn't matter. She followed the wall along, away from her starting point. The farther it went, the harder her heartbeat, the tighter her breaths became. When she found the corner, finally, she was smiling. Four metres at least. There was a chance.

She rounded the corner, tracing it out until she reached the curved opening. The next section of the tunnel. She ran her hand along the smooth rim, careful not to lean too far, to lose her balance. She couldn't see the cable and had no hope of finding it in the dark if she fell.

Garbled words of encouragement bounced down and echoed around the chamber. She ignored them, following the curve right down until it met the floor. Her fingers crawled across the cable dangling at its centre, and she wrapped it around her wrist, just in case. As she did so, her fingers brushed against something, a familiar canvas. Her backpack! Her hand lashed out automatically, overeager in the dark. Her clumsy fist connected with it on the side, sending it teetering over the edge.

She hurled herself forward, down the slope. Her left hand hunted, zeroing in on the clips scraping against concrete. The cable snapped taut against her wrist, her right shoulder once again bearing the brunt of her dive.

"Haha! I got it! I got it!" She yelled, lying face down, dangling over the abyss. To the echoes of her jubilation, and the father's enthusiastic but unintelligible response, Brita slid her feet down and around and pulled herself upright on the lip of the tunnel. With a heave she was standing once more, her pack clutched tight in her fist, excited shouts from above and below resounding in the darkness.

She nestled into a dank wet corner and opened the zipper, then plunged her hand to the bottom in search of her torch. Her fingers touched on cold, smooth metal, and she closed her eyes. Next step. What was the next step. She pulled it out, depressed the switch. The light was so bright that even from behind her closed lids, it was blinding.

Slowly she opened them and took in her surroundings for the first time.

She was right. The rusty door protruding from the wall opposite was an access point for what should have been a maintenance module. She didn't waste time wondering about maintenance of what, instead quickly sweeping the beam across the floor. Yes! The emergency portal, sitting right in the middle, still in its pouch. A little farther along, her damp schematics, lying in a puddle, and a battered pen, right up against the lip of the downward slope. Her knife, her camera were nowhere to be seen.

She pulled in the pouch, rifling through the contents. Everything was there, everything they needed to get out, down here, with her. She looked at the cable, at the 250 metres of tunnel she could never re-climb. She looked up at the door, ignoring the questions echoing down from above, and carefully picked open her sodden schematics.

Torch clamped between her teeth, she traced her way through sheet after sheet of plans until she found the tunnels. There they were—four parallel hollows, snaking down the mountainside. She let out a breath, edging just a little farther away from the mouth of the next downward section. They were over 800 metres long!

She ran a finger along the plans—there. 250 metres down, a maintenance hatch on each tunnel. And if there was a door for people, there must also be...aha! A stairwell, for access, running all the way back up... to the main courtyard. The courtyard filled with guards, waiting and watching. She let the torch drop into her lap, muttering to herself as she held her head in her hands.

She traced the length of the tunnels and the stairwell, forlorn, hoping that this time they might lead elsewhere. There was another access hatch in each tunnel at 500 metres down. The stairs ran even farther downhill, all the way to the turbine generator building, right at the bottom. For all the good that did her. She kicked at the drawings, but they were stuck to the damp floor.

She stared at her shoes, her father's shoes. What if... She rushed to the iron door and put her whole body weight onto the lever. It moved.

She yanked again. And again. Movement. Just a little each time. How long had this door been shut? Had it ever even been opened? She heaved. Heaved. Until, with a scratch, the catch broke free from its rusty bindings and the door swung inwards.

Fresh air gushed over her. She hadn't realised just how dank and cloying it had been down in the depths until she was exposed something different. She stepped out into the starlight and sucked in a lungful of clean air, grateful for the moment of respite, the chance to stretch her neck to the heavens. The metal platform on which she stood was narrow, the door to the next tunnel less than a step away.

With a surreptitious glance up, she attacked the lever of the second door with just as much vigour as the first. It yielded much quicker, but with no less screeching fanfare. She winced at the noise, but there was nothing to be done.

After stepping back to grab her torch, she flashed it through to the second tunnel, sweeping it across the floor. It looked just the same as the first, only it was empty—there, in the corner! The beam locked on to just what she desperately needed to see—the remaining half of her boot, the one Solomon had lost through the closing Gateway. She clambered across to examine it, only to drop it with despair.

She swung the torch around once more, but knew she wouldn't find it. The other shoe—the one with the emergency Gateway, with the cables and dialling module still attached—was nowhere to be seen. She had a spare power pack in her bag; it would have been perfect.

Unintelligible questions wafted down from up above. They must have been beside themselves waiting for an update. She had no idea how to tell them, or whether they'd even understand her when she did. She stepped back out onto the platform, shut off her torch, and stared down the stairwell, down to the turbine hall, where her lost boot would probably be.

The turbine hall! She darted back to her drawings. Damp as they were, the draft had blown them all over. She gathered them back together, searching for the one she needed. There, all four tunnels running parallel downhill, into the turbine hall. One big cavern, with her way out inside.

53

"Brita! Please!" Hugo, standing inside the tunnel, right at the edge of the slope, could no longer keep the panic from his voice. The only sounds he'd heard in the last couple of minutes had been the shriek of metal against metal, and the echoes of their own words bouncing back, unanswered.

"Anything?" Mariska sounded just as panicked. He turned back, shaking his head. "What could have happened?"

"I don't know." Horrid scenarios chased one another through his mind, each one worse than the last. He stared back down into the depths, and—

He jumped, pointing down the hole. "The light! The light is back!"

"It's back?"

"Yep. She must have just turned her torch off or something." She was okay. He sagged against the curved tunnel wall. The diffuse yellow glow had sprung into existence not long after Brita's excited screams that she'd found the backpack had echoed up the tunnel. Then, just after the rasping metal had pierced the air, it had gone dark. He let out a long, slow breath, keeping an eye trained on the bobbing light below.

"Hey, what should we do if those fucking thugs come back?" Mariska was still on the camp bed, but she was upright. A little water, a little food, a little rest, and a little hope. Together, they had worked their magic. He doubted he would have had her resilience if Stanley and his cronies had gone after him as hard as they had her.

"I know what I'd like to do."

"Get in line, old man." She laughed. It looked like it hurt, and she convulsed with a racking cough.

He spared one last glance at the torchlight below, his daughter's proxy, before stepping out of the tunnel and back into their enormous holding pen. He fetched her a fresh bottle of water.

"At the very least, we could make this"—he waved a hand loosely at the cable dangling down into the depths—"a little less obvious." He dragged over the canvas bags and spare blankets and arranged them along the edge of the hole, obscuring the makeshift anchor and the first few feet of the cable.

"If you lay out the canvas, you could pile the blankets so it looks like Brita is sleeping."

"Good idea." He set to it, stuffing and arranging the canvas bags and spare food just so. He was just about done when the cable whiplashed, jerking the anchor and toppling fake-Brita's torso.

Brita's voice reverberated up from the depths, but it was too distorted. He couldn't make out a single word. He scrambled to the lip of the slope, heart in his mouth.

"What?" The light was still there. "Did you catch that, Mas?" A slight shake of the head, just enough to make it clear she hadn't, but not so much that it would cause too much pain.

"Pull up the cord!"

He got it this time. He reached back, grabbed a blanket for his knees, and started pulling. If the Stanley, or Solomon, happened to walk back in right now, so be it.

His arms tired quickly, though he was helped by the cable getting lighter and lighter as he went. Sweat broke out on his brow, and the ache in his shoulders, which had never really gone away, was back with a vengeance. Hand over hand, he passed the first knot, then the second. The cable made a tangled mess at his side.

Heart pounding, he could feel he was almost there. Just a few more pulls. Three, two, one...and there it was—the end of the cable. It was tied around a small pouch—an emergency Gateway. With arms like jelly, he loosened it and dragged himself out into the light. He collapsed down beside Mariska and took a long swig from her bottle.

She took the pouch from his hands, unfolding the scrap of paper that had been tucked inside. She read it, lips silently mouthing each word, a look of concern spreading across her face.

"What does it say?" He wanted to snatch the paper back, read it for himself, but he could barely raise his arms.

"She says, umm, she can't get back up. It's too steep. But it's all right, she's found another way home. Her boots, down at the bottom of the tunnels..."

Mariska paused, a look of sadness falling across her battered features. Hugo stepped towards her. "What? What is it?"

"She says to wait for Jorge as long as you can, but don't..." Mariska let her hands fall to her lap and scrunched the note in her fist. "Don't wait too long."

Hugo told himself she was just trying to protect them. That she just didn't want them to get hurt. That she knew what she said wouldn't matter, they'd do what they had to, no matter what.

— ◆ —

"You want turn?" Yosip asked. The Ukrainian was sweating, and he paused for a drink of water. Stanley watched as Jorge's pleading eyes traced the path of the bottle: from the table, up to Yosip's lips, and back to his side. The reporter was desperate.

Stanley pushed himself lazily to his feet. "Yeah, why not—"

"Stan!" Solomon's voice echoed down the corridor.

Stan rolled his eyes. Perfect timing. He shouted back, "Yeah, boss?"

Nothing. He glanced across at Yosip, who was taking another long pull of water. He shrugged.

Goddammit.

He pressed a finger into Jorge's chest. Watched him squirm.

"Don't you go anywhere, champ. I'll be back."

Stanley bumped a sweaty, blood-spattered fist with Yosip and left them to it.

What a fucking mess this was, he thought. At least tonight would be the end of it, one way or another.

— ◆ —

Brita watched the cable jerk out of sight, the tiny payload on its way back up to where it would be useful. As soon as it disappeared into the darkness, she did too—out the door and into the night. The stars bathed the stairwell in a soft grey light, just enough to see by. There was no need for her torch.

Not that she would have risked it, regardless.

The outside air was cool and dry, and she enjoyed it for the five minutes it took to travel the 500-odd-metre descent. Sweat dripped down her back onto her already sodden shirt, her backpack bouncing lightly with each step. The two great tunnels funnelled her onwards, the turbine hall looming below.

She was tired, but her footsteps were light, buoyed by her success. Her father and Mariska had a way out. And Jorge too, if luck fell their way. And if not...

She didn't want to think about if not. She had to think about getting home. About exposing Solomon. While Jorge was in the hands of Solomon and his mercenaries, it was the best thing she could do for him. The only thing.

She reached the bottom of the stairs and found another door, the same design as the others. Like something out of a submarine. She leaned hard on the handle. Nothing. Not a millimetre of movement. Looking around, she jumped up on the railing and took aim with a boot, but she only managed to crack her ankle with a misdirected kick. She swung her good leg at the door in frustration, and it bounced outwards with an almost mocking creak.

It was already open.

She rubbed her shin ruefully, pulled her torch from her pocket. Sliding through the open door and back into the darkness, she gave the door a playful tap with her boot as she passed. The space inside was humid, and the smell of pine that had sat in stagnant water for far too long washed over her. She swung the door closed behind her and flicked the torch on.

Light played off the shimmering water, bouncing, dancing, and revealing four dark wooden crates, evenly spaced and massive, taking up most of the volume of the cavernous space. She bent down and fumbled for a rock, or a pebble, something. Her fingers closed on a lump of concrete, and she tossed it out. It dropped into the water with a plop and ripples radiated outwards, breaking up the smooth surface.

She directed her torch beam straight down. The water no longer shimmered as the light broke through the surface. A muddy brown sediment covered the floor. Her hand dipped down, the water coming up to her wrist before she reached the bottom. Even that movement swirled eddies and raised sediment, clouding the water. Reducing visibility to zero. She shook her hand dry, spraying droplets all over, disturbing the once-mirror-like surface even more.

She swung the torch beam to either side. Ripples made their way into the open mouths of the four tunnels. There was nothing for it. She stepped gently into the water, holding her breath against the cold that was sure to seep into her boots. It was even worse than she was expecting—the water was warm, the kind of sickly warm that made her feel as if it was clinging to her skin. A shiver ran up her spine, but she planted the other foot, just as gently. The tepid water was just another obstacle between her and the next item on the list.

The final item.

She held the torch-beam high, aiming it down into the water to minimise the reflections. There to the left. The other boot. Two quick steps and she was on it, pulling it from the water. The spiked black copper of the Gateway's frame trailed behind it. She tried to lift it free, but it was too long. It dragged through the sediment as she stood, stirring up an impenetrable cloud.

She flipped the boot over. *No!* She twisted, violently, searching the now muddy water in vain. *It should have been right there!* But it wasn't. The dialling unit was nowhere to be seen, hidden under the mud. She screamed in frustration, squeezing the boot tight in her fist—the only movement she could make that wouldn't muddy the waters even further.

All right, Brita, calm down. Throwing things won't solve your problems. Think.

Three deep breaths, eyes closed. One. And two. And three.

She stepped back slowly, making sure to lift her feet all the way from the water, limiting the damage. She set the boot down on the metal grating, gathered the wiring into a bundle, and stuffed it down inside.

With both hands free, she took two long steps back to the mouth of the tunnel and started a systematic sweep. It had to be here somewhere.

54

"Read this." Solomon slapped three sheets of notepaper into Stanley's hands as soon as he entered the corner room. "Make sure ah haven't missed anythin'."

Stanley rested his shoulder against the dusty concrete and rifled through the yellowing paper, and eyed his boss.

Solomon was agitated, dishevelled. Unable to stand still. This wasn't a boardroom or a private retreat. He looked like a man way outside his comfort zone, trying to pretend to the world that he was still in control. The contract he'd drafted, if you could call it that, was a distillation of everything that had gone wrong. Water damaged, tattered edges. So thin that Solomon's pen had torn through it in two—no, three places. And clause after clause of convoluted legalese. Grasping for a clean solution to a fucking mess.

"You copied these from the old contract, right? Word for word?"

"Yessir, ah did," Solomon said, as if it had been the obvious play.

"Even this one?" Stanley jabbed a finger at clause 13.2, deep on the second page. "Maintaining the Stora branding? She balked at that last time..."

"Ah'd like to see her fuckin' try it now."

Solomon slapped the concrete, his shoulders twitching. Stanley looked back at the contract. It was way too much. What they needed was control, nothing more. Solomon paced, and Stanley knew, with a sinking feeling in his gut, that his boss was trying to be too clever. Again. He wanted to hand Volodymyr Gateway, get the fucking Slavs off their backs, but he'd seen how powerful Gateway was. How it really would blow everyone out of the fucking water. He wanted to keep a piece of that, if he could help it.

And who wouldn't?

Stanley folded the contract but didn't hand it back. "This will take Brita down to about 1%, right?"

342

Solomon was staring out the window, his knuckles pressed on the concrete. Far below, a headlight flashed around the curve of the mountain and disappeared. "It's all that she deserves."

Stanley pursed his lips. Solomon would do what he wanted, as always. He knew he was making a losing argument even as he started. "She's already shown us she's volatile. That she'll take crazy risks if she thinks there's even a tiny chance she can keep it all for herself." *She thinks just like you do, boss* is what he wanted to say, but he knew he couldn't. He folded the contract one more time, slapped it against his palm. "And you want to take it all away, leave her with nothing?"

"Damn fuckin' straight ah do."

"How do you see this playing out—"

Solomon turned from the window, slowly. The only controlled movement he'd made all night. "With me winnin', and her losin'."

"Why would we take such a risk? Especially when we can bypass both of them. Take what we want *and* keep them onside. In the tent. I can call the cop—"

"No. Enough talk. Ah'm finishin' this fuckin' thing, right fuckin' now."

Solomon snatched the contract out of Stanley's hand and shouldered his way through to the corridor. *And I'd been having such a lovely time with the reporter, too,* Stanley thought.

Dammit. Here he was getting that feeling again. He ran the back of his hand across his chin, checked his pistol was still in its holster, and followed his boss back into the compound.

■ ● ■

Hugo sat on one of the empty cable roundels. He'd dragged it up the stairs onto the gantry and set it behind the barred door into the cavern. He held a metal rod with both hands. A weapon. Another find from the rubble pile. To his right, directly in front of the door, Mariska leaned against the railing, her jaw set. They were waiting.

The emergency Gateway was out of its pouch, stuck to the wall behind him. The dialling module hung from battery pack, fixed at chest height. All he had to do was touch that button and they were home-free. But for now, they were like coiled (if a little battered) springs, ears pricked for the sound of any approach.

The rod was heavy in his hand. He tested the weight—it wasn't so different from the podgy bar he'd wielded back in his navy days, but those days were long behind him. *When that door opens,* he wondered, *will I be able to do what needs to be done?* Did he still have it in him?

He glanced up at Mariska's bruised face, the angled stance she'd taken that protected her ribs. He tightened his grip.

He visualised the action to come. Footsteps, a curt word or two, spoken in a language that Mariska understood, that might give them a vital clue. The cross brace, lifting from its holder, the door opening outwards with a screech. The judgement call—was this the right moment? The perfect opportunity? Or would they fire their solitary shot only to find that Jorge was elsewhere, corridors away, a half dozen armed mercenaries between them and him. What would they do then? Jam the door shut? Take a hostage of their own?

"Do you think she's made it back already?" Mariska asked.

He pulled himself back to the present. How long had it been since he'd pulled the pouch, and Brita's note, from the depths of the tunnel? Five minutes? Surely no more than ten. Was that enough time? Maybe, maybe not. It was definitely enough time for something to go wrong.

"I hope so," he said. Mariska's knuckles were white on the railing. She must have been thinking the same thing. "But she's out of our reach. Out of everyone's reach. It's Jorge we need to worry about."

"Mmmm." Mariska didn't look convinced, but what else was there to say?

"I..." He cut himself off, cocking his ear at the door. Was that a footstep? He flicked his gaze over to Mariska—she was staring right back at him. He hadn't imagined it; there it was again, and another. And, if he wasn't mistaken, the footsteps were accompanied by the sound something heavy being dragged. He hoped, with a queasy stomach, that it was Jorge.

He knocked the rod into the flat of his hand

"Quiet," Mariska whispered, bringing a bent finger to her swollen lips. A patter of conversation reached them. "I need to listen."

— • —

Yosip had Jorge's left arm. One of his interchangeable grunts had his right. Technically, the journalist was conscious; however, Yosip's body blows had taken their toll. Together they lugged him down the central corridor, towards the holding pen, his feet trailing along behind.

Stanley stepped lightly, avoiding the thin trail of sweat and blood Jorge was leaving in his wake.

"Sir," Stanley said, peering around Yosip's shoulders. "There are no guards on the door."

Solomon sniffed. "Take it up with Yosip."

Stanley bit his tongue. When the boss was in this mood, there really was no point. He blinked, trying to force the exhaustion from his eyes, and let his hand fall to the holster on his hip. Just in case.

The two mercenaries had reached the door, and a short argument ensued over who was going to open it. Solomon hovered, impatient, his fingers beating a rapid pattern on the handwritten contract he clutched to his chest. Stanley paused a step or two behind and glanced back down the corridor, towards the main entrance, wondering if it was too late to call for reinforcements.

He didn't trust that Gundersson woman one bit.

She was too much like his boss.

Yosip grunted, twisting and heaving Jorge into his subordinate's arms. The kid hissed and took the reporter's full weight, his forearms deep in Jorge's armpits, his fingers locked together across Jorge's chest. The reporter's head arched back in pain, teeth exposed.

Yosip, free of his burden, raised the bar and pulled the door inwards. A dry metal screech filled the corridor, and Yosip stepped back, making space for the kid carrying Jorge to enter.

Without clearing the room.

*Yosip, what are you doing...*Stanley stepped forward, pulling his pistol free—

The kid took a step, then another, both boots across the threshold.

Stanley held his breath.

The kid craned his head around, for the first time looking where he was going.

He balked. Jorge slipped.

"What? What is it—"

"Shcho? shcho tse—"

Stanley, Yosip, they both shouted at the same time.

"Madyar, vona—"

"Het z dorohy."

Yosip muscled the kid and Jorge out of his way, and everything turned to shit.

⸻ ❖ ⸻

Mariska lay on the gantry floor beneath the handrail, her back to the coming action, one arm dangling over the edge. She'd heard Yosip and another of the guards—she didn't recognise his voice, but he sounded young—arguing over who should go first. The crossbar rattled and the door shrieked, and she used the sudden clamour as cover for three deep, painful breaths. As the door swung inwards, throwing a shaft of harsh, fluorescent light across the platform and down into the cavern, she pushed the third and final breath from her lungs and slumped as if unconscious.

Come on, Yosip. Come and get me.

She held a ten-inch length of PVC conduit in her hand, hidden beneath her body. Fixed to one end was Brita's razor blade.

A boot slammed down on the metal grating. She felt it before she heard it. A second step, then a gasp.

"What? What is it?"

An exclamation, in both English and Ukrainian.

"The Magyar, she's—"

"Get out of the way."

A crash, something heavy being dropped. She prayed that it was Jorge, that Hugo had managed to hold his nerve. A second set of boots, a hand on her shoulder—

Mariska exploded upwards, makeshift shiv slamming into something soft, her hand slick. She let it go, grabbed onto whatever she could, and yanked down. Hard. Bones snapped, sharp and wet.

She was on her feet, chest heaving. Had she shouted? Had she screamed? She looked down. Three bodies, crumpled in a heap. The young boy's. Jorge's. And Yosip's, lying at her feet. A red stain spread from his side, his head twisted at a horrible angle, bent up against the handrail's upright—

Rattattatat! Rattattatat!

Deafening. Blinding. Mariska cowered, hands over her ears. Someone grabbed her by the elbow, and she let them.

"—Mas, come on!"

It was Hugo. He tugged her across the doorway, let her go and grabbed Jorge with one hand, the other waving the rifle back at the door. She felt numb.

Blat! Blatblat!

Bullets crashed through the chamber. She hauled the battered reporter. It was all she could manage. Hugo dragged her, dragged them both, and they tumbled. The wall shimmered and she fell, not onto hard, rusted grating, but onto carpet. More hands; more crashing, deafening noise; and then silence.

Then darkness.

— • —

Faint echoes of violence echoed eight hundred metres down, finding Brita on her hands and knees, combing through the now completely opaque water. The sounds, they should have been paralyzing. She should be worrying that the crash was Solomon bursting through the door just in time, that the muddled, distorted scream was her father on his knees.

She should be up there with them. But she wasn't. She was down here, soaked through and frustrated. And maybe that's what she was hearing. Solomon, bursting into the cavern in triumph only to find that he was too late, that they'd already gone.

Yes, that was it. That's what it had to be. And soon she'd be gone, too. The Gateway cables were tacked up on the wall, ready to go. The charged power pack was in her pocket. All she had to find was the bloody dialling unit—

A staccato burst, and its resonating echo, shattered her delusion. She clamped her eyes tight, squeezing the mud between her fingers. Jorge had come of his own volition. Mariska even more so. And her father... he'd been the one to bring Solomon into this in the first place. What happened up there was out of her control. She'd done all she could.

Her only task was to look out for herself.

— • —

Stanley stared at the empty wall, two fresh, smoking divots where Jorge's smug head should have been.

"What—what the fuck is goin' on?" Solomon screamed.

Stanley ignored him. He lowered his pistol to his side and surveyed the damage. The kid lay on his feet beside the door, a red, weeping welt rising on the back of his neck. A heavy bar, more rust than metal, lay on the grating by his hand. He started down, intending to feel for a pulse. The kid moaned.

"Stanley? Yosip?"

Stanley slipped his gun back into its holster and stepped over the kid's back, but stopped at the doorway. There was no point going any farther, not with Yosip's neck at such an angle. Not with the massive red stain that had overtaken his right-hand side. He glanced down through the grating and found his confirmation: a puddle of blood on the cavern floor, directly below.

"Jesus H. Christ..." Solomon crept through the door and stopped, taking in the carnage. "Stanley, what..."

"They're gone. The reporter, the old man, your pretty new friend."

Stanley gripped the railing, training his eye on the scene below. The camp bed, the canvas bags, piled together in front of one of the tunnel openings. *Why in god's name did we give them beds? Blankets?*

"Fuckin' where?"

"An office somewhere. London? Who knows. All that matters is they're not fucking here."

Solomon joined him on the railing. Shouts echoed down the corridor, followed by sprinting footsteps.

Too fucking late.

"What about Brita?"

"She wasn't with them," Stanley stated.

He spotted the empty cable spools, tucked away in the far corner, and snapped his focus back to the incongruously placed camp bed. And the jumble of white cable just visible underneath. Right before the far-left tunnel opening. Through which he'd thrown Brita's backpack. And Gateway.

Clever girl.

He pulled his phone from his pocket, shoved it into Solomon's chest.

"No more games, boss. I'll get the girl. You call the cop. Let's finish this fucking thing."

Stanley had never spoken to his boss like that before, given him an order. He didn't wait to find out how he would take it. He paused at the door for just long enough to snatch an assault rifle from one of the slack-jawed guards that had arrived forty-five seconds too late. Why weren't they in here, watching the goddamn prisoners—

No. No point going over and over mistakes that couldn't be changed. Mistakes for which Yosip had already paid the ultimate price.

He slung the rifle over his shoulder, checked the magazine, and started down the steps. Halfway down he vaulted the railing, landing catlike on the puddled floor below. He stalked towards the dark opening, rifle held out in front.

On the threshold he turned, nodded to his boss. In response Solomon put the phone to his ear. Good. At least Marlowe could be trusted to do as she was told. And as for Brita...

Stanley smiled. He reached down, grabbed the white cable, and followed her down into the dark.

55

Brita forced her wrinkled, waterlogged fingers to relax. The only thing she could do was get herself home. Maybe with the evidence she'd collected—no, even that was thinking too far ahead. The silence from up above spurred her into action. She pushed herself to her feet and trudged back to the starting point: the three-metre-wide tunnel mouth.

She sat on her haunches, staring out over rippling water. Her torch flickered, dimmed. How much longer until she was totally in the dark?

Her search area was an expanse of four, maybe five metres of water before the first of a series of huge wooden crates—packed with unassembled turbine components—which prevented any farther view into the depths of the hall.

The lone boot had been lying no more than a metre from the mouth of the tunnel, the tangled cables trailing behind it. It was heavy and would have been easily slowed by the water. The dialling unit was much lighter and could have bounced much farther…but no. She kicked at the edge of the water. She'd searched all the way between the shallowest area at the lip of the tunnel, right up to the edge of the crate. She must have missed it. There was only one thing to do.

Start again.

She got back down on her hands and knees and began sweeping in a semicircle, left to right, the palms of her hands just brushing along the silty bottom. Clatters and scrapes echoed from up above. No more shouting, no more bullets. Not for a full minute at least, maybe two. If they'd been caught, or worse—she shuddered, trying to push what "worse" might mean to the back of her mind. If they'd been caught, surely there would have been more yelling. Solomon couldn't help himself.

Maybe the silence meant they got away.

It was a comforting fiction, at any rate. The only reality she could let herself believe.

She came across a gouge in the sediment: where the shoe had been, where she'd dragged the cables up from the mud. The only anomaly in a stagnant pond, un-

349

touched for decades. She edged outwards, trying not to lose hope—what was that? Her fingers brushed against something. It was only small, but it was there. Her heart pounded as she scrabbled about under the surface, dragging it above water and into the light...

No, it was just a rock. That lump of concrete, from when she'd first stepped through the door. *Goddammit!* She flung it at the crate, and it ricocheted sideways, landing in the water half a dozen yards to her right. She brought the torch to bear on the side of the crate. The rock had left a notch on the edge of one of the cross braces. She must have hit it at just the right angle.

Actually, there were two dents on that cross brace. One was wet, dripping from the recent impact, but the other was dry. Well, as dry as rotten pine could be in this place. The freshly exposed wood in both notches was bright—nowhere near enough time had passed for the damage to age. *What if...*She flicked the dying beam across to where she thought the rock had landed. The ripples were faint, already three or four metres wide, but they were still there.

She fixed the spot in her mind and crawled over, right in front of the other tunnel. She set her bearings and bent down, fingers playing across the subsurface in an intense, radiating pattern. Immediately she rediscovered the rock. Best to leave it where it was. A waypoint, if she were to lose her place.

Her bedraggled fingers were combing a sweep close to the mouth of the tunnel when they struck dead on a square object. This had to be it. It had to be. She ripped it to the surface, brought her torch to bear...Damn. It was her body cam, screen cracked and water leaking from its innards like blood. She pocketed it, choosing to take its appearance as a sign she was on the right track, rather than...no.

She didn't want to think about rather than.

Her focus had to be absolute. Only the water, her fingers, and the ground they covered existed to her. And so she didn't notice that the scrabbling and scraping sounds that echoed from the tunnel mouth were getting louder.

Getting closer.

"Brita? Is that your torchlight I see?"

She froze, as if a switch had been flipped and she'd been thrown into suspended animation. Her thoughts devolved into an unintelligible buzz. Only instinct made her flick off her torch, plunging the hall into darkness.

"I thought so." The voice was icy cool, even through the garbled echoes. Terrifyingly playful. *Miss Gundersson? My name is Stanley. Welcome to Kolkata.* She shivered. It could only be him. "I found your maps. Very resourceful."

He's at the landing, oh god, he's at the landing. She swept back and forward with her hands in a panic, crawling away from the opening. Her boot scraped over something, and she spun to grasp for it—

Damn it, just the rock!

She clutched it tight in her fist and kept hunting, fighting the rising panic, forcing herself to maintain a semblance of pattern to her search.

"Very resourceful. Don't you go anywhere, now. The boss still has a contract for you to sign."

Stanley's words echoed and died, and beneath them the scraping steps resumed. Small circles, then bigger circles. It was the only way. She spun quickly; she knew she was rushing. Taking the risk that she'd overlook the one spot she couldn't afford to miss to make sure she covered as much area as she could in the time she had left.

A double click, metallic and dangerous, reverberated down the tunnel. The regular scraping was replaced with a rising hiss. *God, he's sliding the rest of the way!* She had only seconds. She flailed out, desperately searching. Nothing. She couldn't wait a second longer. She darted for cover, each panicked footstep sending a riot of crashing waves outwards between the crates.

Just three more steps, two—she stepped on something. His approach was so, so loud. She stared wildly behind her, swooped, plucked whatever it was from the water without stopping, without thinking. Only once she was out of sight did she stop, back pressed against the wooden crate, heart pounding, eyes shut tight despite the darkness.

The choppy turbulence, the most this cavern had seen in a decade, covered her tracks.

Behind her a mighty splash. A bright torch beam playing across the ceiling. It would take him a second to get his bearings. She crept to the very back corner of the crate, as far from him as she could get, and, finally, checked the object in her hand.

It was all she could do to stop herself from sinking to her knees with relief. It was the dialler, intact. She tucked the lump of concrete beneath her armpit, eased the power pack from her pocket, and slotted them together, wincing at the soft click.

"I told you not to go anywhere, Brita."

The torchlight played in the narrow alleyways between the crates. She listened for his careful, sloshing steps but could not tell their direction. Only their proximity. She fought to still her breathing, calm her trembling hands.

"Come, Brita. You don't have one of your Gateways down here, or you'd already be gone. You're beaten. You need to know when to quit."

He was between the third and fourth crate, she was sure of it. Her Gateway frame was tacked to the wall just on the other side of this crate, next to the opening of the closest tunnel. And so far he hadn't seen it.

All she had to do was get there.

She hefted the lump of concrete, felt its weight. It was now or never.

"We caught your friends, your father. You wouldn't abandon them, would you?"

She hesitated. The torchlight swung violently as he rounded a corner, shining onto a patch of water that was empty only by chance.

He's goading you, Brita. It's not true, she told herself, as if she believed it. *It's not true. It can't be.*

She lobbed the lump of concrete as far as she could, aiming for the water behind the far crate. She squeezed her eyes shut, waiting to hear it clatter onto a wooden crate top. Instead, she heard a soft splash, followed by a brace of sharp sloshing steps. The torch beam swung away, and she slid along, back to the wood, edging closer and closer to freedom.

"You can't hide for long, Brita. You're no hero."

She leaned out, just far enough to be able to watch his rake-thin silhouette drift away, sloshing steps distorting the reflected light in a crazed pattern across the ceiling. She turned her attention to the Gateway—only four metres away. The connecting plug, just visible in the reflected light, dangled inches above the surface of the water. The dialling unit was clutched firmly in her hand. All she had to do was get there and plug it in.

Stanley stopped, sweeping the space behind the farthest crate. This was the best chance she'd ever get. Deep breaths. *You can do this. On three. One. Two.*

She abandoned her cover, splashing across the short distance. An indecipherable shout, barely audible above the rushing blood in her ears, was followed by the sweep of the torch beam. She shielded her eyes from the bright light, used it to make sure of her grasp on the connecting plug, and rammed the dialler home. She waiter for the telltale shimmer, but there was nothing.

She froze, frantic. The unheard shouts were getting closer.

The button!

She fumbled, the dialling unit slipping between her sodden fingers. A tiny black switch, and she couldn't find it.

Bullets crashed, chips of concrete flying into her face from above. A warning shot—

There! Just above the connector port.

The dank grey wall flickered with a blinding golden light, a Malaysian sunrise in full swing. Blinded after so long in the dark, she dove forward, tumbling onto soft carpet as a wild spray of bullets crashed through the windows above her head. She yanked the power pack loose, cutting the bullets, Stanley's desperate anger, off midstream.

The wall was just a wall again. She slumped back, eyes closed, relief fighting against worry, about her friends, her father—

A shadow passed over her face. She looked up, found her father looking back.

56

BRITA AND HER FATHER were ushered through another hastily configured Gateway, direct to Ming-Xia's home. Mariska, Jorge, and Ming-Xia were already there; the eastern wing had been converted into a temporary hospital. A family friend had been drafted in to treat the wounded. Discreetly, of course.

"How?" Brita asked. Time had become a loose, unfathomable haze. "They can only have been back, what, five or ten minutes?"

"Mas and Jorge, yes. Hugo, too, though he refused to be seen to, when he learned you hadn't come back yet." Anita nodded. They sat together on one of Ming-Xia's couches, shoulder to shoulder. She felt the Bhutanese damp and mud seep into the soft leather, and didn't care one bit. Her father lay across from them, already asleep. "But your first attempt to get back left our gracious host a little worse for wear."

They'd been on the other side, in Ming-Xia's office, waiting, Anita said. Without warning, the wall had shimmered and disappeared. They'd seen Brita and Hugo, and Ming-Xia had reacted first. Anita had been speechless at Hugo's condition. Then had come the shouting, Hugo hurling himself and Brita towards the portal, only for the portal to die, flashing shut, Ming-Xia crying out in pain.

They'd figured out only later that Solomon had shot the Gateway handset out of her hand.

Ming-Xia was lucky her fingers were still intact.

Brita flitted from bed to bed, ignoring Anita's orders to get some rest. Ming-Xia, awake, her arm in a sling, was a fount of enthusiasm. She rejected wholesale Brita's regret, her apologies for dragging her into this, instead gloating over her brand-new scars. Her doctor didn't think there was any structural damage, and there was a brace standing by for when the swelling went down.

Mariska drifted in and out of sleep. The wounds on her fingers and her face had been treated, and the bruises would fade with time. There would be worse to come, though, Brita knew, tough as Mariska was. But that would come later. For now, she was safe, among friends.

Of all of them, she spent the most time with Jorge. He had yet to wake. She marvelled at Ming-Xia's resources—her family doctor had built a private hospital, with staff, in record time. Monitors beeped away, tracking Jorge's vitals.

She sat and waited, holding his hand, and tried not to think about why Ming-Xia would need to know a doctor who could manage all this at such short notice.

A hand on her shoulder roused Brita from her slumber. She blinked the sleep away, confused at the plush blanket tucked around her chest. At where, exactly, she was.

The regular, insistent beeping of Jorge's heart rate monitor brought it all rushing back.

"Afternoon, sleepyhead." Anita's smiling face was crouched at her side, eyes lined with concern. "Lord knows you needed it."

"What time is it?" Her tongue stuck to the roof of her mouth, and her teeth were all fuzzy. She needed water, and to brush her teeth.

"It's about two in the afternoon, and I'm afraid we need to talk about what comes next. We're set up in the dining room. Come in when you're ready, okay?"

She looked around—only Jorge remained in his bed. Otherwise, the impromptu emergency ward was empty. "Why? What's happened now?"

"Let yourself wake up. We'll be waiting." Anita gave her arm a squeeze and left her to chew over exactly what she meant.

Everyone was seated around Ming-Xia's long, elegant dining table. Someone had even set up a screen, and Garfield's concerned face, blown up to the size of a dinner plate, dominated the rear wall at the table's far end. A half second after she entered, he gasped.

"Brita, thank Christ. They told me you were all right, of course, but until I saw it with my own eyes..."

"Thank you, Garfield. It's good to see you." Brita caught Anita's gaze, and her friend pursed her lips. She ran a quick headcount. Everyone was here. She pulled back an empty chair and lowered herself into it. "What exactly have they told you?"

"Not much, I'm afraid. Just that you'd been 'recovered,' and that everyone was unharmed. Though, by the looks of things that was a bit of a white lie."

"Right. So he doesn't know…" She glanced at her father, who shook his head. He'd finally managed to have a shower while she was asleep, and had his wounds cleaned. He had a crisp white bandage wrapped around his head.

"Know what, Brita? What the hell's been going on?"

"I suppose I'd better start at the beginning…"

Unsurprisingly, Garfield blanched and blustered his way through the entire story, from Gateway to Lloyd and the raid on his offices, Solomon and the dinner party, Sandeep and the kidnapping, her escape, Jorge and the hostile takeover. By the time she reached the end of the rescue, he'd fallen silent, apparently drained of even the capacity to react.

Describing it to him, Brita found herself doubting the reality of her own memories. Her own actions, in the cold light of day, seemed brazen, reckless. Idiotic. When she'd finished, Garfield merely blinked.

"I've never heard so ridiculous a tale in all my life. Honestly, and no offence, Hugo, but do you really expect me to believe that you invented teleportation? And that Richard Solomon, one of the wealthiest men in the world, would go so far as to kidnap you in order to steal it? I mean, really—"

Brita sighed. If she was being honest, she didn't blame him. She turned to Anita. "Can I have your handset, please?"

Anita raised her eyebrows, questioning, before a flash of understanding lit her gaze.

"Garfield, can you please go to my office?"

"—and to think…I'm sorry, what? What good will that do?"

"Just do it, please? For me?"

Garfield sighed, as if he were the one who'd just fought his way free of the clutches of an international criminal gang. "Fine, fine. Though I don't see…"

The screen went blank as Garfield disconnected the call. Brita turned to the duffel bags, still nestled in the corner of the room, pulled another Gateway kit free, and pinned the frame to the wall. She called Garfield's mobile. "You there? Good. Close the door, and make sure the windows are set to opaque. My desk phone is about to ring. Answer it with the blue button."

Brita dialled, and a Gateway portal shimmered and faded, revealing a portly Garfield barely three yards away, still bent over her desk. He turned, slowly, and blinked. Twice.

"I thought…" He blinked once more, then straightened. Adjusted his tie, as if it made a difference. "So this is what you've been keeping from me this whole time." He approached, inspected the threshold, and stepped through as if it were just another doorway and he'd been walking through such doorways his entire life. He shot his cuffs. "Hugo, my apologies. I can see why you were so insistent that I stop Brita from signing that bloody contract all those months ago. Ha-ha."

Brita ended the call, and the ghostly portal shimmered and disappeared. She rounded the table and handed Anita back her phone. Garfield pulled out a chair on the opposite side of the table, beside Hugo. They sat at the same time.

"I take it if I were to look outside, I'd discover I was in Kuala Lumpur, is that right?" Garfield asked, as if he were discussing the weather.

"Have a look at your phone, Mr Overton," Ming-Xia said, pointing to the weight in his jacket pocket with her bandaged hand. "Your SIM will tell you much faster than your eyes."

"Hmmm, yes. I imagine you're quite right, Ms Peng. A pleasure, by the way." He affected a seated bow and turned to Brita. "So, Solomon's whole gambit: the kidnapping, everything. It was a ploy, a cover for a hostile takeover? So he could take control of this?"

"It wasn't a fucking ploy, Garfield," her father interrupted.

"That's not what I meant, Hugo, and you know it. I'm not here to diminish the hardships you've all endured, so don't go twisting my words."

Her father fumed, but Mariska placed a bandaged hand over his and shook her head. Garfield pursed his lips and clasped his hands before him on the table. "What I'm trying to get at is simply this: when I received calls from Toby at Vector, or Andrew Hanson at RBS, informing me that this was one scandal too many, that they were jumping ship. It was all part of the same sordid plot?"

"Yes, I'm afraid so." Brita nodded gravely. "Solomon managed to take control of roughly 29% of Stora in those first forty minutes. We're very grateful you put the trading halt in place when you—"

"31%." Mariska croaked.

"What?" Brita and Anita both blurted the question in unison, though only Anita continued. "No, that can't be right. I've run the numbers at least three times—"

"What do you mean *you've* run the calculations? Did you get appointed CFO while my back was turned? My analysts have been working for thirty-six hours straight, I'll have you know—"

"Oh, give it up," Anita shot back. "If you were halfway competent you would have put in that trading halt the moment you heard the news, and...oh, it doesn't fucking matter. Your analysts were only looking at half the picture. I wasn't, and there is just no way. 29% is the most he could have gotten."

Mas shrugged, telling Anita that her maths didn't matter. Not when she didn't have all the information at hand. "He flipped Sato. Yesterday afternoon. Used his Ukrainian thugs to squeeze him, then rode in like a knight in shining armour."

The room fell into a stunned silence. She met Anita's gaze. Solomon had come so much closer than either of them had thought.

"Is anyone going to fill me in on who in God's name this Sato character is, and why he had 2% of our company to just give away when the fancy struck?"

"For Christ's sake, Garfield. Sato Katsubashi was one of Gateway's early investors. He provided seed funding to help get the project off the ground."

"Off the ground and behind my back, you mean."

Her father, Anita, they both caught her gaze, looking to her to lead the way. But what could she say? He was right.

"Hmmm, well. I'd like to say I'm surprised, but sadly..." He sighed, and a look of malice flashed across his brow. "I suppose now is as good a time as any to let you know I received another phone call, this morning. From Lloyd Hargreaves."

A horrible weight took hold of Brita's intestines, rose up through her chest, and locked her breath at the base of her throat. Whatever Lloyd Hargreaves had had to say, it couldn't possibly be good. Garfield's lips curled into a nasty smile. He wanted to drag this out for as long as he could, extract maximum enjoyment from her—

"For fuck's sake, man!" her father shouted, slamming his fist on the table so hard that his water bottle jumped and toppled over. "What did he say?"

"Oh, nothing much. He complained about his legal troubles, about how expensive lawyers are, and how difficult it is to pay them when one's assets have been frozen by the City—"

"He's talking out of his arse, Brita." Her father spoke over the top of him, but Brita waved him to silence.

"—then he mentioned the strangest thing. An anonymous tip-off, from a friend, that one of his assets had been mysteriously released, free to be sold to the highest bidder." Garfield leaned forward, grinning, and dropped his chin onto his steepled fingers. "And you'll never guess what it was."

Brita sank back into her seat and dropped her gaze to her lap. She didn't need to guess. She knew. She'd known it the instant Garfield had uttered Lloyd's name.

"That's right, Brita. Lloyd sold his 20% stake in Stora this morning. And I think we all know who to."

The room, the people, Garfield, they all faded away. She'd lost. After everything. He'd beaten her.

He'd won.

"No, that's bullshit," her father shouted, from what seemed like miles away. "I don't buy it. There's no way."

"Call him yourself; he'll tell you the exact same thing."

"I will—"

A cough from the hall silenced her father, silenced everyone. Roused Brita, just enough to look up. Jorge hunched in the doorway, leaning on his IV drip for support. "Don't bother," he said, his voice little more than a pained whisper. Anita half rose from her seat, but he waved her away and dropped his phone onto the table. "I can do you one better."

He hit call, and the phone rang out across the room three times before it was answered.

"Jorge. Not a good time. You'll have to be quick."

"Harvey, you're on speaker. I'm here with Brita Gundersson."

"Jesus, you sound like shi—did you say you're with Brita? You know where she is?"

Jorge waggled his eyebrows at her. He wanted her to talk, to give proof of life to whoever this was. God, it was the last thing she wanted to do. Right now, she wanted to disappear for good. And why was Jorge calling him anyway… A memory flashed: a stocky little cop, escorting her from Lloyd's foyer, and giving Jorge a wave from the top of the stairs.

"I'm here, Harvey, and I'm fine, by the way. We actually met at Britannia, a couple of months back, and I wanted to ask—"

"Good god, your voice is a sound for sore ears! Jorge, where on earth did you find her?"

"Not important. What's this I hear about Lloyd fucking Hargreaves somehow selling his stake in Stora, from right under your bloody noses?"

The line fell silent. Well, almost silent. The entire room heard Harvey muffle the receiver and curse Jorge to the high heavens.

"Jorge, old chum, I don't know where you heard that—"

"From the horse's mouth, that's where."

"Christ."

"Christ is right, Harvey."

"This wouldn't have anything to do with your Ukrainian mobster pals, would it?"

"I'm afraid it very much might. And you know what that means."

"Yes, yes I do."

Harvey fell silent, contemplating the implications of Jorge's revelation. Quietly, almost as if she didn't want to attract attention, Mariska raised her hand. Jorge nodded.

"Harvey, does the name Marlowe mean anything to you?"

Harvey coughed, and Brita blanched. Marlowe, that was the name of the detective that had arrested Lloyd. The name of Harvey's boss.

"It's good to know you're safe, Ms Gundersson. I'll, uh, I've got to go. You get back here as soon as you can. Sounds like there's quite the mess for you to untangle."

Harvey coughed once more, and the line went dead.

So Solomon had corrupted even the City of London Police. She couldn't win. They were outflanked, outgunned, outplayed at every turn.

"So that's it then. He's won..."

Ming-Xia railed against giving up. Anita said surely there was still something they could do, something they could try, but Brita's shoulders sagged. She'd done everything, absolutely everything, in her power to keep Gateway out of Solomon's hands. Pushed herself right to the line... she allowed herself a guilty glance over at Jorge. She'd even strayed over it once or twice. And still it hadn't been enough.

It was over. All over.

She fumbled, trying to slide her hands into her pockets, but only succeeding to catch a nail on the hem. Goddammit, she couldn't even do that! She jammed her fingers down, needing some sort of outlet for her anger, her frustration—

And she found the body cam, hiding at the bottom of her pocket.

She looked up, wide eyed. Everyone was staring at her.

"Brita? Did you hear me?"

Her father was on his feet, his fists on the table. She pulled the camera into the palm of her hand, curled it into her fist. Met her father's gaze. She hadn't heard a word.

"I said he might own the company, but you're still the CEO. So you can sell it to me. Gateway. Right now." He scrabbled for a sheet of paper, a pen. "There's five of us here. Five out of eight. That's enough, right? A quorum? I'll resign from the board, give you everything. My 20% stake. Ming-Xia, Anita, Mas, split it however you like. We have to get Gateway off Stora's books."

Brita stared at him, speechless. No, not speechless. Processing. There was something here. A way out. A path to victory. But before the idea could coalesce, take shape, Mariska intervened. Her friend, her protégé, grunting with the effort of just pushing herself to her feet, her trembling, bandaged hands, pressed into the tabletop.

"Don't, Brita. Don't do this."

"Why not, for God's sake?" Her father scribbled as he spoke, his pen flying across the page. "I'm telling you. This is our chance, right here, right now."

Behind him, Jorge stumbled, and Garfield helped him to a chair before he collapsed. Brita hardly noticed. She turned the camera over and over in her hand, her mind racing.

"Brita—"

"Mas, what's gotten into you?" Her father stopped, pausing his scrawl to put a hand on her shoulder, one eye on Jorge, wanting to ease her back to her seat. "You're just going to let him take it? After what he did to you? To all of us?"

"He's shown you what he'll do. The lengths he'll go to. Gateway is corrupted. Solomon stained it the moment he touched it." Mariska shrugged him away, her eyes never leaving Brita's, as if it was the same old Mariska, determined and headstrong. But Brita heard the strain in her voice, the pain she was holding at bay. "You know what we have to do. You know there's no other choice."

"Mas, you know how important Gateway is, how many people it could help if we do it right. It's only corrupted if we let him take it."

Mariska's strength seemed to fail her, her battered body forcing her to sit. Brita's heart ached to see her friend like this. To see the broken woman Solomon had turned her into, no longer driven by ambition and by pride, but by fear.

"You have to kill it, Brita," Mas whispered, and Brita could only offer a sad smile. "We have to kill Gateway."

"What?" Garfield, Anita, Ming-Xia said, the trio exclaiming in unison.

Their eyes turned to her father. He blustered. "I don't know what she's talking about."

"Don't play dumb, Dad. We know how paranoid you are. You told us, that first night. If you couldn't have Gateway, then no one could." Brita scoffed and glanced purposefully over at the duffel bags stuffed with Gateway prototypes from his storage unit. Including the little black SD card. The last resort. "Or have you forgotten?"

The pen in her father's fist creaked, and his knuckles turned white. "It doesn't have to come to that."

"But it has, Hugo," Mariska pleaded. "Nothing will keep Gateway out of Solomon's hands. It's too late." She sank back into her chair, her eyes closed. She looked so incredibly tired. "Far, far too late."

Garfield asked about wiggle room; her father refused to concede, as if the force of his anger could turn the tide. Anita's eyes met Brita's. Her face was drawn, her lips thin and tight. *You too?* Brita raised her eyebrows, and Anita turned away. The scale of Solomon's influence, the pervasiveness of his reach had defeated even her.

Her father fired back, Garfield too, but Brita wasn't listening. Her free hand had made its way to her chest, to the microphone that still wound its way around the underwire of her bra. She looked past Mariska, past her father, to Jorge, ashen faced, slumped against the wall. Despite everything, he caught her gaze, smiled, and dropped his hand to the microphone secreted within his belt.

She reached into her top, ripped out the microphone, and slapped it down onto the table. The talking ceased. It was all pointless anyway. She uncurled her fist and set the bodycam down beside it.

This. This was her path to victory. The way she could keep Gateway pure. Keep it within the family.

"What's that?" her father asked.

Brita slid the camera towards him. It rattled across the table. "The one thing Solomon and Volodymyr can't ignore."

"Brita, please." Mariska stared at the camera, eyes wide with horror. She raised her hands to her face, then pressed them together in front of her lips, as if she were praying. "When I said there would be casualties, that they couldn't be helped, I didn't know. I didn't know how bad it would get..."

"I remember what you said, Mas. I listened. I got my hands dirty, right down into the muck." Brita reached across the table and pulled Jorge's phone in front of her. "This is what you wanted. You chose the winning side."

"Not like this." Mariska's voice cracked. "Not anymore."

Brita scrolled through Jorge's contacts and smiled at Solomon's number, right where she'd expected it to be. By the time she'd hit dial, Mariska had pushed herself away from the table and left the room.

57

SOLOMON'S PHONE BUZZED IN the pocket of his Ukrainian army jacket. He considered leaving it to voicemail; today was a momentous day, and business could wait. But it could be Volodymyr, and that was a phone call he wouldn't dare miss.

He leaned back on the courtyard fence overlooking the valley and gazed up at the Himalayas, bright in the afternoon sunlight. He pulled his phone from his pocket and answered without even glancing at the screen.

He knew it was Volodymyr. He could feel it in his bones.

"What can ah do for you this fine afternoon?"

"Solomon."

He stiffened, his shoulders suddenly tense. It was Brita.

"Ah take it you've heard, then."

"I have."

"And this is what, a surrender? A desperate attempt to salvage somethin' from the wreck?"

"No. Not quite." She paused, and Solomon's throat tightened. She didn't sound like a defeated woman. At all. "I'm calling to offer you a deal."

"Yer offerin' me a deal? Oh darlin', ah'm not sure you've quite grasped the situation—"

The line crackled, and it was no longer Brita speaking. He was listening to his own voice.

"You got the restraints? Good. Cuff 'em."

"Gladly." Clanging steps, ringing out across the hollow of the cavern, almost loud enough to drown out Stanley's words. Almost. "We caught your friend, by the way. Yosip's softening him up as we speak."

"Who?"

Solomon cringed at the callous eagerness in his voice.

"Your buddy, the reporter."

The recording ceased. Solomon gritted his teeth.

"Ah don't know what you think that proves—"

Rapid, strained breathing, hissing through clenched teeth. Then his own voice, from the far side of the room.

"Yosip. Yer guys, they got any paper?"

"Yes. In truck."

"And a pen?"

"I've got one, boss." Stanley again. The microphone even picked up the rustle of him fishing his pen from his pocket. "Whaddya need it for?"

"Brita's cracked. She took one look at what ah did to her friend and collapsed like a shanty town in tornado season. Ah need to draft up a contract. Then, Yosip, mah friend, you can call Volodymyr and tell him Gateway is all his. And he can leave me the fuck alone."

Solomon pinched the bridge of his nose and squeezed his eyes tight. "Fuck."

"Fuck is right, Solomon. I doubt Volodymyr is going to be very happy to hear that."

Fuck Volodymyr. He could survive this without even breaking a sweat. But him…Solomon shook his head. *That goddamn reporter.* The recordings she'd just played him were terminal. He knew it, and so did she.

"What do you want?"

"It's simple. Gateway dies, and what happened in Bhutan dies with it."

Solomon sucked his teeth, his mind racing. "What do you mean Gateway dies?"

"What it says on the tin, Solomon," Hugo said, butting in. "You don't get it, I don't get it, Volodymyr doesn't get it. It disappears, gets forgotten." He paused, as if considering whether this was something he really wanted. "It's too dangerous, anyway. Too powerful to risk it falling into the wrong hands."

"Volodymyr always gets what he wants. He won't just give up."

"Maybe, maybe not. But he won't like having his most profitable investment exposed to the IRS, to Interpol, either, would he? I imagine his friends in the Kremlin would like it even less. And I doubt that would make you very popular at all…"

Jesus. He pulled the phone away from his face, clenched tight in his fist, and made to fling it out into the abyss. It was all crumbling down around him. This was meant to be his moment of triumph, the day he finally broke free!

"Do you really think those little snippets of audio are gonna to save you? Are you really that naive?"

"I've got video, too." Brita again. "It makes damning viewing. You should tell your lackeys that if they're going to try to destroy evidence, they need do a better job."

"What about Jorge?" If he knew anything about that Spanish prick, there was no way he would stay silent.

"Don't you worry about him. As long as Gateway stays dead, his pen stays silent."

The fight drained out of him. She had him beat. "And Stora?"

"Keep it, sell it. Do whatever you like with it. I only kept it for Gateway, and Gateway…"

"You'll really do it? Really kill it, after everythin' you went through?"

"Richard." She paused, with an agonising, excruciating sympathy. "Darlin', it's already done."

Before he could stall, before he could bluster, think of anything else to say, she'd disconnected the call. He turned, bent over the fence, and gazed down into the valley, at the four hydro-tunnels disappearing down into the mist. He shoved his phone back into his pocket, and it clattered against another.

Against Brita's. The handset he'd taken, when he'd caught her red handed.

He pulled it out, swiped it open. Nothing. He checked the power. Nothing. Held it down. Hit reset. Booted it to BIOS. Nothing. Nothing. Nothing.

And it had been seventy-six percent charged, not half an hour ago.

He knew, he'd checked.

"Fuck."

He flicked the Gateway handset, the sleek, black, invaluable, useless brick, over the edge. As it fell into the chasm, he turned, not waiting to hear it land, and walked back inside.

— · —

EPILOGUE

Jorge hugged his parka tight around his chest. The weather had turned, wind gusting down the man-made tunnels of Canary Wharf, but he kept walking. He really shouldn't have been doing this, not with his ribs, his punctured lung still on the mend. But he wanted to see it for himself.

At the final pedestrian crossing he pressed his buds deeper into his ears and hit play. Last night's special report with Frank Darabont mingled with the sounds of the London streets.

"Less than a fortnight after her shock resignation as CEO of Stora Telecom, Brita Gundersson has announced the formation of a new company with her father, and Stora founder, Hugo Gundersson..."

The lights turned green. The wind lost out to the high-frequency burr of the crossing lights. It even drowned out Darabont's smug, self-satisfied voice. Not that it mattered. He'd watched the video so many times that morning that he could picture the footage in his mind. Brita, smiling, staring through the barrage of flashing bulbs, photographers lining up to take the definitive photograph of her and Hugo's long-awaited public reunion. Smiles a mile wide as they gushed about their excitement at finally having the chance to build something together. Frank explaining to the audience the story behind the new company's moniker as the camera panned to one side. An amalgam of the four founders' names: Brita, Hugo, Anita Kingston, and Ming-Xia Peng. Garfield Overton was there too. Somehow he'd managed to cling to the Gundersson coattails for one last ride.

And every time, Jorge noticed the conspicuous absence. The woman missing from the picture. Not that Frank ever mentioned her name. He probably didn't even know she'd ever existed.

He stopped, hands thrust deep in his pockets, and faced the new BH-MAX headquarters from across the street. He'd expected...actually, he wasn't sure what he'd expected, but it was just a building. Grey concrete and grey steel, mirrored glass

365

windows reflecting gloomy grey skies, with a generic, artificial sign glowing at the top. A drab, uninspiring office building, just like all its neighbours.

He tapped his buds, silencing Frank for good, and turned back into the wind. Strange how when Brita had needed him, when she'd been vulnerable, she'd seemed different. Like she didn't have the same gloss that other billionaires had. Like she was who she'd told him she was: a leader who cared about her employees more than her shareholders. Who cared about doing the right thing more than the bottom line.

Like she might actually have been different.

He thought back to that final phone call. He hadn't known where she'd planned to take it. Had he actually agreed to give up his story for the greater good? Or had Brita just taken his assent for granted? It had been impossible to argue after the fact, when clearly she was right. Better to kill Gateway, let Solomon walk free, than let the likes of Volodymyr Uvorvykishki control it. And how free was Solomon really, having cost Volodymyr his promised new toy?

Besides, he'd been drugged up to his eyeballs for the pain. He'd barely noticed Hugo, frantically scrawling on a piece of paper for the entirety of the call. He'd gleaned no meaning from Hugo passing that piece of paper to his daughter to read and to sign. Nor from Brita sliding it to Anita, then Ming-Xia, and finally Garfield.

He'd been too focused on staying conscious. Too determined to hear Solomon capitulate to Brita's terms. Too damn tired to wonder why Hugo would give up on Gateway without so much as a fight.

He hadn't noticed that she was no longer sitting at the table, but he remembered now. Remembered the look of betrayal on her face as she'd walked away.

His foot rolled on an uneven cobblestone, and he winced, the jolt travelling from his hip, up his side, and along his ribs. Betrayal. That was an emotion he understood.

He pulled up her number, hit dial.

She answered on the second ring.

"Mariska? Jorge. Have you seen… you have?" There was anger in her voice, and a steely determination. "Yes, infuriating. But sadly, not a surprise." He paused, glancing up at the silhouette of an airliner jetting across the clouded sky. "Listen. If she's going to rebuild it, then the world deserves to know the whole story. The real story. And I think you should be the one to tell it."

Acknowledgements

Project Gateway started with me daydreaming one day about how cool it would be to not have to commute to work, to dial up the office and just step on through.

It stayed as a daydream for a long time, until 2019 in fact, when I read *American Psycho* by Brett Easton Ellis and, for some reason, decided that maybe I could write a novel too. I toyed around with a couple of scenes (Brita was called Boris, it was set in Stockholme, and Gateway had been invented by Sven who wasn't related to Boris at all...)

Then 2020 happened, and we all got locked inside for months on end. Which gave me the time I needed to actually sit down and write it. So, thanks Dan Andrews, I guess?

Putting macro-scale ecological and economic factors outside of our control to one side, there are so many people who deserve thanks for the roles they played in bringing this book to life.

My very first writing group: Mum, Dad, John, my brother Patrick & my cousin Alison. Thank you all for putting up with the very first drafts of individual chapters, usually without much context. Every project has to start somewhere, and you all got in on the ground floor.

My first readers: Caitlin, Grace, Mum and Dad (again), Pam and John (again), Ben, Luke & Kyle, Lendyn, Toby, Tegan & Nandita. Your feedback on the first (complete and readable) draft was critical in shaping the *Project Gateway* that everyone else gets to enjoy today.

My various writing groups and workshoppers, for letting me critique their work, and providing their honest feedback on mine. Every little bit helps.

Mum and Dad (again, again) for reading all of the subsequent drafts, and providing enthusiastic feedback despite having read it more times than they can count.

My editor, Stephanie, for catching so many mistakes (and teaching me how quotation marks are *meant* to work), and my cover designer Brie, for turning my half-baked sketches into the awesome book you're holding in your hand.

And to Caitlin, for your encouragement, patience, and for trusting me enough to tell me what you really think.

Thank you for reading *Project Gateway*

I hope you enjoyed reading it as much as I loved writing it. If you think others will enjoy *Project Gateway*, then please consider leaving a review. Reviews help show readers that picking up a copy of *Project Gateway* is worth their valuable time. They make a bigger difference than you may realise.

Review at Goodreads

I'd Love to Hear From You!

If you have a question, want to suggest a topic or character for my next flash fiction adventure, or just want to say hello, then this is the place to go. You can send me a message direct, or sign-up for my monthly newsletter.

Get In Touch!

www.ingramcontent.com/pod-product-compliance
Lightning Source LLC
Chambersburg PA
CBHW010423170726
48283CB00011B/3023